Brian Stableford

THE INSUBSTANTIAL PAGEANT

Brian Stableford has been writing for fifty years. His fiction includes include eleven novels and seven short story collections in a series of "tales of the biotech revolution"; a series of metaphysical fantasies set in Paris in the 1840s, featuring Edgar Poe's Auguste Dupin, most recently *Yesterday Never Dies* (2012); and a series of supernatural mysteries set in an artist's colony, most recently *The Pool of Mnemosyne* (2018). Recent novels independent of any series include *Vampires of Atlantis* (2016) and *The Tangled Web of Time* (2016). He also translates antique works from the French, with particular interests in the Symbolist and Decadent Movements, *roman scientifique* and the *fantastique*. The current volume is the second in his Morgan's Fork series, being a sequel to *Spirits of the Vasty Deep* (2018).

BRIAN STABLEFORD

THE INSUBSTANTIAL PAGEANT

for Andrea

THE INSUBSTANTIAL PAGEANT

And like the baseless fabric of this vision,
The cloud-capped towers, the gorgeous palaces,
The solemn temples, the great globe itself—
Yea, all which inherit—shall dissolve,
And like this insubstantial pageant faded,
Leave not a rack behind.
Shakespeare, *The Tempest*

I
The Sister

None of the three doorbells had a name stuck to the panel beside it. Simon had no hesitation in pressing the middle one: the bell of the flat that had been his own just a few weeks before. The answer was immediate.

"Hello?"

"It's Simon Cannick." He was expected. There was no need for any further explanation.

There was no need for a reply either. The buzzer sounded; he opened the door and went up to the first floor. The door of the flat was already ajar; his sister—or, to be strictly accurate, his half-sister—was standing behind it, watching for his approach through a narrow crack, still partially in hiding, as if she were reserving the right, if she did not like the look of him, to shut the door in his face.

If she had any such temptation, she resisted it. The door opened, but she stepped back behind it, semi-defensively. It wasn't until she had closed it behind him that she turned to faced him, and he extended his hand; even then there was a recoil of sorts, a hesitation in the manner in which she met his eyes. He thought that the handshake was the safest gesture, in the circumstance, far safer than an attempted hug. It was; she took the hand, and shook it briefly; he thought that he could feel the tension as she gathered her courage.

"Marianne?" he said, as if to make sure, although there could not possibly be any reasonable doubt.

"That's right," she said. "Would you like a cup of tea or coffee?"

"Yes, please. Coffee, black, no sugar." He was grateful for the politeness. The journey had been more arduous than he anticipated, and he was thirsty. The thought that he only had a few hours before he would have to repeat it in reverse was a trifle annoying now, although it had seemed in the planning to be a sensible move, limiting the planned encounter in order to scout out the ground, before deciding whether a more extensive second contact was desirable.

Marianne ushered him into the room that he had always thought of as "the front room," because it overlooked the street, rather than "the study," although it had been the room in which he worked, for ten hours a day, seven days a week, during the years he had lived in the flat. She vanished into the kitchen after a vague hand gesture inviting him to sit down.

The room looked eerily unfamiliar, precisely because the furniture was mostly the same, and had not changed its position; only the superficial details had changed, including the array of photographs on the sideboard. With the exception of his desk, the furniture had not been his; he had always assumed that it belonged to "the landlord," not knowing that the landlord was actually Eve—which is to say, his grandmother, and Marianne's. There had been a great many things that he had not known, while he was still living in his cocoon of innocence.

He took half a step toward the sideboard, in order to examine the photographs, presuming that his mother must be among them, and his niece, as well as pictures of Marianne in her younger days; but his tread veered, almost of its own accord, as if by instinct, and moved toward the bookshelves. He was glad to note that they were still bookshelves, with not a trinket or a soft toy in sight, and that they were crammed full. Marianne was obviously a reader. He began to scan the shelves immediately, curious to discover what kind of reader she was, but before his eyesight could gather the information necessary for a summary judgment, his gaze was trapped and held.

Some of the books on the shelf at eye level were his—not in the sense that they were books he had owned, but had somehow forgotten to take with him to St. Madoc, but books that he had written.

That was a surprise in itself, and not just one cause for mild amazement, but a package of surprises, which he unpicked with further astonishment.

Three of the books were relatively recent print-on-demand titles, and bore his own name on the spine: *Legends of the Grail, Dealings with the Devil* and *The New Archetypes of the Unconscious*. The others were old, dating back to the early eighties, and were signed with two different pseudonyms. They included *The Alien Gift, The Angry Darkness, Gateway to Tomorrow, The Suburbs of Paradise* and *The Gardens of Armida*. They were American paperbacks, of novels that had not been published in England, easy enough to get at the time, even in Bristol, but only if one knew where to look—not the sort of thing that could be picked up casually in a city-center bookshop. He plucked two of them off the shelf; there was no scribbled price inside indicating that they had been bought second-hand. They had been read, but not maltreated.

He glanced at the worktable near the window that had replaced his own, in the same position; it too had a computer and a monitor on it, not quite as large as his own, but up-to-date, with a router tucked in between the two. It would, therefore, have been very easy for Marianne, simply by looking at his Wikipedia entry—which she would inevitably have done once she had learned the name of the second beneficiary of her grandmother's will—to be fully aware of his bibliography, pseudonyms included, and there would have been every excuse for the kind of curiosity that might have led her to order a few of his titles from Amazon or Abe, but the juxtaposition of the titles from two different phases of his career still seemed a trifle odd.

The two books that he had lifted from the shelf were still in his hand when Marianne came back into the room carrying two mugs of instant coffee. She set them down on the coffee table, and repeated her gesture of invitation. He replaced the books on the shelf.

"I thought about putting the books in a pile on the table," she said, "but it seemed a little . . . I don't know, like showing off. I thought about hiding them too, but . . . that would have been silly, wouldn't it?"

Assuming that it was a rhetorical question, in no need of an answer, he sat down in the armchair that had been indicated to him and reached for the mug, the inevitable modern-day buckler for use in wary conversations.

He had no idea what to say, so, naturally, he said something foolish. "The novels aren't my best work, I'm afraid."

"I quite liked them," she told him, sitting down on the sofa. "I was a lot younger then, of course."

He took a few seconds to contemplate the implications of that remark, while he also seized the opportunity to study her carefully, having not really had an opportunity, or the courage, to do so previously. She was short, quite small, not unlike Felicia in her build, with similar blue eyes and similar spectacles. Her hair was black, though—presumably dyed—and cut short, in a kind of bob that seemed almost as anachronistic as that label. Her nose and chin were broader than Felicia's. He could not see any evident resemblance to himself. He knew that she was a little more than ten years younger than him, which meant that she would be fifty-eight next birthday, which meant that in the early eighties she would have been in her early twenties.

She was studying him with equal attention, taking advantage of the same tacit opportunity and necessity, letting the pause in the conversation drag on—which was fair enough, given that it was his turn to speak again. As the topic had already been broached, however ineptly, he thought it safe to say: "I'm flattered to think that you were reading my books all those years ago. It must have been quite a surprise to find that I'd written them."

"Oh, I knew that you'd written them," she said—and must have immediately deduced from his reaction that she had given the wrong impression. "Not *you* as in my half-brother; you could have knocked me down with a feather when my grandmother gave me that little news item, but *you* in the sense that Raoul Abbot and Joaquin Burkett were both Simon Cannick."

That did not serve to clear up Simon's confusion.

"But how . . . ?" he began

"My husband was a fan—not of you, specifically, but of the genre. He had access to information of that sort even before the internet—he had an encyclopedia." Simon remembered the encyclopedia, but he was still one step behind the argument. He could see a little triumphant smile at the corners of her lips; she obviously knew something that he didn't, and was enjoying the advantage for a moment—but she didn't make him suffer in suspense for long.

"We've met before, Mr. Cannick," she said. "That's why I was interested to know about your pseudonyms way back then. And that's why, as I say, you could have knocked me down with a feather when Gran told me that you were my brother. The old cow must have known for years that you were living in her house, but not a word, to me or to Mum. I could have strangled her . . . not that there was any point, as it was practically her last gasp when she finally came clean, and she could hardly talk."

Simon took a long sip from his protective cup.

"I don't think she realized that I was her grandson until quite near the end," he said, feeling that he ought to defend Eve, "and even when she'd deduced it, she couldn't be entirely sure . . ."

"Oh, I know that," said Marianne. "I mean that she must have known for years that *Simon Cannick* was living downstairs . . . although, to be fair, I don't suppose she had any reason to think that I'd be interested in the name. You don't remember me, of course. No reason why you should. After all, you had thirty-some students in a class and a different class every two years, so hundreds over time—but I only had the one English teacher at A level."

"You were in one of the classes I had when I was teaching part-time at the college?" he said, although he felt a little foolish merely stating the obvious.

"That's right. And you helped with the second-year play—again, something you probably did every year, thinking of it as a chore, or a farce. But it was the only time I was ever . . . well, I suppose you can't even call it being on stage, but it was still performing, to an audience. For me it was . . . out of the ordinary."

"What was the play?" he asked, for the sake of saying something rather than because he thought it might shake loose an ancient memory.

"*Hamlet*. I was Ophelia. Oh, don't worry, of course you can't remember. To you, it was just routine. I was still Marianne Richardson then, not even the kind of name that might stick in your memory, and certainly not pretty enough to be worth noticing particularly. Frail enough to look the part, maybe, but too drab. Luckily, the competition wasn't strong."

Simon was still a trifle dazed, not just by the coincidence but by the faint suspicion that it might not have been a coincidence. His habits of thought had taken a severe jolt in recent weeks, and even though coming to meet members of his biological family, nearly sixty-nine years after his abandonment as a tiny baby was, in a sense, a step back into the "real" world from the madhouse of Morgan's Fork, he knew that he had left that "real" world behind him, all the more so as his biological family were Murdens too, distantly connected in some weird way to the neider.

"I had no idea," he said, trying to stay in contact with the conversation and refusing to let his mind wander. "It had never occurred to me back then to look for my birth-mother and any siblings I might have, and if it had, I'd have started looking in Birmingham, where I was . . . found."

"I was born here," she said. "Gran and Mum moved to Bristol long before I was born, probably shortly after . . . well, I can imagine why they didn't want to stick round in Birmingham, but it was just an accident that they came to Bristol. When I told Mum that you'd been living within spitting distance of her for most of your life, she was . . ." She paused, slightly puzzled. "In fact, come to think of it, no, she wasn't . . . I was going to say amazed, but that wouldn't be the right word. I don't know what she was. You'll be able to judge for yourself at two o'clock, I guess. Would it have made any difference, do you think?"

"Would what have made any difference?" Simon asked, having lost the thread of her thinking.

"If you'd known back in the seventies that one of your pupils was actually your sister?"

That was not a question that he had asked himself. "I have no idea," he said, honestly.

The tiny smile had gone. "Me neither," she said. "Should it make any difference to us now, do you think, that we've each discovered a sibling?"

"Would you have written to me if it didn't?" he countered. "Would I have written to you? A trifle belatedly, maybe, but we both had more urgent matters to cope with. And the letters crossed in the post, so the idea had obviously come to us at the same time, implying that we both felt that there was some reason for . . . well, *this*." He raised the mug slightly, and made the ghost of a circular movement, intended to signify their meeting rather than the room.

"I suppose so," she said, and added quickly, as if in a hurry to get in first: "So what was yours?"

Simon thought that it was not an occasion when the gentlemanly thing to do was say *Ladies first*.

"As I said in the letter," he said, carefully, "I felt that I ought to give you the opportunity make contact with your—our—grandmother's family, even though our grandmother, and her mother before her, presumably had reasons for cutting them out of their lives entirely. Eve never told me anything about her background, and I still know almost nothing about Lilith, except that she was James Murden's aunt, but I thought that you might like to know about the family, just as a matter of curiosity. Also, I thought that you and your mother might like to know a little about me—although, plainly, you already know practically everything there is to know, if you've looked me up on the internet and bothered to buy a few of my books—a few more, that is. Then again, it wasn't until I got to St. Madoc and fell into . . . my present situation, that I discovered my relationship to Eve. All her solicitor told me before I left was that she felt bad about her death causing me to lose my home, after all I'd done for her—not that it was very much—and wanted to give me an alternative."

"That wasn't the whole truth," Marianne observed.

"Evidently not," Simon agreed, "but I didn't know it at the time, and by the time I found out . . . anyway, it seemed that there were loose threads hanging in the story, which seemed an offense to my writer's mind: threads connecting me to our mother, and to you, not to mention . . . you have a daughter of your own, I believe."

"That's right: Zoe. You can meet her, if you like, after the scheduled appointment with Mum, if there's time. Zoe has a daughter too, Krysten. It's a recurrent pattern, it seems, going at least as far back as Gran's mother—except for you. You're the odd one out. You know that it wasn't me, don't you?"

"What wasn't you?" Simon asked, lost again.

"Who forced you to leave—who sent you packing, off to the wilds of West Wales. If anyone had asked, I'd have said that you could stay—in fact, I'm surprised that it was even possible to throw you out; I thought sitting tenants had rights."

"I think that law changed," Simon said, vaguely.

"I could just as easily have moved into Gran's flat—I'm on my own, after all—but as you'd already gone . . . I suppose Gran might have thought that Zoe would move in with me, with Krys, and perhaps that we could take Mum out of the home, but if she thought that she was bringing the family together again, as some kind of final good deed . . . well, I won't say that she didn't know us very well, because I think she knew us well enough, even though none of us ever went to see her. You must think badly of me, leaving some random downstairs neighbor to look after her for all those years, without ever showing my face, but . . . there were issues."

Simon nodded, in what he hoped was a sympathetic manner, and realized too late that she might think that he was agreeing with her judgment that he must think badly of her. "I gathered that there were issues," he said, hastily, "not from anything she ever said, but from what she wouldn't say. I asked her more than once about her family, and although she didn't actually say that she had no one, she gave that impression. But she can't have hated you—she left you the house, after all. And perhaps she really did think that it might bring you together, and that it would be a good deed."

"It won't. Mum says that her Gran—the woman you just called Lilith, I presume—used to say that there was a family curse, and that when Mum said that she didn't believe in curses, her Gran—Lilith—used to say that not believing in it wouldn't protect her from it. I don't believe in curses either, but . . . well, things do run in families. It's a horrible thing to say, I suppose, but you might have been better off out of it."

So might you, Simon couldn't help thinking. *I might not be doing you any favor coming here. But, like poor Mephistopheles, we aren't* out of it. He didn't want to broach that subject, though, not in the course of this meeting, not today. This was just a scouting mission, to find out how the land lay.

Even so, he risked saying: "I've heard talk of the same kind in Wales. The problems seem to have taken a different form in that branch, but . . . as you say, some things do run in families, for various reasons."

While he was speaking, his eyes veered to scan the photographs on the sideboard, and he felt a twinge of regret that he hadn't gone that way to begin with, instead of making a beeline for the bookshelves. Even at this distance, he could see that all the photographs were of women of different ages and different eras: not a single husband or father in sight.

He must have frowned slightly, but Marianne was obviously thinking along different lines, and mistook the reason for the change in his expression.

"Yes," said Marianne, "it is difficult to tell us apart, in photographs taken in our younger days—Zoe and me, especially. Like peas in a pod a generation apart. Bob . . . my ex . . . used to say that he hadn't made any genetic contribution to her at all . . . what is it? You've heard mention of that among the mysterious Murdens too, have you?"

Simon supposed that his expression must have changed again, not to one of amazement, but, perhaps to something more akin to his mother's reaction to being told that she and the son she had abandoned at birth had been living in such close proximity, unknown to one another: a muted awareness of the hand of Fate, or something vaguely similar.

"Yes, I have," he admitted, pensively.

Marianne was already on her feet heading for the sideboard. She plucked two of the pictures out of the array and brought them back to Simon.

She handed them to him with a slight hint of challenge. "Me, on my wedding day," she said. "Zoe, on hers. I can tell the difference. Nobody else can. There are couples like that in St. Madoc, too?"

"Not any more," said Simon, "and not for a long time . . . but yes, there do seem to have been cases in the family of . . ." He hesitated, not sure how to put it.

He needn't have bothered. She knew. Perhaps that should have seemed unlikely, but somehow, it didn't. Once again, he thought he recognized the hand that wasn't Fate but something odder, and perhaps more sinister, whose true nature he was no closer to working out now than he had been when he had woken up from his dip in the sea beyond the sea, in spite of racking his brain by day and sleeping with Felicia by night in the meantime.

"Virgin birth?" she said, flatly. "Parthenogenesis? I wasn't a virgin, I can assure you, when Zoe was born."

"In fact . . . ," Simon began, but stopped, not wanting to sound like a schoolteacher, even though, it seemed, the last time Marianne had clapped eyes on him, he had actually been her teacher.

"It's okay," said his half-sister resuming her seat on the sofa. "I didn't go to university, but I'm not an idiot. I passed my A levels—thanks in some small part to you—but . . . I'll go into that another time, if there is one. Bob, as I say, was a science fiction fan. He explained to me that even if Zoe was a clone, as he put it, that didn't mean that it wasn't a sperm that had started the abnormal egg developing, just that the sperm hadn't been able to mingle its genes with the ovum because the anomalous ovum was already diploid. He said that it isn't as rare as people might think, but that people often don't notice, because daughters are expected to look like their mothers, and that even identical twins often don't look identical, even if they're only born minutes apart rather than eighteen or twenty years. Krysten doesn't seem to be a clone of Zoe, though, nor am I of Mum . . . thank God." Quickly, she added: "Because of the arthritis, that is. She's in a bad way, as you'll see shortly." Equally quickly, she went on: "So what else runs in the Murden family?"

Simon had the strong impression that she wasn't just changing the subject for the sake of the conversational flow. She had something else in mind. But what? So had he, of course, and he would have bet a thousand pounds to a bent sixpence that his hidden agenda was a lot bigger and a lot weirder than hers . . .

A bent sixpence? he repeated, querying his own train of thought. *God, I'm old. How long have we been decimal?* But there was no point in his mind reflexively dodging an issue that had to be addressed, even though he had to be very careful with its boundaries.

"There's not much family left to run, I'm afraid," he said. "When I arrived in St. Madoc, the Abbey still had five Murden residents; now it's down to two."

"Including you?"

"No," he said, warily. "Why would you think . . . ?"

"The solicitor who came to get Mum to sign the sworn declaration that she'd abandoned you in Birmingham, on whatever the relevant date was, said that it was needed to prove your entitlement to inherit the Abbey. He said that the DNA test that had already proved that you were her son hadn't been obtained legally, and might be challenged in court, but that her statement would establish your parentage solidly and unchallengeably. So I assumed that you were now living in the Abbey."

"Things don't move that rapidly," Simon told her. "Your grandmother's will might have gone through probate on the nod, but James Murden's will is a more complex matter, especially if it's challenged . . . and, the fact that the Murden solicitor is taking precautions implies that he thinks it might be. He's warned me not to expect an early result. There's still a wide river to cross before I get my hands on the seven million."

"*Seven million!*" Marianne exclaimed, in what was definitely amazement. Obviously the solicitor hadn't mentioned that aspect of the legacy. He strangled in embryo the suspicion that Marianne and her mother might be taking an interest in him because they had sniffed a possibility of a share in his unexpected legacy.

"I have a strong suspicion that by the time the complications and contests have been ironed out, a big bite might have been taken out of that by legal fees, but yes, your grandmother does seem to have pitchforked me into a situation that is . . . enviable—unwittingly, I presume. Just in time, though. If James had gone another week without discovering that I was Lilith's great-grandson, and had died with his previous will still in place . . . then there really would have been a fight over the estate."

"The previous heir apparent must really hate you, then," she speculated, off-handedly, her thoughts seemingly elsewhere.

"That's part of the problem—James's previous will, according to the solicitor, didn't actually name an heir. It made what provision it could for Felicia, Melusine and Cerys, but he couldn't leave the Abbey to any of them because there's an entail attached to the inheritance limiting it to male descendants. There would have been a contest between what James called 'the distant relatives' and it would have been up to the court to decide who the most direct male descendant of Seymour Murden was, or whether to abolish the entail and allow Felicia or Melusine to inherit the Abbey in spite of the ancient restriction. That really would have soaked up the seven million. It wasn't until the solicitor explained all that to me that I realized why James regarded my advent as something of a gift from Heaven, even though he didn't know me from Adam. The distant relatives, he did know, and God only knows what the wrangling would have done to poor Felicia. She's in a bad way even as things are."

He cursed himself for letting his tongue run away with him. This wasn't the way the meeting should have gone, and he wasn't at all sure how it had. But Marianne seemed fascinated. "And Felicia is . . . ?" she prompted.

"James's sister. A little younger than he is—was—but still a centenarian. A clone of her mother, apparently."

His sister did not blink at that statement, but centenarians were by no means as rare nowadays as they had been a generation ago, and their own grandmother had almost reached the magic number.

"And Melusine?" she asked.

"James's cousin—but she disappeared on the night he died, and there hasn't been any trace of her since. The other Murden currently resident at the Abbey is Cerys—she's only twenty-two, the sole hope of the Murden posterity, in that sub-branch of the family, given that James's daughter, Megan, is as old as I am."

"The solicitor mentioned another recent death—a lady even older than James?"

"Ceridwen. Yes. Much older . . . although hardly anyone believed the birth-date of 1789 she always cited. Even James and Felicia had doubts about it."

Marianne frowned slightly. "Did you believe her?" she asked.

That was a good question, dangerously close to the boundaries he had set himself in advance for the present conversation. He knew that he could wriggle out of it easily enough, but it suddenly seemed to him that it would be cowardly to do so. "I believe that she believed it," he said, trying to ignore the ominous metaphorical sound of splintering boundaries, "and it wasn't for me to doubt her word, or to call her crazy. I've been called crazy too many times myself to bandy the charge about carelessly. Maybe that proves that I am crazy, but if so, so be it. There's no point in trying to cover it up, if you and I are actually going to become better acquainted."

"Are we?" she said, bluntly.

This time, he did decide to duck, not wanting to make up his mind until his initial curiosity was satisfied and he had a much better sense of the lie of the land. "I don't know," he said. "What you think?"

"Oh, I think we've been acquainted all along, without knowing it. You've forgotten me, but I haven't forgotten you. Now I know that Simon Cannick is my brother—not to mention Raoul Abbot and Joaquin Burkett—it adds an interesting extra dimension to the relationship, but the acquaintance was already forged. Not that I had a crush on you, way back when, although one or two of the girls thought they did, especially when you declaimed Hamlet or Byron in class. You were perfectly safe, though—everyone knew you were screwing the Domestic Science teacher."

"Wasn't it called Home Economics in the seventies?" Simon stalled, reflexively. He remembered Magda; he hadn't had so many girlfriends that he had forgotten any of them.

"Whatever," she said. "Did you marry her, in the end?"

"No."

"Pity."

"Why? Did you like her?"

"She wasn't my teacher—I only ever saw her in the corridor. I only said it because . . . I don't know. Isn't it always a pity when these things don't work out?"

"It is in novels," he said, with a slight sigh. "But you might be right. Perhaps I should have asked her."

"But you married someone else instead?"

"Eventually."

"And it didn't work out?"

Simon realized that he hadn't been meeting his sister's gaze for some little while, and looked at her directly, as if trying to hold off the interrogation directly, given that the coffee mug, which he had replaced on the table, had proved utterly impotent as a shield.

"Obviously not," he said, "or I wouldn't have spent the last seven years living downstairs from my grandmother without knowing it."

He must have sounded slightly sharp. "Sorry," she said. "Not criticizing. Pot and kettle, and all that. Family curse—not a single marriage lasted, and some didn't even try. Runs in the family. Even my genes have the allergy, it seems. Sorry, I'm a little out of my depth here. This isn't the way this meeting was supposed to go, is it? I really don't have any kind of script for this situation, even though they have TV shows now that get people back together with long-lost families. I gather that there's supposed to be hugging and weeping, but maybe that's just for the camera . . . I'm not much of a hugger, until I learn to feel comfortable with people. I hope you don't take offense at that."

"Not at all," said Simon. "Me neither. It runs in the family."

"And how. Meeting me must be the easy part, though, for you. I must admit that I'm a little fascinated as well as anxious at the prospect of introducing you to Mum. I don't know whether it will play out as comedy or drama, but it should be interesting, for a semi-innocent bystander. Does that sound cruel?"

"No," Simon said, automatically, only fifty per cent sure that he wasn't lying. "Why only semi-innocent? How can you possible think that you have anything to feel guilty about?"

"If you knew me better you'd know that I can always find something. Ignorance is no excuse, isn't that what they say? I never knew that I had a brother, but . . . well, in a way, I think I should have known. If I had . . . but that doesn't matter now. Maybe I'll explain later . . . if we're going to get acquainted . . . better acquainted, that is. Are we?"

Simon realized that she too thought that she was under examination, and that she too was scared that she somehow might fail to pass muster, and that even though they were both far too old to obtain any possible existential or emotional benefit from having a brother or a sister, she couldn't help wondering whether somehow, they might.

"St. Madoc isn't really a village any more," he said. "It's just a collection of holiday homes. It would be almost deserted at present if the DSS weren't using a few cottages as emergency accommodation for families it has to shuffle around because of the chronic housing shortage. In a matter of weeks they'll all be out, and the holidaymakers will be back. Perhaps you'd like to come down for a weekend, whenever it suits you. You can have my cottage all to yourself—or yourselves, if you want to bring Zoe and Krysten—while I move into the Abbey for a few days. It's a hell of a place to get to—the arse end of nowhere, as Megan puts it—but you have a car, so it won't be too bad."

"You don't?" she queried, stalling.

"No. I don't drive. I was going to get a very expensive taxi to the nearest railway station until the landlord at the Mermaid—that's the local pub—suggested that I get one of the local boatmen to run me down to Fishguard Harbor. Cheaper—but also slower. Anyway, I hope you'll come . . . if you'd like to. It will give you a chance to meet the remaining Murdens . . . and for the two of us to have a much longer talk."

"I would like to," she said. "I have a lot of questions, as you've probably gathered. I'm sorry if I'm a disappointment to you."

Simon was startled. "Why do you say that?" he asked.

"Well . . . you're a writer, you've published hundreds of books. And a scholar. I'm just a school secretary. That's all I've ever been, except a mother for a while, and if you believe my daughter, I was no good at that . . ."

Simon guessed that she had almost added that at least she had never abandoned a new-born baby in a shop doorway, but had thought better of it.

"You're not a disappointment," he said flatly. "And if you've built up great expectations on the basis of the fact that I was used to declaim Shakespeare and Byron in the classroom and half a dozen of my books, you're the one likely to be disappointed when you find out that I'm as dull as ditchwater in person."

"I don't believe you," she said, equally flatly. "You probably think that I haven't read the newer books, and just bought them for show, but I have, and others besides, and believe me, in a competition, you'd leave the ditchwater standing." She grinned to underline the joke. She did not, however, attempt a hug as yet.

"I don't know yet how precious a sister might be," he told her, attempting to match her artificial grin, "but I know exactly how precious readers are, and I have enormous respect for people who do real jobs, unlike me. So there isn't any way at all you could have disappointed me."

He couldn't tell whether there were tears forming at the corners of her eyes, but he could feel a suggestion of them in his own, so such things obviously weren't just for the cameras after all.

Marianne stood up. "I'll get the car keys and my coat," she said. "It's nearly showtime, and we wouldn't want to be late for the big scene, would we?"

II
The Mother

Angela Richardson was only eighty-three, having given birth to Simon while she was still at school, even younger than her own mother when she had given birth to her. In today's terms, Simon thought, that wasn't so very old, given that even centenarians like Felicia could still be fit and healthy—but Angela had been suffering for years from a severe rheumatoid arthritis, which was playing havoc with her joints, causing her limbs to seize up and inflicting a great deal of pain. She was wearing a heavy ankle-length skirt and a cardigan with voluminous sleeves, so the deformity of her elbows and knees wasn't obvious, but her stance, even while seated, betrayed the fact that all was not well in her stature. She had a pronounced dowager's hump, so Simon deduced that she must be suffering from osteoporosis as well, unless the symptom had other possible causes.

Marianne had told Simon that their mother was still capable of going from one side of a room to the other, but only just, and that it was an ordeal; current theory was, however, that patients should be forced to be as active as possible, lest their joints should atrophy. Independent life would have been impossible for her, and she had been in the home for more than a decade. Angela, at least, had every excuse for not having visited her own mother during that interval, and for not having been able to go to the hospice when Eve had decided to make her deathbed confession, leaving the duty of hearing it and relaying it to Marianne.

The nursing home had to provide care around the clock, seven days a week, and had to be accessible to visitors on Sunday because that was the day when most people found it most convenient to visit, but there was still a reduced staff on duty and a kind of Sabbath gloom hanging over the place. The care assistant who greeted them told Simon that Angela could have received his visit in her bedroom, in private, but that she had refused, on the grounds that it would have required an arduous journey from the common room, and then another in order to insert herself back into the home's standard routine.

"Don't worry too much about being watched and overheard," the assistant advised him. "Most of the guests are half-blind and three-quarters deaf even when they're awake, poor things. There will be some interest, though. The rumor has gone around, inevitably."

Simon didn't bother to ask exactly what information had run around, because he had no intention of correcting any misapprehensions that had crept in, even if it turned out that he was in a position to do so.

The "guests," as the care assistant had put it—the elderly inmates—did indeed pay attention when the group entered, suspending conversations and the clicking of one game of dominoes, but Simon was amazed to see that most of them were looking up from the screens of mobile phones or tablet computers. He was used to seeing younger people poring over such devices on trains, buses and even walking along the streets, but to see people who were older than he was, in their eighties and nineties, sick and impaired, also making use of instruments that had always seemed to him to be too awkward and inconvenient for his own eyesight and fingers, make him feel even more out of place in his own epoch. When Ceridwen had proudly showed off her iPad he had thought it evidence of her uniqueness, but apparently, it was merely par for the course, and he was the anomaly.

Angela's armchair—which was on castors, like something out of a furniture museum—had been moved into a corner, and an improvised *cordon sanitaire* arranged around it. It was the corner furthest from the French windows, and the day was cloudy, so the light was a trifle gloomy, even at two o'clock in the afternoon, but Simon didn't mind, and assumed that his mother would have no objection either.

The awkward introduction was, to say the least, skimpy. They all knew who they were and why they were here. They took their allotted positions almost in slow motion. Marianne's chair was beside Simon's, facing the old woman who had given birth to them, establishing a precise isosceles geometry in spite of the fact that Simon was a complete stranger who had only met his sister for the first time two hours previously.

"I don't know what I'm supposed to say," was Angela's opening gambit. "'I'm sorry' and 'It wasn't me,' don't really measure up, do they?" There had been no hugs, and—so far, at least—no tears. Angela's build and features were broadly similar to Marianne's but sharper and somewhat contorted.

They were not clones, but the family resemblance was obvious, in spite of the troubles inflicted on Angela by age and illness. Again, Simon felt like someone apart and alien, in spite of Megan's DNA test and Angela's sworn statement.

"I realize that you were in a difficult situation," Simon said, speaking very calmly. "I understand why Eve—your mother, that is—thought that it was necessary to do what she did. I'm not harboring any resentment or anger against either of you. In the event, it worked out for the best. The Cannicks, who adopted me, were good parents. I understand, too, why Eve didn't want to tell me, when she realized who I was, although it wouldn't have made any difference to my attitude to her if she had."

"You'd still have done her shopping and kept going up in the evening to keep her company?"

"Yes, of course."

"She probably knew that. That wasn't what she was afraid of . . ."

That was an obvious hook, but Simon hesitated, and didn't ask the question that was being held out to him.

The old lady looked down at her painful body, with a curious expression of contempt and hatred. "You'll have to forgive me if I'm a little sharp," she said. "I didn't take all my meds this morning. The morphine is a godsend, but it makes me too woozy to hold a sensible conversation. The downside of not taking it on time is the pain backlash. Maybe the joy of seeing my long-lost son ought to compensate for that, but it doesn't—no reflection on you. Maybe I would feel something other than pain if I didn't have the pain, but as things are . . ."

"I understand," said Simon.

"No, you don't," she said. "You can't. But it doesn't matter. Anyway, you can see why you never saw me at my mother's flat. I could never have got up those stairs. Don't hold it against Marianne that you never saw her either. That's my fault."

"No, it isn't," said Marianne, quietly.

"Don't be greedy," said her mother. "My mother never wanted to let me have my share of our guilt, so I don't see why I should surrender an atom of yours. Let me have it all—isn't that what mothers are for?"

"Zoe certainly seems to think so," Marianne muttered.

"You can talk about yourself some other time," her mother retorted. "This is my time. It might be the only opportunity my only son ever has to call me an evil bitch and an unnatural monster."

"I don't . . . ," Simon began, but was not allowed to finish.

"I know. The whole point of leaving you in that shop doorway was so that you could be adopted by nice parents and brought up as the kind of nice boy who would never call his mother an evil bitch or an unnatural monster, and who might grow up to be an accountant or a solicitor . . . or an English teacher."

The belated addition sounded suspiciously like damning with faint praise.

"And a writer," Marianne added, not very helpfully.

Angela's hand twitched, as if she would have liked to raise it an imperious gesture forbidding further interruption. She had something to say and was already worried that she might not have time to say it before the lack of morphine sent her to the abysm of unendurable agony.

"There's no point in beating about the bush," Angela said, curtly. "You know what my mother did for a living back then, don't you?"

"She was a prostitute," Simon said, blandly. "It's not a big deal." He carefully refrained from adding any comment about it appearing to run in the family, having no intention of mentioning Megan Harwyn beyond her name and her status as James Murden's belatedly acknowledged daughter.

"So," said Angela, "you might be able to figure out how she felt when her fourteen-year-old daughter, whom she had been absolutely determined to prevent from following in her professional footsteps, turned up pregnant."

"I imagine that she was a trifle disappointed," Simon ventured.

"You didn't know my mother. You might think you did, because you held her hand when she was ninety-some, but you have no idea. She was incandescent with rage. But I'm not going to whine about what a hard time she gave me. The point is that it worked. Once she'd covered up my . . . slip, she went back to work on my behavior with a fervor you can hardly imagine. And eventually, she got me respectably married, and she thought that was the end of it. In a way, it was . . . but it wasn't. I don't know what Marianne's told you, but in my mother's tunnel vision, it all worked, not just for me, at least partially, but for Marianne, and for Krysten, and we still have hopes of Krysten's babe, in spite of . . . anyway, Mum never knew about that. For Mum, we were all respectable."

"Thoroughly respectable," Marianne echoed, in a whisper that wasn't exactly an ironic contradiction, but certainly wasn't a wholehearted endorsement.

"Shut up," said Angela. She was looking directly at Simon, and it was to him that she continued addressing herself. "My mother never told me why," she said, "but my grandmother dropped hints, when she tried to smooth things over. I didn't understand them at the time. But since then . . . no, I'd been lying if I said that I now understood them any better, but . . . I'm curious. According to that smarmy git who got me to sign a sworn statement that I abandoned you in a cardboard box sixty-odd years ago, you're James Murden's heir."

"That's right," said Simon. "I only met him very briefly before he died, though."

"Struck by lightning?"

"Electrocuted, yes, after the Abbey's lightning conductor was struck."

"Lucky sod. No chance of a death that quick in these parts, I can tell you. But he also mentioned someone else: a grandmother. You didn't meet her, by any chance?"

"I did," Simon confirmed. "Again, very briefly, but yes."

"But she can't possibly have been the same person that my grandmother referred to as *her* grandmother, could she?"

That was a far more blatant hook than the first one, and Simon got the impression that it would pursue him if he didn't bite right away.

"She did claim to have been born in 1789," he said, as blandly as possible, "and perhaps she was. Not many people believed her, though."

"Had four children by three different men, none of them her husband? Not the daughter of the man married to her mother? The origin of the family curse, after sleeping with the Devil?"

Simon sat up straighter. "Certainly not the last of those," he said, diplomatically skipping over the other two. "There is a family tradition with a supernatural element, but it doesn't concern the Devil. Personally, I liked the old lady, very much."

"Yes, but you liked my mother too, so you're obviously no judge of character. *An evil bitch and an unnatural monster* was my grandmother's verdict . . . and if the old lady really did live to be two hundred and twenty-eight, maybe she *had* made a pact with the Devil, don't you think?"

"No, I don't," said Simon.

"Well, maybe not. But if she really was that old, then she really might have been my ancestor, and yours?"

"She didn't make that claim. She only suggested to me that she might be a several-times-great aunt, and if what little I've so far managed to piece together of the genealogy is accurate, then that might well be what she actually was, rather than my direct ancestor and yours. In either case, though, I don't believe that she was evil, or in the least monstrous. Would it really matter if she had a slightly riotous youth, by the standards of whatever day that might have been?"

"Not to me—I'm at death's door and in eternal torment already, but even though Marianne thinks I don't give a damn about her, and that circumstances seem to prove that I never gave a damn about you, I can't help taking an interest now in what my grandmother insisted was a family curse. My mother was convinced that she'd beaten it, but she was wearing blinkers right up to the end. You've written books about the Devil, so Marianne tells me, but she also says you take the piss out of everything. That might not be wise. Denying the curse won't have protected the two of you from it, if it's real."

"It's not a curse," said Simon, and immediately regretted his careless phraseology.

"It?" his mother queried, pouncing on the indiscretion. "So there is an *it*? What is it, then?"

"There are some odd patterns in the family heredity," Simon conceded, "but they have nothing supernatural about them, or if they do, it's nothing to do with the Devil."

"What about mermaids?"

Simon had no idea how much, or exactly what, Lilith might have told her granddaughter about Murden family traditions, but there was no earthly point in denying that part of the legend.

"Mermaids, yes," he said. "There's a rich family tradition of legends concerning morgens—which is effectively Welsh for mermaid—and there's an old depiction of one in what remains of the Abbey's chapel. The formation of three headlands, Morgan's Fork, is even named after them, although the spelling has been Anglicized over time."

"And ghosts?"

"Obviously," Simon agreed, wondering where on earth—or beyond the earth—the old lady was going with this line of questioning. "What old family doesn't have its ghost stories?"

Angela Richardson nodded, in apparent satisfaction. Obviously, he was endorsing tales that she had heard in her childhood, and which had recently come back to mind for some reason. He had a strong suspicion that he knew at least a little about what that reason might be.

She was studying his face, speculatively, and not in the manner of a birth-mother studying a long-lost son she has just rediscovered—at least according to the images of such reunions provided by mawkish TV shows.

After a pause, of which Marianne did not try to take advantage, the old lady, through slightly gritted teeth, wincing against the stubborn pain of her incompletely medicated arthritis, said, point blank: "Have you seen him?"

"Who?" Simon parried, knowing that it was pointless.

"Don't play dumb, Jason. I'm your mother, and I'm dying. The Black Monk, of course. Have you seen him?"

Simon had the impression that a Rubicon was running torrentially at his feet, although the carpet of the nursing home common room was perfectly solid, and the room itself was somnolent almost to the point of catatonia, in spite of the eyes and ears that were doubtless straining for gossip fodder, even while most of them were pretending to be concentrating on tiny glowing screens or very old-fashioned dominoes.

"Yes," he said, simply. "More than once. But I didn't die. And for the record, my name is Simon and my mother was Maud Cannick. You just gave birth to me." That was one of the things that he had firmly decided in advance not to say, but for precisely that reason, it had been on his mind, and the interview had gone so differently from the way that he'd imagined it that he had completely lost his footing.

She tried to smile. "Thank you for that," she said. "I needed it. If you hadn't had a little dig at me, I'd have had to do it all myself." She turned to Marianne. "You see?" she said. "I do care about him, in spite of old appearances. Sometimes, appearances are misleading."

Marianne obviously knew what her mother was implying by that remark, but her attempted reply was cut off by another curt: "Shut up, I'm talking to Jason." Once again, the old lady was staring straight at Simon. "And I know full well that you call yourself Simon, but I've been calling you Jason in my mind for sixty-nine years, since before you were even born, and I'm not going to stop now. If I'm damned for that as well as all my other sins, so be it. It's not one of those I repent. How did the old lady die—the indirect ancestor?"

"Quietly, in her bed. She'd been bed-ridden for a long time, but she didn't seem to be in great distress when I saw her—quite buoyant, in fact."

"Lucky her," muttered the arthritic. "Two hundred and twenty-eight! And I'm only eighty-three, and already damned. If that's for what I did to you . . . but it isn't, is it? It's just a freak of chance, like a lightning bolt."

Simon refrained from telling her that the lightning that had killed James had struck the Abbey precisely because James had had a lightning conductor erected on its roof. "When did you see the Black Monk?" he asked, curiously.

"The last time, you mean? Last night—and the time before that was the day that Marianne told me that she was bringing you to see me. I'd seen him before, though, both in dreams and *out there*. Never his face, though. He doesn't have a face, you know."

"I know."

"But you're not taking the piss out of him? The Devil and other things you wrote about, but not the Black Monk?"

"I didn't mock the Devil, either. I'm not a satirist. I was examining the history of the idea from an objective point of view, taking it as axiomatic that the Devil is a human invention and delusion, designed and deployed for human reasons. I consider ghosts in the same light even though I've actually seen some. That I saw *something* is undeniable—but exactly what I saw, and the precise fashion in which what I saw exists, other than in my mind, remains an open question."

"And the mermaids?"

"That too. It's a waste of time getting hung up on the question of whether these things are real or illusory, because the distinction isn't nearly as clear as we'd like to think. But I am certain that the Murdens never made a pact with the Devil, and that any oddities of the family heredity are perfectly natural. I understand that you're in severe pain, but you aren't in pain because of a family curse, or as a punishment because of anything you've done, to me or anyone else. As you just said yourself, it's a freak of chance. And I'm sorry I corrected you when you called me Jason—I didn't realize that you'd given me a name before you gave me up. As I said, I have absolutely nothing against you. If I had a good mother, it's because you and Eve took the necessary steps to make sure that I got one, so far as you could. In my judgment, that's to your credit."

"La la la. What about the other one?"

"Other what?"

"You're playing dumb again. The other ghost. Have you seen Glendower—the guardian?" She pronounced the name without the Welsh inflexion.

This time, his parry was not playing dumb. "Guardian of what?"

"Merlin's cave, of course, and his cauldron—the holy grail."

Simon was far more surprised by that than the references to the Monk and Glyndwr. Everyone knew about the ghosts, but references to "Merlin's cave" were few and far between in the documents that James had translated and partly catalogued, and speculative associations with the grail legend very sparse indeed. References to the mysterious space beneath the Abbey as "the cauldron" were also sparse, even though that, so far as Simon could presently judge, was the real heart of the family legend. It was almost as if it were deliberately not being mentioned. James had never used the term in speech, always using his own invented terminology of "the vitreous cocoons." The core of the secret had evidently remained something only confided to initiates, never to be specified or elaborated in writing, or—supposedly, at least— in conversation beyond the Abbey's walls.

"What did Lilith tell you about the cave?" he asked, warily.

"That it was Merlin's, and that the Murdens are really Merlins, and that the Abbey and the cauldron had always been theirs, even in the days of its founder. Have you seen it—the cave?"

"Yes," said Simon, and waited to see what the next question would be.

"And is the holy grail really there?"

"No," said Simon, confident that it was true. Whatever the vitreous cocoons were, they were not the holy grail. He could not resist adding: "And it's not really Merlin's cave either. It existed long before Wild Merlin, and even before Saint Madoc's time." He had to suppress the urge to go on, so much had such questions been on his mind since he had started sifting through that part of James's legacy—the part not caught in what might yet become a dense legal tangle.

James, he knew, had dismissed all speculations about possible links between the Abbey and Arthurian legend as irrelevant fancy. As a good scholar, James had known that the linkage of Merlin with the legend of the holy grail had been forged by Robert de Boron at a relatively late stage in the evolution of Norman Arthuriana, a long time after the Welsh poems about Myrddin Wyllt, from whom the Murdens fancifully claimed descent. He had considered concoctions of that kind superfluous. James had thrown out the cauldron of Annwn too, considering it to be further Norman fantasy, irrelevant to his own quest for understanding, but Simon, coming at the question from a slightly different direction, was not so sure about that.

Simon remembered that Alexander Usher had made no mention of the holy grail during his long lecture about the legend of Saint Madoc and the history of the Murdens—but it had occurred to him since that that particular absence might have a different significance. When Ceridwen had asked him whether he thought that the Reverend might have a hidden agenda, he had leapt to the conclusion that she was worried about him seeking evidence of heresy and compacts with the Devil, and Usher had confirmed that by the fashion of his own dismissal of the idea; but he wondered now whether both of them might have had a very different hidden agenda in mind, which at least one of them had been intent on keeping hidden.

"And Glendower?" said Angela Richardson, jerking Simon out of the reverie into which his mind had wandered, unbidden. "Did you see him?"

"Oh," said Simon, dragging his attention back to his present situation, from which he felt direly guilty for allowing it to wander, even momentarily. "As a matter of fact, I thought that I did see him, once, not long after James showed me the cave. I'm not so sure now, though; I was very light-headed at the time, not quite myself."

"You saw him because the treasure he's guarding is part of your inheritance?" It was almost not a question, more like a self-satisfied conclusion. And, in a way, Simon thought, it was a correct conclusion; custody of the vitreous cocoons would, indeed, be part of his inheritance if the will got through probate successfully—the important part, certainly from the viewpoint of the neider, although he still had no clear idea, as yet, as to exactly why they were so important, and only the vaguest idea of what they actually were, in spite having "slept" with the neider.

"Perhaps I did," he said, thinking it safer than quibbling about the various misconceptions under which his birth-mother might be laboring. "But I'm not certain, as yet, to inherit the Abbey and the millions. There will be problems, in spite of the sworn statement you kindly signed."

"The smarmy git didn't seem to think so. You don't have to worry, by the way. I have no designs on the money. You know why my mother left the house in Bristol to Marianne and not to me, don't you?"

Bewildered by the apparent change of subject, Simon simply said: "No."

"Because the council are paying for my care here, and I don't have a brass farthing. If I'd inherited a substantial asset, they'd have been after me to pay my whack, and their calculations of cost . . . well it would probably have been necessary to sell the house to pay the bill, given that this filthy bone-rot has been killing me so slowly, leaving my blood and brain intact while eating away the skeleton. So my mother, with her usual miserly instincts, skipped a generation, with the cottage in St. Madoc as well as the Bristol house and the cash. Nothing I could do with money anyway—although if you cared to steer a little in Marianne's direction, I don't suppose she'd object. That little pothead Zoe certainly wouldn't."

"Mum!" Simon's sister protested, in what seemed to be an authentic tone of outrage.

"Don't interrupt when I'm talking. I told Marianne to buy your book, obviously, but she says it's mostly about the south of France, with hardly a mention of England, let alone Wales, and only mentions Merlin to say that his entanglement with the story was accidental."

She was talking about *Legends of the Grail,* which Simon had seen on Marianne's bookshelves. He had started that essay with the axiomatic assumption that the story of the grail had been invented by Chrétien de Troyes and that the English and Welsh legends were simply copies imported and spread with the Norman conquest; the bulk of his own examination had concentrated on the elaborations of the legend claiming that Joseph of Arimathea had brought the grail to the south of France in the company of Mary Magdalen and two other Maries, where it had been mysteriously hidden ever since.

"It's a big subject," he murmured, defensively. "I couldn't cover everything in a single study."

"I'll try to stick around long enough for you to do the sequel, then," said his mother. "But if you find the grail before then, do let me know. If it really is a magic cup, even though your book takes the piss out of the idea, I'd be glad to have a swig, being in dire need of a miracle."

Simon presumed that she was joking.

A young man materialized at his elbow. Simon assumed that he was another care assistant until he said: "Mr. Cannick, I'm the duty physician. I'm a little concerned about the length of time that this interview is lasting. You can see, can't you, that your mother is . . . ."

"Oh, bugger off, you jumped-up schoolboy!" Angela interrupted. "I know how much I'm hurting far better than you do, and how much I can stand. I haven't seen my son for the best part of sixty-nine years, and he hasn't even had a chance to tell me what an unnatural mother I am yet. I've got a bell— I'll ring it when I . . ."

This time, she interrupted herself, with a gasp that tended to endorse the physician's opinion as to the extent of her tether rather than her own.

Simon stood up, concerned. "I didn't come to cause you further pain, Mrs. Richardson. Quite the contrary. If I'm . . ."

"Shut up!" she snapped. "You can go, you can go . . . and I won't even ask you to come again, or tell me that you forgive me, or any of that bullshit. I only have to say one thing more for now, and it's for your ears only. *You* and *you*, start walking. And Jason, bend over and put your ear very close to my mouth. Don't worry, I won't try to kiss it . . ."

She gasped again. Marianne and the doctor both seemed inclined to protest, but Simon raised both his hands, palms forward and fingers splayed, as if to push them toward the door of the common room. "Just give us a minute," he said. "Please."

They didn't exactly go, but they did hesitate, and Simon bent over, as instructed. He thought, in spite of the strange path that their conversation had taken, that Angela Richardson was going to say something affectionate or apologetic, or perhaps ask him to look after Marianne and Zoe.

"I have a message for you, Jason," she whispered. "*As above, so below.*"

At first, he thought that there had to be more, and that she had simply paused before delivering it, for dramatic effect, or to draw breath—but he realized, after ten seconds or so, that the old cliché was the whole of the message. He straightened up, and looked at her quizzically. She was looking at him in the same way, except for the added agony.

"Sorry," she muttered, seemingly disappointed. "I thought you might know what it meant. Maybe I am going doolally after all. I almost had myself convinced, there."

"I don't understand," said Simon. "How did you receive this supposed message?"

"In a dream—but not an ordinary dream, a Black Monk dream. I should have asked you about the dreams instead blethering on about the other ghost. For your ears only, remember, and urgent."

"But where does it come from?" he asked, bewildered in spite of the conclusion he had immediately drawn that it must be the neider that was using a bizarre channel of communication—for reasons he could not begin to fathom, since it had gone to such elaborate pains to set up a direct link to his own unconscious, albeit one that did not seem to be working effectively as yet.

"Where do you think?" she said, sinking back into the armchair, her face screwed up and her breath hoarse. "*From hell.*"

The way that the two words were spat out gave them an electric intensity, and Simon felt suddenly certain that Marianne and the anonymous duty doctor—who had clearly heard it—were looking at him reproachfully, as if it were his fault, as if his coming here had caused the flare in his mother's agony . . . as, in a sense, it had, given that she would surely have consented to take her morphine if she hadn't had the timetabled meeting with him, the appointed confrontation with the fruit of what was presumably her worst sin.

III
The Niece

"I'm truly sorry about that," said Marianne, when they were back in her yellow Renault, heading north, first down and then up the slopes of the Avon gorge. "I thought it might be bad, but I didn't expect all that. Are you okay?"

"Yes, of course," said Simon. "Perhaps it was a bad idea for me to come; it seems to have stirred all kinds of things up in her mind that might have been better forgotten. I'm the one who should be apologizing, not you."

"I arranged it," she countered. "I can't even use the excuse that I was trying to do a good deed, that I thought it would help her. I didn't think that . . . and I didn't think it would do you any good, either. No good intentions at all."

"I don't believe that," Simon said, flatly. "None of us knew what to expect, but we all volunteered, and I don't believe that any of us went into it with any intentions that were less than good. And for what it's worth, I found it, to say the least, interesting. I only regret that it might have done her harm, and caused you unnecessary anxiety."

"Don't worry about that. I haven't had a pang of anxiety about her for years. I don't get any pleasure out of her being in pain and round the twist, but I'd be a liar if I said that it breaks my heart. I really don't feel anything . . . and there's no earthly reason why you should. At least you've done it now — you can cross it off your bucket list."

Simon couldn't think of a response to that remark that wouldn't qualify as undiplomatic, and he had other things on his mind anyway, so he said nothing.

After a few seconds had ticked away in pregnant silence while the car was stuck at a red light, Marianne continued, in a tone that she seemed to be softening deliberately: "To be honest, I'm not in the least surprised that she's going crazy, stuck in that place for years, hardly able to move. The doctor says that it might be a side-effect of her arthritis, which he describes as 'atypical' to cover up the fact that he really doesn't know what's happening to her or why. He's suggested that tiny fatty plaques might be forming in her brain, like the ones that produce the symptoms of Alzheimer's. They used to call senility second childhood, and the doctor says that it's very common in senile dementia for old memories to begin coming to the surface again. I never met Mum's grandmother, obviously, and Gran—your Eve, that is—always said that her mother—Lilith, that is—was completely off her rocker, so God only knows what sort of stories she passed on to Mum on the sly, or what Mum's imagination is making of them now she's digging them up again. But it might have been a mistake to humor her to that extent . . . except that you weren't just humoring her, were you?"

"No," said Simon.

"You really have seen the Black Monk?"

"Yes—but practically everybody does, out there in the vicinity of Morgan's Fork. The local ghosts are always in the mind, as a resource for the brain to employ when it receives optical information that's insufficient to permit accurate discernment. The brain invents more of what we see, on an everyday basis, than we assume. Places, houses and villages, really can be haunted by ideas, which prompt the production of images when the light is poor. The credulity of children listening to ghost stories is a rich source of sightings, sometimes throughout life, and when people get old, and their eyes become less efficient at feeding the brain the information necessary for seeing and hearing, the brain invents, often dredging up ideas and images from the remote past. In any case, the Black Monk is such a common motif in urban folklore that there are similar legends in dozens of places, and the poor fellow's practically a cliché. Even though it's many years since monks were a common sight in English streets, it's not surprising that the relevant ghosts crop up everywhere."

"I remember," she said. "That argument's in your book on the new archetypes of the unconscious. That was a difficult one to follow, but I think I can see it now. Some of what Mum was saying, by the way, was new to me. She told me to get your book of grail legends, but she didn't say why at the time, and if she really has been calling you Jason in the privacy of her innermost thoughts all her life, she certainly never mentioned it to me . . . although I suppose she wouldn't, as she and Gran had so carefully failed to mention that you had ever existed. God, we're a mess. But you really can't blame her for thinking that she's getting hallucinatory messages from hell, given that's where she goes when she skips her meds . . . where she is, beneath the blanket of the medication."

"I don't blame her," Simon said. "Not in the slightest—not for anything. Even if the message was hallucinatory, she thought she was doing something good, or at least necessary, in passing it on. And . . ." He stopped, not wanting to go there.

Sometimes, though, even saying "and" is saying too much.

"And what?" she demanded.

"And it's something that runs in the family," he said, although that wasn't exactly where his previous train of thought had been headed."

"Getting messages from Hell?"

"Getting messages . . . or things that we interpret as messages."

There was another pause, although there was no red light and the traffic was flowing freely. After a few seconds, she risked: "You too?"

"Oh yes," he said, and deliberately refrained from throwing the question back at her.

After a gap that was more a hesitation than a pause, she said: "It worries me—the craziness that runs in families . . . and the other things. It seems that we've both avoided the arthritis, though—the doctor had a DNA test done to check that I didn't have a pair of the recessive gene that's now thought to be responsible for Mum's variety of the disease. There are certainly some who'd say that I'm showing distinct signs of craziness, though. I put it down to the menopause, and the fact that I've been on my own for a long time . . . longer than you, it appears, if your marriage lasted into your sixties. That must be a family record, by a long way, at least for our branch." She hesitated again, as if trying to select the least worst alternative at a conversational crossroads, and then added: "You never had children?"

"No. I was married for a long time, it's true, but I was in my late thirties when I tied the knot, and my wife was even older. I could have married earlier, I think—I had already had one long relationship with another teacher at the college before Magda—that's the one you remember—but . . . well, somehow, I kept letting the opportunities slip away. I had my writing, you see. That always kept my personal relationships a little more distant than marriage."

"Do you regret now that you didn't marry sooner and have children?"

She was probing, but that was only natural, Simon thought. Siblings were, among other things, a natural basis for comparison.

"I think about it, sometimes," he admitted, "but I tell myself that I wouldn't have been any better at being a father that I was at being a steady boyfriend or a husband, and that the children I never had probably dodged a bullet in not being born. But I have a niece, don't I? And a grand-niece—and, it appears, a great-grand-child?"

"Don't pin too many hopes on the niece. Considering that Zoe and I are identical twins twenty years apart, it's surprising how different we are and how abysmally we get on. Or perhaps it's because we're too alike that we've always seemed to rub one another up the wrong way. Or maybe I'm just a lousy mother, like . . . sorry, you don't want to hear that. But you can't get much lousier than stuffing a kid into a cardboard box and leaving him in a shop doorway, no matter how much you can go on now about how she was only trying to give you a better life than she and her whore of a mum were capable of providing. If I were you, I wouldn't have been nearly so restrained about calling her an evil bitch and a monster . . . even though that might not reflect well on me. I talk too much, don't I? Don't answer that. Anyway, we're here. Zoe lives way up there. I've told her that she can move into Gran's house any time she likes, but . . . well, let's go up, and let's hope that she'll be on her best behavior for once in her life."

The elevator took them up to the seventh floor of an eight-story building, and they moved along a vinyl-floored corridor to number 707. Marianne rang the bell, and waited. Zoe knew that they were coming and had been sent an estimated

44

time of arrival by text before they had climbed into the car in the nursing home car park, but she wasn't a clone of her mother to the extent of waiting behind doors left carefully ajar in order to see what was coming.

The physical resemblance, however, would have seemed uncanny if Simon hadn't been forewarned. Although Zoe was in her late thirties rather than her late fifties, she was already showing sufficient signs of aging to imply that she was on exactly the same downhill path as her mother.

Zoe's opening conversational gambit was also in complete contrast to her mother's and grandmother's. She looked Simon up and down with an overt insolence, and then looked him straight in the eyes and said: "So you're the famous Simon Cannick who wrecked my mother's life?"

Marianne blushed crimson, and opened her mouth to protest, but was so confused that she couldn't find adequate words, torn between wanting to issue a sharp denial and wanting to apologize on her daughter's behalf.

"Did I really?" Simon said. "And how, exactly, did I do that?"

Marianne tried to interject: "You didn't!" but Zoe waved away the protest.

"You mean she hasn't told you the story? *Hamlet?* The school play you directed?"

"It was a college, not a school, and I wasn't the director," Simon corrected, mildly, "but I believe that I did assist with a production of *Hamlet* in which your mother played Ophelia. So?"

"She really hasn't told you? God, she repeated the story so many times when I was young that I thought it was on an old vinyl record with the needle stuck. That's supposed to show her age, not mine, by the way."

"She's exaggerating wildly," Marianne said. "I might have repeated a silly anecdote two or three times, but . . ."

"Get away!" said Zoe. She turned back to Simon. "She was so proud of once having been taught by a famous author that she hardly ever shut up about it, even after what you said."

"But what did I say?" Simon queried. "And how could anything I said about *Hamlet* have ruined anyone's life?"

"It didn't!" protested Marianne.

"That's not what you said twenty years ago. She fancied the boy who was playing Hamlet, you see, and thought playing Ophelia would be a good chance to get off with him, until you told the cast that when Hamlet tells Ophelia to get to a nunnery, he didn't mean a nunnery with nuns, but was using the word as slang for a brothel, and everyone split their sides laughing, especially Hamlet, because . . ."

"That's enough!" said Marianne. "And you're missing the point of the story completely. The reason I mentioned the incident, *one or twice*, is that I had previously assumed that that Hamlet simply didn't understand how Ophelia felt about him, and didn't realize that she was offering him a path to love and happiness, but when you explained what he was really saying, I realized that he was actually being nasty, and that he did understand, but that he was deliberately humiliating her, that he was really trying to hurt her . . . and that he succeeded. And I told the story as an illustration of a realization that I made, or thought I had made, around that time, about the actual attitude that men in general have to women in general. But I never said that you wrecked my life, except perhaps as a kind of joke, and in fact, I've always been grateful to you for pointing out something that I hadn't realized, as a conscientious teacher should. I shouldn't have brought you here—I should have known that she would just try to show me up. As if Mum didn't do enough to give you a bad impression . . ."

"Oh, lighten up, Mum!" was Zoe's response. "It was just a joke, damn it. Mr. Cannick can see that, can't you, Mr. Cannick? Or shall I call you Uncle Simon? Seems a bit late, given that the family waited until you were a senior citizen before letting the dark secret of your existence out, but I don't mind. Personally, I'm surprised that you even condescended to reply to Mum's letter. I'd have thrown it in the bin."

Dismayed by Marianne's seemingly genuine distress and having no idea what to do about it to smooth things over, Simon was glad to see a loophole of sorts in the rich tapestry of Zoe's misconceptions.

"In fact, my letter wasn't a reply to your mother's," he said. "I had already written to her asking whether we could meet. The letters crossed in the post. The initiative was mine, and I'm extremely sorry that I seem to have caused some disturbance. That wasn't my intention. And if it had been the case that Marianne's letter had reached me before I'd written my own, I would have been delighted to receive it, given that it was such a nice gesture, expressed so courteously. And I'm very pleased to meet you too, Zoe."

Zoe laughed. "Very good," she said. "You really are quite glib, for an obsessive curmudgeonly recluse."

Zoe had obviously looked him up on the internet too, Simon realized, and had gone further afield than his Wikipedia entry, to flippant self-deprecating remarks he had made in an old online interview, where he had described himself in exactly those terms.

"I compose a lot of dialogue in my head," Simon said. "I'm told that it's mediocre, but the practice at least allows me to reel it off when required. Are your daughter and granddaughter not here? I would have liked to meet them too?"

Zoe's artificially cheerful face darkened suddenly. "No," she said, "they're not. Mum didn't tell you about that, then? Decided to leave that particular item of dirty linen in the drawer?"

"Of course I didn't tell him," Marianne put in. "I didn't say anything about Krysten except her name."

"And the fact that she's got a sprog," Zoe said.

"Actually," Simon put in, "Marianne hadn't mentioned that. It was her mother who did."

"Bloody typical," said Zoe. "Mad old cow. Well, since you're one of the family, I suppose you ought to know. Krys doesn't want to live here any more, because I'm the mother from hell. Her first choice would be to live with her good-for-nothing boyfriend, but he's more your average get-thee-to-a-nunnery type than the settling down type, so now she wants to move in downstairs from Mum, and Mum probably thinks that with that leverage she can persuade me to move into the top flat, once it's properly disinfected. No chance. If I'd had my way, of course, I'd have followed what now appears to be family tradition and stuck the sprog in a plastic bag and left her in a Tesco trolley, but it isn't that easy nowadays to dump babies, with all the CCTV and the like, and I didn't know at the time that it was a family tradition. Such is life. So there you are. Nice gestures and courteous letters notwithstanding, is this really the kind of family you want to belong to?"

That seemed to clarify some of the reasons for Zoe's present hostility to her mother, Simon thought, but he was vaguely impressed by her ability to use a word like *notwithstanding* in a sentence. Once upon a time he would have expected that from any teacher, even at primary level, but until recently, his daily routine had involved watching TV quiz shows in the interval between finishing his afternoon work session and eating his evening meal, so he was well aware of how far twenty-first century standards had slipped.

Feeling that he now had an image to live up to, he searched for something glib to say. "I can't imagine a better one," he said, after only the slightest of pauses. "If ever there was a family with everything, this seems to be the one. An embarrassment of riches, in fact. St. Madoc is going to seem extremely boring to you, if you accept my invitation to come and visit me there."

Zoe turned to Marianne, presumably intending to say: "What invitation?" but her mother got in first.

"Apart from the ghosts, that is," she said, responding to the suspicion that she might find St. Madoc boring "Not to mention Merlin's cave and the holy grail. With all that going on, I really can't see myself being bored. And I'm longing to see the mermaid in the chapel, and to meet Great Aunt Felicia, who's a hundred years old. You really ought to come, Zoe. Mr. Cannick has kindly invited us both to stay in his cottage. He says we can have it to ourselves for as long as we care to stay, while he moves into the Abbey . . . and I'll bet that it's full of his books. I'll have plenty to keep me amused, even if the ghosts don't show up."

Zoe looked at Simon.

"I do hope that you'll be able to accept the invitation," he said. "You'll be very welcome, whenever it's convenient for you. Raven Cottage isn't palatial, but it's comfortable, and it certainly makes a change from Bristol."

Zoe refrained from making any response to the offer. "You must have had a fine old time in the anteroom to the cemetery," she observed. "Granny was on good form with the ghost nonsense, I assume . . . and you agreed with everything she said, like a dutiful son, in spite of the cardboard box? So now you've promised Mum that if she comes to stay with you for a weekend break in the back of beyond, she can see the Black Monk, the mermaids and the holy grail?"

"I'm not able to make any promises regarding the ghosts and the mermaids," Simon said. "In fact, I suspect that I'm correct in saying that St. Madoc might well seem a trifle boring . . . but the cottage is, indeed, filled with my books, and I hope they might provide some distraction. Once the seasonal visitors begin to trickle in, in a couple of weeks or so, the local pub will become a lot livelier, though, and if the distant relatives come down in person, the liveliness might even turn violent. If you're really lucky, I might get stabbed in the back while you're there. Being the heir presumptive to the Abbey and seven million pounds seems to have made me a fine crop of enemies. If all the daggers people looked at me during the funeral service that Felicia held for Ceridwen and James in the Abbey's chapel had been real, I'd have been cut to ribbons."

"Seven million pounds?" Zoe repeated, incredulously. "You've inherited *seven million pounds?*"

"And an Abbey," Simon pointed out. "Don't forget the Abbey, complete with resident ghosts and legends. But I haven't inherited it yet. The will has to get through probate, and it seems entirely possible that there might be challenges, from people who've been gathering evidence to support their own claims to be Seymour Murden's most direct descendant for years, and to whom my advent must have come as a horribly nasty shock. The legal process will take a while, and I'll have to avoid falling backwards into any daggers in the meantime."

"Even so," Zoe said, "forget everything I've just said, and welcome to the family, uncle dear. Is it incest to marry a half-niece, or are we more like cousins?"

"I suspect that it would be incest, morally if not legally speaking," Simon said, getting into the swing of the game, "but I'm way too old anyway, for a lovely young woman in the prime of life, like you."

"Millionaires are ageless," she told him. "The older the better, in fact. Krysten must be legal, though. A half-grand-niece can't be any more consanguineous—is that the right word?—than a cousin."

Simon paused to admire the use of *consanguineous*, sure that the query was an affectation rather than an expression of uncertainty. A certain literariness obviously ran in the family.

"Stop it, Zoe," said Marianne. "You might think you're being clever but you're just being disgusting. Anyway, we only stopped in for a few minutes, all of which you've contrived to waste completely, with your stupid sense of humor."

"Story of my life, according to you," Zoe muttered.

Her mother continued, emphatically: "I've got to drive Mr. Cannick to Parkway now, and you're going to leave him with the worst possible impression of us. I should never have brought him here."

"You really think dear old Granny would have left him with a better impression if you'd ended the tour at the living waxwork museum? Here, at last, you get a little wit and sanity—don't you agree, Uncle?"

"To tell the truth," said Simon, "the whole day has been extremely interesting. It certainly makes the boat trip to

Fishguard and the long train journey worthwhile, although I must admit that I'm not looking forward to the return boat trip at dead of night. The so-called Morgan's Fork fishing fleet is exceedingly slow, but another pleasant amenity in good weather, if you do come to stay. I hope you will—both of you, and Krysten too, if possible."

He extended his hand for a civilized farewell gesture, but Zoe was having none of that. She threw her arms around his neck and kissed him on the cheek. "I leave the handshakes to Mum," she said, blithely. "More her style. Pleased to meet you, Uncle, and *au revoir*—or do I mean *à bientot*. You're the translator, not me. But not *adieu*—that I do know."

"*Au revoir*," said Simon. "Soon, I hope."

Marianne led the retreat, still blushing and seething. In the elevator on the way back to the ground floor, she said: "I am *so* sorry, Mr. Cannick. I was afraid that it might be awkward, but I had no idea that it would be that bad."

"I can see what you mean about being far from identical, even though you look so similar," Simon remarked. "The looks might just be coincidence, and you might not be genetically identical at all. But there's nothing to worry about. I quite like her sense of humor, and it certainly unwound any tension there might have been. Don't be angry with her, please. And please stop calling me *Mr. Cannick*."

"Sometimes I do see a lot of Bob in her," his sister said, with a sigh, choosing to pick up his first remark rather than his request that she refrain from being angry, "and it can hardly be his parental influence. When we split, he wasn't exactly eager to take full advantage of his rights of access, any more than he was to keep up his maintenance payments. Zoe blames me for it all, of course. She thinks I drove him away. Maybe I did. I certainly seem to be driving her away. Is your invitation to visit you in Wales still open, or do you want to withdraw it? I wouldn't blame you."

"I'd be delighted to see you in St. Madoc, at any time you care to visit," he assured her. I really would like the chance to get to know you better—and Zoe is very welcome to come too, at the same time or separately. As I said, I can't promise ghosts or mermaids, and certainly not the holy grail, but it's a pleasant spot regardless—a wilder coast than the Severn estuary, and a strange little island connected to the mainland by a concrete bridge, with an Abbey, chickens and a donkey named Pamphile, and legends by the score. I'm a stranger there myself, obviously, but it's my home now, and my true homeland, and there's a sense in which it's still the homeland of all of Lilith's descendants, even though she fled from it."

"From the curse," Marianne reminded him.

"So she seems to have thought. But it's not really a curse, and she seems to have remembered that there was a treasure too. That isn't what she might have thought it was either, but I've certainly found a treasure of sorts there, even if the will fails to pass through probate and all I end up with is Raven Cottage and a few loyal cousins. They've already been immensely valuable to me, and I'd like to think that you, and Zoe, might be equally valuable, once we become authentically acquainted."

"I can see why Mum called you Jason," she said, as they climbed into the Renault.

"Really," said Simon, "Why?"

"Because you're a hero," she said, with an apparent sincerity that he found quite touching, even though he couldn't believe that she actually meant it—especially given that the name seemed to have been attributed to him while he was still a tiny embryo in the womb, who could easily have turned out to be a girl.

IV
The Restaurant

When the train from Swansea finally pulled into Fishguard Harbor station, after what seemed to have been an interminable second leg of the journey, even though he had had plenty to occupy his thoughts, Simon was unable to feel the slightest hint of relief. The prospect of the journey by boat along the coast, now that it was already dark and the experience no longer had the appeal of novelty, seemed distinctly dispiriting.

Given that, he ought to have been very glad to find Megan Harwyn waiting for him on the far side of the ticket barrier, with the tacit promise of a much faster journey back to St. Madoc by car, in a BMW much plusher than Marianne's little Renault. His first reaction, however, was one of slight dismay, because it represented a further complication to a day that had already thrown up more than he had anticipated and more than he felt that he could easily handle, in his present state of mental being.

"I sent the boatman back," Megan said. "I paid him off. I knew which train to meet because there are only six a day on Sunday, and the others were all at impracticable times. There's a small restaurant a little way along the waterfront that opens on Sundays, and the car's parked just a little further along the quay, so I'll be able to feed you and get you back at pretty much the same time that Cerys and Felicia would have been expecting you, if they can be bothered to wait up. You don't need to fall on your knees and kiss my hand—a simple thank you will do."

Simon couldn't actually get the "thank you" out, and he realized that he was more confused than he had thought, without quite knowing why.

"It's okay," she said, deliberately misunderstanding his awkward hesitation. "You're not a millionaire yet, so there's no reason why you shouldn't allow a rich cousin to buy you dinner. No obligation. And I need to talk to you. The last couple of weeks have been so busy that we haven't really had a change to catch up with matters that are now of mutual interest, especially with you spending two nights out of three at the Abbey. This way."

He followed her, meekly.

"You seem a little washed out," she observed. "I hope it's just the train journey, and that meeting Mummy went as well as it could, in the circumstances."

"I can't honestly say that it went well," Simon admitted. "My birth-mother is in dire straits, discomfiting to see—but my sister seems nice and my niece, to whom I also paid a flying visit, seems . . . lively. Angela hadn't taken her morphine because she wanted to maintain what little clarity of mind she has left in order to check me out . . . and also, I suspect, to punish herself a little. She's old, and . . . well, in sum, that segment of the day was every bit as awkward as you might expect a meeting between an agonized old woman and the baby she abandoned sixty-eight years previously to be. It was interesting, though."

"Sometimes, cousin, I think you overdo the detached, I'm-an-objective-observer act. *Interesting!* I take it, then, that she didn't beg for your forgiveness on bended knee and you didn't throw your arms around her and cry *Mother!*"

"Not exactly—and not just because her knees don't bend any more. Are you and I calling one another *cousin* now?"

"It's what we are," she countered. "But no, I was just trying it out for size. Let's continue to use our names, like the good next-door neighbors we also are. Shall I meet my other cousin—your sister, that is—some day?"

"I hope so. I've invited her to come and stay in Raven for a weekend, when she can get time off from work. She works in a school, so it must be pressured, but I presume the pressure eases during the Easter break. Easter isn't until mid-April this year, but . . . I suppose it depends how eager she is to come and pick up the dialogue where we left it. I hope I haven't put her off. I tried to make a good impression, but, as you can probably imagine, it wasn't easy. Then her daughter set out deliberately to embarrass her, paying off some petty grudge of her own. Marianne might be sitting at home now thinking that it was a really bad idea and wishing that she hadn't bothered."

It was only after he had stopped rambling that he realized that he had probably missed the point of Megan's question, and that the reason she had queried the likelihood of Simon introducing her to his newly-discovered sister might relate to a different anxiety. It was too late to add anything, though, and too touchy a subject to raise anyway.

"The restaurant's just here," said Megan. "I've eaten here before. The view's better in daylight, because it overlooks the harbor directly—the windows get splashed at high tide when the wind's up. And the tide will, in fact, be high in an hour or so, so at least we'll be able to see all the harbor lights reflecting from the swell. The halibut's usually good, and the brill, although nowadays, sea bass and lemon sole are the reliable standards. The fishing in the Channel isn't what it used to be."

Slightly to his surprise, Simon realized that Megan was rambling too, clearly uncertain of herself, perhaps because of the unusual step she had taken in driving all the way to Fishguard to meet him, and perhaps, also, because the last couple of weeks had been so busy, even once the farcical funeral was out of the way, that they really hadn't had a chance to catch up with all sorts of matters that were, indeed, now matters of mutual interest. He had been lax in that regard . . . partly because, as she had observed, he had been spending more evenings and nights at the Abbey than at home. He took note, a trifle belatedly, of the fact that Megan had assumed that she would be returning him to the Abbey, not the cottage, and that Cerys and Felicia might even be waiting up for him, in spite of the lateness of his anticipated arrival. He wondered what deductions she might have made about that.

He ordered sea bream with "new" potatoes and mixed veg. They got a table overlooking the water without any difficulty, the restaurant being less than half full—understandable on the Sunday of the first week of March—but the view wasn't exactly picturesque, given the darkness and the fact that Fishguard was a busy commercial port rather than a tourist spot. The water outside the harbor walls was probably choppy, but the expanse in front of the quay on which the restaurant was located was almost flat calm. It did reflect the harbor lights, but the lights themselves were a trifle garish, too obtrusive within the visual field to allow the eye to concentrate on the water, even though the quays were almost deserted for the moment.

Megan wasn't drinking, but she insisted that Simon have a glass of Pinot Grigio, and carefully waited until he had taken a capacious swig and made serious inroads into the bream before she finally broached the subject that was uppermost in her mind.

"I've been approached," she said, "twice in one day. I wanted to tell you about it, first of all to let you know where I stand, and secondly to give you a warning. I know both of the men who seem to be actively exploring the possibility of challenging the will, Bernard Pallister and Douglas Jefferson, from way back, and they might cause you difficulties if they have a mind to do so. Have either or both of them approached you?"

"About what?"

"I'll get to that in a minute. Am I right in assuming, then, that you haven't heard from either of them?"

"Yes."

"Well, it's possible that they're creeping up on you, and only contacted me first in the hope of finding out how the land might lie. Perhaps you'll be approached tomorrow, or the day after—but the more ominous possibility is that you won't, because they're already taking aim at you."

"Looking to challenge the will, you mean?"

"Of course."

"On what grounds?"

"How should I know? They've probably each got a clever lawyer looking for loopholes or possible dirty tricks to play. Even if they don't find any plausible grounds, they might do it anyway, in order to put pressure on you, to try to force you to make a deal."

"What sort of deal?"

"There's a lot of family history you don't know. I'm out of touch myself, since James never talked to me and the dribs and drabs of information I got out of Dougie, Bernard and a couple of the other relatives in the days when they were clients never added up to much. Even Dai's probably out of the loop now, although Dougie used to be quite thick with him back in the day. James hadn't tried to call one of his famous family meetings for thirty years when he died, and although Bernard still owns property in St. Madoc and Dougie owns a couple of cottages in Morpen, it must be nearly as long since either of them actually came to stay. Not that I'd know, necessarily; both of them had got to the stage of cutting me dead in the Mermaid a long time ago. I'd like to think that it was because Dai had told them that I was no longer on the game, but it's far more likely that they no longer thought I was attractive enough to be fuckable. I know for a fact that they hadn't given up on whores entirely, and still haven't; they just wanted fresher meat, and still do."

Simon had no idea whether he was supposed to react to that little tirade by telling her that she didn't look bad at all, for seventy, but thought it far safer to say nothing at all and wait for further explanations.

"Anyway," she said. "You know about the great Murden schism. You might or might not know that for a long time, when he first inherited the Abbey, James wanted the family to organize some kind of co-ordinated plan for the management of what had been the whole Murden estate. Exactly what he had in mind, I don't know, but I do know that Bernard and Dougie had very different ideas about how that plan might work—and that neither of them could begin to get his own scheme off the ground without James and one or two of the others aboard.

"Because of the way the schism worked out, Bernard's family mostly inherited immovable property—houses—while the previous generation of Jeffersons mostly got farmland . . . circumstances probably not unconnected with the fact that Bernard has built a career as a property developer and Dougie became a wholesale dealer in farm produce. I don't know any details, but I'm pretty sure that Bernard's grand plan for managing the hypothetical reintegrated estate, back in the seventies, involved demolishing all the old cottages in St. Madoc, Morpen and along the coast and launching a large-scale construction project of some kind. Dougie wanted to reorganize the farms, amalgamating the various fragments of land and streamlining the whole agricultural production process, possibly involving large facilities for various sorts of livestock. He might have changed his mind since, because he seems to have found it more profitable in recent decades to let his own land lie idle and collect fees for what I believe the jargon calls set-aside, although Brexit might put an end to that malarkey if what I see on the TV news is reliable."

"The economic context must have changed out of all recognition since the seventies," Simon observed, wincing because he had just accidentally imported a couple of fish-bones into his mouth with a chunk of bream, and was wondering whether it would look more disgusting if he used a finger to try to fish them out or separated them out carefully with his tongue and then spat them into his napkin.

"Of course it has," Megan agreed. "And they must both have been caught on the hop by James's death. Back in the seventies they must have expected him to die within five or ten years, and the possibility of him living to a hundred-and-whatever must have seemed exceedingly remote; as the decades went by, though, they must have begun to think that maybe he was going to go on forever—and then, *pow!* They might have updated their plans now and again over the years, but they'd probably fallen into obsolescence by virtue of neglect. If they were sane people like you and me, they'd just shrug their shoulders and say: *Well, it's too late to bother now.* But they obviously aren't prepared to do that . . . not, at least, without taking thorough soundings . . . and they obviously want help dredging the family mud."

"And now you're officially recognized as James's daughter, with a right of access to the documents kept in the Abbey . . ." Simon left the sentence dangling because he had finally managed to spit out the fish-bones, less discreetly than he would have liked. He took a swig of Pinot Grigio.

"That's doubtless part of their thinking," Megan agreed, a trifle cagily. "Personally, I think that both of them should have thrown the towel in back in the eighties, but when these rivalries set in, positions tend to harden, and although the dreams are put on the back burner, they never really die. While I was playing leper at the funeral and had plenty of time for looking on from the sidelines, I noticed that neither of them said a word to one another at the funeral, but that Dougie had quite a long chat with Felicia, which seemed to cause her some annoyance."

Simon couldn't help feeling a twinge of guilt about the reference to Megan "playing leper" at the funeral. He had, as it happened, taken note of the fact that all the "distant relatives" were conspicuously avoiding her, and had even thought that he ought to make some effort to ease her isolation, but his first responsibility had been to Felicia, who had been in dire need of both a support and a shield, and he had hardly quit her side.

"I remember," he said, reacting to her observation. "Little dark chap, a trifle slimy, tried to cut me out of the conversation. He wanted to go down into the crypt 'to see his old friend James laid to rest and to pay his respects to his ancestors,' and was reluctant to take no for an answer. Felicia said that he and James had never been friends, and weren't far off being enemies."

"That's right. You can be certain that he had some other reason for wanting to get into the crypt than the one he gave, although I can't imagine what. Anyway, the fact that he and Bernard both called me must mean that they're at least thinking of dusting off their old plans, to see whether a tweak here and there could still make them profitable. If one or other of them were actually able to get his hands on the residue of the estate, of course, it would be plain sailing from then on, but even without that, there might still be a deal to be done if you were to prove more tractable than James, or if pressure could be brought to bear on you to make you knuckle under. If one of them contacts you imminently, it probably means that he's decided to try friendly persuasion; if not, it almost certainly means that they're both looking hard for some potential leverage. You haven't, by any chance, told anyone about any ideas you might have for the future management of what's left of the estate if the will is proven?"

"I've discussed a few pie-in-the-sky ideas with Felicia and Cerys," said Simon—and then had second thoughts, and added. "Although I might have given Alun Gwynne grounds for thinking that I was sympathetic to his utopian ideas for trying to create what he called a real community . . . and Dai must have seen the effusive way he thanked me for giving James the nudge that persuaded him to meet with the Morpen DSS tenants."

"That would probably be enough to generate an impression, but it won't have done any harm. In any case, if they haven't changed since the seventies—and they probably haven't—they'll still be the kind of men to look for leverage first, even if they eventually decide to try negotiation. They're the kind of people who always play dirty, if they can find a way, as evidenced by their approaching me. They were very vague about the size of the bribes they were tacitly dangling, but that's understandable, given that they have no clear idea of what I might be able to offer. I got the strong impression that they're unaware that they're in competition with one another as well as you, but whether I could start an auction, if I wanted to, is anyone's guess."

"You don't want to start an auction?"

"No, I don't, and not just because I don't have anything to auction. But I thought I ought to warn you that they might come after you—and to warn you that, if or when they do contact you, you shouldn't take anything they say at face value. Obviously, you don't have to tell me if they do call, but my input might be useful before you respond to any offer that either of them might make, or react to any threat they might make."

"What kind of threat?"

"Again, how would I know? I just know that they're no strangers to making threats. Let's hope, though, that the situation doesn't get messy, for your sake."

Simon gave the prospect of the situation getting any messier than it already was a few moments' thought, while removing the last of the meat from the bones of his bream and then laying down his knife and fork. "It's not my own sake that worries me," he said, "so much as Felicia's. She's in a rather fragile condition at present, understandably, given that the narrow society she's been living in all her life has just been blown to kingdom come. But no one's likely to attack her, are they?"

"Probably not. But now I've turned them down and I'm legally established as James's daughter, I might be in the firing line myself . . . and so might your birth-mother, since she signed that document establishing your identity."

"You think they might try to discredit that in court, as well as your illicitly obtained DNA test?"

"Yes, I do—but I don't think they can cast any serious doubt on you being a Murden, no matter how much they'd like to do so. They'll have to be more ingenious than that if they hope to disqualify the will or break the entail . . . and trying to break the entail might be just as hazardous for them if they succeed as if they fail, because that would throw the whole situation into chaos for years. They're only a couple of years younger than me, so they don't really have years to waste. Disqualifying the will made on the eve of my father's death might have the same effect, if what the solicitor has told me about the previous will is true. The battle for the estate might then become a fight over shards, from which no one could get a big enough slice to make the hassle worthwhile. But they're not nice people—they might fight just for the sake of being perverse, especially if they each find out that the other is thinking along the same lines, which they're bound to do, sooner or later."

When the waiter came to collect the plates, Megan merely glanced at Simon's empty glass before ordering a second glass of wine for him, without bothering to consult him. He wasn't sure whether she was just asserting her authority as hostess, or trying to get him tipsy. He knew that there had to be more on her mind than possible challenges to James's will, and it wasn't too difficult to imagine reasons why she might think it worth trying to loosen his tongue a little.

"Wouldn't the sensible thing to do be for them to join forces?" he asked her, being in no rush to change the subject of the conversation.

"Probably, but they won't necessarily be sensible about it . . . and if they are, that might make thing worse for us . . . I mean, for you."

"No, it's okay," said Simon. "We can be us. Even if things don't get messy—and I must admit that I've been rather afraid myself that they might—I'd still get considerable comfort from the thought that someone is on my side, apart from Felicia."

"And Cerys," she pointed out, although there was a hint of question in her tone, which might, Simon feared, be only too justified.

"And Cerys," he said, even so.

"But you're not entirely sure of her. And you're even less sure of me, in spite of what I just said. Well, I can't blame you for that, even in advance of any slander you might hear from Bernard or Dougie."

The dessert menu arrived, along with another glass of Pinot Grigio, from which Simon took a substantial sip, thinking that a little loosening of the tongue might be a good idea. "I'm grateful for your support, Megan," he said, "and for your taking the trouble to declare it—all the more so as you don't know me from Adam, any more than your father did." He left it there, without posing an explicit question.

"So why am I doing it?" she said, asking it for him. "Well, I'm not looking for a bribe from you, any more than I'm interested in anything Bernard or Dougie might offer. For one thing, I have more than enough money for my simple needs, and for another, I'm not a prostitute any more and I take a certain belated pride in the fact that I can no longer be bought. It really pisses me off, in a big way, that those bastards both seem to be taking it for granted that I can be—and not only that, but they seem to think that because they used to pay to screw me forty years ago, and treated me with utter contempt then and since, that they somehow have some entitlement to my good will. Not so. If they let well alone, I won't bother them, as a matter of professional courtesy, but if they poke the tiger, believe me, the claws will come out. So that's why you'll have my solid support in any contest with them . . . mostly."

"Mostly?"

"Right. That's sufficient. I'm not asking you for any more. But there is something you might like to do for me, if you were that way inclined."

"What's that?" Simon asked.

"Don't play dumb, Simon," she countered, sounding not unlike his mother, although she was only a matter of months older than he was. "You know what. The family secret. I know James told you, a couple of days before he died. I know that the whole lot of them threw their arms open wide and treated you like the prodigal son, even though, as you just pointed out, they didn't actually know you from Adam, and even before I dropped my bombshell. Just like that, the unholy three told you the secret they'd been keeping from the whole world all their lives, and from poor Cerys too, if my guess is correct. Well, I'm a Murden too, now, officially and legally. So I think I'm entitled to know, and I can't ask my father any more. But I'm not trying to strike a bargain; you'll have my support regardless, against Dougie and Bernard and any other nuisances that might yet crawl out of the woodwork."

It's not the ones in the woodwork that worry me, Simon thought, but didn't say. *They might come from far stranger places than that.*

"I'm not trying to strike a bargain either," Simon assured her. "Your father ought to have told you everything years ago, for more reasons than one. He was far too stubborn for his own good, in my opinion. If I haven't told you everything already, it's because . . . well, things really have been very busy these last few weeks, and more confused than you know. Going to see Marianne was supposed to be a day off, in a way, a chance to think about something else . . . but it didn't exactly turn out that way"

"I'm sorry if I've spoiled it," she said, in a tone that was far more ironic than apologetic.

"That's not what I was implying," he hastened to say. "My mother . . . it's not her fault, obviously, but my visit provoked memories, things her grandmother had told her about the Murden family curse. It connected with things I've heard from James, and Felicia . . ."

"The grandmother in question being my great-aunt, Lilith Murden?" Megan queried, although it appeared to be a rhetorical question, because she went on: "I did some research into your genealogy after we met in the pub, that first night, as you know. Lilith's fully documented, and so is her father, Malcolm Murden. The connection from him to Rhys Murden is rock solid, and I can't see an assailable breach anywhere, but if, as you say, Dougie wanted to go down into the crypt to see James's ashes stowed away, it's probably because he wants to take a look at the tombstones, in the hope of finding some discrepancy with the documents."

Simon laughed. "In that case, he's welcome—there are no tombstones, and hardly any inscriptions of any sort. The Victorians do seem to have made a few token gestures in the direction of bringing their own burials into line with newly conventional funerary practices, but before that, the Murdens seem to have been just as secretive about their dead as everything else. Apart from scribbles on the flyleaf and half-title of the seventeenth-century family Bible, which has always been quietly rotting on the lectern in the chapel, where anyone can look at it, they didn't even keep a register of births, marriages and deaths, unless it's buried in some covert in the library I haven't found yet. Alexander Usher would have been just as disappointed if James had let him go down to inspect the masonry."

"You've looked at the annotations in the family Bible?" Megan prompted.

"Yes. There's nothing there but a list of names and dates, and a lot of those have been crossed out, presumably because the people in question left the Abbey and were struck off the family register. Some death-dates are filled in, but a lot aren't. I didn't see anyone looking at it during the funeral, but it was in plain view, and it would have been easy enough for Jefferson or anyone else to take a peek . . . or photographs, now that mobile phones are so versatile. I don't see how anything that might be written there, or not written there, could provide grounds for attacking James's will."

"Nor do I, but if Dougie or Bernard could prove that the conditions of entail requiring the Abbey to be left to a direct male descendant had been breached at some time in the past, and that James had no entitlement to inherit it himself, that might be a legally viable argument against your entitlement to inherit the estate from him. Then again, if the documentation could be proved to be corrupt—which might not be excessively difficult, given such dubious inclusions as the old lady's supposed age of birth—the chain of inheritance might be breached that way. As Alexander Usher told you, there have long been suspicions that the claims to extraordinary longevity made for certain members of the family, going back centuries, are fake, based on family members taking on the identity of their predecessors."

"But there are no doubts about the ages of James, Felicia and Melusine," Simon said.

"Probably not," Megan agreed, "but if it can be established that even one person who appears in the census records as a single individual was actually two or three individuals assuming the same identity, that contagion of doubt might spread to the entire branch of the family that has occupied the Abbey since Rhys Murden died, way back when. If that branch can be proved rotten, the possibility might exist of proving that another branch is sturdier, and has a better claim to the Abbey, the estate and the seven million . . . and the holy grail, if it really exists."

"The holy grail?" Simon queried, not believing for an instant that the mention was mere coincidence.

"Metaphorically speaking, obviously. There are too many legends round the family secret for any one of them to be believable, but everyone knows that there *is* a secret, and while no one knows what it is, imaginations run free. You know that Alexander Usher is coming back to St. Madoc tomorrow?"

"Yes. He's asked me to meet him in the Mermaid . . . and I'm beginning to think that he isn't just interested in the architecture of the building."

"Of course he's not. Why do you think he was up to his knees in mud on his last morning, trying to reach Nyder's Cave? He wanted to get into the crypt, and not just to look at the stonework."

"He was wasting his time, just like Jefferson. Air does filter through from Nyder's Cave to the crypt, but it comes through fissures that only a snake or an eel could get through."

"But he doesn't know that. And he doesn't know what the family secret is, any more than I do, and that whets his curiosity. He didn't mention the holy grail when he was filling you in on local history, but that isn't because he doesn't know that particular legend, and James must have mentioned it to you when he gave you his version. Dai Mermaid's always happy to chat about the so-called Celtic grail, and even the Cardi scum know about that and the Cauldron of Annwn, as well as all the other tall tales. I know as well as you do, though, that it's a load of rubbish . . . unless you're about to tell me that there really is a magic cauldron buried beneath the Abbey, once owned by the witch after whom Ceridwen was named?"

Simon contrived a brief ironic laugh. "Actually," he said, "there is. It certainly isn't the holy grail in the sense that the Reverend might understand the term, and it's certainly not the cave where Viviane might or might not have trapped the Merlin of Arthurian legend in suspended animation—in fact, I don't know what the hell it is—but it's certainly there. I've been in it."

Megan had picked up her spoon, ready to plunge it into the newly arrived dessert, but her gesture had been interrupted as soon as he began speaking. She looked at him sharply, to make sure that he wasn't joking, but she didn't bother to challenge him on that basis. She waited for him to continue.

"As I was saying a few minutes ago, before I interrupted myself," Simon said, very calmly, "the other reason why I haven't tried to tell you the secret since James died, apart from the fact that my time has been unusually pressured, isn't because I'm keeping it from you, but that I'm not at all sure that I'd be doing you any favors by letting you in on it. A month ago, I was living in Bristol and perfectly sane; now . . . well, there's a rich literature about secrets that are too dangerous to know, because knowing them drives you mad. I used to think they were absurd, but I'm not so sure any more. Not only do I think that I might be mad, but I think that anyone else I tell might be mad as soon as I've told them. I'm trying to lead Cerys into it gently, step by step, but the measured approach is just making her more impatient and frustrated. As for what I'm going to tell the Reverend tomorrow, if he presses me to let him into the crypt . . . I'm torn between telling him to go to hell metaphorically and showing him the way literally, just to serve him right for being too inquisitive . . ."

He stopped, uncomfortably aware that Megan was, indeed, looking at him as if he had just revealed unmistakable signs of madness.

"I told you so," he said. "Are you sure you want me to carry on?"

V
The Family Secret

For a moment or two, Megan Harwyn actually seemed to be in doubt, even though the intention of obtaining from him, either by means of persuasion or leverage, what he was about to tell her, was at least half of the reason why she had driven all the way from St. Madoc to Fishguard to intercept him on his homeward journey. Simon suspected, though, that her apparent doubt was illusory. He felt sure that curiosity would win, and that everything he had just said to her could only have served to whet her appetite. Crazy or not, she wanted to hear everything he was ready to tell her—and more, if she could winkle it out of him.

"Are you suggesting," she queried, her voice dripping sarcasm, "that the reason that James has kept me out of the family for all these years is that he wanted to protect me from it?"

"No," Simon said. "The reason that James refused to admit that you were his daughter until Ceridwen finally managed to bully him into it doing it posthumously, even though everyone in the family—and, so far as I can tell, everyone living within a ten-mile radius of Morgan's Fork—knew that it was true, is that he was stubborn, and once having told the lie, he couldn't let go of it. On the other hand, I suspect that the reason he delayed telling Cerys for so long really is that he was trying to protect her from the consequences of knowing it. Felicia certainly thinks that he's been trying to protect her all her life, by refusing to let her in on certain aspects of the secret that Ceridwen and Melusine knew.

"As I say, I'm not sure that James wasn't justified in delaying letting Cerys in on the secret—but I think that she's entitled to know at least as much as I know, just as you are. I also feel obliged to warn you, though, as I've warned her, that the secret might be dangerous, at least to your mental health. I can't seek or obtain your informed consent, because of the obvious paradoxicality, but I do feel that I need your uninformed consent to be informed. Even if James was too stubborn to realize that he needed your help, I'm not—all the more so since you've just volunteered it. But like you, I'm not trying to strike a bargain. If, when you've heard what I have to say, you want to withdraw your offer of support and not to have anything further to do with me, I'll understand."

"I'll take that under advisement, as the legal jargon has it, and let you know my decision in due course. In the meantime, get on with it. We haven't got all night, have we?"

"Fair enough. I'll tell you everything I know—and I'll show you the magic cauldron too. But it will take time; we're already on dessert, and it's a long drive home. I can only make a beginning now, and it might take weeks to get through the thousand questions you'll have, most of which I won't be able to answer with any certainty. Tomorrow, though, I'll give you a copy of the memory stick that I gave Cerys, which James was compiling before he died, so that you can begin sifting through the so-called evidence yourself. Maybe, given time, you can make a better fist of it than he could, or me."

"Oh," she said, sounding slightly surprised, "that's different. For a moment, there, I thought you were going to say there are initiation rituals, as in the masons, or even that women couldn't be admitted to the inner circle."

"I suspect that there probably were initiation rituals at one time," Simon said, equably. "But women always seem to have been in the inner circle, as you put it, at least since the days when Owen Murden was given the Abbey by Henry VIII . . . especially women like Ceridwen and Felicia . . . and my niece Zoe, it seems."

"Sorry, you've lost me."

"Female children identical to their mother—clones, we'd call them nowadays, or parthenogenetic births. As Marianne was telling me, a few hours ago, it's not as uncommon as people used to think, and it's not supernatural, although it must have seemed so in Saint Madoc's day . . . and in Seymour Murden's, come to that. Ceridwen's unusual influence within the family seems to have stemmed originally from the fact that she was both the daughter of some such unusual birth and that at least one of her four children was similar . . . although it's hardly surprising, if it's a genetic anomaly, that it repeats, albeit inconsistently. Felicia's never had a child, but Zoe's daughter doesn't seem to be identical."

"Oh," said Megan. "Well, to get back to the original point, do you really think that knowing the secret has driven you mad, and that it might drive me mad too . . . like my father?"

"I don't know—but I never got a chance to put the thousand questions to James that I would now like to ask him, and my research with Felicia isn't making much progress as yet. If only Melusine would come back, we might be able to take a mighty leap forward in understanding, but so far, we haven't seen any sign of her."

"Melusine's alive?"

"Yes."

"Where is she?"

"Somewhere under the water. Wherever she took me when she tipped me off the bridge the night the Abbey was struck my lightning."

Once again, that had the effect of making her stare at him as if he were, indeed, completely mad. But he had warned her, and she had obviously made a resolution not to rush to any sort of judgment. Her face cleared, she swallowed a spoonful of crème brûlée, and then manifested a truly creditworthy serenity. "Don't you think it would be better to begin at the beginning?" she asked.

"Absolutely. But you've already heard most of the beginning from Alexander Usher—the difficult bit is detaching the slim thread of truth from the vast tangle of legend. I'm far from confident in James's success in doing that, and he was unsure himself, but he was certainly the only expert, and he was a fine scholar and an intelligent interpreter. I'm inclined to trust the greater part of his interpretation of the legend of Saint Madoc and the Murdens' centuries-long intercourse with the morgens."

Megan paused for thought, but she had almost run out of crème brûlée, and it didn't require much chewing anyway, so the potential for symbolic rumination was limited. Eventually, she said: "You're telling me that my father believed that Saint Madoc really did sail into the Atlantic and make a deal with the queen of the Morgens to bring back some sort of treasure—a cauldron, according to Dai Mermaid's version of the story—which is still buried in a cave under the Abbey?"

"Yes and no. James believed that Saint Madoc did sail to the west of Ireland, and perhaps all the way to the Sargasso Sea, although I have my doubts about that. He also believed that some kind of a bargain was struck, not with the morgens *per se*, but with the neider, the master and probable creator of the morgens."

"Neider as in sea serpent?"

"More like a giant hydra, with tentacles capable of being mistaken for sea serpents. The neider definitely exists, although I suppose it's conceivable that I only dreamed that I was inside it, trying to make telepathic contact with it."

He was going too fast; it was too confusing. Megan took a deliberate step back, to the beginning—or, at least, to the legend of Saint Madoc, "And the deal that the Abbey's founder made with . . . whatever . . . involved a cauldron?"

"Yes, but not quite the kind of magic cauldron that features in the Mabinogion and other fragments of Welsh folklore—the kind that Lewis Spence and others have tried to connect with the Arthurian legend of the holy grail. It's something much weirder, way beyond the scope of Saint Madoc's imagination, or Myrddin Wylt's, or Seymour Murden's . . . and perhaps mine too, although I'm doing my best. But it does exist; as I say, I've been inside it, and I can take you there if you want, so that you can see it for yourself. If you do go down there, though, you won't be the same when you come out."

"Mad, you mean?"

"In the eyes of others, yes. Perhaps your own, too. Perhaps only intoxicated, and perhaps only for a while. I thought I was still thinking clearly when I came out, but I started seeing and hearing things that probably weren't what I thought I was seeing and hearing. James was with me, but whether he experienced any after-effects, I don't know. He'd been down there many times before though, so his mind might have adapted. Felicia's been down there several times, and so has Melusine, but I can't advance either of them as a convincing example of people who have come to no harm there. In my judgment, neither of them is mad, any more than James was . . . but they're certainly different.

"I'd like to think that I'm not mad myself, obviously—but even if I am, I still need to try and think this through, to explain and rationalize it. James dedicated his life to that quest, and that's what he was leaving me in his testament. The Abbey is just the shell, and the seven million is just spending money. The real legacy is the puzzle—the problem. I think there was more hope than conviction in his choosing me as an heir, but he'd probably reached the straw-grasping stage. And he had Ceridwen on his back too. She was convinced that I'd been chosen and brought by the neider, and that I'm part neider myself; she almost had me convinced of it too, for a moment."

He was still going too fast. Megan backed up again. "So, this cauldron thing has been underneath the Abbey since the Abbey's founders buried it in 400 A.D. or thereabouts?"

"The story James put together is a trifle murky on the matter of its origin. The makers of the legend of Saint Madoc represent the entity underneath the Abbey as something that Madoc brought back from the island he visited, whether that was one of the Bermudas or a Caer-Ys much closer to home. Ceridwen seems to have believed that, but James wasn't so sure, and I'm even less so. It's possible—probable, in my opinion—that the cauldron was already on the tine when Madoc's missionaries arrived, and that the Abbey was constructed on top of it, perhaps because it had already been a sacred site for some time. The early Christians often built their churches on sites sacred to the pagans they were intent on converting.

"It's also possible, although this is pure speculation on my part, that the deal that Madoc made with the neider was intended to help the neider form more productive links with the vitreous cocoons—that's what James called the contents of the cauldron. I suspect that the neider wanted, and perhaps needed, the help of both morgens and humans in order to try to build a chain of communication between its own world and the vitreous cocoons, in order to link up with a facility that the vitreous cocoons had, and still have, for communication with intelligences elsewhere."

"Elsewhere?" Megan queried.

"I can't be more specific—that's one of the key pieces of the puzzle. The contents of the cauldron are some kind of exotic matter, which has links to other exotic matter, perhaps very distant matter, billions of miles away in other solar systems, or within the stars themselves, or perhaps displaced in spatial dimensions we can't perceive."

Megan put down her spoon, which she had been holding in her right hand even though there was no longer anything for it to spoon. She looked at Simon's glass, which was empty again, with a kind of envy that only designated drivers can experience. "I see what you mean," she said.

Simon was surprised by that, and it must have shown.

"Oh, not about what you just said—I mean about not being able to know the secret without going mad. Except that you're really not mad, are you? You're probably saner than you have any right to be, in the circumstances."

Simon almost smiled, knowing what a considerable imaginative leap that was. He had been able to make it because he had had a lifetime of professional training in making imaginative leaps, for the sake of confecting imaginative fictions with at least an appearance of plausibility. For someone whose sanity was more securely anchored, someone essentially down-to-earth, it seemed to him to be quite an achievement.

"I wish I could be sure," he said. "But no, I don't think that I'm mad yet, in spite of having to believe so many strange things in order to sustain that conviction. Nor was James. He simply accepted the evidence, bizarre as it is, and tried to make sense of it. Others had tried before him, including some who were doubtless just as intelligent, but they didn't have adequate conceptual tools with which to work. James hadn't either, but he did his best to keep up as new ones became available. I probably don't myself, but like James, I might be able to get a little closer than those who came before me, by standing on their giant shoulders and peering hard into the gloom. I hope so, because I think that the matter is becoming urgent."

"Why?"

"I wish I knew. After centuries of quiescence, the neider has evidently been stimulated into action, perhaps sooner than it would have preferred. As the neider told me the first night I arrived in St. Madoc, via Lenore, in the clearest message I've been able to receive thus far, although the neider had to make use of my own memories and stocks of knowledge to formulate it in words: *Time is out of joint; the storm is up and all is on the hazard; and certain stars shot madly from the spheres.*"

"Which means?"

"The phrases are borrowed from Shakespeare, so the precise wording is a trifle archaic and oblique, but precisely because it was the first communication, and completely unexpected, it seems to have come through the well of the unconscious relatively unpolluted. There have been other messages since; you might have received some yourself, without understanding them, or realizing what they were. It seems to run in the family, including the Bristol branch. I'll need more pieces before I can begin to put them together properly with any degree of confidence, but the fundamentals seem clear enough. Something has happened, or is about to happen, and things could get messy.

"It would help enormously if a more effective channel of communication could be established than fugitive fragments of dreams. James was trying, and so is Felicia. I'm sure that the neider is trying too. Taking Melusine was a bold move, but thus far, it doesn't seem to have paid any obvious dividends. Taking me temporarily was a logical move too, but the returns on that one also seem to have been painfully limited. If that stupid lightning bolt hadn't killed James, we might have made much more rapid headway together, but the best laid plans of mice and men . . . anyway, you're beginning to glimpse the picture, I hope . . . because if you're going to help, and I truly hope that you can, you're going to have to get up to speed quickly, at least as quickly as I did when it was sprung on me."

After a few seconds of silence, Megan signaled to the waiter and asked for two espressos and the bill.

"Well," she said, eventually. "That wasn't what I expected, or anything like. You might need to be careful who you tell that to, because if certain nasty minds got hold of it, they'd probably try to have you committed. Not easy, in this day and age, but not impossible either. The old lady was working with James on this puzzle, you say—and had been working on it with others long before that, if we can believe the birthdate she put on her census returns?"

"Yes and no. She and James had different ideas about exactly what was going on and what it all might mean—but she was by far and away his most prolific link with the neider, precisely because she lived so close to the edge between sanity and apparent madness. I don't think he appreciated her input as much as he should have done. Losing both of them in such quick succession is a terrible blow to the cause, but we just have to soldier on. Unless, of course, you want to back out and have nothing to do with it, now you've begun to glimpse how much danger there is to your own sanity."

"You have to be joking," she said. "I'm seventy years old and I've wasted the last thirty years of my life twiddling my thumbs in the arse end of nowhere, trying to poke my father's dormant conscience. There comes a time when a strong dose of insanity is the only thing that can stave off the utter tedium of growing old. I knew I was right to jump for joy when I saw you moving in next door, but I had no idea how high I should have been leaping. This stuff is manna from Heaven, as far as I'm concerned, and way better than anything I could have imagined. Do you really think it was wise to tell Cerys, though? She's got a lot more to lose than you or me. Presumably that's why James kept her out of it."

"She'll need to make her own decision, but if she wants to cut and run, I certainly won't blame her. On the other hand I'm not at all sure that running does any good. My mother certainly isn't out of it, and nor, I suspect, are any of her descendants. Running away from the Abbey doesn't seem to have done your great-aunt Lilith as much good as she hoped."

Megan insisted on paying the bill—in cash—but she allowed Simon to put a fiver in the pot for the tip.

"The car's just along the quay," she told him, when they turned left outside the door. Simon walked to her left, but he was careful to keep a safe six or eight feet from the edge of the quay, where there was a sheer drop to the surface of the water, some eight or ten feet below. They were walking rather hesitantly, almost in slow motion.

"And you've actually seen this neider thing?" Megan questioned. "On the night of the storm, when you turned up the next morning with two black eyes and bruised all over? You hadn't fallen in at all—Melusine had pushed you in, and dived in with you?"

"That's right," said Simon.

"Why? I mean, why did Melusine push you?"

"In crude terms, because the neider told her to do it. It summoned her. It had a firmer grip on her than anyone else, except Ceridwen. The storm created, or was associated with, a mental disturbance on Melusine's part that enabled the neider to make use of her. I think it's still trying to secure its mental link with her, in order to use her as a mouthpiece far more effective than poor Lenore. Obviously, it's having difficulties . . . complex difficulties. I'm trying as hard as I can to pick up messages, and so is Felicia, but maybe the effort itself is counterproductive. There might be several reasons why my birth-mother, for the moment, is a better receiver."

Megan stopped, so Simon stopped too. She looked at him quizzically. "Angela Richardson told you that she's received a message from the neider?" she queried.

"No, she told me that she's received a message from Hell—a message for me."

"Which was?"

"As above, so below."

"That's all?"

"Yes. She didn't know what it meant, although she must have heard the phrase, and must have some vague notion of its implication."

"It's ancient mysticism," Megan said, seemingly wanting to demonstrate that she was capable of keeping up intellectually. "It means that the microcosm—which is to say, human being—reflects the macrocosm: universal being."

"Actually," Simon said, "it's not that ancient, although it pretends to be. It comes from a fake alchemical document, the *Tabula Smaragdina,* or Emerald Tablet, which claimed to be a twelfth-century Latin translation of an earlier Arabic document. Thirteenth-century scholars of alchemy—mostly monks, probably including those at St. Madoc's Abbey—were fascinated by it, and Isaac Newton translated it into English during his occult phase. It still had a big reputation during the nineteenth-century Occult Revival, especially in Theosophist doctrine. It is, as you say, supposed to say something about the relationship between human and cosmic being, the microcosm and the macrocosm, but it doesn't actually say very much. It's one of those portentous remarks that, as philosophers are wont to say, is either trivial or false."

"So why would the neider want to send it to your mother as a message?"

"I have no idea. I'm not sure that it's actually from the neider. I'm not even sure that it's actually a message. Maybe my mother is simply going crazy, and her dreams are dredging up the kind of pseudo-intellectual froth that she associates with her idea of me because of the little she knows about my writing. On the other hand, maybe it really is a cosmic revelation that would enlighten me, if I only had the brain of Isaac Newton."

Automatically, he looked up, as if in hope that the macrocosm might supply some helpful comment by way of the stars. It didn't. There were no stars visible. There was nothing above him but impenetrable darkness, between the dazzling glare of two high-powered street-lamps.

Megan evidently decided to drop that line of enquiry, and backed up again to something that seemed more relevant. "But where did you actually *go*, when Melusine took you into the water?" she asked.

"I don't know. I was already in an altered state of consciousness, probably hallucinating. It seemed to me that we dived down to the seabed and kept going, into a cocoon of exotic matter, where the neider lives, or is rooted. I can't be sure. I definitely fell in the water, but after that . . . I didn't drown. It really was like being cocooned, or transported back to the womb. It felt safe."

"And you were under the water all night?"

"Yes," he said.

Simon was about to try to explain, in his customary pedantic fashion, that the neider evidently had some means, when it cocooned someone at the interface of its own exotic space, of feeding oxygen to the blood so that its prisoner didn't asphyxiate, when something surged out of the water in the harbor, rising over the edge of the quay and continuing to rise until its tip was level with his eyes.

Then, swaying so that the tip in question was directly in front of Simon and Megan, the tentacle moved sideways, and the tip split like a pair of eyelids to expose a yellow eye with a lenticular pupil. Although they were between two of the tall lamps along the edge of the quay, there was plenty of ambient light coming from various directions, and the eye reflected that light, glistening almost to the extent that it seemed phosphorescent. It seemed to Simon to be meeting his astonished gaze and looking deep into his eyes, all the way to the inner darkness of his mind.

Music crashed into his consciousness with thunderous loudness, and it only took a couple of seconds and three or four notes for him to recognize it. Almost as soon as he had put a name to it, the eyelid closed again, and the long tentacle fled, not sinking vertically in a reversal of the fashion in which it had risen but moving horizontally, like a whiplash. The splash as it hit the surface of the water was audible, but not very loud. Ripples spread, but soon died away, and the tentacle itself disappeared completely.

VI
Driving in the Dark

Simon became aware of a sharp pain in the back of his right hand, which he imagined momentarily as a snake-bite, but when he looked down he saw that Megan had grabbed his hand and had clutched it convulsively, digging two of her long fingernails into his flesh and drawing blood.

"Ow!" he said.

She did not let go immediately, but the grip relaxed, and she withdrew the claws.

She didn't apologize. In the variegated light, he could see that her face was very pale. He looked round. In spite of the Sabbath gloom, in the direction from which they had come there were people outside the restaurant, chatting. There were also people visible in the other direction even though the quay was largely empty of workers, but they too were going about their business as if nothing had happened. He knew, however, that it had not been a hallucination; the simple fact was that the other people had not seen the tentacle, even though it had been clearly visible, let alone the yellow eye. Only he and Megan had seen it.

He had turned his attention to the back of his hand, and was feeling the pain, when the door of a car slammed, some twelve or fifteen feet away. Megan had run to it in a panic, pulling her push-button door release out of her coat pocket.

When Simon had joined her, climbing into the passenger seat of the BMW, she was holding on to the steering wheel with both hands, and staring straight ahead through her windscreen.

"That was real, wasn't it," she said, tersely.

"Yes," he said.

"Tell me what you saw," she commanded.

"A tentacle came out of the water in the harbor. Then it opened an eye—a lidded yellow eye. Then I heard the music."

She turned her head sharply. "What music?"

"The opening bars of *Also Sprach Zarathustra*, by Richard Strauss."

"The music from *2001: A Space Odyssey*?" She was much the same age as he was; she might well have seen the movie in a widescreen cinema, in its full glory.

"Yes," he said. "You didn't hear it?"

"No."

"You didn't hear anything?"

"No . . ." The *but* was implied rather than articulated.

"You saw something else? Or felt something."

Her hands on the steering wheel were still clutching it tightly; her arms were rigid.

"I don't know," she said. "No." It was a transparent lie. She continued to hold her position.

Simon sympathized. She had taken it all in her psychological stride when it was all just words, playing with ideas. It had amused her: imaginative manna from Heaven, as she said. But actually seeing the neider, and having it look into her . . . that was something else. And whatever else she had seen or felt, instead of the music, had disturbed her.

80

But why here? he couldn't help thinking. *Why now? What the Hell does it think it's playing at?*

"It's okay," he said, aloud, in a far less hysterical tone. "It really doesn't mean us any harm. Quite the contrary; it's trying to communicate, but it doesn't know how. It's only with immense difficulty that it can employ material form. It really is very alien, and our minds must be as far beyond its imagination as it is beyond ours. But it seems to be trying to tell us something, and it can't do it directly, because it has to channel it through the unconscious part of our minds, where the signal can pick up all manner of noise and imagistic detritus. It picked up fragments of Shakespeare the first time it tried to contact me; this time it picked up a fragment of music, but trying to figure out what the music is trying to signify . . . my first hypothesis might have been Nietzsche's book about the *übermensch*, but I think your instinct might have been right; what those few bars now signify to me, and to almost everyone of our generation, is the scene in the movie where the first spark of alien inspiration creeps into the ape's brain. Not a flattering suggestion, I suppose, but I can't quarrel with its aptitude. I just wish it could take us a little further forward."

"But the message was intended for you?" she queried, hoarsely. "I just happened to be there."

"I honestly don't know. Maybe it wasn't a message. Maybe the eye was just an eye looking into us in order to try to gather information. Maybe the music I heard was just a prompt, a spur, to produce a mental reaction that it wanted to gauge. And perhaps I'm the one who just happened to be there, while it was taking a look at you, measuring . . ."

"Shut up," she said, tersely.

He obeyed, and waited. Eventually, he thought, she would relax, and would then pull herself together.

"Sorry," she said, after a full three minutes. "I'm being stupid. There's no need to act like an idiot over something so simple. What were you saying about the neider having to channel its communications through the unconscious?"

"People tend to think of telepathy as a matter of transmitting images of speech or pictures from one conscious mind to another, but that's just a plausible impossibility—there's no possible mechanism for it. Such mind-to-mind communication as can exist, employing energies inaccessible to our ordinary senses, seems to be between the unconscious parts of two minds. Very frustrating, obviously, because the contents and workings of the unconscious parts of our minds are, by definition, not directly perceptible by consciousness; but the unconscious part of the mind can provoke conscious images, and routinely does. The most familiar irruptions occur in dreams, but there are more than we realize in waking states of the mind. It's difficult to decode the images, and to deduce what might be happening in the unconscious to produce them, all the more so if the unconscious part of the mind is reacting itself to some kind of stimulus from elsewhere. What's happening is more like empathy than telepathy, the things transmitted being more akin to feelings than speech, and it's sometimes easier for the conscious mind to respond to the provocation by producing music rather than speech or pictures; but that, or something like it, is what seemed to me to be happening when I was cocooned by the neider, and I'm sure of that much, even if most of the rest inevitably remained enigmatic."

She mulled that over for a few seconds, and then said: "So the message can get confused in passing from the unconscious part of the recipient's mind to the conscious?"

"That's putting it mildly," Simon replied. "Looking back on the seeming communications I've received, I suspect that they've been considerably polluted by input from my own unconscious. And that's only half the problem. Assuming that the neider is possessed of a consciousness too, which is attempting to import specific material into the unconscious part of its mind or transmission, the message could well get garbled in the transmission phase as well as the reception phase. Add to that the fact that the neider's consciousness and human consciousness might be more different, more alien, than we can imagine, and you can begin to glimpse the problem involved in trying to figure out what a snatch of *Also Sprach Zarathustra* might be trying to tell me."

"Or why your own mind is reacting that way to a provocation, if it isn't trying to tell you anything at all," she reminded him.

"Or that," he admitted.

"Better hope that you were right and I was wrong, then," she observed, sourly.

"Pardon?"

"Better hope that you were right about the music being a message intended to suggest Nietzsche to you, urging you to step up and be an *übermensch*, and not just a random nudge from some alien slab that thinks you're a stupid ape."

Simon was by no means sure that it was a matter of either/ or. He suspected that the truly significant thing about the encounter was not the nature of the image that had been transmitted to or produced by his mind but the location in which the encounter had taken place, distant from Morgan's Fork. Was it possible, he wondered, that the reason the neider was having difficulty getting messages to him there was because the proximity of the vitreous cocoons was impeding rather than assisting the transmissions?

"You're right," was what he said aloud, to Megan. "That is, indeed, the better hope. After all, it's what all of us ought to be striving toward: taking control of our destiny, to the extent that it's possible, becoming creators instead of passive members of the human herd."

"Amen. And how's that working out for you?"

Simon wasn't certain whether or not she was trying to make a joke in order to regain command of herself, but he assumed that she was. He was prepared to be a trifle flippant himself, in that event. "Not well, so far," he admitted, "but it's not entirely my fault. I can't help feeling a trifle miscast. Personally, if I were the neider, I wouldn't have picked me to carry its torch. How desperate must it have been to find an heir for the Abbey at short notice in order to have settled on me? I'm not obvious *übermensch* material, am I? Talk about scraping the bottom of the barrel."

"False modesty doesn't become you, Simon. I haven't read much of your work yet, but I only have to know that you're a writer to know that you secretly think that you're an intellectual superman. So stop whining, and let's get on with the job, shall we?"

She finally switched on the ignition, and backed out of the parking space. Half a minute later they were on the road heading north, away from the lights of the port, and those of the town.

Then, once again, she said: "Sorry. Don't mind me. It's just that . . . well, you wouldn't understand."

"Probably not," Simon agreed. "There's painfully little I do understand. But whatever it is that upset you, I'd like to know, if it isn't too painful to tell me. Every little helps in the erection of the edifice of understanding."

"Is that supposed to be a joke?" she snapped, but immediately corrected herself. "No, of course not; it's just your unconscious mind giving what passes for your intellect a little nudge. But there was really no need for me to react like that, and there's certainly no need for me to continue reacting. Yes, to set your mind at rest, when that filthy yellow eye looked into mine, I felt something. Specifically, I felt as if a big prick was being rammed up my you-know-what. Nothing that I haven't felt ten thousand times before, obviously, but believe me, nothing's been up there for so long that it's a wonder the bloody thing hasn't scarred over. Satisfied?"

"It's not what I expected," Simon admitted. "But it's been one of those days where the unexpected is ubiquitous."

She muttered something inaudible under her breath, which he thought unlikely to have been complimentary. After another pause, she said: "Given that I've just confessed something intensely personal for the sake of your curiosity, will you give me an honest answer to a personal question, in order to help me settle a question that preys on my mind sometimes?"

"Yes," he said simply, hoping that he would have the guts to do it.

"When I suggested to you once that you might have met one or two of my clients, you said that you didn't use prostitutes. Was that true?"

"Yes."

"Never, or just hardly ever"

"Never."

"Don't relax—that wasn't the question. Why not?"

That, again, was unexpected, although he thought he could understand why she was asking. "You want an honest answer," Simon said slowly, "and I'd like to think that I could give you one, but it's one of those things where people aren't always honest with themselves. Maybe I just had an abnormally low sex drive and never felt the need that propelled others. Maybe I was just too timid to go shopping. Those aren't the answers I give myself, but I can't swear absolutely that the answer I give myself is honest."

"Give it to me anyway."

"Well, I never had sex with anyone just for the sake of the orgasm, or for scoring notches on an imaginary bedhead. What I always wanted from sex, and sometimes thought I got from it, was *being wanted*, before, during and after. And all you can buy from a prostitute is the orgasm, anything else is fake. You'll probably tell me that it's just as fake with anyone else, and that I was fooling myself thinking that there was a difference, and you might be right, but if so, with my wife, and the girlfriends I had before my wife, I was fooled; with a prostitute, I couldn't have been. I don't disapprove of prostitution; there's a demand, so there's a supply. Some of the supply is exploitation, and a lot of it desperation, which casts a shadow over the whole business, but I only disapprove of the exploiters and I only feel sorry for the exploited and the desperate. That's all I can say. You're in a better position than I am to judge how common or rare that is."

"Don't be ridiculous," she snapped. "Given that people who feel like you do would be excluded from my sample by definition, how could I possibly compare their number with people who don't?"

"Fair point," he conceded. "Why did you ask?"

"I wanted to get a sense of how much of a hypocrite you are. Having a suspicious mind, I thought that the only reason why you would make a point of not using prostitutes is that you secretly despised them, and were only pretending not to disapprove. I wanted to know whether I'd committed myself to defending and helping someone who was just as bad, in his own way, as the fuckers I hate. But at least you've given me a plausible story, so I'll give you the benefit of the doubt, even though I know you're a professional storyteller, and dead wrong about one part of your argument."

"Which part?"

"I wouldn't have told you that you were fooling yourself thinking there was a difference. That would be ridiculous. If there were nothing real to fake, there'd be no point in faking it. If what you say is true, you were absolutely right: what you had with your wife and girlfriends was better, while it lasted. Far better. So much better that you'd have been a fool to pay for the mere illusion. Mercifully, there are a lot of fools in the world."

"Mercifully?" Simon queried.

"Bad choice of words. You know what I mean: it's still my source of income, even though it's been a long time since I did any of the donkey work myself."

"I'm not so sure that I was absolutely right, or even that it's possible to be absolutely right. The difference between real and fake isn't that clear, and there are a lot of degrees in between. There's almost always an agenda in wanting someone; it's never pure. Or maybe I'm just a cynical and an embittered old man."

"Maybe," she agreed. "Imagine what that makes me."

"Not so very different, if you really agree with my argument."

"All the difference in the world, darling—that *darling* was fake, by the way."

"I think I could have worked that out. I realized some years ago that nobody was ever likely to want me again, sincerely, because that kind of wanting, in essence, is a reaction to visual stimuli that I can no longer provide." Mentally, he made one important reservation, but it wasn't one that he was going to spell out for Megan Harwyn.

"If you're fishing for a compliment," she said, "forget it."

"I wasn't. Are you?"

"No—but not for the same reason as you. I know how many desperate men there are in the world, and I flatter myself that I could still hook one, good and hard, if I wanted to, even at seventy. But I don't. So I can do without the compliments and I don't go fishing for them. And if you feel tempted to tell me that that's a pity or that you feel sorry for me, suppress the temptation."

"I'll be careful," Simon promised. There was another silence while the car headed into the darkness, with only its headlights and the white line in the middle of the road to guide it. It had started to rain, but only lightly, hardly more than a drizzle.

Eventually, he said: "When you said back in the restaurant, that you were ready to help me, if Pallister or Jefferson does decide to challenge the will, what kind of help did you have in mind?"

"I'm good with computers. I've already done the genealogical research in which Dougie, at least, seems to be hoping to find some grounds for a challenge to the line of succession. They're doubtless scouring the web for anything they might be able to use against you, but that cuts both ways. Even if you and your nearest and dearest aren't squeaky clean, I'm willing to bet that you're a lot cleaner than they are. If they want to play dirty, I can play dirtier. I've had practice. So, if you find yourself under any sort of attack, don't suffer in silence. I'll be better able than you are to figure out where it's coming from, and, if necessary, to retaliate."

"Is that why they contacted you?" Simon asked. "Because they wanted those skills in their side?"

"No. They don't know me. They probably have a vague idea of how I make my living, but they don't know me at all, in any sense but the biblical, half a lifetime ago. From your viewpoint, I'm a secret weapon."

"I'm glad you're on my side, then," Simon remarked.

"And you're cynically wondering why. It's complicated. Not as complicated as the family secret, obviously, but tangled enough. Put it down to the enemy of your enemy being your friend, if you like. The bastards could have welcomed me to the family, you know, at the funeral. They could have told me that they were glad that James had finally come clean. They could have decided to forget a past that's older than their children. They could have behaved like nice people. But no. Once a leper, always a leper. I forgave you for barely glancing in my direction, because I knew that you were looking after Felicia, but them? There's no way I'm going to let the estate—my father's estate—fall victim to their predation."

"Even if it turns out to be a poisoned chalice rather than a holy grail?" Simon queried.

"Absolutely. Even if your friend the neider has a very funny way of introducing himself. Hold the bastards off. Don't even give the Reverend Usher the chance to pry, let alone Dougie Jefferson. Don't worry about him, by the way, if he does rear his ugly little head I can take care of him, and Bernard too."

"How?" asked Simon, uneasily.

"You read the newspapers; you know how easy it is to inconvenience people by disrupting their cyberspatial dependencies—even innocent people. These guys aren't innocent, and they aren't very clever at covering their backs—a fatal combination, if push comes to shove. It probably won't, but I mean what I say. If they start hitting below the belt, at you or anyone else. I'll trash their lives."

"Have you done things like that before?"

"No comment."

"You do know that that sounds even more like a yes than a simple yes would have done?"

"No comment—but I'll put a hypothetical case to you, if you like. You probably think that I build and service websites for whores in order to make a nice commission, and you wouldn't be entirely wrong, but the other reason is that selling sexual services through the internet is a hell of a lot safer, if it's done carefully, than working the streets. There's a common presumption that prostitutes can't be raped, which has the consequence that they get raped all the time, sometimes violently. But if anything like that happens to a girl who does all or most of her touting via the web, her encounters tend to leave an electronic trail. Lots of clients think they can cover that trail up, or lead it into dead ends, but relatively few of them are clever enough to do that properly. Hypothetically speaking, if something like that happened to a girl using a good web maintenance service, that service provider might well have means of making sure that the perpetrator didn't do it again. But personally, I would never do anything illegal, you understand. Absolutely never, darling."

"I see. Well, as I said, I'm glad to have you on my side. I certainly wouldn't want you as an enemy."

"You certainly wouldn't. So you'll keep me up to date with all developments, won't you, and let me know if anything happens that might interfere with my right of residency in the Abbey? Not that I intend taking it up, mind—I'm happy where I am. But if you need anything, my skills are at your disposal, for genealogical research, or any other kind. Don't ask me to go in the water, though. I'm not sure that I like your friend the neider, and the kind of responses he provokes. Messages of that kind I can do without. Do you really believe that Melusine will come back?"

"It's not a matter for belief, but I can't see the point of the neider keeping her indefinitely. If she doesn't come back, she can't be of any further use, so far as I can see, but if she does, she'll be the ideal go-between, if the neider can succeed in making clear to her what it wants to communicate to us. Presumably, that's not simple, but it can't be impossible. We'll see her again, I'm sure of it—some of us, at any rate. So, do you want to see it?"

"What?"

"The family secret. The Cauldron of Annwn. The vitreous cocoons."

"Of course I do. When's good for you?"

"Tomorrow, if you like. I'll pop next door to Sanderling after lunch, between one and two, if you like—my working routine has gone to Hell, so you won't be interrupting—and we can walk over to the Abbey. I've got my own key to the padlock on the gate, although it's rarely locked during the daytime now James is no longer around to enforce discipline, and I'll pick up the keys to the other padlocks in the morning. We won't need to go through the house—we can get into the chapel through the western door, and we can go straight down to the Underworld to take a look at the stew in the cauldron. Then, when we meet Alexander Usher in the Mermaid in the evening, we'll both have the advantage of first-hand information about what he's really looking for."

"He won't want me there. He disapproves of prostitutes, even ones who gave up providing services directly half a lifetime ago."

"He'll just have to ask himself what Jesus would do won't he? Anyway, he's probably the least of our worries. I don't want to let him into the crypt, even though there's nothing there that would interest him beyond his fascination with church architecture, but saying no to him is only a problem in tactful diplomacy. Dealing with the two gentlemen who tried to recruit your help in going after me might be more awkward, and dealing with the neider . . . well, that's out of this world."

"So it seems. And I'm not at all sure that I can help you with that one. I'm curious to take a look, but after hearing all your blather about exotic matter and the unconscious, I'm not at all sure that I can provide much signaling for trains of thought of that kind. It's a little outside my field—but hey, I can learn. Whatever your alien friend might think, I'm not just a receptacle for phallic symbols. It really is disillusioning, you know, to learn that all an alien intelligence stranger than the human mind can supposedly imagine is just a prick, like any common-or-garden Neanderthal."

"I can see how it might be disappointing," Simon agreed.

"Liar," she countered. "You think it was just my reflexive reaction to the unfamiliar contact, that the rape-nightmare was all in my mind, and not the alien's."

"The thought had crossed my mind," Simon admitted.

"Well, don't read too much into it, even if it's true," she said. "First reactions aren't always the most revealing. We're nearly there—do you want me to drop you at the bridge to the Abbey gate, or do you want to call in at Raven first?"

"Since they're only forty yards apart, it hardly matters, but yes, drop me at the cottage gate. I'll have to pop in first to check the computer, since I don't possess a fancy mobile phone. I'll go over to the Abbey afterwards. Cerys and Felicia will probably have waited up, in order to find out how things went in Bristol."

"Probably. Can't blame them for being curious about new cousins. I'll drop the inquisition now, just to prove that I can be tactfully diplomatic, as you've been so obliging in answering my other stupid questions. I do hope things work out as you'd like them to with your Bristol family. I'll be very interested to meet them if they do visit. Better sooner than later, mind—things could become hectic once the tourist season gets under way. Good night, Simon."

The BMW had drawn to a halt outside Raven Cottage while she was speaking. There was a light on inside the study; someone was in the house. Megan made no comment on the fact, although she must have noticed it.

When Simon had climbed out and closed the door, the car executed a neat three-point turn and drove off again, past Sanderling Cottage, in order to turn left beyond the Mermaid and go to the row of garages where Megan kept the car. Simon opened the door of his cottage and stepped inside.

VII

Further Approaches

Simon had assumed that the visitor who had let herself into the cottage in order to wait for him, presuming that he would stop off there before going to the Abbey, was Felicia. It was, in fact, Cerys. She was curled up in an armchair in the study, reading one of Simon's books—not a novel, but one of his more recent works, signed with his own name: *Dark Matter, Dark Mind*. She didn't seem to have got very far.

"I'm sorry," she said, before he could even say hello. "I needed to talk to you, in private. I figured that you'd call in to check your email before going to the Abbey. I hope you don't mind."

"Not at all," he said. "Do you mind if I switch the computer on and see whether there's anything needing urgent attention before we start?"

"Go ahead," she said, and waited patiently until he turned away from the screen, swiveling his chair to face her, and nodded to her.

"How did your mission to Bristol go?" she enquired, politely.

"It was interesting. My birth-mother, unfortunately, is suffering badly from rheumatoid arthritis, with complications. She hadn't taken her pain medication because she didn't want to be sedated when she met me. It might have been a poor decision. My half-sister Marianne was pleasant, her daughter Zoe apparently less so, but I might have caught her at a bad time. What is it you want to talk to me about?"

"I've been offered a job," she said, bluntly. "Two of them, in fact."

"That's good," he said, neutrally, even though her tone had not implied that it was, and in spite of the fact that he already had a sneaking suspicion where the offers might have come from.

"No," she said, "it's really not. They both want me to go for interviews on Tuesday, at the Ivy Bush in Carmarthen. I don't think either of them knows that the other has made the same move, but I doubt that it's a coincidence. And the offers are fake."

"You don't believe the jobs exist?"

"I believe that they intend to offer me employment—just not the employment they're pretending to offer."

Simon nodded. "I presume that we're talking about two of your distant cousins, Bernard Pallister and Douglas Jefferson, and that you're assuming that they want to recruit you as a spy in the enemy camp, to dig up something they can use to attack James's will?"

"You presume correctly. It was, indeed, Cousin Douglas and Cousin Bernard. How did you guess?"

"You're not the only person they've contacted. They seem to be moving in step, albeit independently. What are you going to do?"

"Obviously, I'm not going to spy for them, but I thought I ought to consult you to ask how you wanted me to handle it. I could simply decline both offers by text, but it has occurred to me that I could fix a time at Ivy Bush to make sure the two cousins arrived together and watch the fur fly. It might be amusing—and, more to the point, it might get them squabbling with one another instead of trying to think up ways to do you down."

"I think it would be better for you to send a polite refusal to each of them, and not to attract any anger against you. I hear that the men in question aren't nice people."

"Who told you that?"

"Megan Harwyn. They made the same approach to her."

"Was that her car that just dropped you off? I thought I recognized the sound of the engine. You were supposed to be coming back by boat."

"She wanted to talk to me in private too, about the two cousins, and other matters, so she drove down to Fishguard Harbor and paid the boatman off."

"That must mean that she's not going to help them either."

"Yes, it does. And I'm very grateful for her support, as I am for yours. Do you mind if I ask you what I've done to earn it?"

"It isn't just you they want me to dig up dirt on, is it? They've probably got private detectives beavering away in Bristol for that. They'll want me to give them ammunition they can hurl against James or Ceridwen, or even Felicia. Absolutely not. I owe James everything. There's no way I'm going to turn on him, even though he's dead. James left the Abbey and what's left of the estate to you, and that's the end of the matter, so far as I'm concerned. Douglas and Bernard weren't interested in employing me when James put out feelers last year asking them to help me find a job, so they can go fuck themselves now, if you'll pardon the expression. Good for Miss Harwyn, though. Did you have to offer her a bribe?"

"No, and I'll forget that the thought even crossed your mind. She has her own reasons for fighting the good fight, which appear to be sound. I have told her about the family secret, though—as much as I've told you—and I've volunteered to show her the vitreous cocoons tomorrow afternoon. You can come too if you like."

"Is that wise? To show her, I mean?"

"I don't think it can do her any harm, and I do feel an obligation of sorts, given that she really is a member of the family."

"I mean, is it wise for you to take her down into the crypt? I haven't really got a handle on this bizarre situation yet, but you told me that it was after you went down the first time that you saw the ghosts. I know you were trying to warn me that it might mess with my head a little if I wanted to see the vitreous cocoons, but I thought at the time that if I were you, I'd be more worried about myself. James took you down, I know, and must have gone down a dozen times before, albeit spread over a hundred years . . . but I'm not sure that was a wise move on his part."

Cerys had obviously been thinking hard about the matter—which was, Simon thought, a good thing. "Are you saying that you'd rather steer clear? That might be a sensible decision. I certainly wouldn't criticize you for making it." *If you think you really have a choice*, he carefully didn't add.

"Actually, I haven't quite made up my mind about that—in fact, that's the other reason why I wanted to talk to you. I'm not sure whether I ought to stay in St. Madoc, but . . . there are complications."

And how, he thought, and tried to choose his words carefully.

"You're already in on the family secret, I fear," he told her, "whether you go down to see the cocoons or not, and you were already thoroughly entangled with it even when James was scrupulously keeping you in the dark in order to conserve the option for you of leaving with a relatively clean slate. I did hesitate as to whether to tell you more, for reasons you probably understand now, but you seemed rather resentful of James's determined secrecy, and I know that he intended to tell you. That's why I gave you the memory stick containing all his research. But now I'm effectively in James's place, I'm beginning to understand the difficulties he had in deciding what to tell you, and how, and in what order. I certainly can't promise you that you'll ever be able to figure it out, because he didn't manage it in a hundred years, and I'm still completely at sea, but for what it's worth, if the will is ultimately proved, you know that you'll have a right of residency here, and you'll also have a real job. I'm going to need a lot of help running the estate, and you're the ideal person to provide a large slice of that help—the only person who is ideal, in fact."

"And that's precisely why I have to make a decision. Before James died, he and I had several long discussions about my options, and the necessity of keeping them open. Two of the options we discussed were going back to university to do a postgraduate course, and doing some kind of educational training elsewhere—a PGCE, or nursing training. I applied for admission to three different courses, starting in September, and I've been accepted on all of them, provisionally."

"It sounds like a wise move," said Simon. "So what you're worried about, I assume, is whether you'd be able to take up one of the offers if you want to? Don't worry about that. If I'm to be James's heir, I'll take on all his responsibilities. If you need financial support to do any sort of course, anywhere, I'll provide it. If you think it best to get away from St. Madoc entirely, and build a career in Swansea, Cardiff or somewhere in England, you have my blessing. I wouldn't blame you in the least."

She nodded to thank him, but didn't exactly jump for joy. He supposed that keeping all her options open didn't make it any easier to choose one. What she actually said, though, was: "And you'll look after Felicia?"

He raised his eyebrows slightly. "Of course."

"I know you've been very kind to her these last few weeks, and I know that Grandmother asked you to do that, but . . . that isn't going to go on forever, is it?"

"Why not?"

"Well, among other things, because I've heard you saying to her in so many words that what you and she have isn't a marriage, and I've heard her agreeing that it isn't . . . but I wonder what's going to happen to her when it stops being whatever it is and she's all alone. She's already lost James, Grandmother and Melusine. I honestly don't think she can take any more, and I can't simply abandon her. I owe her too much."

"She won't be alone," Simon told her, firmly. "What we have isn't a marriage, but it isn't going to end any time soon, unless one of us dies. Have you talked to her about this?"

"No, of course not. She'd tell me to go if I wanted to, even if it would break her heart. What about Miss Harwyn?"

Wrong-footed, Simon could only say: "What about her?"

"Felicia's frightened. Obviously, she doesn't confide in me—she still thinks of me as a child—but I know that she's frightened, and that one of the things she's frightened of is Miss Harwyn."

"Why?"

"Because she thinks that Megan will . . . well, she'd probably say *set her cap at you*. Why settle for a right of residency when she could be lady of the manor?"

Simon laughed. "I can assure you that she has no such intention," he said, thinking that he probably could make the assurance in question, "but even if she had, I haven't. When I told Felicia that what we have isn't a marriage—and by the time you heard me say it and heard her agree, it was just a private joke between the two of us—I wasn't trying to reserve the option of marrying someone else. What Felicia and I are trying to do is something unique, something that only the two of us can do. It's way beyond marriage, but it's already forged a bond between us that's . . . well, I can't say unbreakable, but please take my word for it that it's nothing trivial. She *is* scared, and understandably so, but believe me, the setting of Megan Harwyn's cap is one thing she doesn't have to worry about."

"She drove all the way to Fishguard to intercept you tonight," Cerys observed.

And she ended up staring into a cyclopean eye at the end of one of the neider's tentacles, with an unwelcome tactile reminiscence of olden times, Simon thought. But that was one of many things that he had no intention of telling Cerys, at present.

"She did that for the same reason you came here," he said. "She wanted to tell me about the advances the cousins had made, and to assure me that so far as she was concerned, as you put it so poetically, they could go fuck themselves."

Cerys nodded, but her face still hadn't cleared; she was still anxious. "She could help you run the estate," she said. "She knows it better than me, and she's probably a lot smarter."

"She doesn't need a job," Simon countered, blandly. "She has her own business, which is lucrative . . . and legal."

Again, Cerys nodded, as if to signify that she would add that point of information to her mental balance-sheet, but more likely to confirm that it was already there. Then she said: "Was it very difficult, seeing your birth-mother, after all these years?"

He only hesitated slightly before saying: "Very. I tried to make as light of it as humanly possibly, but . . . it was hard for both of us, even apart from her physical pain. It hasn't done her any good for her old troubles to come back to haunt her after nearly seventy years. I feel truly sorry for her . . . it must have been much harder for her than it was for me."

"But your sister is . . . pleasant?"

"Yes—and I'm not trying to damn her with faint praise. Visiting the nursing home was hard on her, too, obviously, and she was understandably anxious about the whole situation. Her daughter didn't make it any easier for her. But it turns out that I once taught Marianne A level English, and because of that, she's read a number of my books, so I wasn't a complete stranger, by any means. I've invited her to visit me here, because I felt guilty about deliberately having arranged things so that I wouldn't have much time there today. I hope she'll come, so that we can have a real conversation . . . although, in the circumstances, I'm not entirely sure that it would be doing her any favors if she got to know me better."

"You could let her in on the family secret, show her the vitreous cocoons," Cerys observed. The irony in her voice was carefully discreet. She was still wary of Simon, understandably.

"I suppose I could," he said. "And perhaps I should. One of the things I learned today is that running away didn't free Lilith from what she called the family curse—a phrase you've used yourself, if I remember correctly. And it's not only her who continued to have bad dreams. They all know about the Black Monk. Even my niece."

"You don't have to drop hints, Uncle Simon. I've already got the message. Going to Swansea, or even New Zealand, won't separate me from my past, and even if I refuse to go down into the crypt, I won't be able to stop the thing that's in the crypt creeping into the utmost depths of my being."

"I fear so," said Simon, after a momentary hesitation. "It's hardly possible to get further away, psychologically, than I was for the first sixty-eight years of my life, but when the neider started stirring again, it was like releasing an elastic band. Here I am, wrapped up tighter than a mummy. And whether I go down into the blue again tomorrow or not, I'll never get back to the state of mind I thought I was in before. The illusion is shattered. I can't get out, any more than the neider can. But there are degrees of involvement. You can still get away—perhaps not fully, but to a distance. You can't destroy your unconscious mind, but you can keep it down. Repression is a useful ability to have. Don't forget that you have an enormous advantage that none of the rest of us has. You're young, and beautiful. You still have every prospect of a rewarding and successful future out there in the real world: a career, marriage, and children. Not one of the rest us made the most of that opportunity when we had it, to the limited extent that we did have it, but I suspect that we all regretted it eventually. So the sanest advice I can probably offer you is to grab it with both hands. Go to Swansea, or Bristol, or New Zealand, build a career, find a nice man, get married, have kids—and remember James and Felicia fondly, as an aspect of your past from which you've moved on."

"Is that what your Bristol relatives have done? Success-fully?"

That was a challenge he couldn't meet. "It's not a curse," he said, carefully. "Just because others have failed, it doesn't mean that you won't succeed."

Cerys's gaze, always disconcerting, was far more so at present than it had ever been before. Simon knew that she was trying to read his mind, and that what she probably imagined that she was reading was that he actually thought that she was a Murden, and always would be, and would never be able to get away from it no matter how hard she tried. Should she even be grateful for him making the effort to lie? He had no idea.

All she said, in the end, was: "They're not really cocoons, are they?"

"I don't believe so," he admitted.

"James's theory is wrong."

"It wasn't a theory—just a hypothesis. He was a good scholar, and an intelligent man; he knew that it was faulty, in need of refinement, if not replacement. I don't know that my hypothesis is any better. Like him, I have the dire suspicion that it's faulty, that I'm missing a vital piece of the puzzle, but I'm pretty sure that the thing underneath the Abbey isn't part of the neider, although the neider has been trying for centuries to make better contact with it, if not actually to annex it and fuse with it. A year ago, maybe as little as a month ago, that project didn't seem particularly urgent to the neider. Now it does. As to why, your guess is probably as good as mine."

"But you're trying to figure it out?"

"Of course."

"Hoping that Melusine will come back with news from the deep?"

"Yes."

"And sleeping with Felicia?"

He hesitated, but only with slight embarrassment. Cerys lived in the Abbey; she knew perfectly well what Felicia's sleeping arrangements were, give or take a few minor anatomical details. "Yes," he said.

"But so far," she said, "it isn't working."

It wasn't a question, so he didn't feel obliged to issue a correction. Instead, he said: "If we make a breakthrough, we won't hide it from you. If you want to be the first to know, you only have to say the word. For the time being, though, I only have guesswork."

"But the thing beneath the crypt is definitely alien?"

"I don't think there's any doubt about that. Very alien. At least as alien as the neider—but whereas the neider originated from somewhere down below, from a further Underworld, perhaps the center of the Earth, I suspect that the thing in the crypt came from the other direction. And just as the neider is still connected, in terms of its dark mind, if not its dark matter, with the center of the Earth, the thing in the crypt is still connected mentally, if only in terms of vague feelings, with something up above."

"Something in the stars?"

"Probably."

"Only probably?"

"We can only see the stars up there, save for a few planets and a little reflective dust—but what we can see is only vulgar matter. We have no idea what might be up there that we can't see."

"Dark matter." Again, that wasn't a question. She might not have got very far with the book, but she'd got past the fundamental definitions and the basic ideas.

"And dark mind," he confirmed

"And it's dangerous?" That *was* a question.

"Probably—but not actively hostile. I don't think it means us any harm. What frightens me more than anything else is that the neider seems to be frightened—and if the neider's frightened, then there might well be cause for alarm, if not stark terror. But what can we do, except keep trying to understand?"

"So why are you advising me to run away, if you're not running away yourself?"

"Because the rest of us have nothing much to lose by staying, whereas you might have a lot to lose. If the rest of us turn out to be insane, it would be criminal to drag you down with us. You still have a future, or at least a chance at one. Maybe you can have it here as easily as somewhere else, which is why I'm telling you that if things go on as they are, you'll always have a home, and a job, here. But you do have to think about that future, and do what you can to secure it. It's getting late, by the way. If Felicia's frightened, as you say . . ."

"Of course," she said, immediately getting to her feet. "I'm sorry to have taken up so much of your time, selfishly. But . . . you just said that no one else had got away. Does that include all the people you saw today? All of Lilith's descendants?"

"I didn't meet all of them. I didn't see the one who must be about your age—Krysten—but I know that's she's just had a baby, and that she and her mother are at daggers drawn. They certainly don't give the impression of being a happy family, but who am I to judge? I found out my real name, though—well, not my real name, but the name my mother gave me while I was still in the womb. She called me Jason."

"After the Argonaut?"

"Probably not—but who can tell? Maybe so. Maybe, at least, it's a name I ought to try to live up to, now that I know it, even if it's not real, and I really am a Simon, and a Cannick rather than a Murden."

He opened the door for her and locked it behind them, and they walked to the Abbey together.

VIII
The Cloud-Capped Towers

"I'm sorry," Simon said, as he came into Felicia's bedroom. "Cerys was waiting for me at the house. She needed to talk to me."

Felicia was already in bed, but not lying down; she was sitting up, holding a book. Simon wondered whether he ought to be grateful that wherever he went, he found people reading his works with earnest attention. It ought to be every writer's dream, he supposed, but he couldn't help feeling that there was something slightly ominous about it. It was as if it were a kind of message in itself, a suggestion that he was now living one of his own plots, with all the drama and brooding menace that implied. He had never regretted being the kind of writer who avoided cliché to the extent of rarely providing conventional happy endings, but he had to confess that happy endings had their good points, for characters as well as readers.

"I know," she replied to his apology, mildly. "She warned me in advance, and I gave her my blessing. I saw you walking back, from the window. You don't have to apologize. How did it go, with your mother?"

"Not well. It wasn't her fault, or mine. She's in a lot of pain, and the only way out of it is morphine. But it wasn't a disaster; I think we established the vital information, in spite of everything. More than I expected, in fact. She had a message."

"Ah! From the neider?"

"Perhaps. From Hell, according to her, but I'm not at all sure what she meant by that."

"The hot core of the Earth, perhaps?" Felicia suggested. "The parent intelligences of the neider?"

"Possibly, but on the train back to Fishguard, I remembered something Eve once said to me, not long after I moved into the flat downstairs from hers. I was working on *Dealings with the Devil* at the time, and I was holding forth, as I was always wont to do if given the slightest encouragement, talking about Dante and the imagery of the Inferno. And she said that it was all too lurid and crude. Hell, she said, wouldn't be fire and ice, but a darkness so intense that neither earthly nor celestial light could penetrate it, where the only punishment was absolute loneliness. At the time, obviously, she must have been feeling lonely herself . . . but I can't help wondering whether she might have said the same thing to her daughter, if she saw her at all in those days."

"And what was the message that came from the Hell in question?"

"As above, so below."

"Is that all? It's not exactly helpful."

"Perhaps not. Nor was the second message I received, in a distinctly crude and lurid manner, in Fishguard Harbor. A tentacle came out of the water and opened a sinister eye. It scared Megan Harwyn half to death. She came to Fishguard to pick me up, instead of the boat."

"I know. I saw the car drop you off, from the window. Douglas and Bernard have contacted her too, then?"

"Yes. She won't help them. In fact, she promised that if they try to smear either of us, or James or Ceridwen, she'll put a stop to it. I believe her. She knows them quite well, apparently."

"I expect she does, or did. I doubt if she can put a spoke in their wheel simply by threatening to tell their wives that they used to pay to screw her forty years ago, though. I'm not up to date with family gossip, but I'd be astonished if they were still married, at least to the same women they were married to then. They both brought a plus one to the funeral, whom they passed off as trophy wives—pathetic, at their age—but they might have been hired for the day. They're the kind of people who like to keep up appearances at rare family gatherings."

"I didn't really pay much attention to the names that were reeled off at the funeral—there were so many, and they all looked at me as if I were a maggot in their sandwich. Douglas was the one who wanted to go down into the crypt, I know, but I can't remember Bernard."

"Tall, burly and bald, thinks he's a sharp dresser but just looks like an out-of-date spiv. Still a local landlord, having inherited some of the slices csigut up during the schism, but not a rentier. I think he's what they call a property developer. Wealthy, apparently, but that might be just show. Douglas puts on a better show, aided by the fact that his dark hair is only just beginning to thin and go gray, even though he can't be any younger than you; he's 'in trade,' as grandmother would have said, a middleman between farmers and retailers, I think, with a fleet of lorries. Also seemingly wealthy, but again, it might be mostly show. They were on opposite sides of the chapel and I can't remember them talking together, before the service or in the house afterwards. They both looked at you as if you were something loathsome when I introduced you to them, especially Douglas, when he couldn't get rid of you in order to talk to me in confidence, but, as you say, their naked hostility wasn't enough to make them stand out in that particular crowd. The women with them I didn't know at all, but whoever they are, I doubt that they can provide Miss Harwyn with any leverage for blackmail."

"I don't think that's what Megan had in mind—but that's not important. Cerys says that you're frightened that she might have designs on me. She hasn't, and it wouldn't matter if she had. You do know that, don't you?"

Simon had undressed completely while Felicia was delivering her verdict on the possible challengers of the will and he climbed into bed with her as he finished. She was wearing a long silk nightdress, still being slightly apprehensive about showing her naked body, although it was remarkably well-preserved for her age—better than his own, he thought.

"I know that if Miss Harwyn did have designs," Felicia said, maintaining the conspicuous mildness of her tone and manner, "she's clever enough to keep them hidden from you, and that any illusions you have about being immune to seduction are just that. I know how easy it is for women to seduce you, even if they're more than a hundred years old. But that doesn't frighten me. In a way, I'm glad that I can still feel such sharp twinges of jealousy at the absurd thought that you might screw Megan Harwyn, or the even more absurd thought that you might have screwed Melusine under the water, without even being able to remember it. It's reassuring to know that I still have that much capacity for feeling."

Simon knew that something was wrong. Felicia had not put her arms around him yet. She had not even moved over to his side of the bed, or tried to ease him over to hers. That was odd, because she always made the first move, ever since the first night when he had found her sitting on his bed reading *The Bells of Ys*, and he always let her, because he was always afraid of making it himself.

"We've shared a lot of dreams," he said, mildly, "or tried, at least, even though I don't seem to be improving much with practice. I can't even hold on to a few fragments of memory of what I dreamed. I wouldn't know about them if you didn't tell me about them. Even so, I think you probably know me by know, perhaps better than I know myself, but in that case you must know that . . ."

He stopped, because it had occurred to him that what he was saying was ridiculous. Must know what? And why must she? How, in fact, could she know what to read into his dreams, and about whatever feelings he might experience in them, which might not even be his? And how could he possibly know that what she told him about what she had read, and felt, was all there was to tell, or even whether it was the truth. He thought that he had gleaned the impression that she was genuinely fond of him, that she might even love him, and not just because she had never expected to have sex again, or to enjoy it if she did, or to be able, on nights when they didn't actually have intercourse as such, to be able to lie in someone's arms, comfortably, pleasantly, gladly, to feel wanted . . .

"Don't panic," she said. "I do know you, as much as any-one could . . . certainly better than you can. What frightens me isn't you, it's me."

He risked reaching out and putting a hand on her shoulder. She didn't flinch or make any move to repel it, so he put his arm around her, and moved closer. And he waited for her to explain.

And that, he thought, *is me in a nutshell. I never know what to do, except wait for people to explain. And she knows that about me. She knows that it's what I'm doing. She knows that I'll never, ever know what to do sufficiently to take the initiative, to do the right thing instinctively.*

"You don't know me at all," she said. "Neither do I, any more. When I sneaked into your bedroom that night, while you were in the Mermaid with the clergyman, I was acting completely out of character, and when I went back to the cottage the next day, and then again . . . I watched myself doing it, and I thought: *What on earth are you doing, Felicia? This isn't you.* And then I thought: *Oh, shut up, you old fool. What on earth have you got to lose? You've been knocking on death's door for thirty years and more, and too scared to live your life for seventy. If not him, who? If not now, when? If he tells you to get lost, you're no worse off. And if he doesn't . . . well, who knows?*

"And I was right. I didn't have anything to lose, and I would have been a complete idiot not to do what I did, just as I'd been a complete idiot not to do anything at all for the previous seventy years, letting my life drain away. And even if I'd thought ahead, it would still have been the right thing to do, and it still is, and still would be, even if it weren't as pleasurable as it is, as exciting as it is, and as interesting as it is. But precisely because it is so pleasurable, etcetera, it's no longer the case that I have nothing to lose. Now, I have a lot to lose, and more than I could ever have expected to have. So I'm frightened. I'm frightened of losing what I now have, and of no longer being what I now seem to be, and going back to being the pathetic rag of a human being I was before, and will be again if things go badly.

"I'm not frightened of losing you to Megan Harwyn, or any other scheming hussy, because I know that you're just as frightened as I am, of different things. I know that whether you're capable of loving me or not—and for what it may be worth, I think you probably are, and not just because you turned out to be capable of having sex with me even though I'm a hundred years old, and without even thinking about Cerys while you're doing it—you know full well that you need me, more than you've ever needed anyone in your life before, and more than you'll ever need anyone again. You tell yourself it's because you think that the link between your unconscious mind and mine, and the links between mine and what you call the dark minds, are the best chance you've got of figuring out what the hell is going on here, or at least of making up a decent story about it, but that's not the real reason. You needed me because you needed someone, and I was here, and I still am.

"You'd still need me if the things beneath the Abbey had disappeared, the way Grandmother and Jonathan hoped they might, spirited away by the kindly neider. You can't feel that need, but I can. I could, almost as soon as I saw you for the first time. I hadn't made a decision then—at least, I hadn't made a conscious decision—but I knew, when I looked at you across the table while you tried heroically to look as if you were enjoying the makeshift meal that Edith had skimped together at short notice, that you had a need. Grandmother knew it even before she saw you. I suppose I'm lucky that she could hardly stand up. If she'd been a hundred years younger . . .

but she wasn't, and I won, even beating Melusine, whatever might have happened to you under the water. I won, and now I have something to lose. So I'm frightened.

"But really, it doesn't matter. Even if I lost it all tomorrow, because you got struck by lightning, or Cousin Douglas hired a hit man to take you out of the path to the Abbey and the seven million, I'd still be ahead. I'd be devastated, obviously; I'd cry my weight in tears, and probably die of grief, but I'd still be ahead. Nothing can take away the last three weeks, or this moment, here and now. I'll always have had it, and it will always have transformed my life. I'll always have won. And the very fact that I'm so frightened only goes to prove how much this has been worth, and how much it is worth, and how much it will be worth if I can help you to get want you want and bring this bizarre story to some sort of conclusion.

"Because that's what you need, even more than me, and I'm lucky that you think that I might be your best chance of achieving it. Perhaps it's what I ought to need too, and there was a time when I thought it was, when I wanted to sleep with the vitreous cocoons in the hope that I could share their dream, and find out what they were, and what they wanted — but it wasn't that easy. It just disturbed my mind, and made me feel sick. And over time, I stopped caring about it. It became a matter of indifference to me. Perhaps that's criminal. Here am I, privileged to live on top of something that might be the magic cauldron of Welsh myth and legend, the cauldron of rebirth and metamorphosis, and it simply became a matter of indifference to me. Not to James — James never stopped trying, heroically, to make sense of it. But his way of trying was conducive to patience, to hard intellectual labor, to decades of obsession. I'm not like that. That wasn't me.

"And now, I only care because you care. I only need it because you need it, and I need you. But I am trying; believe me, I'm trying. Do you remember a book you wrote, thirty years ago and more, called *The Gardens of Armida*?"

"Of course," said Simon. "It's one of the ones that I gave to Cerys the second time she came to Raven, and I saw a copy earlier today on Marianne's shelves. She read it back in the eighties. She even knew I'd written it. I'd been her English teacher when she did her A levels at the college. I didn't remember her, though. She gave my memory several jogs, but nothing surfaced, not the ghost of an echo. The book, though, I remember. My *Tempest*. I was churning out novels for the US market at the time, and the seeds of all of them were classic plots capable of transfiguration. Other people did the same—there was already an early science fiction movie that had transfigured *The Tempest*, so I had to make mine different. It was easy enough—all I had to do was steal a few ideas and images from elsewhere and stir them into the mix—*Gerusalemme liberata* is where I stole the Gardens of Armida. Always steal from the best: Shakespeare, Tasso, Poe . . . there's an alternative world somewhere, I guess, in which *The Tempest* was on the syllabus that year instead of *Hamlet*, and Marianne would have played Miranda instead of Ophelia, and I wouldn't have accidentally provided a cue for the boy she liked to fall about laughing at the implication that she was a slut, and . . . but I'm blethering. Why did you ask whether I remembered the novel?"

"It's one of the ones I borrowed from Cerys, and read—the one I liked best. I loved the idea of your *femme fatale*, the Prospera who stands in for Prospero in the plot, and who builds that entire fantasy landscape in which the crew of the stranded starship get lost. There's a passage that you stole directly from the play, about cloud-capped towers and gorgeous palaces, from the speech in the original that ends about us being such stuff as dreams are made on, although you slyly didn't take the quote that far, refraining from spelling out the implication crudely, before the illusion collapses in the climax of the novel, and the contrived dream dies. And I tried to put that together with your theory in *The New Archetypes of the Collective Unconscious*, in which you propose that the conscious mind isn't just a passive recipient of archetypal images—that even though it's working blindly, the conscious mind can and ought to try to manipulate and reshape the archetypes, and that it can monitor and measure its progress by examining the images transmitted into consciousness, especially in the arena of dreams.

"So that's what I've been trying to do. I've been trying to depict the arena of our shared dreams, imaginatively, as something akin to the Gardens of Armida—not the ones in Tasso but the ones in your novel, the products of a manufactured illusion, complete with cloud-capped towers and gorgeous palaces. I hoped that it might help, that it might provide a kind of substrate into which you and the dark minds could feed imagery, in the hope that we might be able to obtain a kind of symbolic language for communication . . ."

Simon raised his head. "That's brilliant! Why didn't I think of that?"

"You did. I got it all from your books."

"Which makes it all the more stupid that I didn't put it together myself. I finish a book, and I move on. I don't forget it, exactly, but I put it behind me and concentrate on the next one. *New Archetypes* was just playing with ideas. I didn't take it all that seriously at the time, but I've been dredging it up routinely these last few days, just as example and illustration, without even giving serious thought to the question of how I might actually apply it. It might just work . . ."

"It already has," Felicia said. "That's what I'm trying to tell you. For the last couple of nights, I've been trying to filter those images through from consciousness to my dream—our dream. I was hoping that it might help you remember, if there was something in the dream that touched a chord. The first night, there was nothing evident, but last night . . . I would have told you this morning, but you had to get up so early to catch that boat, you were out of the door before I was properly awake. I've been thinking about it all day . . ."

The penny dropped. The experiment had worked, Simon realized, or Felicia thought it had. She had succeeded in introducing something of the imagery on which she had concentrated her conscious mind into her dream, and hence into his. But something else had crept in: something nightmarish.

The problem with borrowing the plot elements from the *Tempest* to shape a novel of your own, he thought, was that you had to take Caliban, because Caliban was the source of drama and threat, and a science fiction novel needed that even more than a Shakespearean melodrama. You not only had to take Caliban, but, if you were writing something that was going to sell to an American paperback editor, you had to build him up, the way that he had been built into a frightful monster in *Forbidden Planet*, by a natural process of melodramatic inflation.

In his *Gardens of Armida* the transfiguration of Caliban had been a life-form native to the planet where Prospera—the *femme fatale*, as Felicia put it—had constructed her enchanted gardens in order to seduce the Rinaldo-equivalent starship pioneer. It hadn't been exactly malevolent—Simon had never liked using stock villains in his plots—but it had been dangerous because of its inherent nature . . . just as he had begun to imagine the neider.

He had a vague memory of waking up that morning in mid-dream, and having carried over the imagery of the dream into wakefulness, just for a moment or two; but his conscious mind had concentrated entirely on the matter of getting dressed in a hurry, and setting forth to catch the boat that was to take him to Fishguard, and any fragments that had survived briefly had vanished into forgetfulness, returning to unconsciousness.

But Felicia would have remembered; that was her gift.

"You saw the neider?" he queried. "Something akin to a hydra, or a sea-serpent?"

"No," she said. "In fact, I'm not sure that what we saw was mine at all. I'll take responsibility for the cloud-topped towers and gorgeous palaces, because they were the images on which I was focusing, the images I was using to try to provoke a reaction in the unconscious, but there wasn't any sea in the image that formed in the dream, or anything that made me think of the neider. The towers were very distant, at first, on the horizon. We were moving toward them, along a road through a desert, but not a Sahara of sand; it was a sparkling desert, but not salt either, or gemstones; it was scintillating, but not crystalline—more like scales, perhaps snakeskin, and very uneven, rugged. But that wasn't really what seemed important; what was important was in the distance.

"The palaces were beautiful, marble and glass, and the towers too, and the clouds that capped them were white and fluffy, and soft . . . but their sky was only a patch of sky, or a corner, because they were so far away, the horizons . . . and the rest of the sky was swarming with clouds of a different sort, which might not actually have been clouds at all, but something mimicking clouds, or perhaps camouflaged against a background of storm-clouds. And that sky was dark, and angry, like a Van Gogh storm scene, if you can picture that.

"In that sky there was a star . . . just one . . . or perhaps a planet, but red and fiery, and growing. At least, I thought, at first, that it was growing, but then I realized that it was coming closer, that it was falling. And my first thought was that it was falling upon the beautiful city, that it was going to topple the towers like matchsticks and smash the palaces like snow-globes . . . until I realized that it wasn't going to fall on the city at all, but on the desert, and more specifically, on us.

"Then I wanted to run, because I thought we still had time to get away, but you wouldn't move . . . I tried to get you to move, but, you wouldn't, or couldn't . . . and then I thought that it would be futile anyway because it was us . . . or, more specifically, you . . . that the red star was homing in on. Then I thought that I could still get away, but that you couldn't, and I decided that if you were going to die, I was going to die with you, so I stayed. And the star kept getting bigger, and bigger, and I realized that it had much further to fall than I had thought, and that it had already been falling for a long, long time.

"You were looking around, as if in search of help. And you told me not to worry, that it would be all right. But I knew that it wouldn't be. I kept looking back and forth, from

112

the infernal star to the towers of the city, which were beginning to glow red with reflected light: blood red. I realized that they would be doomed too, because when the red star collided with the earth, there was going to be an almighty explosion. And then the towers disappeared, in the blink of an eye, and I remembered that they weren't solid, that they were just an enchantment, an illusion, and that they could escape, but that we couldn't. The desert was reflecting the starlight too, like a vast, jagged expanse of bloody snakeskin, undulating . . . and that's all."

"You woke up?"

"I don't think so. The vision ended. I don't think it was followed by darkness. Something else began, only I can't remember what it was. Not nothing, but nothing with which my senses and intelligence could connect—perhaps I was trying to imagine dark matter, or dark mind, in spite of the paradoxicality. Perhaps it was a gap in consciousness, a rent in time, but it wasn't *nothing*, and it wasn't simple darkness. I lost track of space and time alike. I don't know how long it was before I felt your body—your actual body—move, and you slipped out of the bed, and I watched you get dressed through a crack in my eyelids, and I saw you go out, and I remember thinking: 'He's going to meet his mother. I hope it goes well.' Then I drifted back into semi-consciousness for a while. I must have dozed for some time, because it was first light when I woke up again, and checked the clock. Then I remembered the dream, and before I even got dressed, I put on a dressing gown and I went to jot down notes, the way I always do, to fix it my memory. Do you think it was an attempt at communication by the neider?"

"Possibly," said Simon. "It does seem to be trying hard. I had actually wondered whether it was trying to get through in Bristol and Fishguard because it was being blocked here, but if the disruption of your dream really was the work of the neider . ." He trailed off, unable, for the moment, to follow the train of thought.

"You think it might be some other intelligence, working through the vitreous cocoons?"

"I don't know. The tentacle with the eye was definitely the neider, or a neider, but the other two manifestations—it might be wise to stop thinking of them as messages—might have come from elsewhere. We have no idea how many entities we're dealing with here, or where the others might be located, but something woke the neider up from a long dormancy within the last few months . . . or the anticipation of something coming."

"From the sky—like my red star."

"Perhaps so.

"You think that part of the dream might be a prophecy, then?"

"Absolutely. In fact, it's straight out of the lexicon of prophecies of doom, only four horsemen, a Whore of Babylon and a beast numbered 666 short of a standard apocalypse. But such visions are invariably symbolic. The one thing of which we can be fairly certain is that a literal red star is not going to fall upon the Earth, hitting the bull's-eye at Morgan's Fork. That's not the way my *Gardens of Armida* ended. I didn't do literal apocalypses, even then. I didn't do token marriages either, of course, so Prospera and Rinaldo didn't exactly ride away into the sunset together when the illusion perished. Not that what I did or didn't do back then is of any relevance to the current script, which I'm not writing, but merely trapped in. Let's focus on the important point."

"Which is?"

"That you actually managed to insert some imagery into the dream by conscious effort. Now that the breach has been made, perhaps you'll be able to do it again, repeatedly."

"You want me to try?"

"Of course. And if I try too, perhaps . . . well, who knows? What we need to do, if possible, is to move the gorgeous palaces from the horizon to the foreground, and, if possible, to get inside them. If possible, we need to find and confront Armida/Prospera, the dream-weaver."

"Do you think that's possible?"

"Why not? It will only be a symbolic representation, of course, but that's what dreams are all about. What other meeting-ground is possible between our consciousness and a Dark Mind except a symbol accessible to both parties? That, after all, is what the tentacle with the eye was, even though it was presumably material. It's what the neider itself is, and morgens: symbols in flesh, and presumably blood. And the Black Monk has only the faintest material component; he's almost all symbol."

His eyes scanned the tightly packed bookshelves that filled one entire wall of Felicia's bedroom; there was a semblance of alphabetical order in the arrangement, but it was compromised by all kinds of arbitrary additions and insertions, a creeping chaos at the fringes of a heroic order.

Felicia followed his eyes. "Well, yes, obviously," she said. "The most apt inspiration must be in there—but the words *needle* and *haystack* come to mind. Perhaps we should just stick to *The Gardens of Armida* . . . or go back to the model."

"Perhaps," said Simon, still pensive. "But I suspect that the entity whose advent, or impending advent, has disturbed the neider is at least as strange as the neider, and they haven't yet succeeded in establishing clear communication, even with apparent effort on both sides."

"What did the tentacle with the eye put into your mind?" Felicia asked.

"What came to mind," Simon said, a trifle pedantically, "was the first few bars of *Also Sprach Zarathustra.*"

"That's one of the pieces you've got on your computer's music center?"

"Yes it is. I hear it at irregular intervals while working. Maybe it's just trying to tell me to get back to work. In fact . . ." This time he stopped dead, not wanting to voice the thought that the same idea might conceivably explain the sensation that had afflicted Megan Harwyn.

Felicia did not press him to continue. Instead, she said: "It's very late. Are you tired?"

"Yes—but my mind is still going like an overloaded express train. I'm in that peculiar state of mind when I'm intensely weary, but can't switch off. I think I might have overdosed on adrenalin—I tried to have a nap on the train from Swansea to Fishguard, but couldn't drop off then either."

"There might be a way to dissipate your excess adrenalin and induce drowsiness," she said, "if you're feeling up to it."

He tried to laugh, and managed a smile. "I might be," he said, warily. "It's worth a try."

IX
Unreliable Memories

The next morning, when Simon woke up, long after the time when his working day had started for the past seven years—he was horrified, on picking up his wrist-watch from the bedside table, to see that it was after nine o'clock—his first thought was that the intercourse might have been a mistake, and that it must have plunged him into a truly deep and dreamless sleep and hammered the last nail into the coffin of his long-sacred routine. His second thought was that the first part of his first thought had been foolish, that he knew perfectly well that there had been no mistake, and that he was embarked on a new life now, in a new world, where "sacred routines" had no place. On the other hand, it still seemed rather peculiar that, not only did he not remember having a dream, but that also he had a firm conviction of not having had any, of having slept like the proverbial log.

That was possible, he knew. He was aware of published research suggesting that it was not, and that everyone invariably had dreams while they slept, but he was not convinced; he was well aware of Heisenberg's Uncertainty Principle, which states that the act of observation affects the properties of what is being observed. The methods by which sleep researchers attempted to detect dreams, he suspected, were themselves generators of dreams. Perhaps lots of people did invariably have dreams, but it remained possible that a least some, at least some of the time, did not, and that when people wake up convinced that they have not dreamed at all, they are right. Sometimes, in his opinion, the human mind really did take a break, the dark half as well as the conscious part.

Felicia's bedroom had an *en suite* bathroom, with a walk-in shower—a facility for which Simon was profoundly grateful—and he let his mind wander as the hot water ran over him and he spread soap over various parts of his body with an automatic facility, still not entirely awake.

He knew that it was far more common than most people thought for them to dream while they were awake, in more ways than one. For instance, the first night that he had spent with Felicia, when he and she had lain down on his bed in Raven Cottage, fully dressed, simply holding one another, what he had remembered the next morning was a waking experience, trains of thought that he had followed consciously, with a high degree of control and reason; but it had also been a dream of sorts, reveries being, in essence, waking dreams, which participate in both the condition of consciousness and that of dreaming. Felicia had eavesdropped on Simon's stream of consciousness that night, not in the sense of picking up the words that his mind's voice had been narrating to his mind's ear, but in the sense of picking up the emotional undercurrent that accompanied them, an echo of the subconscious part of the idea-stream, feeding it and feeding off it. She had read Simon's depression, his loneliness, his self-dissatisfaction and his ennui, and she had thought, poor angel, that it was a reflection of her own, having been reluctant to admit, to begin with, that she and he were, to some extent, twin souls.

She knew better now. She and Simon knew one another, and themselves, a little more intimately.

The previous day, Simon had mentioned in passing to Marianne, while pontificating in his customary self-defensive fashion, that in circumstances where the eye or the ear picks up information from the environment, without quite picking up enough to permit the mind to form a full and coherent picture of what is being seen or heard, the mind improvises, and makes up the deficit with the aid of the imagination. Usually its guesses are correct, or, if they are in error, the error is anodyne and unobtrusive. Sometimes, though, it fills in with something that is mistaken: a visual or an auditory hallucination.

Simon knew that such things happen much more commonly than people might think, and there are circumstances and individuals in which it happens routinely and often. People losing their sight are particularly prone to visual hallucinations as their mind struggles to cope with the loss. People suffering intoxications, or psychotropic disturbances, or concussion, are very prone to see things that are not there. Those kinds of hallucinations are also dreams of a sort. Once upon a time, eye-witness evidence of crimes had been considered highly reliable; then lawyers and psychologists had begun comparing different accounts by witnesses of the same event, and had come to realize that people very often saw the same thing differently, because all of them, to some extent, were making up a slight dearth of authentic sensory information with products of the imagination: with dreams.

So what? Simon thought, as his mind gradually became more active in spite of the slightly soporific effect of the hot shower and the ritual cleansing.

Well, for one thing, his train of thought continued, knowing that, and thinking about it hard over the last few weeks, had made him reappraise certain things that he had seen or heard. He did not doubt that he had seen or heard them, or, at least, seen or heard *something*, but he had begun to doubt that he had seen and heard *everything* that his memory told him that he had seen and heard, and that had made him wonder how much of what he "remembered" had been prompted by his unconscious mind—his dark mind—rather than by photons hitting his retina or sound waves stirring vibrations in his eardrum.

For instance, Simon was still convinced—he *knew*, beyond any shadow of a doubt—that Melusine had tipped him into the sea on the night when he had slept with the neider. But he had just been hit in the face by the bars of a metal gate. He was "seeing stars," which he knew were hallucinatory. He had also seen that Melusine had a morgen's tail and that she had ridden a wave, and that she had plucked him from the bridge over the gully separating the tine from the Welsh mainland. But now, in retrospect, he was not sure that the event had actually happened in the precise way that he had seen it. He was not convinced that the tail, in particular, had not been a hallucination prompted by his unconscious mind. In fact, he was very close to being convinced that it must have been a hallucination, because the timeline of Melusine's disappearance simply had not left room for an actual physical metamorphosis into a morgen.

Not only did Simon hope that Melusine would return, therefore, when the neider had finished with her, but he hoped that she would return with legs, and not as a literal morgen.

More seriously, perhaps, he was no longer convinced that the conversations he had had with the ghost of Owain Glyndwr and the Black Monk, not long after his sojourn in the underworld beneath the Abbey, had happened in exactly the way that he remembered. That the ghosts had been, in some sense, a real presence, he did not doubt. That he had heard speech in his mind's ear that was at least partly generated by the entities in question, he did not doubt either, but as to how much of the speech he had decoded had originated from them, and how much from his own unconscious, he was no longer sure.

And that had made Simon think much longer and harder about the nature of the "telepathy" that Lenore had employed to plant the neider's first and most explicit message in his mind, and which the Black Monk had employed to tell him certain strange and interesting details about his personal history. Plainly, he had supplied the words himself,

because no words had been spoken in the sense of gener-
ating actual sound waves—in the former case borrowing
from Shakespeare—but how much more than the imaginary
sounds had his unconscious provided? And to what extent
was "his" unconscious really "his" anyway?

In the same way that we often dream while awake, adding fragments of dream to our actual sensory experience
without being consciously aware of it, our unconscious mind
is active in other ways. We all perform all kinds of familiar
gestures automatically, exactly as he was doing at the moment, no longer needing the conscious mind to order a set of
actions that he went through every morning, mechanically.
In fact, he knew perfectly well that active conscious direction
played only a small part in all his everyday actions, hour by
hour, and that it was the same for everyone—so much so that
hardly anyone ever gave a thought to the fact that so much
of what they were doing was being done without a thought,
unconsciously.

In recent weeks, however, Simon had been forced to think
about it, to pose himself the awkward questions, and to return
to them continually. *What constitutes that unconscious mind?*
he had wondered, over and over, while his mind was free to
wander because, as now, when he was drying himself with
a bath towel, he was following a series of familiar gestures.
*What exactly is it that works so hard in supporting and filling in
the gaps of our feeble and fugitive conscious existence?*

It was, Simon knew very well, a commonplace of psychoanalytic theory that each of us has a "personal unconscious"
that is idiosyncratic and characteristic, an aspect of a particular self. How that personal unconscious is formed and how
it evolves over time remains uncertain and controversial, but
of its existence there can be no reasonable doubt. We all have
personal hang-ups of which we are not consciously aware,
but which can sometimes be dragged up from the unconscious. Psychotherapy might often be inept and inaccurate,
but it is not inherently ridiculous; its ideative foundations are
sound and its efforts, in their fashion, heroic.

It was also a commonplace of psychoanalytic theory, he knew, that there is a "collective unconscious" that is a feature of human minds in general, which operates in a similar way in all human minds. How that fraction of the unconscious mind is formed and how it evolves is also controversial, but there is no doubt that it is, in some sense, innate and hereditary, that it is analogous to instinct in animals. Exactly what archetypes it contains is difficult to determine, and it is even more difficult to determine whether consciousness or other forces can act upon those archetypes, mutating their raw material so that they become, to some extent, personalized.

Can our consciousness really do that? Simon had wondered, publicly, in more than one of his writings. Can it cause mutations in the unconscious, of which we can only become aware when the altered elements begin to feed their effects back into consciousness?

Yes it can, Simon now thought, aided by Felicia's prompting. It is obviously not easy, but it can and does happen. The unconscious is, to some degree, mutable, not merely by accidents but also, to a limited extent, by conscious effort, especially if you can get the hang of it. That was what Felicia and Simon had been trying to do since their relationship had begun, and they were trying to find a way to do better, in order to get the hang of it.

The reason they were trying to do it was because they thought—and knew for a fact—that among the other forces influencing their own unconscious minds were other minds. And they knew that it was the case, because the other minds in question were so alien that their interference in their own unconscious minds had become obvious. Had they been human, they would not have been nearly so obtrusive, and perhaps not detectable at all.

Having embarked on that train of thought, Simon had rapidly concluded that telepathy, like dreaming, is much more commonplace than people might think. He had come to believe that we are, in fact, all telepathic, that our unconscious minds exchange information all the time, and that to some extent, the collective unconscious is simply a telepathic phenomenon that we take for granted; how the information is exchanged remained a mystery to him, but that was hardly surprising, assuming that it wasn't merely a matter of dark mind but of dark matter and dark energy. It was, he supposed, a matter of entities and metamorphoses that humans cannot perceive by means of the familiar senses, which are geared to interact with the familiar states of baryonic matter—solid, liquid and gas—and their particular energetic transformations, not with any other states and varieties of matter that might, and perhaps must, exist.

In Simon's view, however, that did not matter; the point was that when things arise in our unconscious minds that are prompted by elements of our unconscious that are, by definition, imperceptible, we have no way of knowing whether those prompters are aspects of the personal unconscious, the collective unconscious, or alien intrusions; they are simply "ours," however odd or bizarre they might seem. The alien might seem odd, but it has to be very alien indeed before it begins to *seem alien*, and even then, we are far more likely to draw the conclusion that the consciousness manifesting alien images is simply "mad," mentally unhinged rather than in receipt of influences that are literally alien. And, in a sense, it *is*, because the distinction between mental alienation and the literally alien breaks down in that context.

It was quite possible, therefore, Simon had concluded, that because all humans are telepathic, presumably to varying degrees, some or most or all of us are not only routinely in contact with other human minds but with other unhuman minds, without even noticing the fact—and, if and when we do notice the alien within our own minds, we routinely misinterpret it as an idiosyncratic product of our personal unconscious: which is to say, as madness.

Simon had got past that routinization of misinterpretation, although he was still bearing in mind the possibility that he might, in fact, simply be mad, along with all the people around him. That was a possibility, he thought, that none of us ever ought to forget, if we hope to remain sane.

But there was a further problem, summed up by the old saying that the truth is rarely pure and never simple, although it would be more accurate to say that it is rarely simple and never pure. If information can, in fact, be passed from the conscious part of the mind to the unconscious part by means of conscious influence upon the archetypes of the unconscious, that process is certainly not simple, and cannot be pure.

At the other end of the hypothetical telepathic link, the problem recurs. When the transferred information begins prompting conscious images, whether in dreams, waking dreams or actual perceptions of real physical objects, it does not do so simply, and it cannot do so purely. There is always interaction, always pollution. The images that surface in consciousness are always compound, partly generated by the transmitting unconscious, itself impure, and partly generated by the personal and collective unconscious of the recipient, to a greater or lesser extent—hence the problem that Simon and Felicia had in decoding any messages that the neider or any other unhuman mind might be attempting to send them, and vice versa.

The message that the neider had sent Simon via Lenore seemed to have arrived relatively unpolluted, beyond its transposition into Shakespearean phraseology, in spite of the inherent difficulties of the method, simply because it had been so utterly unexpected, giving his own unconscious little opportunity or incentive to pollute it with extraneous imagery. The messages it had tried to send him via the ghosts of Owain Glyndwr and the Black Monk were, however, a different matter. He had been expecting them, not only in the sense that he had been forewarned of the possibility of some such communication but, in the case of Glyndwr, because he had been told to expect him, specifically, within a certain time-window. The opportunity for his own unconscious to stick its oar in had, therefore, been maximized.

When Megan Harwyn and Simon had both seen a tentacle emerging from Fishguard Harbor—a tentacle that had opened a yellow eye at its extremity—Simon could be reasonably certain that those aspects of what they had seen had been generated by the transmitter, perhaps with the collaboration, or interference, of the collective unconscious. But when he had heard imaginary music and she had felt an imaginary physical violation, those were undoubtedly contributions polluted by, and perhaps wholly generated by, the idiosyncratic personal unconscious.

Simon's problem was that he was now expecting messages all the time, and on the lookout for them. The innocent state of mind that he had had when Lenore had come tapping at his window on the night of his arrival in St. Madoc was long gone; from now on, he was permanently geared up, mentally, for maximum pollution; his very eagerness to obtain messages was compromising their ability to carry meaning, or at least to carry it clearly. Such was the logic of the situation.

But he and Felicia had to try. They had no alternative.

But such thoughts had been turned over so frequently in his brain that they were now beginning to take on a routine quality of their own, rehearsed and repeated continually, whenever he had half an hour to himself, with only automatic movements to perform . . . just like taking a morning shower and getting dressed afterwards, as he had just done, without thinking about it, with his conscious mind elsewhere, wandering in the abstract and obsessing.

When Simon went downstairs, he immediately went to find Felicia, who had obviously left him to sleep, doubtless thinking that he needed it.

Margaret, the aged housemaid, who was waving a slimline cordless vacuum cleaner around in the hallway, to no great effect—none at all on the cobwebs in the corners of the ceiling, which she could not reach—told him that Felicia had gone out, on to the tine, but there was no sign of her when he came out of the back door, even though the headland was not so large that she could possibly be out of sight.

He paused by Pamphile's stable and patted the animal on the neck, while he wondered where she might have gone. Rhodri, the gardener, was busy in the vegetable garden, but there seemed little point in disturbing him. Logically, there were only two places where Felicia could be, only one of which was easy of access. She must, he deduced, be in the Morgen's cave, sitting on the ledge above the place where the sea waves were lapping at the cliff, staring out over the water.

The deduction proved to be correct. Felicia was indeed waiting there, exactly as he had pictured her, on the lookout for morgens—or, more specifically, for Melusine.

The sky was cloudy, the wind brisk and the water choppy. Over the mourning-dress that she now wore routinely during the day, Felicia was wearing the coat with the hood in which Simon had once mistaken her, briefly, for the Black Monk. She was holding a big book—he recognized her well-thumbed complete Shakespeare, and was oddly relieved to find that it was not one of his—but if she had intended to read it, she didn't seem to have got round to it.

"Anything?" he asked her.

"Not so much as a seal," she said. "No tentacles with eyes, and no snatches of music. Have you had breakfast?"

Simon shook his head. He never had breakfast at the Abbey, where his status still seemed to him to be direly ambiguous. He was not yet the master of the house, even though the servants' deference testified to a knowledge that he soon would be, but even if he had been, the idea of ordering Edith to make and serve him breakfast whenever he happened to get up seemed as alien to him as the giant hydra in the bay. Their old routines had died with James's death too, and Cerys had placed an electric kettle, an electric toaster and supplies of instant coffee and sliced bread in the dining-room, but he did not feel, as yet, that he could use that facility as casually as she did.

"You slept well," Felicia observed. "Not a flicker of a dream, so far as I could tell."

"Should I say sorry, or were you glad of the respite?"

She didn't answer, or even turn to look at him. He reached out and moved the edge of the hood back so that he could see more of her face. "No respite, then?" he queried. "You dreamed without me."

"Not possible, any more," she said. "Not while you're sharing the bed. But sometimes—more often than not, in fact—dreams are just dreams. Our personal unconscious is never idle; it always has its strange work to do. And I can still dream about you, even if you're out like a light."

"And Melusine?" he guessed.

"And James and grandmother. The full set. And more; your mother was there too, even though I don't know what she looks like. I shouldn't have made you that long speech last night. I should have known that it would stir things up. You should never excite yourself like that before going to sleep. Talking about things like being frightened pokes your unconscious in the wrong way . . . it brings the personal closer and drives the alien away. It makes you delve into your memories, but not in any honest way. What it brings into the dream is always distorted."

Simon remembered that she hadn't only been talking about being frightened. "It's probably not a bad thing," he said, more for the sake of kindness than philosophy. "The theory that dreams help us process these things has a certain merit to it. It wasn't a nightmare, was it?"

"No. More a winding back, indulgent wallowing in echoes of things as they were. All my life, there have been three constant presences: Grandmother, James and Melusine. They weren't always the most important, but they were always there. I didn't always love them, and I often wished, idly, that I had sufficient energy to get away from them, but they were always there. I wasn't conscious of the extent to which they constituted my life until they suddenly didn't. But when their ghosts come back in dreams . . . the feelings they evoke are mixed. Not nightmares, no. You were there too, and that ought to have been reassuring, but you were also there in the flesh, out like a light. And there was your mother. A vague presence, but slightly unsettling. I can't be jealous of her too, can I? Because you went to see her for a matter of an hour on one day? Surely I'm not that . . . possessive."

He put his arm around her. He didn't want to interrogate her any further about the content of the dream. Sometimes, as she said, dreams were just dreams. And sometimes, he was grateful for the useful capacity that his own mind had for refusing to remember his own.

"Have you ever looked closely at the lists of names in the Bible in the chapel?" he asked her.

"Of course," she said. "It's always been a puzzle, trying to figure out what the names were that had been crossed out, and wondering why. I looked there to try to find Lilith, when we found out that you were related to her, but her name had been crossed out. James told me that all the crossed-out names were those of people who had left the estate and offended the current head of the family, but I know that there was more to it than that. It was part of a deep secret—the one he wouldn't tell me, because he thought he was protecting me. He was always protecting me, even when I didn't need protecting. I never could figure out why he thought I might be in danger. Why do you ask?"

"Megan thinks that Douglas Jefferson wanted to go down into the crypt to look for tombstones, or inscriptions with birth and death dates. She thinks he might have seen something in the Bible that conflicts with the census records, which might enable him to challenge the line of descent that connects me to Seymour Murden."

"Grandmother said that you were definitely Seymour's descendant. She would know."

"Of course. And you and I know full well that she was a credible witness—but how many other people in the world would be prepared to believe that she was born in 1789? If there are discrepancies between the Bible and the census data, with or without any further checks from inscriptions in the crypt—and we both know how meager those are—there might be a weak point in the line of succession."

"But there can't be a weak point. Lenore knew that you were a Murden, and a neider too, like me."

"Even if she were still here, she would hardly be a convincing witness in court. You and I know exactly what I am—but the law might see things differently, and you just said yourself that there was something James was deliberately not saying about the names scratched out in the family Bible, that there was a secret that he was keeping from you. Do you think that might have had something to do with your being so very similar to your mother, as Ceridwen seems to have been?"

Felicia shrugged her shoulders. "Perhaps," she said.

"That crops up in the Bristol branch too. Marianne and her daughter Zoe seem to be identical . . . physically, at any rate. They certainly don't seem to see eye to eye."

"I know the feeling," said Felicia. "I feel sorry for the daughter. To be regarded, and treated, as if you were someone else's second self creates a lot of expectations. Grandmother told me more than once that her daughter—the one that looked exactly like her, that is—was the most thankless child there ever was. I sometimes felt sorry for her too, although Grandmother said she got her comeuppance when she had a rebirth of her own."

"That was the term she used?"

"Yes. Natural enough, given the story connecting the entity beneath the crypt to the legendary cauldron of rebirth. In those days, obviously, no one had thought of calling them vitreous cocoons. But none of that can have any relevance to your descent and the entail; it only concerns the women of the family."

"I don't know," said Simon. "I'll have to search the library some time, to see whether there are any documents there containing something akin to parish records."

"There's a file full of birth and marriage certificates, but I think they only go back to the early nineteenth century. I think I can remember which cabinet they're in. I'll get Cerys to fetch them down for you."

"Thanks. There was one thing that struck me as odd in what my mother remembered about Lilith. Apparently, Lilith said that the grandmother of the family—by whom she presumably meant Ceridwen—was evil, and had made a pact with the Devil."

"That's just a misunderstanding of her claim to have slept with the neider. *Neidr* is Welsh for serpent. Grandmother wasn't very discreet about that item of information, and other scandalous claims; members of the family who took their Christianity seriously considered her a scarlet woman, and sometimes confused the neider with the serpent in Eden, although they're quite different. I don't remember Lilith very well at all; I was only a little child when she left, so I don't know whether she was religious. Hardly anyone was, after Rhys, so it might have been a bone of contention if she was, but I don't have any idea why she left. I asked James, after you turned up, but he said he didn't know either. I asked Grandmother too, but she only said that it was very unfortunate, and that the mother had handled it very badly."

"This would be another mother who had an identical daughter, I suppose?" Simon guessed.

"I don't know. Quite possibly. The mother was called Lilith too, I think. That happened a lot—children being named after their parents, that is—but it's hardly unique to the Murdens, is it?"

"No, indeed," he said, thoughtfully.

Either his presence had made her ashamed of her laxity, or she had drawn a measure of strength from the protective arm. She shook herself, as if pulling herself together, and stood up. "I'm going back to the house," she said. "You'd better go back to Raven, get yourself some breakfast and change your clothes. You've got a busy day ahead, with Miss Harwyn and the Reverend. I'm coming to the pub with you this evening, by the way. I want to see the Reverend for myself. I won't come down to the vitreous cocoons with you and Megan, because it might give the impression that I don't trust you to be alone with her, but in the Mermaid, with other people around, we can all be on the same side, as it were, with the same tactful purpose. I need to repair my relationship with her, or make a clean start. I never hated her, or even disliked her, but as James's sister . . . at any rate, she and I need to start again, if it's not too late. Here."

As she pronounced that last word she handed Simon the *Collected Works*.

"It's all right," she said, as he raised an eyebrow. "I'm only letting you carry it back to the house for me, because I'm a frail old woman and you're a gallant gentleman who was about to offer. I was going to take another look at *The Tempest*, but it really isn't necessary; I remember it well enough. I can even remember passages, like Ariel's song."

Simon could remember that too, especially the second verse: *Full fathom five thy father lies; of his bones are coral made; those are pearls that were his eyes; nothing of him that doth fade, but doth suffer a sea-change into something rich and strange . . .*

But Felicia, he knew, like Ceridwen, had not had a father, unless, perhaps, it was a sperm that had triggered the development of the anomalous ovum that had produced her, without making any genetic contribution to her make-up. Had that been what Ceridwen had meant when she said—not just to him but to anyone who had cared to listen—that Seymour Murden had only given her his name, but had not been her father? Possibly. But in the early 1800s, people had known nothing about genetics and very little about the biology of reproduction. Ceridwen's similarity to her mother, apparently reproduced in her own daughter, would have seemed supernatural even to people who were not living on top of something that might or might not be the original Ceridwen's magic cauldron, and was, at any rate, something capable of inducing sea-changes into something rich and strange. Had Ceridwen believed that her father was actually the neider, with whom she claimed to have slept herself? Might she, in fact, have been right, in that it might actually have been the neider that had provided, via her mother's unconscious mind, the stimulus that had enabled her to become parthenogenetically pregnant? If so, had the neider been Felicia's and Lilith's "father" too, and was that why Felicia seemed to have had a closer link to it than James or Melusine?

The possibilities, unfortunately, were endless. There was no way through the maze.

Felicia, however, seemed to be following a different train of thought. "In your novel," she said to Simon, "the cloud-capped towers and glorious palaces were parts of the illusion, parts of Prospera's artificial decor—but Shakespeare's Prospero is referring to the real world, isn't he? He's saying that real towers and real palaces will go the same way as temporary illusions, that *everything* is the stuff that dreams are made of?"

"It's a long time since I stole it," Simon said, "but if my memory can be trusted, you're right."

"And the glorious palaces aren't literal palaces so much as symbols for all human endeavor and creation: the entire edifice of human achievement, thought and civilization?"

Simon weighed the book in his hand, but didn't open it in order to refresh his memory.

"That's surely a viable reading," he agreed, "but even if you decode the dream that we had the night before last in that context, as a prophecy of the planet's destruction, it doesn't mean that it's going to happen. The one thing that all prophecies have in common with Saint John's Apocalypse is that they never come true."

"What about the writing on the wall at Belshazzar's feast?"

"The book of Daniel is a work of fiction; the prophet never existed, Belshazzar was never the King of Babylon, and it was Cyrus who actually captured the city, not Darius. Even people who invent prophecies after the fact usually screw them up."

None of which proves, he added *in petto*, knowing that Felicia had no way of reading his conscious thoughts, *that the planet isn't in any danger of instant annihilation by some kind of cosmic disaster, imaginable or otherwise, the idea of which is even capable of frightening the neider.*

X

The Cauldron of Annwn

As Simon emerged from Raven Cottage in order to do his daily two miles, Alun Gwynne, who knew his habits and had obviously been waiting for him, intercepted him.

"I won't keep you, Mr. Cannick," he said. "I just wanted to say goodbye, and to thank you again."

"You're leaving already?" Simon said. "I thought you didn't have to vacate the cottage in Morpen until the end of the month?"

"Technically, yes, but things have moved fast, by the standards of these parts—and it's all thanks to you."

"Me? But I haven't done anything—I can't, until the will's proven. I explained that, and even then . . ."

"You already did it, Mr. Cannick. You set the snowball rolling when you got James to meet us, in the Mermaid. He explained why he couldn't help us either, but he promised to contact the council offices in Cardigan and see if there was any arrangement he could make with them. There wasn't— not directly, with regard to the Morpen lets, but the Murdens used to be important people round these parts, and there are old farts on the council who still remember that. The wheels of local government don't turn unless someone gives them a shove, but once they're in motion . . . anyway, to cut the story short, the housing officer seems to have smelt trouble ahead and thought it might be a good idea to stifle it. He's come to an arrangement with another landlord to let a dozen families—including eight from Morpen and the two Syrian families from Morgan's Fork—take over an entire terraced block of so-called fishermen's cottages up the coast a way. The location's lousy, although it's not that much worse than Morpen for the kind of casual farm work that's available in the area in summer, and the properties aren't technically fit to let, under the regulations, but we've signed an agreement to bring them up to scratch ourselves while living in them for a token rent—it's a bit under the table, but around these parts, everybody has a blind eye. We're not builders, like, but we're all quite handy, and if everything goes smoothly, it could be permanent, so we're grabbing the chance. The Syrians are cock-a-hoop too, and when I explained your part in it to one of the kids, who can speak English, they asked me to thank you. We'll all be out of the immediate neighborhood by six, so you can have the pub to yourself for your meeting with the English reverend, unless the guy from Blackbird drops in."

The Welshman held out his hand, obviously having no intention of accompanying Simon on his coastal walk, and presumably in a hurry, if he had to get back to Morpen to pack up all his worldly belongings, such as they were.

Simon shook the hand warmly. "I'm glad it's worked out for you," he said. "If I do end up owning the Abbey and slices of the village, you'll always be welcome here."

"Thanks again, for everything."

Simon turned right along the coastal path, and had taken half a dozen strides before it occurred to him to wonder who the "guy from Blackbird" might be. He looked over his shoulder, but Alun was walking briskly up the main street, already almost level with the Mermaid. He made a mental note to ask Dai when he went to the pub that evening, assuming that the guy in question wasn't already propping up the bar.

It began to rain before he had reached the point at which he usually turned back, but he had been living in St. Madoc long enough to be used to that. He didn't allow his routine to be interrupted by anything so trivial. The rain turned heavy quite quickly, and he hadn't brought an umbrella—there was no point, because the wind would have rendered it useless— but he was going back to Raven anyway, so he knew that it would be easy enough for him to dry himself off and change into dry clothing before having a light lunch, collecting Megan from Sanderling and returning to the Abbey.

He hastened his pace as much as he could, but the path soon accumulated a sequence of muddy puddles. By the time he got back to the cottage he was soaked to the skin, and he put his clothes straight into the washing machine before going to take a shower. When he came back down again, Megan Harwyn was sitting in his kitchen.

"I've boiled the kettle," she said, "but I've left you to make your own sandwich."

"We've given up ringing doorbells, have we?" he asked, a trifle sarcastically.

"I have," she said, equably, "at least when you leave your door on the latch. You'll have to keep ringing mine, I fear. You've seen my security system. Did you know that there's a full-scale evacuation going on?—the Syrians are moving out, and so are the Cardis from Morpen."

"Yes, I did," he told her. "Alun Gwynne came to thank me and told me what had happened. Apparently, when a Murden says jump, there are still people in the county who start hopping, and don't stop just because he's dead."

"Is that what the Cardi boy told you? That it was James who provoked this?"

"Yes. Isn't it true?"

"Probably. How would I know? Not that it matters. They'd all have been out before April Fool's Day anyway. Dai says that the Syrians couldn't wait to get out—don't like the place, apparently. Not that the dump where they're going is any better."

"You know it?"

"Yes. Used to be part of my beat once, a long time ago. It was on the fringe of the estate—Murden land back in the nineteenth century, perhaps still in the family. James would have inherited it, but for the schism. I've been digging into the land registry records, to try to figure out exactly what you'll end up owning, but to call the situation confused would be one hell of an understatement. Everything's supposed to be on the computer now, of course, but in practice, it's only when something changes hands that the record gets on to the new system, and digging up the old documents would be the Devil's own job, even if they were all in one place, which they aren't—and quite a few might have gone missing forever."

"It's very kind of you to make a start on the job for me . . . or for whoever else ends up with the Murden inheritance."

"Yes, it is, but I did promise to help, and I also thought it might be a good idea to dig into Bernard and Dougie's background a little, as they both seem to be trying to put together a case for the claim that they're the rightful heir. They both seem to be very well off now, although they weren't so flush back in the day. Bernard seems to have done well out of the property boom, even owning properties in backwaters like Cardigan and Carmarthen. So far as I can tell, neither of them actually needs seven million quid, let alone an unsaleable abbey, but it's probably the principle of the thing that's spurring them on. They've presumably been thinking about making a bid for the inheritance as soon as James died for thirty or forty years, off and on, thinking of it all along as their inherent right, unaware that, even if you hadn't materialized, they weren't the only one thinking along those lines. Of course, we shouldn't discount the greed factor."

"Certainly not," Simon said. "In my admittedly-limited experience, the rich are much greedier than the poor. For an old-age pensioner like me, seven million is a fabulous sum, the stuff of miracles, but to a twenty-first century businessman, it's just a nice little deal, a routine operation well within the scope of their everyday scheming, but always worth doing, in order to keep the fortune growing. Then again, if they can break the entail—which would probably be easy in this day and age, if they could actually get legal ownership of the Abbey—the building and the private island would be worth a lot more than seven million, even without the legendary extras for use in advertising."

"That's true. Rock stars buy Scottish islands these days, don't they?—and they're lucky if they get a house and a few sheep as accessories. An Abbey and the legend of Saint Madoc, with rumors of mermaids and the rest, might start quite an auction . . ."

Megan left it there, not bothering to raise the question of what effect it might have on the hypothetical value of the property if the legends in question were proved to have some basis in truth. Simon gave the matter some swift thought, though. "Do Pallister and Jefferson know the family secret?" he asked.

"They certainly know that there is a family secret. How much more their parents and grandparents might have told them, God alone knows, but they won't have believed any of the more fanciful legendry. When they were in the chapel for the funeral ceremony they could see the padlocked trapdoor to the crypt, just as I could, and even though they must have seen it before, I doubt that their curiosity was whetted any less than mine. They were probably both disappointed that we didn't all file down to the crypt to witness the urns of ashes being placed in their allotted cubby-holes, although Dougie was the only one with enough cheek to ask for the favor."

"They wouldn't have seen much, and they'd have risked getting their nice clothes very dirty. There aren't any nice marble monuments down there—just lots of cavities, mostly filled in with exceedingly ancient and friable cement. There are names engraved in some of the seals, but most of them are illegible. James showed me where Rhys's remains are, and Seymour's, at least according to the labels, but the only clear record is provided by the twentieth-century tombs, and there are very few of those, so many of the family having fallen in Flanders' fields, or having run away and never came back, like James's Aunt Lilith. If the relics of Saint Madoc are down there, there's no way to find them. As for the cauldron, that's protected by a second padlocked trapdoor, the key to which is normally kept in the safe, the combination to which is now only known to Felicia and me, unless and until Melusine comes back. I collected both keys this morning, before I left."

"You might want to think seriously about strengthening that security—and installing other measures. I know you lock

the gate over the bridge at night, but the tine is far from inaccessible, you know. If I were you, I'd keep James's revolver
within arm's reach while you and Felicia are snuggled up in
bed together."

Simon mastered the slight electric shock caused by the
reference to his sleeping arrangements without very much
difficulty, and didn't even pause in the consumption of his
lunch. He even managed to say: "James had a revolver?"

"And a shotgun. I think the gardener has a shotgun too.
Mind you, anyone trying to creep up on you via the sea had
better watch out for sea monsters."

"So you think your cousins are likely to resort to . . . unusual measures? And that they won't be put off by the fact
that you and Cerys have both rejected their offers?"

"They've approached Cerys too, have they? That's the
trouble with people like that—they think everyone's a whore.
No, they won't be put off, especially if some slimy solicitor
has agreed with them that they might have a case, and they'll
do whatever they can to back it up. A little breaking and entering would be routine business—and even if they've got
through sixty-odd years without wondering what really lies
buried beneath the Abbey, their curiosity has certainly been
piqued now, and they've had an opportunity to 'case the
joint,' as American melodramas put it."

"And James really had a revolver?"

"Absolutely. I'm surprised Felicia isn't insisting that you
keep it by . . ."

"Okay, you've made your point. Both of them, in fact.
Felicia's coming to the Mermaid tonight, because she wants
to try to make a fresh start with you while there are other
people around to take some of the pressure off. She's never
had anything against you, but she is James's sister, and she
had to take his side while he was alive. It's in your interest as
well as hers to put that behind you. She's your aunt, after all,
and it's not as if either of you is so well equipped with close
friends that you can afford to turn down the opportunity to
make a new one, is it?"

"Ouch. You're right, obviously. If she can overlook the fact that I'm an ex-whore, I can overlook the fact that she's the sister of my deadbeat dad, and we can both settle for being good friends of Simon the laird. A fresh start, as you say. And don't worry—even I wasn't sure that you were actually sleeping with Felicia until you just confirmed it by not denying it. I won't tell Dai, so it'll remain our little secret for as long as you like."

"It's not a secret," Simon said, flatly. "I don't care who knows—but it's nobody's business but mine and Felicia's. Let's go, shall we?"

"Sure." She waited until they were outside and heading for the tine, before adding: "Look that was foolish of me. I shouldn't have said anything, about any of it—but I needed to talk. I couldn't wait for you to come and collect me. I wouldn't normally admit this, but I had a really bad night, and being on my own . . . let's just say that I felt a trifle uncomfortable. I shouldn't have let it get out of hand, but you know how I tend to let my mouth run away with me."

"Did you have bad dreams?" he asked, curiously.

"You have no idea. I'm not the kind of person who gets scared—so I tell myself. I had to train myself out of it, in order to get through the old days. So when I do . . . last night . . . and now . . . I know that there isn't any danger in going through that trapdoor and, my curiosity really ought to be telling my anxieties to shut up and lie down, but . . . it's less than sixteen hours since I saw a fucking sea-snake open a yellow eye and stare at me, while reminding me of the worst days of my life with a little ghostly rape, so cut me a little slack, will you?"

"I thought I was," he said, mildly, as he led her through the gate and along the main drive. He took her around the house, as he had promised; the only person they saw on their way to the chapel was Rhodri, who was toiling in the vegetable garden at a sedate pace appropriate to his seventy-some years. James had replaced the servants' salaries with pensions years ago, so none of them was technically an employee any longer, but they had simply carried on doing what they had always done, within the scope of their declining capabilities; it was their life.

When they were inside the chapel, Simon said: "If I'm not being sufficiently supportive, I'm sorry. You seemed to be handling it very well when you left me at Raven Cottage last night."

"No, it's all right," she said. "The fault's in me, not you. You're being an absolute angel. And if I have to grab your hand again, I promise not to dig my claws in." She held up her hands, to show him that she had clipped the fingernails. Then she turned away from him and went to the lectern where the family Bible was kept. She spent a good five minutes studying both sides of the flyleaf and the half title.

"Anything?" Simon asked, when she had finally finished.

"Nothing that leaps out," she said, frowning. "It's quite a mess, as you say, with all those names scratched out. Happy families, eh? It would take hours to compare all the dates with the online records, to the extent that they can be compared, and it's not at all clear what any discrepancies that turned up would prove."

"Felicia says that there's a file full of birth and marriage certificates in the library. She's promised to get Cerys to get it down. You can look at it tomorrow, if you like."

"Thanks. It might be a good idea. Dougie can't have seen them though, can he?"

"Not as far as I know."

"Good. It's always wise to have more information on hand than your adversary, and documents have a reassuring solidity about them. On to phase two now, then."

Simon paused in the aisle. "You don't have to do this, you know," he said.

"Are you crazy? I've been waiting all my life to be let in on the family secret. It's stupid of me to be nervous. It's not the gateway to Hell, is it?"

Simon wished that he could be more certain of that himself, but he said nothing more while he picked up the electric lanterns that he had placed on the floor in advance, handed one to Megan, and then unlocked the padlock over the trap-door to the steps leading down to the crypt. He led the way down, and moved to unfasten the second padlock in the floor of the cellar, without offering to show Megan around the labyrinth that extended from the space at the foot of the stone staircase.

She was not to be put off. She moved her lantern around, inspecting the darkness, and moved away from the staircase, examining the issues from what Simon thought of as the "vestibule" of the crypt, raising her hand to feel the draught that was coming through the cracks in the stone wall facing north-west.

"I see what you mean about nothing bigger than a snake getting through," she commented. Then she moved toward one of the corridors. She held her lantern up. "This is where my father's ashes have been stored?"

"Yes, alongside the mortal remains of his father and at least a couple of hundred other ancestors, and perhaps thousands of monks and lay brothers—but not Myrddin Wyllt, I suspect, even if he was ever actually here, or Glyndwr, ditto. If you want to visit your father's ashes at some time in the future . . ."

He was too late, she had already disappeared into the labyrinth. The gaps were not wide enough for two people to move about comfortably at the same time, and Simon knew from experience how dirty one could get insinuating oneself around the detours. He waited where he was.

This time, nearly a quarter of an hour elapsed before Megan came back, looking like a Victorian chimney-sweep, her outfit ruined—but it had not been one of her better ones. She dusted herself off as best she could, and did not seem unduly worried by the damage.

"Sorry," she said. "Maybe you should let the Reverend come down here, just to see how filthy he's prepared to get. On the other hand, no—as you say, an awful lot of that old mortar has something that looks far worse than concrete cancer. Imagine what fun a team of archeologists could have, digging out all those old bones with a trowel. If the Reverend Usher really does think there's even an infinitesimal possibility that the holy grail is buried here, he'll probably want to bring a metal detector down to sweep the walls . . . and who knows how many beeps he might get? Do you have any idea what the cryptic scratches on the old mortar mean?"

"No," said Simon. "Nor did James. They're not runes, or any other identifiable alphabet. Bardic symbols in a long-lost code, he thought—but it was pure speculation."

"And hardly any dates at all, even where there are names, except for late nineteenth- and early twentieth-century deposits. Nothing that would make Dougie lick his lips. All to the good. Next step, then."

Simon opened the second trapdoor to reveal the lower staircase: the one that descended into the underworld. He issued a vague invitation with his hand.

"You go first," she said.

He did. "You won't have any difficulty breathing," he told her, as he descended carefully, "and there's no damp, even though we'll be below the level of the sea-bed. You might feel slightly queasy, though."

"You don't say," she retorted, sarcastically.

He led the way, steadily, from the lamplit darkness into the blue.

Except, he realized, as he turned his lantern down, when the ambient light became brighter, that the blue was no longer the same pale sky-blue that it had been during his previous visit—cerulean, he had called it then. It was still the kind of color that a sky might have, but it was more intense. As before, it seemed a long way down, although he lost count of the number of steps, and lost track of time

Eventually, keeping his voice perfectly calm, he said: "I'm at the bottom now. I'm going to take three steps forward, so that you can step forward too. Your eyes will adjust gradually, and you'll see . . . well, what there is to see."

He was no longer certain of what that might be. If the color of the Underworld had changed subtly, what else might have changed, perhaps more radically?

As his eyes adjusted to the light, however, he saw the objects that James had called vitreous cocoons gradually became more precise, still giving the impression, with the aid of that label in his mind, that they might, in fact, be cocoons containing living chrysalids of some sort, and still seemingly vitreous. They gave the same impression of topological exoticism, as if he were looking at a three-dimensional facet of something actually possessed of at least four dimensions.

It seemed, so far as his visual sensations were concerned, that the contents of the cauldron were exactly what they had been before, except that their color was more intense . . . and except that they were themselves, in some fashion that he could not quite define, more intense.

He remembered that the first time he had made the descent, he had felt strangely relieved and relaxed as he had adapted to the alien materiality of the Underworld. It had felt a little like awakening, and a little like coming home, and he had begun to feel strangely powerful and proud . . . except that it had not really been *his* feeling, but a feeling that he was sharing, the consequence of an empathy akin to the empathy he was still trying hard the develop with Felicia. He had been eavesdropping on alien emotions: the emotions, he had naturally assumed at the time, of the entities contained in the vitreous cocoons.

But that was before he had slept with the neider. He thought he had a better understanding now of what the thing in the blue really was: not an array of chrysalids at all, but some kind of sensory device, a link in some kind of communication system. Any minds he had sensed at the time, and empathized with at the time, had not been "in" that very limited Underworld space at all, but elsewhere. And the minds with which he might be able to make contact now, through the same portal, might be entirely different minds.

He had heard music before: not actual music composed of sound waves, but music in his head, which his unconscious mind had transmitted to consciousness as apparent sound by way of translation. He could not hear music now. Nor did he feel comfortable. He felt as if he were being *touched*—but not as if hands or tentacles were running over the surface of his body; it was as if something were touching him internally, albeit with something far less brutal than a probing finger, let alone a penis: something much more tenuous, like gossamer threads trailing through his organs and tissues.

The first time, when James had interrogated him afterwards, Simon had agreed with his guide that he had felt an odd sense of imminence, a sense that something was about to happen, but without any clear concept of what it might be. He had thought at the time that it was probably an artifact of his own imagination, but this time, perhaps because he had the anticipation already in mind, he felt the sense of imminence much more intensely.

Reflexively, he looked upwards, but told himself, even as he did it, that the only reason he was looking up was that his mother had quoted the old saw "as above, so below" to him and that had she not said that to him, he would not have looked in that direction, because nothing that was actually present in the Underworld was telling him that what was imminent was some kind of fall, something coming from the sky.

He felt hot, though, and not merely because his mother had also mentioned Hell: not feverish, or burning, but just *hot*. In fact, he did not feel that he was an object being heated by radiance or combustion, but that in some sense he *was* the heat, not the fuel, and not the flame, but something more intimate than that.

If there were exotic dark matter here, he knew, in some kind of quasi-gaseous state, he would not be able to perceive it directly, but might be able to feel secondary effects of its presence, especially if the dark matter in question were not restricted to moving around him, but could also move through him, which it might be able to do. How could he know? And even if there were no dark matter, if the vitreous cocoons were able to receive and transmit dark energy, which could flow through them not merely into the space in

143

which he was standing, but into the dark that surrounded him, and the crypt above him, and the house above the crypt, incapable of any interaction with the ordinary matter of this world but able to interact with its native dark matter, and its native dark minds . . .

We might already have been invaded, he thought, soberly. *There might be invisible ghosts within the rock of the Tine, the bricks of the house, the water of the bay and our own bodies, without our conscious minds being able to perceive anything but a subtle change in the color of the strange celestial light that seems to be a side-effect of the cauldron's life.*

He did not say anything to Megan. He concentrated on his own sensations, trying to read them more accurately.

The sensation he had of imminence did not seem to him to be a prophetic vision of the kind he had talked about with Felicia a few hours before. He did not feel that what was imminent was the destruction of the world, by fire or by flood, but nor did he feel that it was something glorious, like a blossoming or an apotheosis. What did it feel like, then? An impending advent? Was it a warning, as if by the pricking of his thumbs, that something wicked was coming?

No. Transposing it into Shakespearean terms was no help. He tried to let his mind drift, to open it to intrusion from the unconscious without prejudice.

The neider wasn't my father, he said to himself, for no discernible reason. *Nor was the Black Monk. I needed an actual father, in order to be born male: a Y-chromosome supplier. But the Black Monk told me that he was present at my conception, and that there was a stimulus of some sort, to the fraction of myself—my dark matter and dark mind—that is also a fraction of the neider, or some kind of tenuous connection to it. Did the neider send a message to my mother via her unconscious that she was going to give birth to a boy, and prompt her to name me Jason? Has my role in this been in preparation for sixty-nine years? But if I'm Jason, who's Medea? Felicia? Megan? Maybe no one; maybe that's taking the pattern of symbolism too far. Maybe, in fact, I'm Taliesin, who allegedly drew inspiration from Ceridwen's cauldron, which was the cauldron of literary creativity as well as rebirth. In all honesty, though, I'm no genius, and the Black Monk said that he was only a common-or-garden bard. Are these my own thoughts, and even if they are, are they being prompted to develop somehow? Is there a key in there somewhere, or is it all just confusion? Would I be better equipped if I didn't have so much imagination myself, if I hadn't read so much about exotic folklore, and reprocessed it so much on my own account? Or is that what might actually equip me for the contest to come, might actually provide me with the raw material to become a kind of übermensch? Am I uniquely qualified, because of my particular checkered background? Am I the one writer who could actually pull a story-thread of sorts out of this unholy mess, precisely because I don't go in for stereotyped endings, because I follow the ideas wherever they take me? If not, what on earth am I doing here? Except that I'm not really on earth any more, but wherever I might be instead, wherever I can imagine that I might be. Perhaps Felicia's right, and I have to make a conscious effort to construct some kind of ideative edifice or scenery—an insubstantial pageant, after the fashion of Prospera—which I have to drop into my unconscious deliberately, in order for my unconscious to use it, in order to build a stage-set, into which to draw what it needs to get to me out of the depths of its own deep well of dark mind . . .*

He tried to stop himself wondering whether that made any sense, because he knew that making sense was not the objective, for now, but he could not stop asking the question, and lost the original thread of the sequence of ideas. His mind stopped drifting, and he concentrated his reason again, attempting a more focused process of deduction.

The first time he had descended into the blue, he had assumed that the cocoons were an extension of the neider, that this underworld was the same underworld as the one to which the neider belonged. He no longer thought that. The neider was obviously in empathic contact with the cauldron, able to share the dreams of the users of the cocoons to some extent, but it had the same problems of the inherent limitations of contact via the unconscious as any conscious mind inevitably had: the same problems that limited his own understanding of the neider, the cauldron and the cocoons, and their understanding of him, and their understanding of one another.

It must, he imagined, be as deeply frustrating for them as it was for him.

But what could have alarmed the neider? What could have prompted the neider to take urgent action, after centuries of apparent quietude? Was there, in fact, an invasion? Had something really come *through* the cocoons, from elsewhere, which was invisible and intangible to the neider, as it was to himself, but detectable by the dark fraction of its mind?

There was nothing in the sense of imminence he felt that seemed to signify an explicit threat. Whatever was imminent did not seem to Simon to be physical mayhem, let alone death. But if the vitreous cocoons were merely a communication link, there was no reason to suppose that the mental landscape with which he was in communion at any given moment was always the same. Perhaps the cauldron underwent more spectacular changes than shifts in the intensity of its blueness. If the neider really had been frightened, perhaps it was by something only glimpsed momentarily, something that was no longer sensible, something now in hiding.

"Are you okay?" Simon asked Megan, suddenly remembering his responsibilities as a guide and revealer of family secrets.

"Yes," was the terse reply. And then, after a pause: "Is this it?"

"This is it," Simon confirmed. "I'm sorry it isn't more spectacular."

"I can't see the reason for making such a big secret of it. It's not as if anyone's going to try to steal it, is it? Although, in the age of faith, you'd have thought the first instinct of monks would have been to establish it as a place of pilgrimage, selling it as a glimpse of paradise."

"A lost opportunity. How do you feel?"

"As you predicted, rather queasy and light-headed, almost drunk. It's not really unpleasant. But . . . an acquired taste, I suspect. How about you—can you hear music?"

"No, can you feel . . . ?"

"No, thank God, but I can feel cobwebs inside me, if that makes any sense. And I feel warm. You're right about it being easy to breathe. Is it possible, do you think, that we're overdosing on oxygen?"

Simon had not thought of that. Perhaps some of what he was feeling was, in fact, a set of psychotropic side-effects of hyperoxygenation. In that case, perhaps some of what he had felt when he was in the grip of the neider, when his blood had also been artificially oxygenated, had had the same cause. And if oxygen could be produced here by some exotic chemical means, why not other gases, such as nitrous oxide?

He ceased to take the benignity of the air for granted.

"It's probably as well if we don't stay down here for too long," he said, calmly. "Last time, there were lingering after-effects. I don't want to meet Alexander Usher while I'm still under the influence of some kind of hallucinogen, or any other kind of drug—whether akin to laughing gas, ecstasy or belladonna."

"Fair enough," his guest replied. "Can I touch it before we go?"

That was a question that Simon had not asked James during his first visit, because it had not occurred to him. Why not?

He could simply have said "Yes," and allowed her to make the trial, but that seemed more than a little cowardly. What he said instead was: "I don't know. Let me try."

Two strides took him within what his eyes told him was arm's length of the seemingly solid blue entities. Tentatively, he put out his right hand, ready to snatch it back if the contact was painful.

It was not. Indeed, it did not feel like a contact at all, but his extended forefinger disappeared from sight within the intangible structure. He snatched it back instantly, and it reappeared, seemingly uninjured. He extended his hand again; this time, the whole hand disappeared from view, but again there was no pain, and no feeling of any sort. He tried to snap his fingers, and was able to feel the contact between the middle finger and thumb, but he couldn't hear the click.

"It appears that you can't actually touch it," he said to Megan, "but apparently you can reach through it. Maybe I could even step through it—but where I'd end up, I don't know."

She came to stand beside him, and she repeated the same experiment that he had just made.

"It's some kind of doorway," she said. "You didn't know?"

"No," Simon replied. "James never said anything about this. But something has changed since that last time I was here. It's possible that it wasn't a doorway before . . . or perhaps not a doorway to the same elsewhere."

"But you're not going to try stepping through it?"

"No, I'm not—not without knowing what's on the other side. The fact that my hand became invisible and I couldn't hear my fingers snap isn't exactly reassuring, even though the hand reappeared when I pulled it out, seemingly undamaged."

"Something's changed, you say? What?"

"I'm not sure. The color's darker, and it feels different . . . as if I'm not in tune with the same feelings as before. Last time . . . it seemed more comfortable, and there was something that was translated inside my head as noise—this time, there's silence, and . . . a sensation of detachment."

"I don't feel frightened any more," she said pensively, backing away from the blue, "but somehow, I think perhaps I ought to. I don't feel . . . myself. It isn't an oxygen overdose . . . but it is a kind of intoxication. I think I'd like to go now. I'm not going to try stepping through it either. I've seen it; now I know; for now, that's enough. I won't say that it hasn't been slightly disappointing, but it's certainly peculiar. I've found the bottom step; I'm going to start climbing now. I'll switch my lantern back on when it gets dark."

"I'm right behind you," Simon said.

He found the bottom step himself, and thought that he could see Megan's legs in front of him, going up and up, first at eye level and then above.

As if automatically, without thinking, he looked back into the depths of the blue—just in time to see some kind of shadow flick out of sight. Where it had gone, he did not know; what it had been, he did not know; but he had got the fleeting impression that it had not wanted to be seen . . . although it had taken the risk because it wanted to see him.

Is that just a visualization of my own paranoia? he thought. *Or is it a narrative device that my unconscious mind has fed to my consciousness to pep up my personal narrative? Or is it a hint from the neider? Or the advance guard of another invasion from a world beyond space, and perhaps beyond imagination? And how will I ever be able to tell? But if the cauldron is some kind of doorway, at least sometimes, it presumably works in both directions . . . and whatever is on the other side, might not have the same kind of inhibitions as me . . . as us.*

Then, inevitably, he went back to wondering exactly what kind of communication device the contents of the cauldron might be, and exactly what kinds of entities might be able to use it as a bridge between worlds, now that it had changed its nature. His head was already beginning to spin, and he realized that whether he was drunk on oxygen or not, he was drunk on ideas; that he might not sober up for some time to come; and that he might be left with quite a hangover when the effect eventually wore off.

He was very careful, as he returned to what he stubbornly, but absurdly, thought of as "the real world," to secure the padlocks on both trapdoors.

"You really do need something stronger," Megan opined, seemingly holding herself very rigid, as if she were afraid of losing her balance. "I know those locks have a double locking-mechanism, but they aren't going to keep anyone out who comes equipped with bolt cutters, or even a sturdy crowbar. And as for keeping something in . . ." She left it at that, obviously having realized, following her first close encounter with exotic matter, that the normal rules of exclusion and imprisonment simply didn't apply.

"Nothing's ever come out before," said Simon. "Not within living memory, anyhow. Nothing visible and tangible, that is." But again, he knew, the normal rules of material exclusion weren't applicable.

He went to the lectern, but not in order to consult the Bible; he felt that he needed to touch something solid, which would support him if he felt weak at the knees. Megan went to sit down on one of the benches. "I'm all right," she said, although he hadn't asked. "I'm fine. But I might need to lie down for a while before our appointment in the Mermaid. It will wear off, I'm sure of it."

"It will," Simon confirmed, although he knew that he couldn't be sure. The first time he had reemerged from the underworld, Melusine and Felicia had been waiting for him, indulging in a strange competition for his attention—but then Ceridwen had summoned him. He had felt fine, even elated . . . but Ceridwen had told him that he was going to receive a visit from the ghost of Glyndwr, and he had, followed by an intimate chat with the Black Monk.

Maybe, he thought, *this isn't the ideal time to practice my tact on Alexander Usher. But the timing wasn't my choice.*

"I'll walk you home," he said to Megan, in what sounded to him like an absolutely calm and steady voice. "Then I'll try to get some work done. I've been letting things slide of late. In Taliesin's day, this was supposed to be the cauldron of literary creativity. Perhaps, at last, I'll be able to produce a masterpiece."

Simon didn't produce a masterpiece—but then, he reminded himself, sourly, he wasn't Taliesin. He did manage to do some work on his current translation project, though, and the queasiness did wear off. By the time he went back to the Abbey to collect Felicia, in order that they could go to meet Alexander Usher, he felt completely normal . . . which was, he thought, very probably an illusion, but one to be cherished, at least for a while.

As Simon and Felicia crossed the bridge heading for the Mermaid, Felicia said: "People aren't going to make assumptions, are they, just because we're going to the pub together? I mean, I am dressed in mourning, after all."

"Megan Harwyn has already made assumptions," Simon told her, "and Dai won't be far behind. Alexander Usher might not, being a God-fearing clergyman with his mind on higher things, but what does it matter if he does? We aren't doing anything wrong."

"But what are people going to think? I'm more than a hundred years old!"

"Anyone with any sense will just think *good for you*, and anyone without doesn't count."

She did not seem convinced by the judgment, but she changed the subject and said: "Who are those people over there moving out?"

Simon cast an eye over the adults and children loading up a small van outside Tern Cottage.

"Syrian refugees," he said. "They're going up the coast, with the temporary DSS tenants who've been wintering in emergency accommodation in Morpen. James nudged the county council into making a shady deal with them. It saves them all from being shifted into some ex-B&B in Cardigan that isn't fit for rats, although I suspect that the council are just thinking of it as a cheap way to get their derelict housing stock tarted up."

"Oh," she said. "I'm a bit out of touch with estate and village affairs, I'm afraid. I won't be much help to you when the will's proved."

"You'll be invaluable, as you already are." He paused outside the door of the Mermaid. "Ready to face the adversary?"

"Which adversary?"

"The inquisitive clergyman. Megan's on our side."

"On yours, maybe," she muttered, but was quick to add: "Fresh start. Let's go and give the poor fellow the bad news."

Simon opened the door for her, and followed her in. As anticipated, the pub was deserted except for Alexander Usher and Megan Harwyn, sitting together at a table in company with a bitter lemon and a gin and tonic. The tap room wasn't silent, though; the sound of Dai's television was filtering through from the redoubt behind the bar.

"Reverend Usher," said Simon, extending his hand as the clergyman rose to his feet politely. "It's a pleasure to meet you again. May I introduce Felicia Murden, James Murden's sister. You already know his daughter, of course."

"I'm delighted to meet you, Miss Murden," said the clergyman, bowing awkwardly. "I wasn't expecting a family council," he added, "but it's a privilege. Circumstances have changed enormously, it seems, since I was last here. Can I get you both a drink?"

"Indeed," said Simon, pulling out a chair for Felicia, and nodding to invite her to express her preference.

"Cognac, please," said Felicia.

"I'll have a half of dry cider, thank you," said Simon, and sat down opposite Felicia, who turned to Megan Harwyn and said: "I haven't had a proper chance to welcome you to the family. I really am glad that James finally owned up to his responsibility. It's been a long time, but I remember your mother well—a lovely young woman."

"I don't remember her very well myself," said Megan, regretfully. "It was, as you say, a long time ago."

The clergyman returned with the drinks. "I was deeply distressed to hear about James," he said. "I never met his grandmother, of course, but I was sorry to hear about her too. She must have been a remarkable woman."

"You could say that," said Felicia mildly. "Two hundred and twenty-eight years old, and on her last legs for a hundred. You can see where James and I got our stubborn streak."

"Indeed," said the clergyman, in a carefully neutral tone. "Is Cerys going to join us? She was exceedingly helpful in my research. A charming young woman."

"She won't be joining us tonight," Simon said, and added, mischievously: "You must have finished your paper on the architecture of the Abbey by now."

"Very nearly—but I must admit that I've been delaying a little, hoping that I might be able to gather a few more data. If there's any chance that I might be able to look round the Abbey personally, and perhaps even get access to the library . . ." He hesitated, not even knowing where to direct his enquiring glance, but settled on Simon, his original plan evidently having been to recruit Simon as an intermediary, if he turned out not to be in a position to grant the desired access himself yet.

"That's not my decision, obviously," said Simon. "Perhaps it will be, in time, and I'd certainly be happy to discuss the matter again then, but in the meantime, with the family in mourning . . ."

Alexander Usher glanced at Megan Harwyn, who was elegantly dressed in navy blue. "It didn't seem necessary or appropriate," she said, "in the circumstances, but naturally, I have every respect for Felicia's mourning . . . and privacy."

Felicia said nothing, content to let her defenders deflect any possible assault on her right to continue James's policy of exclusion.

"It really is a fascinating building," said the Reverend, diplomatically, "of great relevance to early church history. The modern structure in relatively recent, obviously, but the site has been continuously occupied by a religious edifice for seventeen hundred years, and the archeological evidence of the foundations and the crypt . . ."

"Longer than that," said Simon, cutting him off casually.

"I beg your pardon?"

"The site has been occupied for longer than seventeen hundred years by a religious edifice. I haven't been able to investigate the matter myself, obviously, but I spoke to James about it at some length in the days before his death. I was hoping to talk to you about it too, in order to see how your research complements his. It's a subject in which I have some interest myself, as you know. You've done a good deal of work on the symbolic significance of church architecture, of course, and I touched on it in my book on the mythology of the Templars. Have you read it, Reverend?"

"I have, as a matter of fact," Usher confirmed, but clearly did not want to be sidetracked into a discussion of the symbolic architecture of Templar churches. "And what kind of edifice, in James's opinion, was on the site before Saint Madoc built his church?"

"Not an edifice, as such, but he thought that the site had a special spiritual significance in the bardic religion—what common parlance calls druidism. There were still bards around, of course, for several centuries after Saint Madoc's arrival, and some of the Christian scholars made observations, albeit somewhat biased ones, about the religion in question and its relevance to the location."

"I would very much like to see those documents, if any still exist," said the churchman.

"Not the originals, or even copies—but some commentaries have survived, in Medieval Welsh. Do you read Medieval Welsh, Reverend?"

"No, but I read Latin. If the documents were written by Churchmen, surely some, at least, would be in Latin?"

"One would think so, I suppose, but apparently not. In fact, it appears that the monastery had numerous lay brothers who were bards—irregular, I suppose, but not unheard of. My research into Breton and Provençal myths and legends suggests that the Medieval church in Brittany, the Midi and the British Isles, in the so-called Dark Ages, wasn't nearly as intolerant of pagan neighbors as the Church of later eras became, when its armed power became unchallengeable and tyrannical, and heresy-hunting was rife. Much earlier documentation was, of course, deliberately obliterated in that era, but pockets survived, in out-of-the-way places such as this one. I can't read Latin, to my shame, let alone Welsh, but James was kind enough to give me the notes he was compiling with a view to writing a history of the Abbey and his family. He had no idea how close he was to the end, poor fellow, in spite of his great age, but he knew that he wouldn't live long enough to write it and when he discovered that I was a member of the family, and a direct descendant of Seymour and Rhys Murden, he did me the honor of being delighted, thinking that we might be able to collaborate in the research and analysis, and that I might ultimately be able to complete the project one day."

Alexander Usher's eyes were almost bulging. "If you could let me have photocopies of those notes . . . ," he began.

"They're in a very rough state, I fear. Without James to guide me, it will take me some time to read, collate and organize them. As I say, I'd really like to consult you about certain sections of them that are presently beyond my scope. I'm sure that a mutually beneficial exchange of information can be arranged, over the next few months, or even years."

"I'll be delighted to help, if I can."

"That's extremely kind of you, and I'm sure that, even though I'm at a very early stage of the research, I have a few tidbits of information that might interest you. Did you know, for instance, that the legendary Black Monk wasn't a monk at all, but a lay brother, and a bard?"

"No," said Usher. "I never read that anywhere."

"But you did know, because you told me, that the monks of Saint Madoc were heavily involved in alchemical research?"

"So it was rumored—not unusual, of course, for Medieval monks."

"Indeed. Did you know that they were involved in what the orthodox faith would probably have described as necromancy?"

"I believe there were also rumors to that effect, and I remember you asking me what my views on that subject were. Are you telling me that the so-called Black Monk is the ghost of a Bardic necromancer?"

"In a way, yes—but not the conjuration of the spirits of the dead as practiced by the Biblical witch of Endor. You know, of course, what the Pair Dadeni is?"

"The cauldron of rebirth in the second branch of the Mabinogi. One of several such cauldrons in Welsh folklore. One of them was supposedly owned and employed by the sorceress Ceridwen. It also features in the tale of Taliesin as the cauldron of poetic inspiration, although that's a late document, and some scholars suggest that in earlier versions, that too was a cauldron of rebirth and metamorphosis."

"That fits in perfectly with my embryonic research. And you're presumably familiar with the work of Lewis Spence on the cauldrons of Annwn?"

"That's more your territory than mine, Mr. Cannick. You're the historian of fantastic pseudoscholarship."

"You make it sound as if that were a bad thing—but I suppose that an Anglican clergyman can't be expected to approve of the work of a writer like Spence, obsessed with the revival of the supposed pagan tradition of British Bardic religion. I'm inclined to regard him as a lovable lunatic myself, but James found his work interesting."

"I'm sorry," Megan put in, "but would you mind not talking in riddles? I can't understand a word of this."

"Nor, I fear, can I," Felicia added, feigning sincerity beautifully. "I fear that James didn't keep me up to date with his research; I never took very much interest in it, alas. Please, Reverend, if you wouldn't mind explaining what you mean more explicitly."

"Well," said Usher, obliged to take the question, since it had been addressed to him, "I'm sure that Mr. Cannick knows far more about this than I do. Lewis Spence was a crank rather than a scholar, and although his books pose as non-fiction, they're very fanciful, and, with all due respect to your late brother, not to be taken at all seriously. Specifically, though, I assume that what Mr. Cannick is hinting at is Spence's thesis that the story of the holy grail was derived, ultimately, from the Welsh myths concerning cauldrons. Spence makes much of a famous Welsh poem called *Preiddeu Annwn*, or *The Spoils of Annwn*, which is about a journey undertaken by the bard Taliesin to recover the cauldron of Ceridwen, which, in that version, is supposed to give prophetic insight. He's accompanied by King Arthur, so the poem is said by some interpreters to be an important link between Welsh folklore and the Arthurian legendry of the grail. Unfortunately, the earliest known manuscript of *Llyfr Taliesin*, the manuscript in which the poem is found, dates from the fourteenth century, long after Chrétien de Troyes, who started the Norman obsession with the grail in the twelfth century, so the notion that the original version of the poem predates Chrétien is purely speculative. Mr. Cannick will tell you that Chrétien invented the story of the grail as a Christian allegory. He's written a whole book on the subject. I've read that one too."

"That's true," said Simon, "but when I wrote *Legends of the Grail*, I hadn't seen James Murden's translations of the manuscripts in the Abbey library, or his fragmentary commentary on them. Naturally, I haven't changed my mind—scholars always go down with the ship of their theories rather than admit that they were wrong and take the lifeboat of humility, but I am, as the Reverend says, an obsessive historian of fantastic pseudoscholarship . . . whereas he, of course, is a defender of the true faith."

"You make that sound as if it were a bad thing," countered Alexander Usher, sarcastically. "In fact, though, I have a lot more sympathy with you than you might think, Mr. Cannick, and if the Abbey library contains any document that suggests a link between the holy grail and the cauldrons of Annwn—any link that predates Chrétien de Troyes, that is—I'd be very interested indeed to know about it."

"That is the problem, isn't it?" Simon said. "The manuscripts that have survived are all much later than the originals from which they're presumably copied or to which they refer, so dating the origin of the ideas is inevitably controversial. James, like us, was a skeptic—but he too was very interested in the ideas that Medieval monks, especially the monks of Saint Madoc, might have had regarding pagan traditions."

"And what were those ideas?" Alexander Usher demanded, flatly.

"Many, varied and complex, so far as I can judge. But one, at least, had run in the family for a long time—long enough to be current in 1789, when Ceridwen Murden was christened, and provided her with a symbolic name."

"Are you sure that the woman whom James Murden called his grandmother was really born in 1789?" Usher asked.

"I am," Felicia put in, softly.

"And that she owed her longevity to some kind of magic cauldron?" The clergyman's voice was perfectly neutral.

"That, I don't know," Felicia admitted, serenely.

"Neither did James," Simon supplied. "He had similar doubts about Owain Glyndwr and the Black Monk, although their longevity is even more remarkable, albeit less corporeal. He had, however, seen both of them . . . as I have myself. Like James, I'm not completely sure that what I saw, and heard, wasn't partly illusory, but like James, I am sure that it wasn't *entirely* illusory."

"Aren't we straying from the point slightly?" the Reverend asked.

"Not really," said Simon. "The point is, is it not, that Saint Madoc built his church on a site that was already sacred in the Bardic religion, because it was believed to contain one of the cauldrons of Annwn: a cauldron of poetic inspiration, which, in Bardic thought, is identical with religious inspiration, and also a cauldron of rebirth and metamorphosis . . . if one can master the operation of it. The monks of Saint Madoc appear to have believed that for centuries, and tried to put it into practice in various ways, with very limited success . . . but perhaps not entirely without success, given the persistence of sightings of Glyndwr and the monk, and certain odd features of Murden family history . . . not to mention the morgens."

"And they too were a product of the Abbey cauldron, were they? If they ever really existed?"

"Perhaps, but I don't think so. The whole point of the Welsh folklore, after all, is that there is more than one cauldron of Annwn. Almost all of Bardic lore has been obliterated, of course, and Lewis Spence's reconstruction of its cosmology is highly speculative. But Annwn, in his model, is the abyss, the realm of chaos, a kind of Hell—which is odd, because it's identified elsewhere with a paradisal realm of delights. Its etymology is intriguing too; in Medieval times it was construed as meaning 'very deep'—which is to say that it's the vasty deep from which Shakespeare has Owen Glendower claim to be able to summon spirits—but other sources suggest that its original meaning was 'underworld.' Its location, in various Welsh myths, is usually said to be underneath the earth, but some sources, including *Preiddeu Annwn*, place it on an island. It's a great shame, I think, that James wasn't able to complete his notes, let alone write his book linking the Abbey to one of the cauldrons of Annwn. It would have been a fascinating exercise in fantastic pseudoscholarship, don't you think?"

"Perhaps," said the clergyman, "But you'll forgive me if I regret the fact that the documents can't be made available to serious scholars, who might be better placed to extract a more judicious history therefrom."

"I can see why you might think that, Mr. Usher, but the fact is that James chose me as his collaborator, and not someone else. That doesn't mean, however, that you and I can't assist one another, as we follow our slightly separate paths. You know my perspective on the Holy Grail, having read my book. What's yours, if I might ask?"

"I don't believe that it's a derivative of Welsh folklore related to the cauldrons of Annwn. Perhaps, as you allege, Chrétien de Troyes invented it as an allegory. And perhaps

Joseph of Arimathea really did take away from Golgotha a cup containing blood spilled from Christ's wound."

"Divine blood?"

"That would necessarily follow, for a sincere Anglican."

"And what do you think of the French version of the myth that has Joseph of Arimathea arriving on the Mediterranean coast of France with Mary Magdalen and two other women also named Marie?"

"I don't make anything of it. It's a myth, as you say. Your book, I think, makes far too much of it, but that's understandable, given that your sources of inspiration are French."

"I'm no longer sure that the reading of the myth that I provided in *Legends of the Grail* is the most interesting one. Recently, I've been paying more attention to the stories alleging that Joseph actually brought the grail to Britain, specifically to Wales, and that the mysterious three Maries relate to various Welsh legends. I do suspect, though, that the story in question really might have been, as Lewis Spence suggests, a transfiguration of Welsh legends relating to the cauldrons of Annwn—specifically, Ceridwen's cauldron."

"That's understandable given your usual approach to such matters, but you'll concede me the liberty to disagree with you and Spence—and other birds of the same feather."

"Of course. I presume that you also disapprove of the apocryphal Gospel according to Mary Magdalen, and the recent suggestion that Mary Magdalen was actually Christ's wife, and not a prostitute, as the early Church branded her."

"You presume correctly. At best, it's fantastic pseudo-scholarship, and at worst, dangerous heresy. Naturally, I wouldn't expect you to agree."

"Naturally. The term 'dangerous heresy' has no place in my vocabulary. Would it help to ease your disappointment at Felicia's refusal to give you access to the Abbey's library and crypt, if I tell you that I'm prepared to affirm, with my hand on my heart, that there is no cup that ever contained Christ's blood in or under Saint Madoc's Abbey?"

Alexander Usher stared at him. "You're implying . . . ," he began—but Simon cut him off.

"I'm not implying anything. I'm informing you that if you were to be given access to the library or the crypts of the abbey, you wouldn't find anything there that a sincere Anglican would be glad to find—just fantastic pseudoscholarship and innocuous heresy. And that's why I can't, in all conscience, advise Felicia to allow you access to the library or the crypt at present, although I do hope that we can continue to compare our ideas in the future. Would you like another bitter lemon? It's my round."

"Yes please," said the Reverend, and waited until Simon returned with a tray bearing a bitter lemon, a Cognac, a gin and tonic and a half of dry cider before he said. "You do realize that you've whetted my curiosity considerably, don't you, Mr. Cannick?"

"I did suspect that I might, but I thought that I owed it to you, as a fellow scholar, to make our position clear."

The clergyman looked at Felicia, and then at Megan Harwyn, as if to make sure that Simon's use of the plural pronoun had their full support. Then he returned his gaze to Simon. "I have to admit, Mr. Cannick," he said, "that you surprise me. When we first met, only a few weeks ago, you knew absolutely nothing about the Murdens, Saint Madoc, or morgens. And now, it seems, you have far outstripped your teacher. I'm impressed."

"I have a long way still to go," said Simon. "And I can only see as far as I can by standing on giant shoulders."

"Of course," said the clergyman. His gaze went back to Megan. "You obviously approve wholeheartedly of your late father's choice of a collaborator, Miss Harwyn," he said, colorlessly.

"I do," said Megan. "He is, as you say, impressive."

Alexander Usher looked at Felicia, who simply said: "I agree with Megan."

"Well then," said the clergyman, "it would be churlish of me, would it not, to hope that James Murden's will remains unproven, and that another heir might be more willing—indeed, eager—to give me access to the crypt in order to continue my explorations, so I shall accept your decision gracefully, as a Christian should. The landlord tells me that your discovery of your true identity enabled you to make contact with your real mother. I hope that went well."

"I was in constant contact with my real mother until the day she died," Simon said, equably. "The lady I met for the first time two days ago merely gave birth to me—but it was interesting to meet her, and to learn something about that branch of the Murden family."

"Does it have the same interesting features as the Saint Madoc branch?"

"Not the unusual longevity, but there were certain other coincidences that struck me."

"Indeed? The genealogy of the family is certainly interesting, but very difficult to track. I now suspect that I confused at least two male members named Rhys, and distinguishing between at least four female members named Ceridwen seems well nigh impossible, at least without access to birth records of some sort, if the Abbey library still has any. The relationship between Seymour Murden and the grandchildren of his second marriage also seems rather murky and confused. I've been in contact for some time with a man who has done extensive research in that area, and we've recently compared and combined our findings, although I hesitate to say that the picture has been entirely clarified. Perhaps you know him: Douglas Jefferson?"

Simon did not react, but Megan Harwyn started slightly. "I know him," she said. "What's your point, Reverend?"

"I don't have a point," the clergyman said. "I'm merely reporting a fact. I have no reason to think that Mr. Jefferson has found anything in the course of his research that would be of any relevance to Mr. Cannick's entitlement to what Mr. Jefferson refers to as the Murden Inheritance, but I do know that Mr. Jefferson has a strong personal interest in the inheritance in question, being a descendant of Seymour Murden himself. The ancestry is particularly tangled in the early nine-teenth century, given the remarkable incidence of bastardy in the family, and the suspicion, which some contemporary members of the family still have, that the apparent longevity of some of the family members is illusory, based on impos-ture and substitution. If rival claims of descent came to court, they might make for a fascinating legal wrangle, devoid of any precedent."

"They won't," said Megan. "Dougie was always a fanta-sist. Trust me, whatever he might claim, it'll just be hot air."

"Doubtless you're right," said the Reverend. "And we can doubtless put our faith in British justice. We're not living in America, after all, where the outcome of any such case would probably be won by the litigant with the deepest purse, and an impoverished author, even one as prolific as Mr. Cannick, wouldn't stand a chance, even with God or the cauldrons of Annwn on his side."

"He also has the truth on his side," said Megan, equably.

"You'll concede me the right to treat that claim with a little suspicion, in view of his evident liking for myth, legend and fantasy."

"Again," said Felicia, "I agree with my niece. Simon has the truth on his side, and if Cousin Douglas intends to con-test my brother's will, he does not. I have no doubt that the truth will prevail."

"That is my faith also," said the clergyman, "but I suspect that Mr. Cannick and I have different notions of the truth, and I have no doubt that Mr. Jefferson has a view of his own. We shall have to wait and see which truth prevails in that particular contest, but I wish you the best of luck, and I do hope that the experience doesn't prove too costly." He picked up his glass and drained the remains of his bitter lemon in a single gulp. "And with that, I think, I had best retire. If I've had a wasted journey, I ought to make an early start in the morning. I have a long drive home."

The Reverend began an unhurried retreat to the upper floor of the Mermaid. As soon as he stood up, Dai emerged from the back room in case another round was wanted, and as he disappeared, the landlord exchanged a nod with his guest. Then Dai turned back toward the table, met Megan Harwyn's eye, and shrugged his shoulders slightly.

"Fancy him being an Anglican," Felicia observed. "He'd have made a fine Jesuit, don't you think?"

"Hot air," said Megan, positively. "Believe me, it will never come to court. I know Dougie, and not just biblically. Trust me; it will never come to court. But it's kind of the Reverend to give us the tip. He might have done us a bigger favor than he realizes." She looked at Simon, with a glint in her eye that seemed to signify that she knew whereof she spoke.

"That didn't go as well as I'd hoped, though," Simon said, pensively. "I fear that I mislaid my tact."

"Nonsense," said Felicia finishing her cognac with a flourish. "You were magnificent. Don't you agree, Miss Harwyn?"

"Oh, absolutely, Aunt Felicia," said Megan.

XII
The Intruder

The three of them walked back along the empty main street at a modest pace, and paused in front of Sanderling before separating.

"Well," said Megan, "that didn't go too badly, as polite brush-offs go. As I said in the pub, I was impressed by the way you out-scholared him, and if he's pissed off, he only has himself to blame, for not being straight with us."

"I wish I were sure that it was the right decision," Simon said. "It might have been simpler just to invite him to the Abbey and take him down into the cauldron, so that he could see it for himself."

"That wouldn't have been nearly as amusing," said Megan. "And given that he's in communication with Dougie, it could easily have paved the way for trouble."

164

"Megan's right," opined Felicia. "It's not his business. He's certainly not one of us, and if he's helping Douglas, he's against us."

It was too dark, given the inadequate street lighting, for Simon to judge Megan's reaction to that contribution, but he assumed that she would be pleased to be included in Felicia's "us."

"You're probably right," he said, resignedly. Privately, however, he couldn't help wondering whether, precisely because Alexander Usher knew one of the rival contenders for the Murden Inheritance, it might have been better to try to get him on side. On the other hand, given that what he could have shown the clergyman in the underworld beneath the Abbey bore no resemblance to anything that the clergyman might have hoped to find, perhaps the latter's first response to the revelation of the cauldron would have been to recoil, suddenly convinced, like Lewis Spence, and perhaps Angela Richardson, that the cauldrons of Annwn were the produce of Hell.

"I'll say good night, then," said Megan, opening the gate of Sanderling and taking the first of the three strides that would take her to the front door. "I have things to do."

"Come to lunch at the Abbey tomorrow," said Felicia, seemingly on the spur of the moment. "Mr. Usher and Simon hogged the conversation so much that we've hardly had a chance to exchange a word. There are so many other things that it might be interesting for the two of us to talk about."

Again, the darkness made it impossible to evaluate the expression on Megan's face, but the tone of her reply seemed genuinely glad. "I'd like that," she said. "Would you like to come into the cottage, now for a nightcap?"

"No, thank you," said Felicia. "I know it's not late, but it's been a long day, and I'm rather tired. You've had a rather . . . unusual day yourself."

"I'm fine," Megan said. "I haven't seen any ghostly guests yet, and if I do . . . well, I've been assured that even the Faceless Monk is on our side. I'll see you tomorrow, then. What time should I come over?"

"One o'clock. The gate won't be locked."

Megan completed the journey to her front door. Inside, the control panel of her burglar alarm was faintly illuminated, and Simon caught a brief glimpse of her face before she closed the door reflexively, preventing anyone from seeing her punch in the code. The lights inside the cottage, controlled from the same console, then went on.

"You ought to get one of those," Felicia observed. "It's too easy to get into Raven. I speak from experience."

"You had a key," Simon pointed out, "and Glyndwr and the Black Monk didn't need one." They paused again outside Raven. "I ought to check my computer," he said. "There were messages last night that required some response, but Cerys was there and I was working all afternoon, so I've let things pile up. Back in Bristol, I could often go through an entire week without getting anything but spam, but my electronic life has become infinitely more complicated since then. I'll see you to the Abbey door and come back for a while, if that's okay. I'll just tidy up the most urgent stuff and come over in an hour or so."

"Of course it's all right," she said. "Take all the time you need. You don't even have to walk me to the door; you have a key to the gate, so I don't need to leave it unlocked."

"I'll walk you to the door," Simon insisted. "It would be unforgivably ungentlemanly to do otherwise, and I have my image to think of. And with this cloud cover, the gloom will be Stygian once we're over the bridge."

She produced a torch from the pocket of her coat. "I've been living here for a hundred years," she said. "I know better than to go out without one after dark."

They headed for the bridge, and Simon opened the gate.

"I'm going to the library for a while," Felicia said, as they approached the building. "I'm beginning to find my way around there, with Cerys's help. I need to start searching the family documents. If anyone can build an accurate picture of the nineteenth-century genealogy of the Murdens, it's us, and if there is going to be a dispute, we need to be prepared."

Simon hesitated before saying: "And what if you find something that supports Douglas Jefferson's case rather than mine?"

Felicia swung the torch that she was holding so that the beam was directed at Simon's face. "I won't," she said. "The truth is on our side. I know that."

Simon wished that he could be as confident.

As she went inside she handed him the torch. "Don't fall in the water," she said. "And look out for mermaids as you cross the bridge."

Simon walked back to the gate, and closed the padlock behind him. There was no sign of any alien presence as he crossed the bridge, and he stayed well away from the absurdly low parapet. He switched off the torch as soon as he reached what he always thought of as "the mainland."

When he opened the gate to Raven, however, he immediately became aware of a figure that moved from the shadow into the path, where there was just enough light from the nearest street light to show him a black hood. He knew that he ought to be able to form a greeting of sorts, because rather than in spite of the fact that his mind had immediately jumped to the conclusion that the Faceless Monk was paying him another visit, but his vocal cords seemed frozen.

Then a whisper emerged from the darkness, saying: "Please don't say or do anything, Mr. Cannick. Just open the door and let's go inside, I beg you."

It wasn't easy to recognize the voice, because it was so utterly unexpected, but he did recognize it, and because of that, he pulled himself together and did exactly as he was asked. He opened the door, let his visitor in, and glanced around at the utterly deserted street, where the only visible lights, apart from the street lamps, were behind the curtains of the ground floor of Sanderling and two upstairs rooms in the Mermaid, Dai evidently having shut the pub as soon as his customers had left. Then he closed the door behind him and switched on the lights in the hall and the study.

His visitor peered into the study from the short corridor, checking that the curtains were drawn and that no one could possibly see in from outside before she condescended to go inside and tip back the hood of her coat.

Before he could exercise his unfrozen vocal cords, she said: "You invited me. You said I could come any time that was convenient—your exact words, or near enough."

"I did," he admitted, and almost laughed. "So why are you lurking in the dark, Zoe, pretending to be the Black Monk?"

"You had people with you," his niece replied, as she collapsed into the armchair. "I heard you say that you were coming back, and I figured that an extra ten minutes wouldn't hurt, after being on the road all day. This is a hell of a place to get to, you know. Do you know that I actually had to walk the last ten miles. Ten miles! Along unlighted roads. I didn't know whether to be glad that there was no traffic or scared shitless." As she spoke, she took off her shoes, wincing. "I've got blisters the size of eggs. God I need a drink. And something to eat—but the drink first."

"I'll put the kettle on," Simon said, moving toward the kitchen.

"That too," said Zoe, "but the drink first, please."

Simon went into the kitchen, switched the kettle on, and came back carrying a half-full bottle of brandy in one hand and two glasses in the other, with a packet of chocolate digestives tucked under his arm. He poured brandy into both glasses. He did not invite his niece to "say when," because he had a suspicion that she might abuse the privilege. Then he placed the bottle on his desk and sat down in his own chair, swiveling it to face hers.

"And to what do I owe the pleasure?" he enquired.

"It's a long story," she said, "but the bottom line is that I'm on the run, and I had nowhere else to go. Everywhere else I could think of was either somewhere the police might come looking, or where I'd probably be in even worse trouble."

"And you had somehow got the idea, after meeting me for all of fifteen minutes, yesterday, that I was the ideal person to recruit as an accessory after the fact to whatever heinous crime you've committed?"

"You're family, apparently," she said. "But for God's sake, whatever you do don't tell Mum. If you feel that you have to turn me into the cops, do it, but don't ever tell Mum. I know I'm thirty-eight years old, with a kid and a grandkid, and I seem to have spent half my life telling my mother that I hate her, but she mustn't know about this, okay? You didn't really wreck her life way back when, but this time, you might."

Again, Simon almost laughed, although he knew that it wasn't an occasion for hilarity. "What have you done?" he asked, quietly.

"Nothing, really—hardly anything. You're a writer, right? And not sloppy love stories or whodunits—edgy stuff. Mum's always told me, in so many words, that the kind of stuff you write is far better food for the head than weed or spice. So you probably don't use the stuff, except maybe a bit of weed way back when, but you're not one of those people who gets all screwed up about it, are you?"

"You're a drug dealer," Simon deduced. "You're here because of what TV cop shows call 'a drug deal gone wrong.'"

"So I'm a walking cliché, with blisters. But yes. You might think the cops are stupid, but it turns out that they're not as stupid as you might think, or I'm a lot dumber. I don't even know why they bother—it's only a year since the damn things were legal. What did they expect to happen when they passed the stupid Psychoactive Substances Act. Did they think it would all just magically vanish? Did they think the demand would just go away? Couldn't they see that they'd just be putting up the price and loading up the courts with unnecessary hassle?" She held out her glass for a refill, wolfing a biscuit while he obliged.

"Anyway," she resumed, "it was actually what TV cop shows call a sting. And I fell into the trap. If they'd had the manpower, I dare say they'd have covered all the exits but they didn't. I legged it, and because I knew the territory, I was able to get away—but I had to leave the spice. There was a lot of it. The people I work with know the score, they'd probably understand perfectly well that it wasn't my fault—but you know how people are. They always want somebody to blame, as long as it's not them. They wouldn't have killed me, but . . . well, I know what they'd want as payback if I couldn't come up with the money, and believe me, it isn't nice. So I need to stay out of their way as well as the police. Bristol wasn't safe, and I didn't know anyone else who lives way off the map. I don't know you, either . . . but you had invited me, in so many words, that very day, and you gave me your address, which I'd seen on Mum's letter anyway. And nobody saw me coming, at least for the last ten miles. I got to Carmarthen by rail, and then had to take a bus, but there was no reason for anyone to notice me. Once it got dark and I was on foot, it was just a matter of sticking to the shad- ows. No shortage of them in these parts, and not so much as a star in the sky. Apart from the four of you in the pub, and the barman, there didn't seem to be anyone stirring in the village, but I didn't want to take any chances, so I lay low behind your fence."

"And if anyone had caught a glimpse of you," Simon said, "they'd have mistaken you for one of the local ghosts, just as I did. Why the hooded coat?"

"To hide from CCTV cameras, of course. You watch TV— you know how it works. I wish I didn't, mind. It was TV got me into this mess. I should never have watched *Breaking Bad*. *I can do that*, I thought—not making crystal meth, obviously, but I knew my bath salts from my silver bullets. I switched from Es to legal Es years ago—a lot of what was being hawked as E back then was amphetamine anyhow, sometimes placed with LSD—and from weed to spice as soon as the supply was steady. The legal high craze actually enabled the products to become much more reliable. When there were actual shops there was some quality control. Once I got involved with the distribution after the Act was passed, though, I wasn't really in a position to pick and choose what I collected from the manufacturers and passed down the chain. Synthetic Es are easy to carry, even in pricey amounts, but demand is king, and the bulk of the demand is for synthetic cannabinoids, the more powerful the better, and bulk is the operative word. It's just refined weed, mind—no reason on earth why it should be illegal, but it is, and if you're caught with a big shoulder bag full of the stuff you can hardly plead personal use. Even as a first recorded offence it could well have been a holiday in Eastwood Park, and even if I'd got away with a suspended sentence or a caution, the job would have gone up in smoke. I'm a primary school teacher, for God's sake. I'd have been stuck as a full-time professional drug runner for life. In fact, I am, obviously. The police will go to the school looking for me . . . I'm never going to work again, am I? What a mess. I need time to think, and make a plan. All you have to do is let me hide out here for a few days and use the phone. Just a few days, and I swear I'll move on. No one will ever know I was here, I swear. If I have to take the fall, I'll take it on my own. I won't tell Mum . . . if you don't. Okay?"

Simon went to the phone and picked it up. He watched Zoe's face while he punched out the number, observing the battle between terror and resignation with a certain sadistic pleasure. Then he said: "It's me, Felicia. Something's come up at the cottage. I might be here for some time. I'm sorry, but it can't be helped."

He knew, as he heard Felicia assure him that it was perfectly all right, that she would be trying to stop herself jumping to the conclusion that he was with Megan Harwyn, and he almost told her what had actually happened, but, quite apart from the fact that it would have panicked Zoe, it was simply too bizarre.

"Don't worry," he said. "There's no reason for concern. It's just something I need to take care of. Go to bed. I'll see you in the morning, if not before."

When he rang off, Zoe had relaxed somewhat, but she also looked puzzled.

"That was the old lady you were talking to outside?" she said.

"That's right," he said. "Your distant cousin. Hopefully, I'll be able to introduce you to her eventually, but perhaps now isn't the right time, given the circumstances. First, we have to make that plan."

"We?" she said, her tone divided between hope and anxiety.

"Accessory after the fact," he said. "Already involved. You didn't think you could leave me out, did you? After walking ten miles and blistering your feet? If you don't mind me saying so, though—and I know I'm a fine one to talk—don't you think you're a little too old to be moonlighting as a drug-runner?"

"Absolutely. I'd rather be in bed with a nice warm husband and my baby daughter sleeping peacefully next door—without a baby daughter of her own, obviously—looking forward to seeing all the happy faces of year four in the morning. Somehow, though, life went off the rails way back down the track. When I joined the gang after the Act was passed and the shop had to close, Krysten was just a pregnant teen, and I thought that I'd have to look after her and her offspring. I was never going to get on to the housing ladder on a primary schoolteacher's salary, stuck in the rent trap in the flat where I'd had to bring Krys up as a single mother after the louse did a runner. My options seemed a trifle limited. So yes, I'm way too old, but I had mum's example before me of what the next twenty years were going to be like if I couldn't get out. She's me, you see, just nineteen years older, and I'm her. It's always been a matter of looking in a mirror, and not liking what we see, hating one another because it seemed better than hating ourselves . . . except that it wasn't, really. And then Krysten, who doesn't look exactly like me but near enough, starting the whole bloody cycle again. I couldn't take it. Like I say, I'm a walking cliché, even in the way I fuck up. You don't know how lucky you are that the family curse only afflicts women."

"Look around," said Simon, with a sigh.

"I have," she retorted. "I see books. Your books. And I've lived with my mother for more than half my life, and even though she didn't know that she was related to a writer and, to be honest, hardly ever mentioned the fact that she'd once known Simon Cannick, in spite of what I said to wind her up when the smug bitch brought you round to the flat to show you off, she never left room for any doubt that books were the summit of human achievement. So no, I don't believe that you're afflicted by the family curse. If appearances can be trusted, you've even got a girlfriend, even if she does look as if she's a hundred years old."

"Tact isn't exactly your strong suit, is it?" Simon observed. "Never mind—it runs in the family. And yes, I love Felicia dearly, and if I'm going to tread on eggshells with your mother on your behalf, I want you to be exceedingly careful around my nearest and dearest, okay?"

"Fair enough. I'm good with the kids, you know—wall-to-wall tact there, nailed down. Once I'm out of the classroom, though, I tend to open the valve. And my feet hurt like hell. Can you squeeze one more glass out of that bottle? I don't suppose there's any chance that you've got any synthetic cannabinoids lying round? No? Blast? No, I thought not."

He managed to squeeze one more glass out of the brandy bottle, and forgave her for the fact that there was none left for himself.

"I'm sorry," she said, after taking a sip.

"What for?" he asked. There seemed to be a long list of possibilities.

"Everything. Turning up like this, when you don't know me. Dumping on you. Saying that your girlfriend looks as if she's a hundred."

"She's actually over a hundred. She got a card from the palace."

Zoe had the grace to look startled. "Good for her," she said. "If I thought I could still pull at a hundred, I might revise my views on the desirability of living that long. For the moment, though, the difficulty seems to be getting to fifty. I've just trashed my whole life by walking into a stupid police sting operation. Of all the bloody idiots in the world . . . I shouldn't have come here, should I? I'm going down no matter what, and all I've achieved by running is blistered feet."

"Not necessarily," Simon said. "We haven't made the plan yet."

"You're serious?"

"Of course. We're family—and whatever romantic notions you have about books, we're fellow victims of the same curse. If we can't help one another out, what hope is there for us?"

"You think there's something you can do to help? Apart from giving me a place to lie low for a few days, that is."

"I don't know. But I can certainly hide you for a while, to give us time to think, and weigh up the options. In fact, if you wanted to disappear indefinitely, I could probably arrange that. The Abbey isn't quite the end of the earth, but it's the next best thing. Disappearing indefinitely might be too costly, though, no matter how much you think your mother and your daughter hate you . . . superficially."

"No need to rub it in. You'd actually be willing to do that, though? Hide me in your Abbey? In Merlin's cave, maybe? You told Gran that it really exists."

"It's not my Abbey yet, and there appear to be people intent on seeing that it doesn't become mine. And there are other complicating factors. But we have some time in hand. The village won't start to fill up with visitors until the end of the month, and although they'll probably start to filter in sooner than that, you should be able to stay here for a while without anyone knowing that you even exist. If it seems like a good idea to smuggle you into the Abbey, that will be simple; the place has a tradition of discretion going back decades. I don't own it yet, but if I ask Felicia, Cerys and the servants not to say anything, they wouldn't breathe a word."

"You have servants? In this day and age?"

"I think they're what's known as old family retainers. James was about to shop around for new staff in Morpen when he died, but everything's in limbo now, and the temporary residents of Morpen have gone anyway."

"James was the guy who left you the Abbey?"

"That's right."

"But he didn't even know you—you were living with Mum's Gran for years, and she didn't tell anyone that she was your Gran as well until she asked Mum to visit her in the hospice."

"That's true, but James and Ceridwen wanted nothing better than to find an heir who wasn't Cousin Douglas or Cousin Bernard. They had their reasons. Crazy ones, possibly, but strong ones."

"Who's Ceridwen?" Zoe asked.

"James and Felicia called her grandmother, but that was to save the bother of trying to remember how many greats to add. She died shortly before James. She claimed to be two hundred and twenty-eight years old."

"Get away!"

"No—if you're going to stay here, even temporarily, with this branch of the family, you'll have to get used to things like that. You only know about a couple of the things that run in the family. There are more."

"Go on."

"Not now. For now, there are other things to consider. We might be able to sort this mess out in a matter of days, with a little luck and cunning. First, the police. As it was a trap, they presumably knew that it was you they were setting the trap for. And they got your shoulder-bag full of drugs. But you were wearing a hood, and presumably this happened last night, while it was dark. They didn't actually catch you in possession of the spice?"

"It was my bag, with my fingerprints on it."

"Inconvenient, but not unassailable to reasonable doubt. The point is that you got away. Proving that the person they tried to arrest was actually you might not be straightforward, especially if you had an alibi."

"I don't."

"Alibis can be provided. They don't have to be true, or even believed; they just have to be a good source of reasonable doubt. You're a thirty-eight-year-old primary school teacher. It's not going to be easy for a prosecuting barrister to persuade a jury that you're a drug dealer, if there's any room for doubt with which a defending barrister can work. Think hard, though: who might give evidence against you, if it did come to court? Not your . . . associates, I presume? What about customers?"

She thought for a moment or two, as requested. Then she said: "Not likely. Nobody has anything to gain by it, and most of them have something to lose."

"So, being arrested might be a risk worth taking, provided that you can get your story in place first, with appropriate supporting evidence. It's just a matter of choosing a plausible alibi for last night and an account of your whereabouts between then and the moment when you surface. But you're worried about your associates too?"

"Well, yes. They're the guys who were running the shop, when there was a shop, but . . . well, although it was all technically legal and above board, they weren't exactly upright citizens even then. Now . . . well, they watched *Breaking Bad* too. As I said, they always want someone to blame when things go wrong. If I can't pay them for the product in cash, they'll want it in kind, one way or another. They'll play rough. If necessary, I could take it, but there's a strong possibility that they might want to involve Krys, and I can't risk that. I might be all kinds of a loser, but Hell will freeze over before I start trafficking my daughter, even if she is an ungrateful bitch."

"But if you could come up with the cash, they wouldn't pursue the matter? And they wouldn't have any objection to your resigning from the operation, given that you've been compromised with the law?"

"Probably not . . . except that I haven't got the cash, and I couldn't . . ."

"Something can be arranged," he told her. "Even if it meant contracting a debt to someone else, it would just be a matter of making sure that it was someone who wouldn't play rough, and wouldn't involve your daughter."

After a pause, she said: "That really isn't why I came. It really isn't."

"It wouldn't matter if it were," Simon told her.

"It would to me," she told him. "You don't know me, and the only time we met I was horrible. And then I ambush you in the dark and confess to being a drug dealer. I'm not exactly looking trustworthy, am I? But I really was just acting on impulse. All I was thinking about was running. I hadn't even planned this, let alone hitting on you for . . . a loan."

"Sometimes our impulses guide us without us knowing it. Now, your school. Technically, I suppose, if you didn't get convicted of a crime, they wouldn't have any grounds for sacking you, but in practice, nobody's innocent until proven guilty once mud is thrown."

"And if I do turn myself in, the police are bound to test me for drugs in the system. That might be a problem."

"Not for long. You just have to wait until your system is clear. In any case, would it actually be the end of the world if you were asked to resign quietly from your present job?"

She thought about that for a few moments too. "Maybe not," she said, "but it would make things damnably difficult. And I don't suppose that there's a primary school within ten miles of this place."

"Not at present," Simon confirmed. "But let's accept the *maybe not* for the time being, and pass on to the next problem: your mother. I can understand why your first thought, after ambushing me, was that I mustn't tell her. But she's going to have to be brought into any plan we can make, on your side. We might not have to tell her everything, but we will have to tell her *something*. So it's just a matter of when we tell her, and how. That's a diplomatic problem, but far from insuperable."

"Tact isn't my strong suit," she muttered.

"Nor mine, to tell the truth, but I'm not completely unskilled. I'm not going to phone her in the middle of the night, although the police might well have gone looking for you there during the day, if they have the manpower to spare. It's best not to leave it too long, though. I'll make the call, if you wish, but one of us has to do it, no later than tomorrow evening, if we're to organize any sort of workable plan."

"You'd do that?"

"Yes. For Marianne as much as, if not more than, for you. And for myself too."

"Why? What do you get out of it?"

"A sister. I never knew I wanted one, and still didn't when I turned up at your door. Now, I think I'd quite like one. And I think—or hope—that she might quite like a brother too. Maybe we're way too old to be of much use to one another, but at our age, anything new that isn't actually toxic is potentially welcome, if only as a novelty."

"And you're sure it can meet the condition of not being toxic, are you?"

"Pretty sure. I certainly have nothing to lose? Has she?"

"Probably not. Okay, you can phone her tomorrow—but you'd better think hard about what to say to her. And don't tell her where I am. She might guess, but if you don't tell her, she won't be certain. Just tell her you've heard from me. And if she goes off the deep end . . . what am I saying? *When* she goes off the deep end, just weather the storm. She'll probably slam the phone down on you, and hate you for at least ten minutes, but . . . you're Simon Cannick, We have that going for us. Like you, she probably didn't know whether or not she wanted a brother or not two days ago, but that was then and this is now. Let's hope I didn't wreck it for you with my stupid tactlessness. But check back with me before the next step. Even if you can handle her better than I can, I need to be up to date and in the loop. One step at a time, right? And in the meantime, you can't tell anyone I'm here. Not Mum, not your girl-friend. Nobody. Okay? And I might need you to make a few more calls that might be too difficult for me. But not tonight. When we've sorted out the details of the plan. Agreed?"

"Agreed," said Simon.

She seemed amazed. "That easy? You're too good to be true. Why are you doing this? You don't even know me, and what you do know there's no reason to like."

"I'm a writer," Simon reminded her. "I like melodrama. And what have I got to lose?"

She looked at her empty glass, as if wondering whether she dared to ask whether he had another bottle. Instead, she said: "And if I did contract another debt in order to get out of this, which wouldn't involve any threat to Krys, how would I be expected to pay it back?"

"I don't know," said Simon, "but it certainly wouldn't involve sex or violence, or anything criminal."

"That doesn't leave a lot," she muttered. "Do you have the money? Even without this business with the will hanging in mid-air until the court sorts it out? You do realize that it's a matter of thousands, not loose change?"

"I can get it," Simon assured her. "It's not a problem. But there are conditions."

"Oh?"

"Firstly, you get out of the drug business. All the way out, for good."

"Fair enough. And?"

"And you do everything humanly possible to stop being angry, with your mother and your daughter."

"Not so easy. Why do you care?"

"I'm a nice person. I'd like to reduce the sum of evil in the world, and add to the sum of love. And when you get to my age, you have no option but to live as if you might not have much longer to live, and you really don't want to go thinking that there are good things you might have done, and ought to have done, but didn't."

"Only if you're a saint," she said. "But you really are trying to play the part, aren't you?"

"Some are born heroes," Simon told her, "some become heroes, and some have heroism thrust upon them. Not long ago, I found that before I was born, my mother named me

Jason, perhaps after the hero. She told me other things of interest, including the fact that she had a message for me, from Hell."

"From the Devil?"

"Not that Hell—a different one."

"You do know that she's crazy, don't you?"

"I know that she was in pain, and that she didn't take her morphine in the hope of having a clearer head when she saw me. Maybe it didn't work, but the effort speaks volumes. In any case, it doesn't matter whether she was crazy or not. If you find out that you've been called Jason all your life without knowing it, you have to make an effort to live up to it, don't you?"

"You're probably crazy too—but I'm certainly not complaining. Have you got any more to drink?"

"Certainly—but I'll have to put the kettle back on to boil; the last lot will have gone cold. I'll make you some hot chocolate; it probably won't help you sleep, but at last it's not loaded with caffeine. Food supplies are a bit low at the moment, because the delivery truck only comes once a week, on Wednesday, but I've got plenty of cans. I'll warm you up some beef stew, and put some bread in the toaster. You can have the spare room entirely to yourself, for as long as you need it. The window overlooks the street, but it's shuttered outside. If you keep the curtains drawn and use the bedside lamp instead of the ceiling light, nobody will be able to see a glimmer, but you'll still be able to read. There are plenty of books in the house."

"It's okay," she said. "I've got my phone. I don't even need the desk lamp."

"Of course you have. I keep forgetting that it's not the nineteenth century any more."

"Are you going to leave me here on my own?" she asked, a trifle anxiously.

"No—by the time you've had something to eat, Felicia will probably be asleep. I'll sleep here tonight—just across the corridor. Tomorrow night, you'll be on your own, but you'll feel at home by then, and we'll know what steps to take next. Your mind will be more at rest. Okay?"

"Okay. And thanks—you really are a hero."

"Not yet—so I really need the practice," he told her, knowing that she would take it as a joke, and hoping that he could mean it as one.

XIII
A Writer's Conscience

Simon left Raven Cottage shortly after ten, having arranged to go back later in the afternoon in order to call Marianne, once her school day had finished, and to take the vital first step in mending Zoe's awkward situation. Both of them had slept late, and he couldn't help feeling a trifle worried as he went through the gate to the Tine, wondering what Felicia might have thought about his unscheduled nocturnal absence, and the fact that he didn't want give her an honest explanation of it, because of the promise he had made to Zoe.

His arrival at the Abbey was something of an anticlimax, however. Felicia was not waiting for him; Cerys was alone, poring over the computer in the lounge.

"She's not out of bed yet," Cerys told him. "She was up half the night with the family Bible, sifting through old documents in the library and talking on the phone."

"Taking to whom?" Simon asked, surprised.

"Megan Harwyn. They started off texting one another—I don't know who began it—and then switched to talking. I gather that Miss Harwyn went straight on to the computer after you left the pub last night and hacked into Alexander Usher's email account, in order to check his exchanges with Cousin Douglas. Then she started following up the things they'd discussed there, looking for clues as to what Douglas has planned. While she was searching cyberspace, Felicia was going through the paper records, such as they are—the scribbles in the Bible I've seen, and they're a mess, but there are various oddments in the library, including several files of legal documents of various kinds. Seymour apparently stored away a surprising amount of paper, and Rhys even more, although almost all of it seems to relate to his engineering projects. I volunteered to help her go through it, but she says that Megan's going to help her this afternoon, and that she knows what they're looking for. Considering that they've spent the last fifty years and more not talking to one another, they seem to have become the fastest of friends in a matter of twelve hours. You must have had a good time in the pub."

"Did they find anything useful?"

"If they did, they didn't tell me—but you know how things work around here. Rule One, Cerys is always the last to know. Don't wake Felicia up, though—she must be exhausted. Why didn't you come over last night? You could have joined in."

"Something came up at Raven."

"Something to do with the will?"

"No, another matter entirely."

"Another matter about which Cerys will be the last to know . . . at least until I've undergone the ritual initiation, like Miss Harwyn?"

"It's nothing to do with that either, nothing to do with the Abbey or the estate. Don't push it, please."

"Okay. But you will let me know, won't you, if anything that's likely to affect my future crops up?"

"Of course. How's your own research going?"

"Slowly. I started out continuing my trudge through James's translations, and his comments, but without him here to explain what he meant by his jottings, it's like trying to do some kind of weird puzzle. So I switched over to your book about dark matter and dark mind, foolishly thinking that it might be easier to follow, if only because it wouldn't have any Welsh words in it. Undue optimism. Considering that you're supposed to be writing popular non-fiction for a non-specialist audience, you're not exactly reader-friendly when you start banging on about exotic states of matter and unconscious minds. Do you honestly understand it all yourself, or are you just bullshitting?"

"And I thought Felicia was a harsh critic," Simon observed, dryly.

"Look, Grandmother told you to be kind to us—she never said a word about us being kind to you, although, from what I can see, Felicia's being exceedingly kind. I'm sorry if I can't match up to her standard, but she'd probably scratch my eyes out if I tried. Can I run a few questions past you since you're here? Felicia isn't, and we still have a while to go before you rush off to do your daily two miles."

"Sure," said Simon.

"Okay. Dark matter: discovered by astronomers, even though it doesn't interact with electromagnetic energy and can't be seen, but they know it's there because if it didn't exist, galaxies wouldn't hold together and rotate the way they do. Dark matter effectively supplies the gravity that determines the structure of the universe. Correct?"

"Pretty much."

"And there's a lot more of dark matter than there is of ordinary matter—about five times as much? But even that's only about a third of the total mass and energy of the universe, the rest being the dark energy that relates to dark matter as electromagnetic energy relates to ordinary matter. Correct?"

"That's the standard theory, at present."

"And the standard theory also thinks that dark matter isn't just superdense forms of ordinary matter, like black holes, but is actually something entirely different—non-baryonic, in the jargon. But we have no idea what it is, or even where it is, except that in some sense, it has to be pretty much everywhere, in order to make the galaxies rotate the way they do?"

"Again, that's fairly standard thinking, although some cosmologists would disagree."

"But according to you—and, to use your favorite phrase, we're just playing with ideas here—dark matter is routinely associated with ordinary matter, to different degrees and in different proportions, and its contribution to local gravity simply gets lumped in with calculations made about the mass of different substances and objects?"

"That's right."

"And you suggest that there are concentrations of dark matter inside the sun, and inside the planets. So that the sun is a dark energy sun as well as a producer of light and heat, and the planets are dark planets as well as lumps of molten iron, rock and gas. And as well as dark matter, you suppose—or at last suggest—there is also dark life, living inside dark suns and dark planets, and that some of that dark life is possessed of dark mind?"

"I have suggested that possibility, yes."

"And as well as all that, you've suggested that there might be strange states of baryonic matter—including the one that you and James called the seventh element when you had your intimate chat before he died—and exotic states of energy analogous to photons and electrons? And that those states of matter might also be associated with exotic forms of life . . . such as the neider, although that's obviously not mentioned in the book?"

"I have suggested that too, yes."

"It's horrendously complicated—you're not a big fan of Occam's razor, are you?"

"It is, and no I'm not—not when I'm playing with ideas. I think, like Haldane, that the universe is not only queerer than we imagine, but queerer than we can imagine—but at least I'm trying to push the imagination as far as it can plausibly go."

"But in brief, you think there's more to human beings than meets the eye when we try to analyze what the weighing machine tells us about our mass: that some of it, however tiny, is exotic matter, and some of it dark matter."

"It's possible."

"And that our minds, to a far greater extent than we realize, are products, not of the squishy parts of the brain that we can see and feel, but of other kinds of matter?"

"It's conceivable, especially given the fact that we have little or no idea how the brain produces the mind, that consciousness appears to be an essentially mysterious production, and the unconscious fraction of our mind is even more mysterious."

"And you think, following that train of thought to its terminus, that although our minds are in some sense anchored to the brain, and that the conscious processes of the mind, at least, reflect chemical and electronic phenomena within the brain, there remains a sense in which the mind, especially the unconscious fraction of it, isn't confined to our brains, or even our bodies? That it's actually more widespread than that, and that the so-called collective unconscious really might be collective, that there really might be an earthly noosphere, a sphere of earthly thought, as well as a biosphere?"

"That's the next step in my hypothetical argument. It's supported by a certain amount of circumstantial and anecdotal evidence, although some people would consider the evidence bogus or tainted. Thousands of years of so-called spiritual experience, with all its associated phenomena, does lend some credence to that way of looking at things—which is to say, the notion that the human mind isn't entirely confined to the prison of the human skull, and that there isn't merely a sphere of human thought, which permits potential communication between human minds, but a sphere of universal thought, which permits potential communication between all minds that exist, everywhere."

"Faster than the speed of light?"

"Light is an electromagnetic phenomenon, and the limiting velocity of light a question of material transactions. Dark energy, and dark minds, might not be subject to any such restriction. But the fact that communication between minds is hypothetically possible doesn't make it easier, any more than the hypothetical possibility of using radio waves for communication made radio communication easy before Marconi. Given the amount of effort that mystics have put in over the last few thousand years trying to communicate with the hypermind they call God, if it were easy, they'd have found it by now. On the other hand, many have believed that they've obtained some success. One can quarrel with their interpretations, or call them all mad, but one can't simply dismiss them all out of hand without using Occam's razor to cut their throats. Personally, I try to look at what they report with a more generous eye, and pose the question of what it is they might be trying to interpret, if they haven't in fact, entirely grasped what's happened to them, because of the difficulties of establishing a rapport between consciousness and the unconscious sector of the human mind."

"And you think the neider is some kind of hypermind?"

"Certainly not. The neider is an individual mind, with a consciousness of its own and an unconscious mind of its own, although sufficiently alien to find it exceedingly difficult to establish meaningful communication with minds like ours, and maybe minds of other kinds—kinds of which there might be several hundreds, or thousands. I think, though, that it's an organism that has been deliberately created, by a process of careful metamorphosis, and part of a chain of attempted hybridizations between ordinary matter, exotic matter and dark matter, but only a little closer than human minds to hypermind phenomena."

"Whereas the vitreous cocoons . . . ?"

"Are conduits of a sort, alive but artificial. They're a device that is designed to assist earthbound minds to contact minds elsewhere. They constitute a kind of portal, at least potentially. The neider and its parent life-forms seem to have been trying to use that portal productively for centuries, presumably without much success. The monks of Saint Madoc tried too, in collaboration with the followers of Bardic religion—druids, if you like—with even more limited mental and conceptual resources, but perhaps not entirely without success."

"Artificial, you say? Made by whom? And where?"

"Good questions. By aliens, presumably, and elsewhere. As to how they got here, the better guess is probably that they fell from above rather than rising from below—but I'm increasingly inclined to hypothesize that they didn't travel through what we think of as space at all—which is to say, the four-dimensional spacetime manifold that comprises the observable universe. If that's true, then they didn't fall from the sky like a meteor, but arrived by a more convoluted route, perhaps more akin to metamorphosis than spatial travel."

"You think the cocoons might have come from another dimension?"

"I think that they probably exist in another metaspatial dimension, and that it's merely intersecting with ours at the point it appears to occupy."

"And they're dangerous?"

"Not in themselves, any more than a lens or a radio set. It's what might come through the portal that might, potentially, be hazardous to us, or to the neider, or perhaps to the entire human race—probably not in the material sense that a bomb might emerge through it that could blow us all up, but in the sense that something might bend or twist our minds, perhaps locally and perhaps worldwide."

"A mind bomb. An explosion of madness."

"That's a very crude way of putting it, but in essence, yes. Destruction is always simpler, and far more likely to happen, as a result of accident or clumsiness, than creative construction. But a radiation of peace, happiness and love isn't inconceivable, as evidenced by the fact that people have conceived it."

"It's not the usual inclination of your plots, though, is it? To judge by what I've read so far the average Cannick *deus ex machina* isn't exactly lavish with peace, happiness and love. His apotheoses tend to be far more moderate, to say the least: small victories against the awful intensity of dark destiny."

"That's very good—do you mind if I steal it?"

"Sorry—I was just trying to sound like you. I've obviously been reading far too much of you. But it's true, isn't it? You don't end your stories by waving a magic wand and setting everything to rights, even though you could, because, within the world of a story, an author can contrive anything, simply by saying that it happens. In your novels, the characters have to settle for much smaller rewards, because you think that's what the world is actually like."

"That's probably a fair analysis," Simon agreed.

"Because that's the way you read the noosphere, or the universal hypermind. That's the message you dredge up from the collective unconscious into the tiny prison of your consciousness."

"That's one way of looking at it," Simon agreed again, even more warily.

"No," she said. "If I'm reading your books correctly, it's *your* way of looking at it. Isn't it?"

"The trouble with belonging to this family," Simon observed, with a slight sigh, "is that everybody knows me better than I do myself. But you're probably right. I write my books and move on. My consciousness moves from one project to another, one imaginary world to another. As a loyal and assiduous reader, at least for the past few weeks, you've been taking them aboard *en masse*, seeing the wood as well as the trees. And you're right; if that frame of mind is consistently present in my creative work, it must be coming, in a trickle if not a flood, from the unconscious, from the sum of the personal and the collective, not to mention the human and the universal."

"And in your particular case, and mine, as victims of the Murden curse, not just the human."

"Perhaps not. If some kind of alien taint, originating from the cauldron or from the neider, really is bred in the Murden bone, handed down from mother to child—perhaps in the dark bone rather than the white—then it would, presumably, come out in my work, in my play with ideas. But if what you're trying to infer from that is that my tendency to avoid conventional happy endings somehow reflects the likelihood, or even the inevitability, that if something bad is coming through the cauldron right now, we're unlikely to win anything but a small victory, you're looking at things from the wrong angle . . . from the reader's angle, not the writer's. You're a writer yourself, so you should know the difference."

"An unpublished writer, awkward, inept and still groping my way toward a primitive understanding."

"That is *not* what I said when you asked me to comment on your work."

"No, but it's what you meant. Like Felicia, I'm a better reader than I am a writer. So explain to me why I'm wrong—why I shouldn't take your creative distillations from the unconscious part of your persistently dark mind seriously, as an account of the way things really work, at least for the victims of the Murden curse?"

"I'm not saying that you're wrong, just that you're looking at it from a particular angle: the reader's angle. From the viewpoint of the reader, the text is set in stone, metaphorically; it what it is, unalterable. But from the writer's point of view it's something unformed and unfixed, constantly undergoing metamorphosis and rebirth, and it's never really finished, even when it takes form somewhat arbitrarily, as a typescript and, if he's lucky, a printed book. Even if his writer's conscience makes him avoid an overgenerous *deus ex machina* that sets everything to rights with the sweep of a magic wand, he always knows that the power was there, that the possibilities were endless."

"But what comes across to the reader," Cerys insisted, "not just of your novels, but of your non-fiction too, is the pessimism. And it's simply true, isn't it, that when the text reaches print it is set, if not in metaphorical stone, at least in literal black and white? It is it what it is, not any of the vague possibilities that might still be floating around in the darkness of your imagination, forever unconscious."

"That's even better," said Simon. "I really will have to steal that argument."

"I'm trying to make a serious point here, Uncle Simon. I'm not just playing with ideas. I'm the one with the future at stake, remember. I'm trying to decide whether I ought to stay here, and join you in the collective madness of living with and within the cauldron of Annwn, or whether to the get the hell out and never look back, even if I am carrying the curse in my dark blood. And I'm trying to figure out exactly how dangerous this thing beneath our feet really is, to me, to us, and to God only knows what else. I'm trying to take your books seriously, as a clue if not a guide. And what they're telling me, admittedly and necessarily looking at them from a reader's point of view, is that there are no happy endings: that the Gardens of Armida always disappear; that all the glittering promises are just a mirage, just an insubstantial pageant, bound to collapse—the real world as well as its illusions."

Simon felt as if he were under attack, subject to mental machine-gun fire.

"You're exaggerating," he said. "You're leaving out the small victories. You shouldn't do that."

"Damning the world with faint praise," she retorted.

He thought that he ought to file that one away for repetition as well, but figured that it would be a failure of tact to say it out loud.

"Pessimism isn't always right, Cerys," he said, in the end, "even if it's the likelier bet. If, sometimes—often, even—it turns out that we can't achieve anything very much, even a measure of understanding, that doesn't excuse us from trying, and it shouldn't make us scornful of small victories. It's not a damnation of the universe to suggest that, most of the time, they're the only kind that we're likely to win."

"And you think we might be able to achieve something here?" she said, with a magisterial sweep of her arm to indicate that "here," in this instance, meant the document displayed on the computer screen, which she had been studying in order to catch up with James's patient scholarship, the Abbey and the remainder of the rump of the Murden estate, and the Underworld beneath it, with the blue cocoons that might be about to hatch disaster.

"I think the neider must think so," Simon said. "Otherwise, it wouldn't have renewed its strenuous, albeit inept, awkward, groping efforts to make fruitful contact with humankind. Whether it will succeed, I don't know. But yes, I think the possibility is there. I think we might achieve something, today, tomorrow, in the next few months, and the next few years. I think we might achieve something good and something lasting."

"But you're looking from the writer's point of view," she said. "And you aren't writing this, are you? You don't have a *deus ex machina*, however parsimonious. You don't even have a pen. You're helpless, unable even to run away."

"Touché," said Simon. "But I'm not yet seventy, let alone dead, and while the possibilities exist, I'm not going to let go of them, at least in my imagination. You have far more possibilities than I have, as we discussed last night. Maybe that makes your choices more difficult, but believe me, it's infinitely better to have choices than to have run out. It probably won't be easy for you, whether you stay here or leave, because life isn't easy, unless you're very, very lucky. But if you want advice, the best advice you'll get from me, verbally or through my books, is not to be scornful of the small victories, even if—especially if—you have to fight like hell to win them. And I'm sorry the books are complicated, and difficult, but that's the way the world is, and my writer's conscience won't let me pretend otherwise, even if it would only take a stroke of the pen to tell the lie. And before you ask, yes, this is me being kind. Maybe not as tactful as I'd like to be, but definitely kind. Whatever you decide to do, you already have the promise of my support."

"So whatever I decide," she countered, with a hint of a sneer, "it will count as another small victory for you, in your secret moral accounts."

"And every time you come out with another smart remark," he said, "I'll chalk it up to the benign influence of reading my books, so we both get the benefit. A win-win situation."

She had the grace to smile wryly, but she didn't thank him for all his philosophical assistance. Simon forgave her for that, still playing the saint.

A bell rang then, apparently having waited politely for their dialogue to finish before interrupting them. It was the bell connected to the push at the gate, although the gate wasn't locked.

"I'll go," Simon said, as Cerys rose to her feet with Pavlovian alacrity. He ran to the front door, and along the driveway.

XIV
Strange Implications

The person waiting at the gate was Megan.

"The padlock isn't fastened," Simon pointed out.

"I know," she said, "but I wanted a quick word with you in private before lunch. I figured that if you didn't answer the bell yourself, Cerys would fetch you for me. It would be far more convenient if you had a mobile phone, like normal people. I texted Felicia, but she didn't reply, so I inferred that she must be still in bed. We were up rather late last night."

"So I heard. Cerys says that you hacked into Alexander Usher's email account and stole all his exchanges with Douglas Jefferson."

"Me?" she said, in mock horror. "That would be illegal, and you know that I would never do anything illegal. And it would be like trying to hack the Church of England, protected by God as well as Norton. If that's not impossible, what is?"

"So you haven't found anything."

"Let's just say that I'm pretty sure that *he* hasn't found anything worthwhile. There's nothing to find in the electronic records but yawning gaps. On the other hand, Dougie does seem to have taken the opportunity, either while he was here for the funeral or on some previous occasion, to photograph the lists of names and dates recorded on the opening pages of the family Bible, along with the crossings out and other symbols. Felicia got Cerys and the gardener to carry the original up to the library, and to pull the files of family documents out of the corner where James had secreted them, so we now have everything Dougie has, and more . . . a lot more, in fact."

"And?"

"The good news is that everything Felicia exhumed last night while we were exchanging notes supports your case, or, at the very least, does it no harm. There are some crucial pieces, capable of refuting a flimsy hypothetical argument—which is all that Dougie has—but the indications they offer are suggestive of . . . peculiarities that might blow up a lot of smoke, even though there's no fire. There might conceivably be further relevant evidence in the crypt, from before the days of cremation, but my brief survey yesterday suggests that there's nothing presently recoverable. Even in the highly unlikely event that DNA could be salvaged from old bones, I really can't imagine that it could ever produce proof of Dougie's suspicions, and so far as I can see, legally, you're absolutely in the clear. For other reasons, though, I wanted to run my ideas past you before confiding them to Felicia, let alone to anyone else. Do you mind taking your daily constitutional a little early?"

"Not at all."

They turned south along the coast road and began strolling, at a leisurely pace. Megan seemed to be collecting her ideas. After a pause, she said: "The hard data in the files is surprising, but could be regarded as merely odd. It does, however, give rise to certain . . . conjectures. Last night, Felicia and I were concentrating on trying to figure out exactly what it was that Dougie suspects, and ways of countering it if he were ever unwise enough to set his suspicions before a court. That, I think, we did, and I think Felicia went to bed satisfied . . . albeit a trifle anxious about your continued and unexplained absence. When she wakes up, though, she'll carry on thinking, and she's a very intelligent woman. She'll be able to see the further implications as clearly as I can. Whether they'll cause her any distress or discomfort, I don't know, but I thought I ought to talk to you first. Did the old lady ever tell you that she had four children by three different men, without ever being married?"

"Yes. It was common knowledge within the family, apparently. Even my mother knew, having got the gossip from Lilith."

"Did she also tell you that Seymour Murden was married to her mother, and gave her his name, but that he wasn't her father?"

"Yes. My mother knew that too, from the same source."

"And you believed her, just as you believed that she really had been born in 1789?"

"I believed that she believed it."

"Well put. She might, indeed, have believed it, if, as I suspect, she was told from birth that she was the same person as the Ceridwen born in 1789."

"But you think she wasn't?"

"That depends what you mean by 'the same person.' The family might not have defined that concept in the same way as you or I . . . or the law."

Simon had no difficulty at all following the implications of that observation. "The family even used the term 'rebirths,'" he said. "Given the mythology attached to the cauldron it wouldn't have been difficult for Murdens, at least in the days before the positivist enlightenment of Rhys the Engineer, to imagine that the daughters who grew up to be identical to their mothers were actually, in a sense, reincarnations of the same person. Alexander Usher said something last night about there being four Ceridwens."

"Indeed. But your Ceridwen, the one James and Felicia call grandmother, was probably sincere in believing that they were the same person as the one born in 1789, reborn in different bodies."

"So she wasn't actually two hundred and twenty-eight when she died in strict biological terms, although she sincerely believed that she had been?"

"No, she probably wasn't—but she was very old, well over a hundred, so she was certainly remarkable."

"And the stories she told about having four children by three different men, and Seymour Murden not being her biological father, are confused?"

"Very confused. The Ceridwen born in 1789 was actually Seymour Murden's second wife, not his daughter, and she did have four children—but her daughter Ceridwen Murden, who wasn't Seymour Murden's biological daughter, because she was a clone of her mother, also had four children. Your Ceridwen was confusing the two, and probably confusing the number of fathers involved as well, who might have numbered three in total, but might not."

"And how many children did our Ceridwen have?"

"None, so far as I can see, which might be why she told you that she was really a great aunt, even though the Ceridwen born in 1789 really was your several-times-great-grandmother."

"Okay. I'm following you so far. How much more complicated does it get?"

"Very. So, the clone was the first Ceridwen's fourth child. The other three might, in the eyes of the family, have been failed attempts to produce her, but that's conjecture. What's certain, however, is that the second of the four was Rhys . . . the first Rhys."

"Usher mentioned that there were two. You think the second took over the identity of the first at some point, and began misrendering his birth-date in official documents?"

"I'm sure of it. So is Dougie. But it doesn't matter. Dougie thinks it might offer him the basis for a hypothetical argument for giving priority to his line of descent, from Seymour's eldest daughter, over yours, which goes back to Rhys, but it doesn't. Legally, your case is rock solid, in spite of a second complicating factor, which Dougie and Usher have also observed."

"But the second Rhys can't possibly have been a clone of the first. Even if he was the son of the first Rhys . . ."

"That's where the situation becomes intriguing. You realize, of course, that there are no birth certificates for any of these individuals, and no official documentation of any of them before 1840?"

"I thought the national census started during the Napoleonic Wars?"

"It's true that the first one was 1801 and that a further census was taken every ten years thereafter, but in the beginning they were simply head counts, with very little personal data. It wasn't until 1841 that a detailed account of the members of every household was recorded. The official registration of births, marriages and deaths began at about the same time, in 1837, but didn't become compulsory until 1875. Prior to 1840 there were multitudinous, albeit rather patchy, parish records of religious marriages, baptisms and burials throughout Wales, many of them carefully collected and subsequently imported on to the web by the Mormons, but the Murdens of the Abbey don't figure in those at all. There are various other kinds of lists useful in genealogical research, but the Murdens hardly figure in those either. Apart from the documents held by the family, there's very little hard information about Seymour, and even less relating to the several Ceridwens—very little beyond the names scratched out in the family Bible when the 'reborn' Ceridwens took on the identities of the one born in 1789. It was the erasure of the name of the second Rhys, and the realization that some of the erasures weren't people struck off the family list on account of some petty treason that first raised Dougie's suspicions. There was enough data in subsequent official records to suggest strongly that the Rhys who became famous as Rhys the Engineer was the one whose birth-date had been erased, not the first one, who was Ceridwen's second child."

"Now I come to think about it," said Simon, "I believe I remember that Alexander Usher told us in the Mermaid when I first met him that Rhys was Seymour's son, whereas James told me later that he was his grandson—but that might have been a simple mistake."

"Perhaps it wasn't. It's possible that James had a reason for thinking that the Rhys from whom you and he were descended was, in fact, Seymour's grandson—biologically, that is, not legally. Legally, he was definitely Seymour's son."

"I see what you mean about the complications."

"Not yet, you don't. The file of birth- and marriage-certificates that Felicia found in the library only contains documents dated after 1840, but there was another file with it containing earlier documents, clearly dated and notarized, which Seymour Murden seems to have taken great care to assemble and preserve."

"What sort of documents?"

"Documents formally acknowledging a number of children as his—certificates of adoption, if you like. There are eight, four of whom were the children to which his second wife gave birth, including Rhys and the second Ceridwen, who seems to have taken over the official identity of the first at some point."

"Why would he have formal documents drawn up acknowledging four children who were legally his anyway?"

"Maybe to thwart any possible contention that they weren't really his—remember your Ceridwen's peculiar allegations about her relationship with her supposed father and the fatherhood of her four children. In any case, the more interesting documentation relates to the documents that don't refer to his wife's children. One of those is for the Rhys who seems to have taken over the official identity of the first. Legally, therefore, that Rhys really was Seymour Murden's son, although he wasn't the child of the first Ceridwen—which puts you in the clear and blows any aspersions that Dougie might want to cast on your origins away. Legally, you're a direct descendant of Seymour Murden . . . as you are biologically, several times over."

"What do you mean by that?"

"For one thing, I mean that there are several instances further down the line of Murdens marrying first cousins, and giving their own children a double dose of Seymour genes. For another, the notes Dougie exchanged with Alexander Usher also took note of another oddity in your ancestry, of no apparent consequence legally, but which intrigued them nevertheless. It was easy for them, of course, to find the birth-certificates of your Evelyne, born in the early 1920s, and her mother Lilith, born at the turn of the century; that latter certificate registers the father of Lilith as Malcolm Murden, a direct descendant of Rhys Murden, and registers her mother's name as Lilith Murden. No record can be found, however, of the birth of that previous Lilith; that's not entirely surprising, given that registration of births didn't become compulsory until 1875, so it's possible that it simply wasn't registered, if it happened in 1874 or earlier. But there isn't a Lilith born in the 1870s recorded in the family Bible either. Again that absence doesn't prove anything, in itself."

"But?" Simon prompted.

"But one of the other formal acknowledgements of paternity carefully made up for Seymour and notarized was for a 'daughter' named Lilith. Not the same individual biologically, obviously . . . but the family, even as late as 1874, in the era of Rhys the Engineer, might not have seen it that way. And if they thought of her as a rebirth from the very start, as they might have done if her own mother was one of a line, and died giving birth to her, that might be why there's no birth recorded in the Bible. That's conjecture, obviously, but the coincidence of names is certainly real."

"So you think that I might be descended, a trifle tortuously, from two of Seymour Murden's adopted children?" said Simon, tentatively.

"At least," Megan confirmed. "Probably more. The whole picture is still more than a trifle unclear."

"Alexander Usher commented on the incidence of bastardy in the family in that era," Simon observed. "I thought
he was just referring to Ceridwen's oft-repeated claim about
her children having different fathers. Maybe not—but you're
implying more than extra-marital affairs, aren't you? You're
dropping heavy hints about possible incest. The Reverend
didn't go that far."

"How could he, given that the only possible evidence
available to him is purely circumstantial? But it seems to me
that, one way or another, there might be a lot of Seymour
Murden in you, genetically speaking. More than there is in
Dougie or Bernard, even though neither of them has been
short-changed in their genetic legacy. The family, of course,
wouldn't have thought in terms of incest at all. They'd have
thought in terms of rebirth."

"Ceridwen said, in so many words, that James was just
Rhys all over again," Simon mused, "but I thought it was
just a manner of speaking. She never said that I was Seymour
reborn . . . but she certainly welcomed me to the family with
a very unusual warmth. But you're implying, I suppose, that
the other four children that Seymour acknowledged legally
must actually have been his biological children?"

"That would depend on your definition of biological children. If the second Ceridwen was a clone of the first, should
she be recognized as Seymour's child? And if the second
Ceridwen gave birth to four children, at least one of whom
was also a clone and one of whom bore a close resemblance
to the first Rhys, might Seymour have thought of them as his
children too . . . and might he have thought that in screwing
their mother he was actually screwing his wife reborn? All
conjecture, obviously . . . but it might help to explain the legal
acknowledgements of paternity."

"That's an exceedingly tangled web of speculations."

"Yes, it is," she admitted, "and we have to remember that
whatever we might think of the links within it, given our
modern knowledge of biology, Seymour and his contempo-
raries would have looked at it very differently, with a different set of concepts . . . and goals."

"You think they were actually trying to produce parthenogenetic children, because they regarded them as in some sense sacred, and that they were doing it by reproducing unions between children who were supposedly the rebirths of couples who had given rise to such rebirth before, not realizing that, in biological terms, only female children could be genetically identical to their mothers?"

"You have to remember that the identity, or lack of it, wouldn't be obvious at birth. It wouldn't be until they were older that the excessive similarities between mothers and daughters became obvious . . . but if observers were on the lookout for similarities of that kind, they probably found them, sometimes, when they weren't actually there genetically . . . and sometimes found similarities between fathers and sons to which they attributed the same sacred quality."

"But they had to keep it secret," Simon observed, "because even relationships that we can now consider to have been between genetically unrelated individuals, like Seymour and his wife's clone daughter, would still have seemed to them to be incestuous in legal and religious terms."

"In terms of laws and religious beliefs they didn't recognize, having their own . . . and which many of them still didn't recognize, even when Rhys the Engineer tried to sweep away the old superstitions and drag the family into respectable Victorian society—which might help to explain some of the tensions within it, including the tension between James and Ceridwen."

"And his protection of Felicia from Ceridwen's hopes and expectations, because she was a rebirth, and might be expected to have a rebirth of her own, if she had any children," Simon suggested, getting into the swing of the game. "And although the idea that the rebirths were sacred was essentially arbitrary, the relationship between the family and the cauldron, and between the family and the neider, by giving rise to quasi-religious experiences, lent enormous support to the idea of the uniqueness of the Murdens and their special heritage . . . or their curse, as dissenters came to think of it. But it's just a story, almost all conjecture."

"Almost all," Megan agreed. "Anyway, I don't know how far Dougie's speculations have gone, given that he has far less information than we have, or exactly what he thinks he can do with the limited information he thinks he has. But I know that everything he's put in his emails is worthless. He and Usher have discussed the possibility that if the substitution of Rhys Two for Rhys One could be proven, it might be arguable that the entail was broken in the mid-nineteenth century and thus can have no legal force today, but that's clutching at straws, and even in the unlikely event that it worked, it would only serve to open a can of worms, in more ways than one. It's difficult to see what the consequences of breaking the entail retrospectively would be, in terms of the probate court's handling of the estate, but they'd surely be chaotic. So, as I said before, all Dougie has is hot air. I think you can forget about him. On the other hand, you might have some concerns about what Felicia might think when she'd worked her way through the arguments and speculations I've just sketched out, as she surely will."

They had arrived back at the bridge to the tine, at the terminus of Simon's standard daily walk. They crossed the bridge and paused outside the gate.

"So what are you going to tell Felicia?" Simon asked.

"I'm not going to tell her anything, except that, so far as I can see, it doesn't matter what Dougie's planning, because we hold all the evidential trumps, and because, if he's too stupid to drop it of his own accord, I can give him a nudge. The rest is up to you. She can make deductions and speculate on her own account. Not that there's any reason why she should care, necessarily . . . and you can probably explain better than I can why she shouldn't."

"It might be difficult for her not to care a little, given that she's supposedly reborn herself, and that James and Ceridwen carefully kept some of the implications of that status hidden from her for a hundred years."

As Simon opened the gate, he thought that he glimpsed another dangling thread of the Gordian knot, and he continued: "But if, hypothetically speaking, Cousin Douglas were able to get the conditions of the entail thrown out by the court, and the competition for the inheritance opened up to further contestants, there might be a lot of them, and Alexander Usher's snide comments about the outcome of long-winded lawsuits being dependent on the depths of the contestants' pockets might come into play. Felicia, for instance, would obviously have a strong moral claim to a share of a divided inheritance, but she doesn't have any money of her own. Nor does Cerys, and I'm far from rich. But as James's daughter, you could enter the lists powerfully armed yourself . . . you're not poor, are you?"

"It's very gentlemanly of you to point that out," said Megan, "but I assure you that I have no interest in trying to put in a claim for a share of the inheritance, and even if I thought that Dougie's argument had any merit, which I don't, I wouldn't want to make use of it. I'd be a complete idiot to involve myself in a fight of that sort, just as Dougie would be. Why on earth would any of us want to encumber the rest of our lives, which might not be very long, with that kind of wild goose chase? It's far better for everyone if the will stands, and James's estate stays intact—not just for you, but for Felicia and Cerys, and, in my estimation, me too. And I'm going to do what I can to make sure things work out that way."

"You're a saint," said Simon, remembering that a similar accusation had recently been laid against him.

She laughed. "No, no," she said, "a sinner through and through, and utterly selfish—but I am on the right side of the law, as well as the side of justice. And I really don't want to upset Felicia. Or, to be strictly accurate, I don't want her to upset herself with what she's found in family records that I asked her to look at. Although she texted me first last night, so she did start the ball rolling, and I dare says that she'd have found everything eventually even without my prompting. Either way, though, I thought I ought to fill you in first, so that nothing would come as a surprise over lunch."

"Very kind of you," he said, although, as they approached the main door of the Abbey, he couldn't help wondering what Felicia might think of the fact that he had gone for a long walk before lunch with Megan, if she still suspected that Megan had covert "designs" — and, he was increasingly beginning to think, she might not be wrong about that.

XV
Off the Deep End

Simon was pensive as he walked back to Raven Cottage after the long lunch, leaving Megan in conversation with Felicia and Cerys. The revelations that Megan had made to him before lunch had inevitably been discussed, but had not seemed to cause Felicia the slightest distress, even though she still seemed to doubt Megan's assurances that if Cousin Douglas did not drop his plan to attack the entail of his own accord, he could be persuaded to do so. In fact, Simon thought that, of all of them, he was the one most unsettled by the new discoveries and speculations, because of the further speculative ramifications that might bear upon the relationship between the Murden family, the cauldron and the neider. He felt increasingly at sea within the vast accumulation of myth and legend over the last fifteen hundred years, within and without the various secretive custodians of the Abbey.

When he reached the front door of the cottage, however, he put such ideas to one side, deliberately. He cast a long glance along the deserted main street, which seemed even more deserted than usual now that he knew that the Syrian refugees had gone and that all of the cottages were, indeed, empty . . . except that a sudden twinge of memory reminded him that he had quite forgotten to ask Dai whether anyone was presently resident in Blackbird Cottage, as Alun Gwynne had suggested in passing. He sought the distant building in question briefly with his gaze, but it seemed as dormant as all the rest.

Zoe was in the spare bedroom. There was a book on the bedside table—one of his novels—but she wasn't reading it.

"Is everything all right?" he asked.

"Yes. I sneaked downstairs for some lunch, but otherwise, I've just stayed here."

"The place is even deader than usual," he said, "but it's better to be safe than sorry. It's time to phone Marianne now—but stay here. I'll feel more comfortable if you're not looking over my shoulder."

She hesitated, but said: "Okay. Whatever you say. Good luck."

"I'm not the one who needs the luck," Simon replied.

He went downstairs, picked up the phone, looked up Marianne's number in the pad beside the machine, and cursed himself slightly for being stuck in the twentieth century, in a world of landlines and telephone pads with pencils.

Marianne answered right away. Simon announced himself and said: "Is this a convenient time?"

"Yes, its fine," she replied. "I've just got home from work. I've been meaning to call you, to apologize about the other day, but things kept getting in the way. Things didn't go nearly as well as I'd hoped, but I hope you won't hold it against us. I really would like to see you again, and to accept your invitation to come to Wales, when I can, but things are a little hectic at the moment."

Simon thought it best to cut to the chase. "Have you had a visit from the police?" he asked.

There as a pregnant silence before she said: "Yes, as a matter of fact. Yesterday. They were looking for Zoe, but they wouldn't tell me why. I couldn't tell them anything. How did you know?"

"I've talked to Zoe."

"Oh." She didn't add anything further, but simply waited.

"She wanted my advice."

"She wanted your advice. Why?" Her tone was artificially neutral, but Simon could hear a certain tension within it.

"Well, you'd made a point of introducing me to her shortly before, and you seem to have built me up somewhat in her estimation. She wanted me to call you because she was afraid that if she did it herself you might, to use her phrase, *go off the deep end*. She thought that you might listen more calmly if I acted as an intermediary."

"The bitch. I'll kill her—no, forget I said that. This is me not going off the deep end. I'm sorry, Simon, truly. Whatever she's got herself into, she had absolutely no right to drag you into it. The little coward should have had the guts to talk to me herself, no matter what. Ringing you is just . . . well, disgusting. It wasn't enough for her to embarrass me in front of you when I introduced you to her. She really is . . . but that's between us. Did she tell you what kind of trouble she's in?"

"Yes. She explained everything."

"I'll bet she did. Well, don't take her word for anything; it's entirely likely to be all lies. It's the drugs, isn't it? I knew, even though the police wouldn't say. I've told her time and time again, but she wouldn't listen. *It's legal! It's legal!* Well, it isn't legal any more, and even when it was, if the school had found out that she was taking them . . . fortunately, they haven't introduced random drug tests to primary schools yet. But the police! They'll have been round the school this morning, I expect. She wasn't there, I know—she phoned in sick—but she's not at home, either. Just the fact that they came looking is going to set warning bells ringing. Oh, the little fool. You have no idea how hard I've tried with that girl . . . and she's a grandmother now, as well. At thirty-eight! When I see her, I'll show her what going off the deep end is."

"Actually," said Simon, "I'd be obliged if you didn't. I'm supposed to be smoothing things over. She won't have a high opinion of my diplomatic skills if she thinks I've only made things worse. And I'd rather like to live up to the high opinion that you seem to have given her of me, if possible. I'd quite like it if we could all get along harmoniously, now that we know that we're related."

"So would I, but . . . well, she had no right . . ."

"I'm sorry you feel like that, Marianne, because I'd rather like to think that she did have the right, just as you have the right. We might have only just found one another, but we are brother and sister, after all. I'm quite flattered by the thought that when Zoe needed advice, she thought of me, and that what you had told her about me had made her think that I might be able to help. I hope that I can. And it will be a great relief for me if I can tell her, when I next speak with her, that it's safe for her to call you without any fear of a hostile response."

"Did she tell you to say all that?"

"No, she didn't. She didn't even ask me to call you; that was entirely my idea. She just told me why she was afraid to do so, and I volunteered. If you think there's any blame to be apportioned here, I'm afraid that I have to accept the lion's share."

"No, no," she said. "You're not to blame for anything. Of course you had to offer. She knew that, the sly little . . . sorry, that's what I'm not supposed to be doing, isn't it? How much trouble is she in?"

"Hopefully, not as much as she feared initially. The police will probably tell you, eventually, that they think that she's implicated in dealing synthetic cannabinoids, but they haven't actually caught her red-handed in possession of any, and I don't think they have enough evidence for the CPS to take formal charges to court. They'll want to interview her under caution, obviously, when she surrenders herself, but I think she'll be able to answer their questions in a satisfactory manner."

"Which means that she's got you to help her cook up some cock-and-bull story to get her off the hook?"

"No, of course not. It means that I've tried to set her mind at rest about the likely course of events, provided that she can answer the questions they put to her. She's told me what she intends to say, and I have every reason to believe that things will work out for the best."

"You mean that she can wriggle out of it, even though she's in it up to her neck?"

"That isn't what I said."

"No, but it's what you meant. I'm not stupid—and neither is she, obviously, if she's been able to twist you round her little finger too. I've told her time and time again that she shouldn't touch that stuff, legal or not, and now it's illegal she can't stop, and she's in it up to her neck, addicted. At least, by the time she surrenders herself, if they do a drug test, it will be negative, won't it?"

"I certainly hope so."

"And if they find her in the meantime?"

"A positive drug test wouldn't be enough to support a charge of dealing."

"No, but it would get her the sack. She's a primary school teacher, for God's sake. I don't say that all the teachers at mine are squeaky clean, but they're careful, and at least we're a secondary. What's going to happen if the police tell the school why they're looking for her?"

"They won't. At the very most, it will make the head monitor her a little more closely. Given time, it will all blow over—and with luck, she'll take heed of the warning. I doubt that she's physically addicted, and you can be certain that the advice that I've given her includes a stern warning to give it up and put it behind her for good. I think she might. After all, as you say, she's a grandmother now, which doubles her parental responsibilities—responsibilities she seems to me to be taking seriously, just as you are, in spite of the inevitable frustrations and resentments that arise within such relationships. I understand that there's been friction between her and Krysten, as there has between you and her, but such things can be fixed, with a little good will."

"So everyone says—but nobody really believes it, except perhaps for people who don't have kids of their own."

"Well, that's true, I haven't had children of my own, but I've got a niece, now, and it would be pleasant for me if I could at least start off my relationship with her on a mild note. I'd like to be able to help her if I can, and if what I'm doing now is the only practical help I can offer, then I'd like to think that it might be of some use to her, if only so that she'll think that your high opinion of me was justified. It's not going to help any of us, is it, if she thinks I'm useless, and that your assessment of me was overly generous?"

"She's not the only one who can wind people round her little finger, is she? You must have got my share, but I suppose I ought to be glad that somebody in the family got it. Or is this the way it's going to be from now on—you and her ganging up on me?"

"I can assure you that that's not what's happening. If there were any ganging up to be done, I'd like to think that we could all be in the same gang, or a least on the same side. And for what it might be worth, I've never had the slightest talent for winding people round my finger. In fact, I've always found social relationships difficult, being a complete misfit. But I have written a lot of dialogue in my time, and I think I'm beginning to get the hang of it. A bit late, alas, but I hope it's not too late, and if the belated skill is going to be good for anything, I'd like to think that it could help me establish a good relationship with my sister."

"How is it working out with your other relatives?" she countered.

"Actually, quite well. I thought I was getting along very well indeed with Ceridwen and James . . . and then they died, which has caused me to put an even heavier investment into my relationships with the survivors. But Felicia is over a hundred years old, and Cerys is only twenty-two. There are age gaps to either side there. You're younger than me, of course, but you're a little nearer my age. I think we might have more in common. And if I can succeed in this embassy—for which I volunteered, remember—I'd think that I was making a good start."

"Okay," she said, "you've made your point. I promise that if and when she finally gets around to calling, I'll be as nice as pie, as long as she doesn't wind me up too much. Did she tell you where she is?"

"That doesn't matter. The point is that she'll come out of hiding when she thinks it's safe, and run the gauntlet of the police interview. To be honest, I think she was more frightened of you than of them. If I can reassure her that you and she can make a fresh start, with sympathy on both sides, that will take a lot off her mind, and a little of mine."

"And she's going to give up taking that filthy stuff?"

"I think there's every chance, if she has support. I'll be glad to do what little I can. If you can persuade her to accept my invitation I really think you'd both benefit from a change of scene, and you'll definitely be interested to see the Abbey and meet Felicia."

"Especially knowing that it's all going to be yours quite soon."

"Quite soon might be an exaggeration; it looks as if the probate process might drag on—but yes, I do believe that one day, it will be mine, in a technical sense."

"Why only a technical sense?"

"Because it will really be Felicia's. She's been living in the Abbey for a hundred years and more. She's its life and soul. I'll only be her official representative, as James was for Ceridwen—her chevalier, or champion."

"Like Don Quixote with his Dulcinea?" she suggested.

Simon was glad to hear the attempted witticism. It gave him the sense of having completed the obstacle course he'd set himself to negotiate. "Absolutely," he said.

"Do they have windmills in West Wales?"

"Mills? They have entire wind farms. But I know better than to tilt at them. I wouldn't stand a chance. I know my limitations." *What a liar!* he thought.

"You know," she said, "I've been thinking hard for the last two days about what kind of brother I'd like to have. When Gran first told me, and it was such a shock, my first thought was that I couldn't ask for anything better than to be related to Simon Cannick—but then the reaction set in, and I was scared. And when I met you in person, I thought again, at first, that it was a real stroke of luck. And then, again, the pendulum swung, and I began to think of all the things that might go wrong. But maybe it will be okay. All along, through every mood swing, I've always thought: well, at least it might be interesting, and what have I got to lose?"

"It might," he agreed. He couldn't, in all honesty, tell her that she had nothing to lose, but it seemed advisable to take one step at a time. "I've been giving the matter some thought too, and everything looks positive from my point of view."

"I don't believe you," she said, flatly. "I was with you at the nursing home, remember. Unless it's a positive to see the mother who abandoned you as a baby suffering."

"No," he said, "that's certainly not what I meant. I was very sorry to see her in that state, but it would be criminally selfish of me to wish that I hadn't seen her because a little of her pain was infectious. It was harrowing, but it wasn't a bad thing that I saw her, and that she saw me. I wouldn't have liked to have appeared to be avoiding her. I hope I might be able to see her again, when she isn't hurting as badly."

"I suppose I hope the same," she admitted. "After all, if you can forgive her for leaving you in a shop doorway, I suppose I ought to forgive her for lesser offences, however numerous they might be. Look, I'll call you back when I've heard from Zoe, to reassure you that I didn't go off the deep end, so you won't think badly of me. You don't have a mobile, do you?"

"I'm afraid not," Simon said. "If I were following my usual work schedule, you'd always be able reach me here during the day, but things are in utter turmoil at the moment, and I'm at the Abbey more often than not. If you can't reach me here, just leave a message, and I'll call you back when I can. Okay."

"Fine," she said. "And thanks. It's really kind of you to take the trouble."

"It's no trouble at all," he assured her.

When he went back upstairs, Zoe was sitting on the bed staring at the screen of her mobile, doing an almost perfect imitation of someone who had not been eavesdropping from the top of the stairs.

"It's fixed," he told her. "It's up to you now. Play your cards right, and it could be the beginning of a beautiful friendship."

"Don't congratulate yourself yet," she said. "There are things that can't be fixed with a single phone call."

"Oh, come on, Zoe," Simon said, a trifle intemperately. "You're thirty-eight years old, not sixteen. And whatever arithmetic says, the gap between thirty-eight and fifty-seven is a hell of a lot smaller than the one between sixteen and thirty-five, especially between grandmothers. You're twin sisters as well as mother and daughter. Act like it, for God's sake."

For a moment, he thought she might go off the deep end, but all she said, eventually, was: "Harsh, but probably fair. Can I use your phone now? My battery's low, and I haven't got a charger with me."

"Yes. I'll leave you to it and go back to the Abbey. If you can square things with your associates, I'll go into town tomorrow and get the cash from the bank. I'll fix up some kind of transport for you, to make sure that you get back safely. I checked the internet, and although cannabinoids can hang around in the body for a while, you shouldn't be in any danger of testing positive by the day after."

"Thanks," she said. "It is a loan, you know. It might take a while, but I'll pay you back. Every penny, legally earned. And I'll still owe you."

"I know," he said. "Remember the conditions. And good luck with your phone calls—all of them."

XVI

The Home Invasion

"It doesn't make any difference," Simon said to Felicia, as he climbed into bed and took her in her arms. "Even if it's true that she wasn't really born in 1789, Ceridwen believed what she was saying, having always been told it. And she really was very old, even if one might want to quibble over the exact number of years. And even if it was one of her other selves who really slept with the neider, it did happen, and she did retain some kind of privileged connection, however confused. If she was party to deceptions, she was far more their victim than their perpetrator."

"I know," said Felicia. "It might have happened to me, if my mother and my father hadn't refused to go along with it. We didn't know about genetics in those days, but father was a no-nonsense type, from what I understand, like James. We owe that to Rhys, I suppose. He was the one who tried to clear out the family superstitions, and banish them from the generations that came after him. Father must have known, or at least suspected, that grandmother wasn't what she believed herself to be, but never thought it wise, or kind, to confront her with it, any more than his predecessors who were part of the deception, and he lived long enough to set the precedent for James—Rhys all over again, as grandmother used to call him.

"James never paid much heed to that aspect of the old stories—deliberately, I suppose. I rarely heard him mention the word 'rebirth,' and he only used cauldron occasionally. For him, it was always a matter of 'vitreous cocoons'—scientific jargon, not myth. But Melusine . . . it sounds silly, I know, but I don't actually know what she really thought. I've been living with her and James for a hundred years, and always knew that they were at odds, and I even shared their dreams, on occasion—but that never really worked. Melusine was always a little bit closer to Ceridwen than I was, as if they had a secret understanding that I didn't share, and from which

James was positively excluded. But I'm sure she didn't know what Megan has just . . . speculated. Not all of it, anyway."

"When Melusine came to see me in Raven Cottage, having said that she had something important to tell me, she did seem strangely annoyed that James had got in first. What she actually told me that evening didn't really contradict what James had said, or add very much. In retrospect, it seems possible that she had intended to give me a different story, but that James had already seen her, and told her, perhaps gloating the while, that I thought along exactly the same lines as he did, that he and I were two of a kind. And when she asked if I might be willing to sleep with her, I thought it was a simple teasing proposition . . . but maybe . . ."

"Don't overthink it," Felicia said, a trifle dryly. "She might have had secrets from me, but I do know her. She was thinking exactly the same as me: *if not him, who; if not now, when.* She wanted your body, just as I did. She wanted to be held, like this, and more, if she could get it. And before you tell me again that you're a physical wreck, and no catch, I repeat: you're practically an adolescent, by Murden standards."

"Whether Melusine secretly believed the family superstitions or not," Simon said, pensively, "if the implications of what you and Megan have found can be trusted, Seymour must have believed them, and generations before him, even those living in so-called Ages of Reason and Enlightenment. It's understandable that James didn't pay much attention to that aspect of the documents, because it's fugitive there, not afforded any apparent importance . . . but that must be precisely because it was the *real* secret, the secret that shouldn't be written down, the secret known only to the initiates within the community, not even to all the monks or all the Bardic lay brothers . . . and subsequently, not even to all the Murdens. They really did believe that the cauldron was part of the spoils of Annwn."

"Probably. But that doesn't mean that all of Megan's fantasies are true. She's trying to handle me with kid gloves, I know, but I can tell that she's imagining incestuous sex orgies intended to conceive special children, with Druid priestesses designated to produce petty messiahesses."

"You're probably right," said Simon, diplomatically. "At least until the sixteenth century, when the Abbey passed into secular hands. The riotous reputation that some Medieval monks had was presumably exaggerated by rumor, and the Bards . . . well, who knows whether druids had regulations of celibacy, and how closely they observed them if they did? Although . . ."

"Although what?"

"Except that there's a persistent mythology regarding numerous pagan religions and cults, backed up with historical evidence relating to Rome, and perhaps also to ancient Assyria, relating to the occult roles of virgins and priestesses. It's everywhere in fiction, although almost all of it is just tall tales and gossip—but Ceridwen's mother can't have been the first; there was already a context of expectation into which she and her descendants fitted, which might have gone back centuries. The monks were known for dabbling in alchemy and necromancy, and early Christianity overlapped considerably with the mystical ideas that became the primal heresies, the first object of intellectual cleansing. It goes back all the way to the *Acts of the Apostles* and Simon Magus. Two of the early Christian writers reported that the Simon in question— no relation, I fear—traveled with a beautiful woman named Helen, allegedly a prostitute, whom he represented as a re-incarnation of Helen of Troy, and as Ennoia: an incarnation of divine thought. That archetype, and variants of it, recur constantly in subsequent legend and literature; it's at the root of the whole mythos of the *femme fatale*."

"There are plenty of references in the documents to the Virgin," Felicia observed. "But you'd expect that of monks."

"Indeed you would. There are Virgins everywhere. In some of the French versions of the myth of the grail, Joseph of Arimathea arrived in the Midi with three of them, all called Marie, including Mary Magdalen. There are churches dedicated to all three, individually and collectively, and places named after them. Nowadays, we only know the orthodox versions of the story of the virgin birth . . . and we also know, thanks to science, that any real virgin births couldn't have been male children, but clones of the mother due to anomalous diploid ova . . . except that the monks of Saint Madoc had no concept of clones, although they did have a concept of rebirth. So, if Seymour thought that he was actually causing what he thought of as rebirths magically, he might have been repeating a pattern . . . even a ritual . . . that went back a long way . . . centuries. It would have been alchemy and secret heresy, from the viewpoint of the monks, but genuinely sacred from the viewpoint of the bards. If they really did practice magic with that intended objective, they can only have had few successes, but it only takes a few to sustain belief, and it stands to reason that the children of that kind of birth are more likely to repeat it, if they're fertile at all . . ."

"But perhaps they're more likely not to be," said Felicia, regretfully. "I . . ."

She was interrupted then by the distant sound of a bell. When she resumed speaking, she said: "That's the bell at the front gate again." She picked up her phone from the bedside table. "I haven't missed any texts. It can't be Megan—she'd have called or texted first,"

While she was speaking, the bell rang several more times, with evident urgency.

A thought occurred to Simon, who leapt out of bed, hastily pulled his trousers on and stuck his feet into his shoes. "I'll go," he said. "Stay here."

He grabbed a shirt and jacket, and put them on as he made his way downstairs. He reached the front door just in time to find Cerys opening it, already peering out into the darkness. She had not turned the vestibule light on.

"It's all right," he said. "I'll go. You stay here."

"Better take these, then," said Cerys, handing him a torch and another object invisible in the dark. "Just in case," she added.

He realized, as he weighed the second object in his hand, that it was a revolver.

"A gun?" he queried.

"It's James's. I've been . . . looking after it since he died."

He didn't give her a chance to offer any further explanation. He ran to the gate.

The bell had stopped ringing as soon as he had switched on the torch, the distant beam of which had told the ringer that the appeal was being answered.

"What the Devil are you doing?" he complained, as soon as he could make out the hooded figure on the other side of the gate. This time, there was no possibility of him mistaking it for the Black Monk. "You were the one who wanted to lie low, remember?"

"That was before," Zoe retorted. "I woke up, and heard someone downstairs in the cottage. I knew right away that it wasn't you, that it had to be a burglar. I was in my underwear, but I put my coat on, grabbed the bedside lamp and crept downstairs—he was in the study. He had a torch. He'd switched your computer on and he was opening the desk drawers. I tried to creep up on him, but he must have heard me. He turned round and tried to stand up just as I brought the lamp down on his head. I didn't hit him where I intended to, but he was off balance and fell. He hit his head on the corner of the desk. There's blood everywhere. I think I've killed him . . . but it wasn't my fault. You'd better come. Is that a gun?"

Simon had unfastened the padlock and opened the gate while she was speaking, and was already moving over the bridge. The light of the distant street lamps allowed him to move more confidently, and he was already running, while Zoe limped along behind him. It wasn't a long way, but he had time to see the lights in Raven Cottage come on—the light in the hallway and the light in the study. He concluded immediately that the burglar was still alive, and was suddenly glad that Cerys had given him the gun. He raised it, ready to take aim.

When he burst into the study, however, ready for action, he found Megan Harwyn kneeling over the recumbent body of a man. There was, as Zoe had said, blood all over the place, mostly on the desk and on the carpet. Perhaps absurdly, his first thought was that he hoped that it hadn't got into his keyboard.

"You probably won't need that," said Megan, looking at the revolver. "Not immediately, anyway. He's still unconscious. You remember Cousin Bernard, I presume? You met at the funeral."

"He's not dead?" Zoe asked from the doorway, as she arrived behind Simon, still limping.

Simon pushed her toward the stairway. "Go back upstairs," he said. "Hide in the bedroom. I'll take care of this."

Megan had come to the study door, and watched Zoe disappearing up the stairs. "I don't believe we've been introduced," she said to Simon, dryly.

"My niece, Zoe," Simon said, swiftly. "I told you in Fishguard that I'd invited her to come down. It's important that no one else knows that she's here. Are you sure that he's not going to die?"

"It looks a lot worse than it is," said Megan. "Head wounds always bleed a lot." She lowered her voice. "I was working on the computer and heard the door. I looked out of the window and saw . . . someone . . . running away. I knew she wasn't the Black Monk because of the bare legs underneath the coat and the way she was limping. So I came round to see what was happening. The door was open, so I came in. Imagine my surprise."

"He had a torch, but it was dark," Simon said. "He only had a split second to see someone behind him, and she was wearing the hood. He lost consciousness, so he might not remember anything, but if he does, it can't be anything definite. If we can get away with it, the story is that it was me who hit him, right? He's in my house going through my desk, I had every right to hit him. He's not going to want to call the police anyway—it's him they'd arrest, not me."

"You're in St. Madoc," she told him. "The average police response time to 999 calls is somewhere between a day and a half and never. And as you say, he'll be in no hurry. Oh, shit, I think he's coming round. You'll have to give me the full story later. I'll take the lead, though. Trust me."

Cousin Bernard was, indeed, coming round. He sat up, slowly, and looked round, as if he had no idea where he was. Then he put his hand up to his head. When it came away bloody, he seemed puzzled. Then he saw the blood on the carpet. Eventually, he looked at the two people standing by the door, watching him.

"Megan?" he said, slowly.

"That's right," said Megan. "You remember Simon, don't you? Of course you do—it's him you came to kill, isn't it?"

That startled Simon almost as much as the man sitting on the floor.

"Kill?" Bernard repeated. "Now just a . . ."

Megan did not give him the time to finish, and she had evidently decided that "taking the lead" meant going on the offensive. She took a long stride forward, in order to tower over the seated man. Simon stayed in the doorway, behind her.

"I knew when I turned down your request for help that you weren't going to let the matter lie, Bernard, but I never expected you to resort to murder. I knew you were unscrupulous, but killing someone just because he came into an inheritance that wouldn't automatically be yours even if he were out of the way . . . that really is a step and a half too far. And trying to make it look like a burglary gone wrong! You watch too much TV. You're nearly seventy years old, man. Don't you think it's time to put your feet up and relax? I'm sure you can still afford the occasional whore, like that floozy you brought to the funeral, if you can still get it up. You're not the strapping lad you once were, though. You really are too old to do your own dirty work. And murder really is way beyond . . ."

"Shut up, you crazy whore!" shouted Bernard, evidently despairing of ever getting a word in edgeways if he waited for her to pause. He evidently regretted shouting, because he winced with the pain it caused him, but he still managed to say, in a more moderate tone: "I didn't come to murder anyone. I knew he wasn't here. I saw him go off to the Abbey, and lock the gate behind him, so he obviously wasn't coming back in a hurry. There shouldn't have been anyone in the house . . . where's the woman?"

Simon's heart sank, but he did not have time to react.

"What woman?" Megan snapped.

"The woman who hit me. I only caught a glimpse, but it was definitely a woman . . . fortyish, wearing some kind of hood."

"A hood, you say?" said Megan, "and you think you saw a face? Oh, that's bad, Bernard . . . that's very bad. You know what people are going to think, don't you?"

"What the hell are you talking about?" said Bernard.

"Don't play dumb, Bernard. You know perfectly well that there was no woman here—that the house was empty. Nobody hit you, you old fool. You saw the Black Monk . . . and you saw his face! You know what that means, don't you?"

"I saw a woman!" Bernard insisted. "It wasn't a monk, it was a woman—and she hit me—with that!" He pointed at the lamp from Simon's bedroom, which was lying on the floor, with its solid base covered in blood.

"Don't be ridiculous, Bernard," said Megan. "The lamp was on the desk, and you knocked it off when you fell. There was no one here—no one alive, anyway."

"You're crazy!" Bernard told her. "No one is going to believe that nonsense. There was a woman here, and she hit me."

Megan shook her had ostentatiously. "You've been away too long, Bernard, and I bet you don't even talk to the other members of the family—you certainly ignored them at the funeral. This is Saintt Madoc, and even though your name's

Pallister, everyone knows you're a Murden—why else would you try to murder the Murden heir? No one will believe it, you say? You always were an idiot. *Everyone* will believe it, you poor fool. You saw the Black Monk . . . and you saw his face!"

Still suffering the after-effects of his fall, perhaps concussed, Bernard Pallister no longer knew which of the two allegations to address first. In the end, he settled for: "I didn't come to murder anyone. No one will believe that." But he no longer sounded convinced that no one would believe what Megan was saying.

Simon opened his mouth to speak, but Megan silenced him with an imperious gesture, to which he was now becoming accustomed—and accustomed to obeying.

"What did you come here for, then?" she said pouncing like a tiger.

Bernard didn't want to answer that, and put his hands to his injured head, as if in urgent response to the pain. He did not attract the slightest shred of sympathy.

"Come on, Bernard," said Megan, sharply. "You're in serious trouble here. "Breaking and entering, burglary—even if you were only pretending, in the hope of blaming your murder on some random thief, there's enough there . . ."

"I knew he wasn't here!" Bernard cut in, shouting again, again unwisely. In his quieter tone, he added: "And I didn't break in. I used a key."

"And where did you steal the key?" Megan snapped.

"I didn't steal it. I've had it for years. I used to come here in summer every year—as you doubtless remember—and things were very friendly back in those days . . . as you also doubtless remember. I got the key from someone who was renting Raven. I didn't steal it, he gave it to me when his fortnight ended. He knew I was family. He thought it was as good as handing it back at the gate. I just . . . never passed it on. I forgot."

"Bollocks," said Megan. "You forgot! You wanted to use it, more like. You came in as soon as the tenant was gone."

220

"Why would I do that?" Bernard countered. The way he spoke betrayed the fact that he knew how feeble it sounded. Even Simon had no difficulty forming a hypothesis.

"Curiosity," said Megan, flatly. "You were looking for something that might give you a clue as to who owned Raven. And when you didn't find anything, you hung on to the key anyway, because you were still curious. And eventually, one way or another, you did manage to discover that the owner of the cottage was Evelyne Augerrand. Maybe it didn't mean anything to you at the time, but at some stage, you checked her out, and discovered that she only had female descendants, which made her irrelevant to your plan to get your hands on the inheritance when James died. Until it turned out that she did, in fact, have a male descendant, who was in your way, and needed to be disposed of . . ."

"Oh, my God!" wailed Bernard. "Will you stop making stupid allegations! I should have known you were in on it when you turned down my request for help. I thought I was just a reminder of a past you wanted to forget, or bury . . . but you've been part of the conspiracy from the beginning, haven't you? God, I bet it was you who thought the whole thing up, and put it together. You've always known who owned Raven, haven't you. She was a whore too . . . God, I've been blind. I should have seen it. You're the supposed mastermind behind the whole damn con—and the woman who hit me was one of your whores. You're not going to get away with this—and if you think you can frame me for a whole clutch of imaginary crimes in order to get me out of the way, you're very much mistaken. I've got your number, you evil bitch."

He tried to get to his feet, but his head wound obviously flared up. He sat down again, in Simon's swivel-chair.

I'm going to have to get a new one, Simon thought. *It's covered in blood. I just hope he doesn't bleed on the keyboard, if he hasn't ruined it already.*

Megan had soaked up the tirade without blinking. Nothing in her expression or her attitude betrayed the fact that she had no idea what Bernard was talking about.

"You haven't got anyone's number, you idiot," she said. "And you're in the shit up to your neck. You're in someone else's home, having got in with a stolen key. You're in his study, with his computer switched on and his drawers open. Even if people believe your story that you knew that he wasn't here, that still makes you guilty of burglary, caught red-handed."

"I wasn't going to steal anything," Bernard insisted, "any more than the first time. I was just looking round, for evidence of his crimes—and yours, it seems. At the very most, I'd just have unloaded stuff from his computer on to a memory stick—which wouldn't have required much effort, since I can see from the screen that access isn't password protected. Maybe that's because there's no evidence on there of the fraud, but now I know that you're in on it—that you probably thought the whole thing up—I know where to look next. And you're not going to call the police anyway, because you don't want me to tell everyone what I know any more than I want to be arrested for home invasion. Black Monk! You really are a piece of work, aren't you? And I used to think you were just a stupid whore who'd believed her mother's lies about James knocking her up!"

Megan was still a model of perfect composure. "In fact," she said, "I was a very intelligent whore, who knew full well that James was my father, and that he knew it too. I was much smarter than you think, and I still am. And I know that your threat to tell everyone what you know is utterly empty, because you don't know anything. In any case, it isn't me who'll be making a complaint to the police, it's Simon. He'd have called them already if I hadn't told him not to bother. You can go ahead now, Simon, if you like—make sure you get the facts on record in the 999 call. I called you from Sanderling to tell you that I'd heard noises in your supposedly empty cottage. You came running from the Abbey and found me already here, having intercepted a burglar who had fallen over and hurt himself after an alleged encounter with a mysterious hooded figure, of whose presence there's no tangible evidence. Tell the operator that we both recognized the burglar, to our amazement, as Bernard Pallister, a distant relative. You can let the police take it from there. They can pick him up tomorrow, presumably at Blackbird Cottage. You do still own Blackbird, don't you, Bernard? Strange that I haven't seen the lights on there, though, and that Dai hasn't mentioned your being in residence. You didn't sneak in, by any chance, so that you could keep watch on Raven clandestinely from there—at an awkward angle, mind, not easy to see, with the lousy street lighting."

Simon wasn't sure exactly how to respond to the cue, but he took a preparatory step toward the phone, reflexively raising his right hand.

"Is that a gun!" yelped Bernard, evidently not having seen the weapon in Simon's hand previously. "He's got a gun! If you were going to plant that, forget it! There's no way you're going to convince the police that I brought it! God, you're actually going to try to frame me, aren't you!"

Simon was about to explain why he was carrying the gun, but again, Megan gestured to him urgently to be quiet. "Actually, that's not a bad idea," she said. "Good thinking, Bernard. We'll wipe your prints off it, Simon, dip it in the blood while it's still sticky, and I'll testify that I found it on the floor beside him when I came to give him first aid. Possession of a firearm will really put the cherry on the cake of the charge sheet. We've got him exactly where we want him. He's out of the contest for good."

"You can't get away with this!" Bernard said. "Do you think I don't know what you're up to? Believe me, I know—and if you're stupid enough to call the police, I'll tell them everything. When it all comes out, you'll be the ones going down, not me."

"He's bluffing," Megan said. "Make the call, Simon—and don't forget the extra detail about the gun."

"You're crazy!" Bernard said. "Do you think that anyone ever believed for a minute that this joker really is Evelyne Augerrand's grandson? I smelled a rat as soon as I heard the story. I knew that the crazy old lady had been bribed into signing that statement about abandoning him as a child. I presume you've squared the supposed sister, too—Marianne. Easy enough to promise her a share of the loot. You think you've got it all stitched up, don't you? Even faked a DNA test—which you doubtless ordered. But you'll never get away with it. Even if I hadn't found any evidence of the fraud here, it was only a matter of time, and if it ever comes to court, my barrister will drive a coach and horses through your stupid story. And I haven't had a wasted trip, because now I know who thought the whole scheme up. Cerys turned me down too, but that's because the two of you have got her fooled too, and that senile old bat Felicia—but you haven't fooled me. I know who you are and I know who you aren't. And you're not going to get away with it."

Megan's composure finally cracked, and she burst out laughing. "Is that going to be your story? Jesus, Bernard, you're even more stupid than I thought. At least Dougie actually found a weak point to attack, even if he has nothing but hot air to attack it with."

"Dougie?" said Bernard. "You mean that little rat Jefferson? What does he have to do with this?"

"Did you think you were the only chancer who called me up begging for help in attacking the will? Dougie was on the phone the same day—and he called Cerys the same day too. He even suggested the same hotel as you for the meeting. She wanted to accept, just to see your reaction when you came face to face, but Simon advised her to decline politely and not to get involved. He'd been asked to look after her, you see, and he takes family duties seriously, being a real Murden. The DNA test isn't a fake, you utter fool, and he really is Evelyne Augerrand's grandson. If the court orders another test, it'll produce the same result. This imagined conspiracy is all in your head."

Bernard was still one step behind. "You're saying that Douglas Jefferson is after the inheritance? And that he's found a point to attack?"

"In his dreams, he thinks he has, but even if he summons up the cheek to spring it on the court as a surprise, it'll collapse like a house of cards on examination. As things stand, we're forewarned and forearmed. Do join forces with him, if you think you can."

"I'll kill the little rat!" said Bernard, unthinkingly.

"Add that to the statement you give the police, Simon," Megan said. "When informed that there was another fraudulent contender for the Murden inheritance, Bernard responded 'I'll kill the little rat.' God, they're going to laugh about this in the Mermaid when the visitors begin to flock in. Dai will have a field day, all summer long. You'll be famous, Bernard: the only man ever to see the face of the Faceless Monk and get away with a bump on the head. Unless, of course, you've got a brain bleed and are going to collapse and die imminently. Come to think of it, you don't look too good. If I were you, I'd stagger back to Blackbird and go to bed."

This time, Bernard managed to get to his feet. He was a tall man, but his attempt to look intimidating in confrontation with Megan Harwyn was woefully unconvincing.

"You're not going to get away with this, you evil bitch!" he said, trying to snarl but not really succeeding. He turned slightly in order to look down at Simon from a height advantage of a full three inches. "You'd better start running now, you little shit," he said. "I've got your number, and I know who's pulling your strings. You haven't got a cat in hell's chance of claiming that inheritance."

Simon reached out and unhooked the receiver from the cradle on the phone. His finger was poised over the 9 button when Megan said: "Last chance, Bernard. Hop it, and we'll let it go, to save all the hassle—but one more nasty remark, and it's crown court. Take your pick."

The big man evidently thought about saying something— probably another empty threat—but changed his mind abruptly, presumably thinking, that, all things considered, Megan's advice to go back to Blackbird and lie down was sound, whether Simon actually called the police or not.

Simon let him out, and watched him walk along the street past the Mermaid, trying hard not to stagger, but not quite succeeding.

"It's not over," Megan muttered, thoughtfully. "Even if he believes me—which he should, if only because it's true—he won't give it up. You could make that 999 call, though, if you wanted to—without mentioning the gun, obviously."

"I'd rather not," said Simon.

"Because of your niece? She wouldn't be in trouble, just for hitting a burglar. Bigger than average man, smaller than average woman . . . no contest. The CPS would never press charges, even if he was stupid enough to insist." She stopped, and looked hard at Simon. "Oh, my God, she's on the run, isn't she? That's why you didn't mention her at the Abbey today. You're hiding a fugitive. I didn't know you had it in you—good for you. Good job I played the Black Monk card, isn't it? Pure inspiration. What has she done?"

"Nothing serious—but being caught up in something here would be one complication too many, as she's supposed to be in Bristol. You handled that brilliantly, by the way—far better than I could have done. Thanks."

"Oh, I enjoyed it, all the more so because the idiot was convinced, for a good three minutes, that I'm a criminal mastermind who had worked out a way to make a grab for the Murden inheritance just in time for James to change his will before he croaked. That really would have been a stroke of genius—and to think that it never crossed my mind."

"Not that you would have done anything about it if it had," said Simon, "given that you would never do anything illegal."

"Oh, absolutely. I suppose I'd better get home now. Don't worry—my lips are sealed. I won't say a word to Felicia, or anyone else, about you having strange women in the house. You'd better go set your niece's mind at rest. And get some new locks, by the way—lots of new locks."

She left, and Simon closed the door behind her. He went upstairs. The door of the spare bedroom was ajar, and Zoe wasn't bothering to stare at her phone.

"Did you hear all that?" he asked her.

"Some," she admitted. "So much for this being a quiet place to hide out. Thanks for covering up. Your friend is quite an actor."

"She's had a lot of practice."

"So I gathered. You don't have to explain anything to me. But . . . the man I hit really was talking nonsense, wasn't he? You really are my uncle?"

"I really am," Simon assured her, although he didn't suppose that he'd have said anything different if he hadn't been. "And I'm also Bernard's cousin, albeit distantly. Family life, eh?"

"What are you going to tell the people at the house, about who rang the bell? You could tell them it was your friend—she told the burglar that she'd called you."

"I don't want to get bogged down in a web of lies, if I can avoid it. I'll stall, for the time being—but they're going to have to know that you were here eventually, and your mother has probably guessed, even though I was cagey with her too. I'll try to get you safely away, first, and save the explanations for later. How did your phone calls go?"

"Okay, I think. I've got an alibi that isn't my mother or my daughter for the time when the sting went awry. The police will know that it's phony but, as you said, they'll also know that it will create doubt if the case ever came to court. They'll threaten, but, on careful reflection, you're probably right that the CPS won't think that the case is strong enough to pursue. I've talked to my associates and promised to give them the money within three days; they've agreed that if I do that, we'll be all square, with no hard feelings, and that it's a good idea for us not to be further associated thereafter. You're certain that you can get me the cash tomorrow?"

"Definitely," said Simon. "I've also asked the boatman to stand by, in order to run you down to Fishguard to catch the train as soon as you have it. It's slow but safe. He won't say anything—not that anyone's ever going to ask. You'll have to square the school, if you can, or resign quietly if you can't, and settle things with your mother. Either way, come back here in a week or ten days, openly, with or without Marianne, and we can try to sort out your future then, if it needs sorting."

"I will," she promised. "Thanks for everything—and thank your friend. I don't suppose you'd care to leave me the gun, in case the big fellow comes back?"

"No, I wouldn't," Simon said, "but he won't. He'll probably scarper as soon as his head stops hammering, ready to try to pretend that he was never here. He thinks that Megan and I were the only ones who saw him, except for you, but one of the Syrians must have spotted him from the cottage next door to Blackbird, before they moved out, and one of them mentioned it to Alun Gwynne, so we can probably prove that he was here and acting suspiciously, if we ever need to. As Megan says, he probably won't give up, but he won't try to look for non-existent evidence here again. I'm going to need a new chair and carpet, though. I only hope he didn't get blood in my keyboard."

"Sorry," said Zoe. "If he hadn't turned round . . ."

Simon raised his hands. "Not your fault," he said. "I have to go back to Felicia now. She'll be worried—unless she's busy talking to Megan on the phone again . . . Don't ask. I'll see you in the morning."

XVII
Nightmares

Megan Harwyn was leaning against the gate to the Tine, talking into her mobile phone. Simon heard her say: "He's here now. I won't keep him long. Goodnight, Felicia." She put the apparatus away, and met Simon's quizzical stare with a frank gaze.

"It's sorted," she said. "I told her that it was me who rang the bell. She was probably watching from the window, but it was so dark that she couldn't make out anything but a vaguely human shape. I told her that Bernard had let himself into Raven to try to raid your computer and that I'd hit him over the head. I've been watching the street, but he hasn't even switched the lights on in Blackbird. He'll probably be gone by first light, knowing that he now has to find out what Dougie's up to as well as worrying about you."

"Thanks," said Simon. "You're going to a lot of trouble on my behalf. I appreciate it."

"No trouble. I haven't had so much fun for years—ever, in fact. I thought last night was amusing, while I was just a spectator. Tonight was something else. The only thing lacking to make to perfect is that it wasn't actually me who hit Bernard over the head—but at least I can steal a little of the credit . . . you're frowning. You don't like my lying to Felicia, even though it gets you off an awkward hook?"

"Something like that."

"You ought to get those scruples surgically removed, before they choke you. I understand, now, why Felicia kept me on the phone for four hours last night. She was afraid that you were with me, wasn't she? She thinks I have designs?"

Simon said nothing.

"Can't even given me a definite no comment, eh? Must be worse than I thought. And now you know that I can run rings round an idiot like Bernard, you can't help wondering whether I'm circling you. Well, I won't try to tell you that the idea has never crossed my mind, or that the reason I decided not do anything about it is that I'm too scrupulous. But I really have sworn off men forever, and I really wouldn't ever get married, even to be the lady of the manor and part-owner of the spoils of Annwn. It's not that I prefer women, worse luck—I'm a confirmed heterosexual, to my misfortune—but thirty years as a full-time whore really can leave you with a seriously nasty taste in your mouth, and elsewhere, which is one reason why it really pissed me off when your friend the neider shafted me the other night . . . except, if I read your thinking right, it was really my own unconscious that shafted me, the bitch. No matter. The point is that I don't have designs . . . not that kind, anyhow. Without wanting to hurt your feelings, I wouldn't want to fuck you if you were the last man on earth . . . but if it makes your ego feel any better, if all the men on earth went up in smoke except one, I wouldn't be sorry if that one happened to be you. Which, now I come to think about it, is probably the highest compliment I can pay. But enough about me. If my instinct can be trusted, your niece is in a pickle."

"Nothing that can't be fixed."

"You see, you can manage a definite no comment when you put your mind to it. Call me cynical, but if I had to guess, I'd say that she needs money, and that you're such a big softy that you're going to give it to her."

"No comment."

"I thought so. Have you got it?"

"Yes."

"In a bank?"

"Of course. So what?"

"So it's not a good idea for you to give her money that you get from a bank. These days, that's hyper-traceable, and we know for a fact that Bernard has eyes on you. Any substantial cash transaction that has a hint of mystery about it is going to attract his attention. It's not wise to give him any opportunity to stir things. Even if you can keep your niece out of the spotlight, he'll be sure to use it against you—and if he did that, I'd feel partly responsible, after tonight. I've annoyed him far more than a vain prig like him can stand. He's got it in for both of us now, and he won't lose an opportunity to take a swipe at you if you give him any ammunition."

"You might be right, but I don't have any alternative."

"Yes, you do. How much do you need?"

"You can't be serious."

"In fact, I can. Why do you think I made that long speech about not having any designs? I meant every word. I don't have any hidden agenda, except fighting for truth and justice. You can pay me back when the will has gone through probate, with interest if you insist. But for the time being, it's best for everyone if you can pay her off with thoroughly laundered cash that has never been near a bank."

"You keep a supply of laundered cash in Sanderling?"

"Of course I do. Old habits die hard, and prudence increases with age."

"You don't even know how much I need."

"As they say in the jewelry trade, if you have to ask the price, you can't afford it. I can afford it. Prostitution is a very profitable business if it's done right—and legally. How much does she need?"

"Five thousand."

"Is that all? I've known Arab sheikhs, and not even genuine ones, who tipped waiters more than that when they'd had enough whisky, in the days when a grand was worth something. Pop round to Sanderling tomorrow morning and I'll let you have it in used twenties, all kosher."

"Why?" Simon asked, genuinely bewildered.

"I just told you. Also, if she's your family, she's mine. We genuine Murdens need to stick together, while the barbarians are lurking at the gates. James wouldn't have done it, of course—which is another reason why I will, being the better half of our little duo. You'd better get back to Felicia now or she'll be worrying again. I'll keep an eye on Raven for you, just in case. Lock the gate—and keep that gun handy. You never know. Pleasant dreams."

And with that, she walked away.

Simon locked the gate, and walked back to the Abbey.

Cerys was waiting for him in the vestibule. "Can I have the gun back?" she said.

He handed it to her. "Be careful with it," he said, and made as if to go past her.

"I know that it wasn't Miss Harwyn who rang the bell," she said. "I know that it wasn't the Black Monk, either."

"Full marks for observation," he said. "Megan has given Felicia a different story. I think she'd like us to back her up. I owe her one—more than one, in fact—so I'm putty in her hands, but you'll have to make your own decision."

"I will," she said. "What took you so long, in Raven?"

"We had a little chat with Cousin Bernard. We had to go slowly because he was bleeding copiously all over the carpet and the chair. He thinks I'm an impostor and that Megan is the mastermind who planned the conspiracy; he was looking for evidence in the cottage and accidentally bumped his head. We told him that he was wrong, but he doesn't believe us. We let him go, but if I find that his blood has buggered my keyboard, I'll regret not having used the gun. Can I go back to bed now?"

"You know that I'm going to want a fuller explanation tomorrow, don't you?"

"I'll try to make time for you in my busy schedule. Sleep well."

He went upstairs. Felicia was sitting up in bed, waiting. Her opening remark wasn't what he expected.

"Does Cousin Bernard have anything he can use against you, or is it just hot air, to use Megan's expression?"

"It's just hot air," Simon assured her. "Except . . ."

"Except what?" she demanded, sharply.

"Except that he now has a more plausible story than the one he had before he tried to search Raven for evidence that isn't there. Now he thinks that Megan cooked up a plot to invent an impostor to bring forward for the Murden inheritance. It's all nonsense, obviously, but given that it was Megan who ordered the DNA test, and could easily have discovered who owned Raven before Bernard did, if she'd put her mind to it, she's a useful addition to his conspiracy theory, especially given her shady profession. Even if he only gets his own people to investigate, it could still cause hassle for Marianne and my mother, and if he can get the police to investigate . . . that could be a nightmare for all of us."

"And if Megan tries to blackmail him, or launch some kind of cyberattack on him, it might make things worse instead of better? Especially if she's not as clever as she thinks she is."

"I don't know," said Simon, thinking that he was swiftly becoming expert in the art of offering a definite no comment.

He had taken off his makeshift clothing, and was about to climb into the bed when Felicia said: "Just a second."

He froze.

"You wouldn't lie to me, would you, Simon?" she said.

His heart sank. "No," he said, hoping that he was sincere.

"Megan would. She told me that it was her who rang the bell, but I know it wasn't. I was watching from the window, through binoculars. They're good binoculars. I couldn't make out who it was, but I know it wasn't Megan. And I know that although you haven't actually lied about what you were doing last night, you have been suspiciously evasive. Who's staying in Raven, Simon? Who hit Cousin Bernard over the head."

Simon sat down on the bed. "Zoe," he said.

It took her several seconds to remember who Zoe was. "Your niece? What on earth is she doing there?"

"As she pointed out when she accosted me when I went back to the cottage last night, I had invited her to come, whenever it was convenient for her. It became convenient a lot sooner than she had expected—too convenient by half. She nearly got caught in possession of a large quantity of drugs—some lab-concocted super-cannabis. The police didn't have all the exits covered, so she gave them the slip, but she had drugs in her system, and she couldn't afford to test positive if they picked her up in Bristol. So she came here."

"How much does she want?"

Simon was genuinely shocked by the cynical suspicion behind that question.

"It's okay," he said. "I'm taking care of it."

"You?" said Felicia. "Not Megan Harwyn?"

Simon knew that a no comment, however definite, would not escape the trap. So he said nothing. That didn't work either.

"Do you still think she doesn't have designs?" Felicia asked.

"It wouldn't matter if she had," Simon assured her. "I have no intention of marrying Megan Harwyn, and no matter what you might think about my weak will, I'm perfectly capable of refusing that kind of temptation . . . now."

"She might not need a wedding ring to become lady of the manor. It's perhaps as well, isn't it, that I know for an indisputable fact that you really are a Murden—because objective observers, who don't have inside information, might well find Bernard's theory plausible, even if they had to assume that you've been duped too."

"I haven't," said Simon.

"I know, but the key witnesses aren't around to support your story."

"What witnesses?"

"Think about it, Simon. The only reason that you can be perfectly sure that you aren't the victim of a plot to pass you off as the heir, cooked up by Megan Harwyn and Angela Richardson and her mother, is your dealings with the neider, which occurred via the intermediaries of Lenore and Melusine, both of whom have vanished without trace. I know too, obviously, but I'm an old woman, possibly crazy—and who could believe otherwise if I were to testify in court that the reason I knew, from the very beginning, that you were a Murden, and part-neider, is that Lenore told me?"

Simon remembered what Megan Harwyn had said, in passing, about Bernard Pallister, Douglas Jefferson, or both, perhaps trying to have him committed, if they found out how close he was to the appearance of insanity. He remembered, too, that he had remarked to Marianne that he had often been thought to be crazy merely on the strength of the books he wrote. It occurred to him that it might be far easier now to make a case for his being delusional than ever before—and that the person now best placed to make such a case, or to secure its outcome, was Megan Harwyn.

And what defense did he have? The truth? That might easily be taken as proof of his madness. He wondered whether it might not have been better to call the police and accuse

Bernard of attempted burglary, and whether it might not have been better still if Bernard had actually succeeded in completing his search and stealing files from his computer, given that there was no evidence therein of any fraud.

"It's all right," said Felicia, "you can come to bed now. But you'll forgive me, I hope, if our dreams are a trifle anxious . . ."

He was just about to obey the injunction when there was a loud tapping at the bedroom window.

Absurd as it was, he thought he recognized the tapping. He ran to the window, stark naked, and fumbled with the lock in his hurry to get it open.

As soon as he had lifted up the sash, a black bird flew in and perched on the bedhead.

Felicia immediately exclaimed "Lenore!" and reached out with her right hand, as if to stroke the creature's head. But the hand stopped halfway, as she evidently realized that she had made a mistake . . . or that, if the bird really was Lenore, something was seriously wrong with her.

The raven was strangely blurred, as if the matter composing her body were having difficulty settling into the shape that she was trying to attain. Indeed, it seemed to Simon that she was not entirely there, that she could not quite contrive to occupy the space that she was trying to fill. It was, for some reason that he could not quite fathom, a deeply disturbing sight. It was as if the bird were a gap in reality, a kind of mirage, or a kind of dream, that was aspiring to reality without being able to achieve it.

The not-quite-bird turned round, with a twisting hop, in order to try to stare at Simon, but its eyes were hazy and the stare was empty. Simon met it regardless, and listened hard for the voice inside his head, which, he felt sure, was about to borrow words from his vocabulary in order to give him a crucial message—or at least to try.

The bird croaked. There was, Simon thought, nothing particularly strange about a raven croaking, but this particular croak sent a chill down his spine. It was an authentic croak, an actual sound composed of waves in the air, but it seemed to Simon be coming from somewhere beyond the world, and it was redolent with desolation.

As the croak scratched his eardrum rudely, words did begin to sound within his head, as if he were subvocalizing them himself—as, he supposed, he must be. But they too sounded as if they were coming from elsewhere, from an alien space that did not, and could not, exist,

"Do not forget . . . the foul conspiracy," the voice said, hoarsely. "The minute of their plot . . . is almost come. Abjure no magic . . . break no staff . . . bury no book . . . open graves . . . wake their sleepers . . . call forth . . . the mutinous winds."

Then the raven turned round again, with a similar swiveling hop, and looked at Felicia—longingly, Simon thought, as if it were begging for a caress. She even extended her head to be stroked . . . but Felicia's hand remained frozen; she was frightened . . . and rightly so.

The raven suddenly straightened her posture and spread her wings. She turned her head, without the bodily pirouette, and looked at Simon again, with half-formed eyes that were gray with panic.

"Too soon!" she said—actually *said*, not by projecting borrowed words into his mind, and not in a desolate croak, but in impossibly human speech, of which no raven except for the fictitious Grip and Poe's famous symbol of remorse had ever been capable.

Then something happened to the not-quite-bird. Simon had no words with which to describe it, although he could not help perceiving a certain irony in her final injunction to call forth mutinous winds. For a few seconds it seemed as if she were, indeed, victim to some kind of existential hurricane. She swirled like a tornado and was swallowed up by a storm that was not in the air but in the fabric of space itself. Her blurring became utter confusion but she did not go gently into that oblivion. She seemed to twist and writhe, as if she were struggling against an irresistible force that was folding her into an invisible dimension, and as she—or, rather, it, as there was no longer anything left of the illusory raven capable of being attributed a sex—did so, it turned a far more Stygian black than it had contrived while it was endeavoring to be a raven. It was ripped to shreds of shadow, completely, but it struggled unavailingly for existence, or at least a phantom presence, for what seemed like an interval of time longer than the twenty seconds or so at which a clock would have measured it.

Then Felicia said: "Lenore!" again, but in a far more plaintive tone.

Simon refrained from saying "Nevermore," and cursed himself for the whim that had tempted him to do so. "Did you hear what she said?" he demanded, instead.

"She said: *Too soon*," Felicia repeated.

"Not that. The Shakespearean message."

"How could I?" said Felicia, quite reasonably, since his was the mind that had formed the imaginary words. "Tell me."

Simon had no difficulty reciting it word for word, even though it consisted of garbled fragments from *The Tempest*.

"But it's no help at all," he complained. "It's just another damned prophecy, advising me not to do what Prospero did and abandon his magic for mere temporal power. What use is that to me? I have no magic to give up, and the temporal power I've been promised is still a distant mirage. If something is about to happen, I don't know what it is, and I can't do anything about it. Why didn't Melusine come? What use is the damned bird?"

"If Melusine didn't come," said Felicia, quietly, "it's probably because she can't be of any use herself. It's too soon."

"Too soon for what?" Simon snapped.

"I think whatever's happening is happening too soon," said Felicia, reading the dream that had been materialized for a matter of minutes. "The neider isn't ready—Melusine isn't ready. Neither was Lenore, but perhaps the neider felt that it had to try. Melusine can't do anything. Neither can

I, it seems. Perhaps the neider believes—or at least hopes—
that you might yet be able to do something, if you can only
muster the creative strength."

Perhaps it does believe that, Simon thought. *I'm the writer,
after all, the supposedly bold follower of ideas wherever they might
lead. What else have I been doing these last few days, except making
my own mystic journey into the mysteries of Annwn, in search of
spoils? Perhaps I just have to complete the journey. But it's too
soon for me too; I don't even have the commencement of an understanding. I'm completely in the dark.*

"Call me Taliesin," he muttered. "Except that my mother
didn't, when I was just an idea whose time hadn't yet come—
and Jason, I'm not."

"No?" said Felicia, completing her hand gesture, moving her fingers gently, as if she were stroking the sleek black
head of a no-longer-lost Lenore, who still had not had occasion to croak *Nevermore,* and who was not, in fact, there. "In
that case, I can forget about casting Megan as Medea. But we
all have to be somebody, don't we? And according to you,
our conscious selves are only fragments of what we really
are—and what we really are is potentially superhuman . . .
did I really just say all that? Nobody talks like that, do they?
What's wrong with me?"

"I don't know," said Simon, thinking that he could think
of at least one person who talked like that, occasionally, "but
whatever it is, it infected Cerys, too, this morning. It's in the
atmosphere, I think—but it's not excess oxygen. It's coming
from the cauldron. Megan and I sensed it yesterday, forcefully, inside the cauldron. It's fishing things up from the
unconscious. I don't think it's toxic. It's a stimulant, of sorts.
Perhaps it's a resource. The cauldron is supposed to be the
cauldron of creativity as well as rebirth and metamorphosis,
after all. But this has happened before."

"What? What do you mean, it's happened before?"

"I don't know. It is just a feeling that I have."

"Déjà-vû?"

"No, not an illusion. I think this really has happened before, and that it's important that it's happened before . . . but I don't know why. It's too soon . . . I haven't begun to understand. And because of that, it's too late to do anything about it."

He had a sudden mental image of a ship sailing . . . or, to be strictly accurate, a ship that had sailed. He cursed himself for the cliché. He felt that he was letting himself down. Where was his writer's conscience?

"I was just playing with ideas," Simon complained, as if by way of an insincere apology, addressed to no one in particular. "But I've written more than one story in which trying to break through the prison walls of consciousness only leads to madness and disaster."

"I fear," Felicia replied—although Simon was not entirely sure that it was not Lenore speaking through her, and something in the vasty deep speaking though Lenore—"that the lifeboat of blissful ignorance appears to have sailed. If we're not to go down with the ship of reason, we'll have to find another way out, and hope that the vasty deep is replete with desert islands."

On which note, Simon climbed back into bed, took his lover in his arms, tenderly, and descended slowly with her on to the pillow, where they sank into a sleep that seemed, to Simon at least, to be utterly dreamless, and hence absolutely lonely.

But he still had a thought, and therefore knew that he existed.

"Do not forget . . . the foul conspiracy," he told himself, with the utmost gravity. "Open graves . . . wake their sleepers . . . call forth . . . the mutinous winds."

But no graves opened, no sleepers awoke, and no winds came, mutinous or otherwise.

XVIII
Obligation

When Simon awoke, there was a moment of confusion when he did not know where he was, or where he ought to be. For a moment, before opening his eyes, he tried to remember where he ought to be. His flat in Bristol? No, he had left Bristol. Raven Cottage? No, that was not where he belonged.

It was not until he felt Felicia's frail, warm body beside him that he remembered where he actually was, and actually belonged.

He opened his eyes. It was already light; the sun had already risen. He turned over on to his back, and stretched his limbs. Felicia woke up. She reached out to touch him, as if to make sure that he was real.

"What happened?" she asked.

It was on the tip of his tongue to say that he couldn't remember. Then he did.

"We had a visitation," he said. "It looked like Lenore. Perhaps it had actually been Lenore. It couldn't maintain the illusion, though. Something was opposing it. When it went away, it left something behind, something in the air. It made us crazy, or at least intoxicated, but only a little, and it didn't last. It's gone now."

"Are you sure?"

"No—but if it hasn't actually gone, at least it's faded. I feel fine."

"But I felt fine last night," Felicia objected, "and I wasn't, was I?"

"You weren't as bad as me," Simon assured her. "and even I wasn't that bad. Anyway, it's light now." He eased his legs out of the bed, but he didn't feel in the least hung over. Perhaps "fine" was an exaggeration as a description of the way he felt, but he didn't feel bad. He felt calm, and resolute.

He walked into the bathroom and took a shower. The warm water soothed him, and the soap soothed him a little more. When he had finished, he went back into the bedroom and began to get dressed. Felicia was still lying down in the bed.

"I'm not ill," she assured him, when he looked at her questioningly. "Not even tired. I just haven't quite caught up with myself yet. Go downstairs—and get some breakfast. Fix it yourself if you can't bear to ask Edith. I'll have a shower and join you."

Simon obeyed. Cerys was in the dining room, absent-mindedly consuming toast and marmalade, punctuated with sips of black coffee, swallowed with what seemed to be an exaggerated caution, while staring at her phone, which she was holding in her left hand, twitching her thumb in the course of some simple-minded game. Simon did not know whether to be offended or glad that, for once, she wasn't reading one of his books.

Without looking up, she said: "The kettle's only just boiled; there's instant coffee in the jar. The bread's a bit stale, but it'll make toast. There's butter and marmalade there. If you want anything else you'll have to go to the kitchen and play lord of the manor." She sounded slightly contemptuous of his craven failure, thus far, to "play lord of the manor."

He made himself a mug of instant coffee and put two slices of stale bread into the toaster.

When he had collected the toast, put it on a plate and sat down opposite Cerys, she finally set her phone down and looked up.

"Sorry," she said. He couldn't tell whether she was apologizing for her impoliteness at being so slow to respond to his entry or for her snide remark. She added: "I had a bad night. My mind was hyperactive. I think there's something in the air. Perhaps it's spring."

"Perhaps it is," Simon replied, although his response *in petto* was that it was anything but. He buttered the toast, but didn't bother with marmalade. He took a swig of the black coffee, but found it too weak and too lukewarm to have the effect for which he was hoping. The toast was too brittle, and also insipid, but that didn't surprise him.

"I haven't made a decision yet," Cerys told him, although he hadn't asked, or even looked expectant.

"That's okay," he said. "Take your time. There's no rush."

"No," she said, "I suppose not. You're not going to tell me, then?"

"Tell you what?" Simon really had forgotten.

"What went on in Raven last night. Cousin Bernard bleeding like a stuck pig?"

Felicia came in just in time to hear the second sentence. "Don't worry about it, dear," she said, in order to save Simon from pausing too long. "It's sorted. Nothing to worry about."

Cerys looked at her with a martyred expression. "Rule One," she said, glancing at Simon, as if challenging him to remember what Rule One was. He concentrated on his toast and coffee. As soon as he had finished it, he said to Felicia: "I have to go over to Raven. I might be gone for a while."

"There's no rush," she told him, blandly. "I won't worry. I have plenty to keep me occupied."

Cerys had returned her gaze to her phone, and was ostentatiously ignoring both of them, although Simon got the distinct impression that her mind was not on whatever game it was that she was playing.

Outside, the sky was dull, but it wasn't raining. He paused on the steps outside the front door in order to take a deep breath. The tide was out and the atmosphere reeked of damp seaweed. The breeze was blowing from the west, but in a lazy, almost desultory fashion, carrying no significant chill. It did not feel like a winter wind, but nor did it carry any significant suggestion of spring, or seem at all mutinous. The sea was gray and empty.

Simon locked the gate behind him, and walked to Raven with a purposeful stride, intending to check in with Zoe before going next door to collect the money that Megan Harwyn had promised him. The street was absolutely deserted, but he was used to that by now. He looked up; the sky seemed uniform; the sun invisible. The whole world seemed dead. He felt a trifle numb himself.

"As above, so below," he muttered, almost reflexively, and then cursed himself, not for sounding like his mother but for sounding like *The Beginner's Guide to Occultism*.

What's wrong with me? he thought. He had no answer to offer, but he knew that whatever it was, he had brought it with him from the Abbey.

He let himself into Raven Cottage and glanced into the kitchen and the study to check that they were devoid of any human presence before running upstairs to the spare bedroom. It was empty. It wasn't until he returned to the study that he took full note of the fact that a good deal of the blood had been scrubbed from the carpet, and almost all of it sponged from the chair in which he worked. There was a note balanced on his keyboard. He unfolded it and read:

Dear Uncle Simon,

Miss Harwyn came back after you had gone last night. She helped me clean up. We got most of the blood out. We had a long talk. She told me that she'd agreed to lend you the money. She said that there was no point taking the boat, because it would be a good deal safer if she drove me to Bristol and stayed with me while I delivered the money and went to the police station. We would have sent you a text, but you don't have a mobile phone. I'll ring you from Bristol when every-thing is sorted, to confirm that everything is fine.

Thanks for everything.

Zoe

Simon's first thought was that he was a fool for not having anticipated that. His second was a vague feeling of resent-ment that Megan had stolen his mission of mercy, although she was, of course, far better equipped to execute it than he was, not only having five thousand pounds in used twenties hidden in her house but a BMW—and a mobile phone. Then he felt guilty for feeling resentful, instead of grateful.

The bloody woman's taking over my entire life, he thought. *Am I never going to be able to take another step without her anticipating it?*

Then the doorbell rang. He went to open it, without having enough spare mental capacity to wonder who on earth it could be.

There was a man standing in the doorstep. He was short, dark, well-dressed but slightly crumpled, and wearing a strange artificial smile: the smile, Simon thought, of a man who had not got as much sleep the previous night as someone nearing threescore years and ten required. It was not a Mephistophelean smile, although, having recognized the man, Simon's first reflexive mental impression was that the messenger was no angel. He had been warned, in fact, not to believe anything that he might say.

"Hello, Mr. Cannick," said the visitor, urbanely. "We met, if you remember, at poor James's memorial in the Abbey chapel. I'm Douglas Jefferson."

"I remember," said Simon, speaking the way he still felt, a trifle numbly.

Jefferson nodded, perhaps glad to be remembered. "Do you mind if I come in?" he said. "I'd like to talk to you, if I may."

Simon stood aside, and silently ushered his visitor into the study. He indicated the chair that was innocent of bloodstains, and sat down himself on the one that was not, gingerly. The imitation leather was still a trifle damp from the energetic scouring to which it had been subjected.

"Sorry about the blood on the carpet," he said, mildly, making a mental effort to pull himself together.

"That's all right," said his visitor. "Bernard Pallister told me what had happened, although I'd already deduced most of it. I was watching from the first floor of the Mermaid. While you were talking to Megan at the gate to the Tine I slipped round to Blackbird to make sure that he was all right. I dosed him with ibuprofen, patched him up, let him rant for a while and then talked some sense into him. I stayed with him to make sure that there were no unfortunate after-effects, but he's sleeping peacefully now. I saw Megan drive away with the young woman—your niece, I presume?"

Simon could not seem to contrive a definite no comment, for the moment, so he simply waited for Jefferson to continue.

"There's no need to worry," the little man said, smoothly, slipping into his discourse with the ease of a practiced salesman. "I've corrected Bernard's misapprehensions. You have nothing further to worry about from that direction. He didn't want to believe me, at first—he's under the impression that we're old enemies—but the truth eventually filtered into his thick skull. I've convinced him that his absurd conspiracy theory is utter nonsense, that Megan Harwyn is innocent of any devious plotting, and that you really are Lilith Murden's great-grandson, and hence a direct descendant of Seymour Murden, via Rhys the Engineer. I'm sorry for stating the obvious, but I thought it diplomatic to let you know that, unlike Bernard, I'm not a raving lunatic. It's important to me that you know that, because I'd rather like us to be friends, if that's possible." He paused for a moment before adding: "Is that possible, do you think?"

"I don't know," Simon said, dryly. "I don't know you well enough to form an opinion."

"That's perfectly reasonable, especially as I suspect that Megan might have given you a rather poor impression of me, which I'd like to amend, if I can. I'm sure that she was amused by Bernard's improvised conspiracy theory, but he really should have taken the trouble to check with Dai, as I did. Dai assured me that Megan was taken completely by surprise when you turned up at the Mermaid on the evening of the day when you moved into Raven Cottage, and that she then set to work furiously to investigate your background, even going to the trouble of collecting a DNA sample.

"I must confess that I was taken completely by surprise by the events that followed with astonishing rapidity, as was Bernard; we had both determined, independently, some time before, that Eve Augerrand owned Raven Cottage and had both discovered that she was Lilith Murden's daughter, but when Bernard made her what he considered to be a generous offer to buy the cottage she turned him down flat, which obviously began stirring suspicions in his tiny but active mind. Our independent investigations revealed that she only seemed to have female descendants, so her branch of the family seemed to be irrelevant to the inheritance. Neither of us paid any further heed to her until James's death. After that, obviously, we resumed our investigations in a hurry. Had Bernard taken the trouble to check the results of the DNA test, as I did, he would have realized that his conviction that a fraud was being perpetrated was mistaken.

"You know, of course, because Alexander Usher will have told you, that I've conducted extensive investigations into the genealogy of the Murdens, so far as that can be done using materials now in the public domain and accessible online. The results were fascinating, in several ways, but you'll doubtless be glad to know that they confirm your descent from Seymour Murden beyond any reasonable doubt. Bernard was less than delighted to hear the news, but that's the character of the man. He has the mind of a property developer. I didn't realize until a few hours ago that he had offered Cerys a job within a matter of hours of my doing so, and I'm now aware that the coincidence must have given the impression that my offer was as hypocritical as his. You must have jumped to the same conclusion yourself, especially after Megan told you that we had both contacted her as well. Perhaps that was a mistake, but I really thought that after all this time, we could let bygones be bygones. Old prejudices die hard, it seems."

He paused and measured Simon with his gaze, as if waiting for a comment on his judgment regarding old prejudices, or perhaps hoping for a witty rejoinder.

"I don't like to form conclusions too hastily," Simon eventually remarked, in what he hoped was a perfectly neutral tone.

"Very wise," said his interlocutor. "And doubtless you're wondering how I came to be here in time to witness the end of your little contretemps last night. I own two cottages in Morpen, and I was informed the day before yesterday by the letting agent that the temporary tenants were moving out a few weeks before the end of their lease, in order to move into one of Bernard's derelict properties along the coast. I thought that it might be a good idea to ascertain whether my cottages needed any work doing before the holidaymakers began to arrive after Easter, and I thought that such an expedition might also provide a good opportunity to pay a courtesy call on the Abbey in order to renew my acquaintance with Felicia and introduce myself to you properly. Felicia isn't immune to old prejudices, but she's cut from very different cloth from Megan, so I was sure that there was every chance of making a fresh start in my relationship with her.

"Naturally, when I arrived in Morpen yesterday afternoon, I thought that the first thing I ought to do was to walk to St. Madoc and have a chat with my old friend Dai, to catch up on the local news. I knew that the pub wouldn't be open yet, so I went round the back to the kitchen door, as I used to do in the olden days. No prejudice there, mercifully, except a little in my favor. In fact he seemed delighted to see me—a fresh face is water in the Sahara to a Welshman topped up with gossip who's thirsty for sympathetic ears. I was surprised when he told me that Bernard had been in residence in his own cottage for two days, but that he appeared to be maintaining the utmost secrecy. I couldn't help wondering what my old adversary might have planned, so Dai and I settled down with our pints in an upstairs room, in the dark, in order that we could keep an eye on what was happening in the street while we chatted, without being observed ourselves.

"We saw you set off for the Abbey, where you're apparently, and quite understandably, spending a good deal of time these days. I must confess that I wasn't entirely surprised thereafter to see Bernard making his way to Raven Cottage and letting himself in. I had even offered Dai a wager on that circumstance, but he refused it, on the grounds that I would certainly win. We were, however, extremely surprised a few minutes later to see the young lady run out in panic and race to the bridge to the Tine. Dai and I were still discussing what we ought to do about it when Megan came out of Sanderling Cottage, went into Raven and switched on the lights. Assuming that the matter was, so to speak, in hand, we decided to sit tight and await developments. As I said before, when you and Megan had made your way separately to the Abbey gate, I went to make sure that Bernard was safe.

"I must say that the incident seems to me to be extremely regrettable, and I would have criticized Bernard severely for his appalling conduct if I hadn't feared inciting his wrath against me while I was trying to calm him down and make him see reason. He's not a bad fellow, really, but he is, as they say, not the sharpest tool in the box. He's quite canny in his business dealings, when he's on familiar turf, as it were, but he doesn't cope well with novelty, and when he gets ideas into his head, he often fails to subject them to the rigorous criticism that hypotheses require before earning promotion to the status of theory. I'm sure that a man with your impressive bibliography understands that very well."

Again, Douglas Jefferson looked at Simon as if trying to gauge his reaction, but Simon wasn't at all sure whether he ought to construe the remark as an inept compliment or a vague insult. "I'm aware of the tendency that many people have to rush to judgment," he said, and immediately cursed himself privately for the pomposity as well as the pointlessness of the reply.

It wasn't the first time he'd been guilty of that particular sin in recent days, he recalled, and it was in danger of getting to be a habit. Nor was it his alone. Even in Raven Cottage, it seemed, there was something in the air—or something within him.

"For what it may be worth," Jefferson continued, "I believe that I've succeeded in making Bernard see that his strategy, in the situation in which we unexpectedly found ourselves a few weeks ago, was completely misguided, and he has authorized me to apologize on his behalf. I've pointed out to him that it's in his interest as well as mine for both of us to make every attempt to work with you, in your new capacity as owner of the Abbey and the rump of what used to be the Murden estate, in the hope that it might finally become possible, after many years of strife and suspicion, caused by grudges left over from previous generations, to combine our different interests and work with a degree of co-ordination.

"I won't bore you with details of family quarrels whose deeply entrenched roots go back to a time before James was born, let alone either of us. Megan might have told you that James made numerous attempts to find such common ground in the 1970s and early 1980s, but couldn't bring about a rapprochement then. We're all much older now, though, and hopefully a little wiser, and the various utopian plans we had at the time have been rendered quite obsolete by economic and political developments in the interim. With Brexit looming, the context of possible future discussions has changed completely, and I think it would be to everyone's benefit to make a fresh start, with a clean slate. Don't you agree, Mr. Cannick?"

"I can see the logic of the argument," Simon ceded, warily.

"Excellent. And then, of course, there is the other matter that, although not urgent, inevitably concerns us all deeply." Jefferson stopped dead, evidently waiting for Simon either to make a guess or request enlightenment.

"I'm afraid that I've only been taking one day at a time recently, Mr. Jefferson," Simon parried, "and I haven't been able to think very deeply about anything while the will hasn't yet been proven and my future is still clouded with uncertainty."

Jefferson looked out of the window at the gray sky, as if its solid cloud were an obliging symbol of uncertainty, laid on especially for the purposes of the conversation. The gray seemed a shade darker now than it had when Simon had first emerged from the Abbey, even though the invisible sun must have been higher in the sky by now, peering down benignly at the opaque mass shielding the coast of Pembrokeshire and Ceredigion.

"Of course," the practiced salesman continued, still comfortably in the groove of his patter. "Well, I hope I can put your mind at rest in that regard. The probate court won't find any fault with the will. If any queries come up, I've been able to gather all sorts of information capable of laying any doubts to rest and I'll be glad to make the results of my research available for that purpose, if necessary. But I've had far more leisure to consider future possibilities than you've so far had, and there is one very obvious question that seems to me to be worthy of urgent consideration, even though the issue hopefully won't arise for some years to come." Again, he paused, inviting a guess or a query.

Simon was beginning to tire of the game, so he simply said: "And what's that, Mr. Jefferson?"

"The question of your own heir, Mr. Cannick. Who, do you think, ought to be next in line to inherit the Abbey and its associated properties? You have no children, it seems."

"No," Simon confirmed. "Have you?"

"I have. Three, including a son. Bernard Pallister has two, also including a son. Nor are we the only cousins you have who are blessed with that privilege. It's a circumstance that encourages thinking ahead, especially for people of our age, nearing the Biblically allotted threescore years and ten."

Simon only paused for thought briefly before saying, in a perfectly neutral tone; "I can see that, if and when the will is proven, I'll have to give that matter serious consideration, with view to making a will of my own and clarifying the situation for all potentially interested parties."

"You're a wise and conscientious man, Mr. Cannick," Jefferson said, sounding as genuine as snake oil. "I will, of course, be very glad to make my genealogical analyses available to you, in order that you can study Seymour Murden's descendancy in as much detail as publicly accessible sources permit—although I dare say that the Abbey has much more elaborate documents in the library than that curious old family Bible in the chapel. Doubtless there are also inscriptions in the crypt, although I've never been down there myself. You probably remember that I requested to go down at the funeral, but that Felicia, quite understandably, didn't think the request appropriate at the time."

"It would have been a waste of effort," Simon told him. "There are very few legible inscriptions, all relatively recent, which contain no data, so far as I can see, that isn't in sources that are much more accessible."

"That's a pity. Naturally, I'll take your word for it, although you surely haven't had time to mount a thorough search. You do seem to have hurt poor Alexander's feelings, though. He telephoned me after his meeting with you in the Mermaid to express his disappointment—it seems that he had formed high hopes of the likelihood of your assisting a fellow scholar in his research. He seems quite convinced now that you have something to hide."

"He's correct," said Simon, "as you must know very well."

Simon judged that Jefferson had been expecting a routine denial, but the other was not thrown off his stride. "The great family secret," he said, increasing the artifice of his perpetual smile. "I was never admitted to it, I fear. Obviously, I won't ask you what it is, although Alexander has certainly raised some intriguing possibilities. But that, presumably, is something that you won't want to allow to die with you. Felicia, bless her, has to be reckoned an unsafe long-term custodian, although she looks exceedingly well for a centenarian, even in mourning, so I assume that I'm justified in thinking that your expectations in that regard are pinned on Cerys. Perhaps, too, you're hoping that she might produce a potential male heir, given time. But you doubtless know enough family history to know how rare it is for Murden women to bear male children. At the very least, you might want to have a Plan B in mind."

"I'm familiar with the eccentricities of heredity manifest in the family history," Simon confirmed.

"Of course you are. You have a grand-niece, too, I believe, who has just had her first child, and might yet have several more. Might I be very indiscreet, though, and bring an item of information to your attention of which you might not be aware, but which might well enter into any future conclusions you make regarding the inheritance of the estate?"

"Go on," said Simon, realizing that the salesman was finally about to get to the bottom line of his meandering tabulation.

"Did you know that Megan Harwyn has a child?"

Simon blinked, but there was no electric shock, no chill or frisson. The immediate, reflexive reaction of his conscious mind was: *So what?* It was hardly a surprise to learn that Megan might possibly have a hidden agenda that was not the one that Felicia had suspected. "No," he admitted, aloud. "I didn't."

"I thought not. Even Dai seems to be unaware of it, and Dai reputedly knows everything. I suspect that I might be the only member of the family who does know. It's a girl . . . a girl who bears a remarkable resemblance to her mother, at an interval of twenty-some years . . . although I doubt that she knows that, never having met her birth-mother since the day of her delivery. She's a mother herself, now. She has a son: a son who is the only direct male descendant of James Murden . . . although, of course, he has only been that descendant, in legal terms, since the publication of James Murden's will. Needless to say, James was quite unaware of his existence.

"You've obviously introduced Megan to at least one of the descendants of your birth-mother, but there's little prospect, I fear, of her making a reciprocal gesture. That's a pity; you might find that you and her daughter have a certain amount in common, although Megan didn't actually leave her in a cardboard box in a shop doorway. Perhaps you'd like to contact her directly—I can give you her address, if you wish. She doesn't know me, but I've monitored her progress at a distance. I thought at the time of her birth that I might be her father, but there were no DNA tests in those days, and I realized when she grew older, and I was able to compare her with her mother, that I couldn't possibly have made any genetic contribution to her composition. That was what finally convinced me that Megan really was James's daughter, because I had heard that the phenomenon ran in the family. I was tempted to mention it to him, but I knew that he wouldn't take it well, so I refrained."

"And why are you telling me?" Simon asked, bluntly.

"Because it's relevant to the questions you'll have to ask yourself, when the will is proven, regarding the future of the Abbey and the configuration of your own testament. Unless, that is, someone takes it into his or her head to challenge the will on the boy's behalf . . . which is, I suppose, conceivable, even though his mother doesn't know, at this moment in time, of his possible entitlement. I have no intention of telling her, obviously, and I assume that you have none . . . but I can't speak for any third party."

At that point in time, almost as if on cue, the telephone rang. Simon turned swiftly and snatched he received from its cradle. He assumed that it would be Zoe, or perhaps Megan, updating him on the situation in Bristol. It wasn't. It was Felicia, in great distress.

"You have to come back Simon," she said, "immediately. Something terrible has happened."

XIX
Damsel in Distress

"I'm sorry, Mr. Jefferson," Simon said, already heading for the door. "Something's come up. We'll have to leave it there."

"Is it anything with which I might be able to help?" Jefferson was quick to offer.

"No," said Simon, already opening the front door of the cottage.

"When can we meet again, Mr. Cannick?" the other said, obviously realizing that there was no time for further diplomatic niceties.

"I don't know," Simon retorted—but then thought that it might not be a good idea to leave Douglas Jefferson with a ready-made excuse for coming to visit him in the Abbey. Swiftly, he added: "If you tell me where I can reach you, I'll call you—later today, if possible, or tomorrow."

Jefferson was already fishing in the pocket of his jacket. He was the kind of man who always had business cards handy, and had long perfected the action of whipping one out and handing it over. Naturally, it was a fancy card, with embossed lettering, so incredibly pompous that it even had a monogram in the top right-hand corner, in a cartouche shaped like an escutcheon, with a Latin motto beneath it. The latter was in tiny print, but it was legible: *Sicut superius sic inferius*.

Simon's first pedantic thought was that it wasn't even correct, that it had collapsed the actual phrase from the Emerald Tablet in order to fit it into the small available space. But it retained the meaning: *As above, so below.*

"You can get me on my mobile any time," Jefferson said, drawing his attention to the number on the bottom right-hand corner of the card. "I won't be any further away than Morpen for a couple of days. We could meet in the Mermaid, any time that it's convenient. I'd like . . ."

Simon did not stop to hear what Douglas Jefferson would like. He stuck the card in his jacket pocket and set off toward the Tine at a run.

"I'll call you," he repeated, shouting over his shoulder.

He had to pause to fumble with the padlock, but he wasn't in so much of a rush that he forgot to seal it again. Then he continued running to the Abbey.

The door opened as he was approaching it, and Margaret came out. She still did much of the cleaning around the house and helped Edith in the kitchen, but she usually spent the greater part of the day in her bedroom on the second floor, watching TV. Simon had never seen her so agitated, so manifestly alive.

"Come quickly, Mr. Cannick," she said. "There's a flood in the cellars and Miss Cerys is drowned. Miss Felicia's in the chapel."

Simon did not pause to ask for further enlightenment from someone clearly incapable of providing it. He ran to the chapel, where he found Felicia, in company with Edith and Rhodri. The cook seemed exceedingly anxious too, but the gardener was putting on an appropriate display of Welsh stoicism, and Felicia seemed quite calm. She was kneeling down, holding one of the electric lanterns that he and Megan had employed two days before when descending into the crypt and the Underworld. She was lowering it carefully through the square gap left by the tipped-back trapdoor, into the darkness—where it disappeared.

It did not disappear because Felicia had dropped it; it disappeared because the darkness into which she had lowered it swallowed up its light, blocking it completely, just as the vitreous cocoons had swallowed Simon's hand two days before.

Felicia looked up as Simon arrived. She didn't waste any time with unnecessary explanations, or frivolous hysteria. She simply stood up, put the lantern down, and turned to the gardener. "Rhodri," she said, "what I want you to do is to take Edith and Margaret over to the mainland. Mr. Cannick will give you the key to Raven Cottage, and I want you to take Edith and Margaret in there. Make a cup of tea, and wait. I really don't think there's any danger here, but if there is, you'll be safe there. Mr. Cannick and I will handle the situation."

The gardener did not even hesitate, let alone raise an objection. Felicia was the mistress of the house now, and Simon the heir apparent. Whatever devilment was at work, it was their responsibility to handle it. Simon gave him the key to the cottage, and the aged trio shuffled off, with no obvious reluctance. When they had gone, Felicia turned to Simon.

"Cerys is missing," she said, succinctly. "We found the trapdoor open. She must have taken the keys from the safe. It could only have been her, because she's the only one of us, apart from you, capable of lifting the trapdoor. She must have gone down; how far I don't know. She isn't responding to shouting. It's impossible to get a light down there. It's not just dark. Something has filled the crypt, but it's not a liquid or a gas. It seems to have stopped rising . . . but there doesn't seem to be anything to prevent it from rising further if it decides to do so. I doubt that closing the trapdoor would work, and we're not going to do that while Cerys is down there."

Simon picked up the lamp. Then he lay down flat on the chapel floor, and peered into the darkness, which seemed impenetrable. He lowered the lantern into the hole. Its light was completely eclipsed. He brought it out again and set it down. Then he reached down in order to feel the steps at the top of the staircase. They were tangible, seemingly as solid as ever. Slowly, he eased his head over the edge, and lowered his face into the darkness. He could still draw breath within it, and the air seemed to contain plenty of oxygen. He could feel a slight air current, and a faint odor that was slightly saline and slightly musty. He deduced that all the matter below the floor of the chapel was still there, still exactly as it had been before. Only the light was absent, its photons somehow deprived of effect, neutralized or metamorphosed.

He could not believe that Cerys would have gone down the steps into that unnatural darkness. When she had gone down, the darkness into which she went must have been ordinary, submissive to the glare of the lantern she had taken. He did not suppose that she had only gone down with a lantern; it was easy to guess what else she had been carrying.

But why? Why had she gone down there, alone?

The simplest hypothesis was mere curiosity. She had been turning the idea over in her mind for days. Did she or did she not want to go to the heart of the family secret? Did she want to stay in the Abbey, with Felicia and its new potential owner, or should she seek her fortune in the wider world?

Simon had offered to escort her down into the Underworld, as he had escorted Megan, but it wasn't difficult to think of reasons why she might not have wanted his guidance, and might have preferred to mount her own exploration, while he was on the mainland and would probably be gone for some time. After all, she didn't really know him, and didn't really trust him. It was perfectly plausible that she had decided to take a look for herself, without even warning Felicia about what she intended to do.

"Did Cerys seem to you to be behaving oddly at break-fast?" Felicia asked him.

"I suppose so, but I didn't pay much attention. I had other things on my mind."

"Me too—and I fear that I might not have paid much at-tention to her for quite some time, wrapped up in my own state of mind. I fear that I've grown used to thinking of her as someone who helps me, and it hadn't occurred to me that perhaps I ought to be the one helping her. But you had a long talk with her on Sunday. Didn't you reassure her?"

"I assured her of my support in whatever she wanted to do—but that isn't quite the same thing, is it? We had another chat yesterday, but there was something of an edge to it. She's always very polite, but I sometimes get the impression that she doesn't like me very much. That would be understand-able, I suppose. It was when I arrived here that all of your lives were turned upside-down. My offering to substitute for the financial support that James has always given her must seem a very poor compensation for his loss. I handled the situation at breakfast very badly—I should have answered her question fully and frankly, instead of confirming her sus-picion that everybody always excludes her deliberately. This is my fault."

"No, it's entirely mine," Felicia insisted, refusing him even a share of the blame. "I didn't even notice that she was troubled this morning, let alone how troubled she must have been for weeks. The poor child's just lost three out of the four people who have been the anchorage of her existence since her mother walked out on her, and the fourth one has been utterly wrapped up in herself, and a total stranger has walked into her life, taking over everything, including me. But she thinks that she ought to be the one who's protecting me, so she hasn't let it show, and she's tried to carry on as normal—except that she knows that things aren't normal, and never were, and she feels . . . well, I can't imagine what she feels, but I know that it isn't you that I should have been sleeping with these last few weeks, and it isn't your depression I should have been trying to coddle and soothe, and it shouldn't have been my own stupid anxieties that I ought to have been trying to cope with. I've let her down, and now . . . she's gone."

Simon moved to put his arms around Felicia, in an attempt to soothe her anxieties but she shrugged him off, because, for the moment, she didn't think that her anxieties deserved soothing, given that she felt, wrongly, that she had let Cerys down. And to make matters worse, he couldn't think of anything to say that Felicia couldn't construe as making things worse, especially "It's not that simple . . . ," or "It's not that bad . . ."

But in fact, he thought, it really wasn't that simple, and it probably wasn't that bad. Cerys might have been in a bad mood that morning, but he had every faith in her rationality and her practicality, and in the resilience of her habitual attitude of resentful resignation. Her recitation of the mantra that nobody every told her anything, that she was always the last to know, was more defensive humor than real complaint . . . although he knew only too well that more true words are spoken in apparent jest than sullen earnest.

In any case, Simon thought, it wasn't really Cerys's fault. There had been "something in the air" for days now. Liminal as its effects had been, Cerys had shown those effects, just as he and Felicia had. And the effects had been intensifying all along, as witness the previous night's visitation by the confused simulacrum of Lenore, which had been so rudely interrupted. Something had already come through the portal, even before Megan had drawn his attention to the fact that it was open: not something solid and material, although it was clearly capable of constituting mirages and casting equivocal shadows, but something nevertheless alive, active, and communicative: something capable of touching human minds, albeit in the same elusive and frustrating fashion as the neider, unable to make itself properly understood via the words and images it provoked. Even if she had been suffering from feelings of disorientation and neglect, and even if those feelings had exploded in a fit of pique, Cerys had not gone down into the Underworld entirely of her own accord. She had been drawn. And the strange darkness that had closed around her was no mere accident, but a trap.

Perhaps, he thought, the entity operating through the cauldron had taken Cerys just as the neider had taken Melusine, in order to try to build, patiently and painstakingly, a dream-bridge to her conscious mind, with the aid of the most intimate physical contact it could contrive.

But why Cerys? he thought, in immediate response to that hypothesis. *Why not me?*

He thought, however, that it was probably a silly question. He understood how the esthetics of story worked. Human and alien minds might have very little in common, apart from the fundamental rules of logic and arithmetic, but if there were any foundation stones of thought beyond logic and mathematics, if there were any fundamental rules of creativity underlying all of narrative, shaping and guiding all storytelling, they had to be reflected in the hoariest of clichés, the most hackneyed of storylines.

If the entity beyond the cauldron understood anything at all about the dynamics of human consciousness, or even if it were merely hypothesizing based on its own understanding, it had to know, or to believe, or at least be prepared to gamble, that if it wanted to make contact with a hero, the best way to lay down a lure was to employ a damsel in distress. That was Rule One of all romance.

"As above, so below," he muttered. "The human mind, in its essentials, reflects the cosmic mind. Fictitious creativity can't work in any other way. The fundamental operations of Dark Mind are bound by the same esthetic principles as petty hack writers starving in their garrets."

He became conscious of the fact that Felicia was staring at him in a fashion that was almost anger, almost disappointment. He couldn't blame her. He was doing what he always did, not merely following his bizarre trains of thought instead of doing something, but overthinking things, as Cerys always accused him of doing.

"What are we going to do, Simon?" Felicia said, sharply and succinctly, trying to drag him back down to earth.

She succeeded. He decided. "You're going to do the hard part," he told her. "You're going to wait. I might be gone for some time."

"But you can't go down there," she said, flatly, although she actually meant the opposite of what she said. "You won't be able to see."

"I know the way. The blue light in the Underworld might well still be visible when I get there. If it's not, that will only make it easier for my brain to improvise. The hallucinations will come, I'm sure of it, produced by my unconscious, carefully polluted by the Other. Whether I'll be able to make any sense of the hallucinations, I don't know, but I'll certainly try . . . and I think the Other, or Others, will be trying just as hard. You shouldn't worry. The last thing they want to do is to hurt me, or Cerys. If they wanted to hurt anyone, it would be the easiest thing in the world for them. They could probably blow the whole planet into smithereens. That's not what they want. They want to communicate, to forge a link, with us, with the neider, and with the dark minds in the earth's core. Except . . ."

"Except what?" Felicia demanded, impatiently. She was not in a mood for dramatic pauses.

"Except that Cerys has taken a gun down there with her, and I'm not entirely sure that *she'll* be able to cope with the hallucinations. If she starts shooting blindly, she might hit me . . . and even that might not be the worst thing that could happen, if there's something else down there capable of being hit."

"She doesn't have a gun," Felicia objected.

"Yes she does. She appropriated James's revolver after he died. She was anxious. It made her feel safer, as a talisman rather than a weapon. She lent it to me when Zoe rang the bell at the gate, in case I needed it. I gave it back to her when I came back."

"Why on earth did you do that?"

"She asked me for it. She's not a child, remember. She's an intelligent adult, and hopefully, she understands enough of what's going on not to panic down there, even when she starts seeing things. We have to trust her."

"If we have to trust her, perhaps we should both wait until she comes back of her own accord. If you're right, and whatever is down there has no intention of hurting her, surely it will simply let her go. As you say, she's an intelligent adult, not a child. Perhaps she doesn't need rescuing."

"Maybe not, but I still have to go. That's the whole point of the exercise, if I'm reading the situation right. I'm the one who needs to make contact, because I'm the one who's qualified. I'm not only more qualified than Cerys, but more qualified than the neider, although the neider probably doesn't think so, even though it knows that I'm a little bit neider myself, more accessible to its psychic probing than anyone else."

"I'm coming with you," Felicia said, firmly. "I might be a hundred and one, but I can still go up and down stairs, even in the dark, and I've been down there more often than you have."

"You don't have to be with me physically," Simon told her. "You're my other half, my twin soul. You'll be with me in the only way that matters. You don't even have to give me a favor to wear around my neck or tie on the end of my lance. We've been together since the first night you came to Raven Cottage, and we'll be together every step of the way—but you can't come down the steps with me. That's not the way it works. I need to be on my own, physically, in order that my mind can synthesize the necessary hallucinations as cleanly and specifically as possible. Your place is inside, in my heart, not beside me . . . and here in the chapel, waiting . . . unless you have to go and answer the telephone, given that Rhodri and Edith aren't here."

He stood up and set the lantern down, figuring that it would be useless, and an unnecessary distraction. If he and Cerys needed to use one when they came back up, they would be able to use the one that she had taken down.

He leaned over, and kissed Felicia on the forehead. She seemed slightly annoyed by that, but it seemed to him the more appropriate gesture.

"If Zoe or Marianne rings here while I'm gone," he said, "as they might, if they get through to Rhodri at Raven and he tells them that I'm here, tell them that I'll ring them back as soon as I can. And if Douglas Jefferson rings, tell him the same."

"Douglas Jefferson?"

"I just had a rather one-sided conversation with him in Raven. He wanted to make friends . . . and also to stab his chief rival for that potentially valuable friendship in the back."

"Bernard?"

"Megan. I'll explain when I come back. For now, I have to pretend to be a hero."

She was only pretending to be reluctant to let him go, because she thought that she ought to put on a show. "You might do better," she advised, hypocritically, "if you stopped pretending that you're only pretending."

"You're probably right," he said, "but you've shared my dreams. You know how limited my capacity for self-delusion is."

She made an inarticulate sound of disapproval and annoyance, grabbed his head and kissed him on the lips. "I won't accept pretence," she told him. "I thought I could, but I can't.

I don't care what you've been for the last sixty-eight years. Now, it has to be for real. Go on—but make sure you come back. It can't be difficult. It's the oldest story in the world, and you've retold it so many times that it's practically second nature."

He forgave her the hint of theatricality. It was in the air, invisible but not inactive. She couldn't help it, any more than he could.

He started down the steps, and disappeared into the darkness, more thoroughly than he had ever been able to do before. He kept his right hand on the dry and dirty wall, and moved his feet with meticulous care. The worst thing in the world, he thought, would be to trip and stumble now. That would really ruin the esthetics of his feigned heroism. He felt the abnormal atmosphere invading him bodily, like a slow tide. There was no pain, although it was certainly tickling his nerves, but there was a slight warmth, like an internal caress. He couldn't tell whether that was just a natural aspect of the possession of his inner being by the dark energy, or whether there was deliberation in it, in the interests of reassuring him that the possession meant no harm.

He remembered the feeling that he had had, suddenly and sharply, that this had all happened before—a memory doubtless triggered by Felicia's assertion that it was the oldest story in the world—but the reassurance of that idea was suddenly undermined by a new anxiety, as he realized that the sensation that all of this had happened before, to other fake heroes, might have a different, and more ominous significance.

He reached the bottom of the stairway, and paused, making a mental map of the short distance that had to be covered between the bottom of one stair and the top of the other. There was no need to take his hand away from the wall; he would have the guidance of solidity all the way.

It was easy. Nothing could possibly go wrong.

He took the first step, and then the second.

And then something wound around his neck, smoothly and swiftly, seizing him by the throat, and squeezing. This was no invasion of exotic substance that could coexist with his organism without disrupting it; this was something physical, material and potentially harmful.

It was all he could do to freeze in position, to keep his hand on the wall, and to insist to himself sternly that he was not about to die, that the tentacle that had snaked around his neck had no intention of asphyxiating him, that it only wanted to hold him in place.

He knew that he was at the utmost limit of the neider's physical reach, that it must have been extremely difficult for the hydra to drive one of its slimmest extrusions through one of the narrow fissures connecting the vestibule of the crypt to Nyder's Cave, and he wanted to cooperate, to help the alien make the most of the desperate contact. But he had no idea what was going to happen next, or even what might possibly happen next.

All he could do was to try to keep very still, to avoid choking himself by resisting the grip, and to wait for his mind's eye to formulate some kind of image. He cursed himself for his ineptitude in doing that; what was the point of having neider flesh integrated with his own, if it didn't make it easier to establish contact with the parent neider?

The image that the parent in question eventually contrived to form in his mind—not unnaturally, since the only primitive fragments of common understanding that humans and the neider had, even after centuries of tentative interaction, were clichés—was the image of the Black Monk, the one that everyone in the vicinity of St. Madoc saw in dubious existential circumstances.

Rationally, he ought not to have been able to discern the figure of the Black Monk against a background of Stygian darkness, but that kind of reason had yielded, at least for a while, to a dream logic in which the blackness that surrounded them both was so very black that the hooded figure was almost pale by comparison. He felt the dark energy that had infused him stirring, but he had no idea whether that was simply a natural turbulence, or whether the dark mind from which that energy had come was taking an active interest in what was happening to him. It felt like a wind blowing within and through him, perhaps mutinous, although he hadn't called it forth—had he?

"Okay," Simon said, audibly, not having to force the words through the noose around his vocal chords. "Talk to me, if you can. Show me, if you can't. Play me music if you can't even do that."

The Black Monk—who, he remembered perfectly, was not a Monk at all, reached up and pushed back the hood that protected the face that no one was supposed to be able to see except when the moment of death was imminent.

Simon recognized the face, and understood the dream-logic of it. They were in a crypt, after all: a crypt whose cracks and crannies were crammed with the dead, many of the older corpses poorly contained by rotten cement that was crumbling into dust. They were ready fuel for hallucination. They were, however, not competing with one another in order to qualify for that kind of manifestation. There was no democracy among the dead. They had a hierarchy; the lower ranks of the dead were deferential to the privileged.

The Black Monk, who was not a monk at all, was Ceridwen. Simon recognized her easily, even though she was young and beautiful rather than two hundred years old, give or take a few rebirths. She was the true Ceridwen, the original Ceridwen of the Cauldron of Annwn, reincarnated many times over. That apparition fascinated him, and he savored it eagerly. The intrusive energy within him, the possessing unconsciousness or mutinous wind, stirred again. This time, he was sure: there was an active interest involved.

"Too soon," Ceridwen told him.

"I know," he replied. "You've already told me that." As soon as he said it, he realized a fuller truth. The neider, speaking through Lenore, had indeed said that to him before—but those two words might well have been the only contribution that the neider had made to the strange visitation. The other message had probably come from another source.

"And you're right," Simon said to the neider's Ceridwen. "We're not ready. I'm certainly not. Presumably Melusine isn't—which means that you aren't. You only have the barest, most tentative understanding of what human consciousness is like, and how you might be able to communicate with it, in spite of centuries of practice with a whole series of Ceridwens, Melusines and their kin . . . and me too. But at least you had the common sense and good manners to throw me back, because you sensed that I'd be far more useful to you in the world than asleep in one of your cocoons, because I needed to be the recipient and interpreter of the message that Melusine is going to bring on your behalf, in time. But events have moved on. I'm needed now to receive a different message."

Ceridwen looked at him fondly, with insubstantial tears in her phantom eyes.

"Don't go," she said.

"I have to go," Simon replied. How much of his longer speech, if any, the neider had been able to understand, he had no idea. Probably very little. But he felt sure that that he could get the essential message across, because he and the neider did have a connection, the commencement of an understanding. It was necessary, he knew, for he and the neider to build on that foundation, to contrive a constructive relationship—but it was also necessary for him to rescue Cerys from the Underworld, whether she really needed rescuing or not.

Ceridwen was trying extremely hard to say something, to formulate comprehensible words. Simon was glad about that—glad that the neider was making the effort, not only trying to match his own effort, but trying to do it on his ground, in his fashion.

"Mortal danger," she contrived to say.

"And how," said Simon. "I've got that—belatedly, I fear, but I'm a slow learner. Yes, I know there's mortal danger, and I think I'm beginning to understand why. This has happened before, hasn't it? And in the past, it hasn't worked out well. James deduced long ago that some kind of catastrophe had put a stop to the attempted colonization of the surface by the dark matter entities at the earth's core, by means of the neider and other artificial material constructions, but he thought of it as a physical catastrophe, an earthquake or the eruption of a submarine volcano. It wasn't anything so crude, was it? It was an accidental side-effect of an attempt at communication via the vitreous cocoons. It was a mindquake, not an earthquake—and that makes so much sense that it almost seems to be on the margin of inevitability, if you only look at it from the right angle.

"The capacity to exchange information between unconscious minds is inherently dangerous, and that's why it's so incredibly difficult to do it constructively, with a measure of conscious guidance. To the extent that the collective unconscious really is collective, not only shared by individual entities like you and me, but various levels of hypermind, from the planetary to the universal, to describe it as a minefield would be the most ridiculous of understatements. We know perfectly well what havoc the unconscious part of an individual's mind can wreak with the mechanisms of consciousness, how utterly fragile and sensitive consciousness is, when the unconscious starts its shenanigans.

"We know what obsession can do, what rage can do, what phobias can do, what amour can do, what even common-or-garden anxiety can do. We know that such shields as consciousness has to protect it from the impulsions of those kinds of turbulence are extremely fragile, and that it happens far more often than not that all the forces of reason and common sense are inadequate to keep the pressure of primal urges at bay. We know what heroism is required of an individual to stay sane, even when the ultimate source of the turbulence is our own petty personal dark mind, let alone the dark mind of a society, or a planet, or something on a far vaster scale and far more alien. Ordinarily, it doesn't overflow beyond a single conscious mind, but it can. There are epidemics of insanity caused by the turbulence of the collective unconscious communicating itself telepathically to a couple, or a group, or a crowd, or nation.

"The forces with which we're dealing here are immense, and immensely difficult to concentrate, to focus narrowly. In a way, it might be easier for them to influence a collective than a single individual consciousness…and if they affect even a single individual mind in the wrong way, they could start a psychic plague that could disrupt a whole species, or a whole world. And it's happened before, hasn't it? To human beings, not just once or twice in history and prehistory, but several times. And when it first happened to the neider, a thousand years ago or more, it really scared the shit out of your makers didn't it? But it didn't stop them, because that's not the way the story goes. That's not the way life and creativity work.

"You came back, in spite of the mortal danger, just as we humans come back, at least when we're pretending to be heroes. So let me go, my serpentine friend. Let me go down into the Underworld and through the portal, assuming that it's possible, because it's necessary. Let me try to confront this entity, whatever it might be, not just for my sake and the sake of the human species, but for your sake, the sake of your species, and for all the dark minds in the earth's core. If not me, who? If not now, when? What have you got to lose?"

Pompous ass, he thought—but only briefly. The atmosphere wasn't conducive to second thoughts of a down-to-earth nature.

Simon knew that the neider actually had a lot to lose—far more than its fragile material existence, lurking on the sea bed. He knew that he had a lot to lose too—more than his own life, and Felicia, and the Murden inheritance. Because, whether he was pretending to be a hero or not, whether he was faking it or not, or just playing with ideas, what was at stake here was massive. But he also knew that he was right in what he had said to the image of Ceridwen, the custodian of the cauldron of creativity, rebirth and metamorphosis, because this really was the way that life, creativity and fiction worked. He had to go on, or the game wouldn't just end, it would become meaningless, beyond black.

He had no idea how much of his speech and thought
the neider had understood, or whether its interpretation of
what he felt was correct, but he sensed the tentacle that had
reached around his neck snap. The terminal fragment became
a snake, and the snake swallowed its own tail, to become an
ouroboros, or a torque. It was a little too tight for his liking,
but he could still breathe. He could see the logic of the move.
He was doubly possessed now, by two different intruders,
who might just be able to make contact with one another
through the intermediary of his dark mind.

"Very well," he said. "Let's call it a favor, in the sense that
Don Quixote would have understood the term. I won't men-
tion it to Felicia—she's not entirely in control of her jealousy.
But thank you."

He didn't bother to say any more. The Black Monk faded
away into the deeper black. Ceridwen made no attempt to
blow him a kiss.

Summoning up the mental map that he had folded away
momentarily, he made his way to the second trapdoor. It was
open, tipped all the way back. There was, as yet, no visible
hint of blue, or any other color, in the darkness below. With
one hand still on the wall, and treading with immense care,
he began the descent.

XX
The Gardens of Armida

When he had descended some twenty steps or so—the point
at which he usually began to lose count and the staircase began to seem endless, the black air was disturbed, but not by
blue; the color that invaded his consciousness was crimson,
a little darker than blood red. He continued descending, and
still had not reached the bottom when he was englobed by
the redness, and he began to discriminate forms within it.
He recognized the vitreous cocoons; there was the same sug-

gestion of a glassy surface, and the same suggestion of a vast number of cells, like the chambers in a honeycomb, in each of which something was stirring: something larval, on the threshold of metamorphosis.

The dark energy that had infused him from the atmosphere, like an alien ghost, was no longer stirring, for the moment. It was on familiar ground; it was comfortable, at home. On the other hand, he could feel the ouroboros around his neck quivering slightly, as if blood were circulating within it, warming an intelligence to consciousness. For the moment, its parent mind was the curious one, and the nervous one. It did not have to open an eye of its own; it was in close, albeit somewhat confused, contact with his consciousness, including all of its sensations, drawing its own intellectual stimulation from those raw materials.

When the cocoons had been blue, however, Simon had been apart from them, and content to be separate, in a space resembling and connected to his own space. This time, he felt that he was inside the multidimensional structure of the vitreous cocoons, in *their* space—and he had not reached a floor. His right hand was still touching something, but it was no longer a cold stone wall. It was warm, and fleshy.

He took his hand away, feeling a slight repulsion. He stopped, in order to take stock of where he seemed to be. He crouched down, and reached out with his right hand to touch the step on which he was standing. It was not a stone step; it too felt more like living flesh, covered with a smooth, warm tegument. He imagined that he could sense life murmuring within it.

Then the step split. So did the wall. The entire structure around him seemed to come apart, and the vitreous cocoons yielded up their chrysalids: he saw them as a vast, innumerable flock of crimson butterflies, because that was the form and color that his imagination attributed to them, but he knew that his brain was merely making the best of visual information that was inadequate, and treacherous, with too much confusion resulting from the temporary and uneasy hybridization of ordinary and extraordinary species of matter. The butterflies flew away, in a swirling cloud, that being what butterflies tend to do in human memory and human imagination.

Then the world turned sky blue, momentarily, before the blue shrank, and became concentrated, and became a sky, extending over a landscape. Simon knew that it was all illusion, but it was a very forceful, very focused hallucination, with all the texture of reality. He could not have seen it without the assistance of the exotic energy that was possessing him, but he doubted that the mind responsible for its construction could have contrived it without the presence and inspiration provided by Cerys and himself. For the moment, at least, the Other had a kind of tentative rapport with its human visitors.

The ouroboros was still fearful, still reserved, on the periphery of the collaboration, but for the moment, it was unresisting, awaiting developments.

The landscape was not vast, because Simon was not standing on any kind of ridge, but rather in a hollow, surrounded by vegetation, beyond which the tops of crystal towers could be seen, capped by clouds. But it was all very stylized; the flowers on the vividly green trees, although undoubtedly growing, were strangely shaped and strangely colored, like the designs of an excessively vivid and rather slapdash imagination. The towers too, although seemingly solid, with the glint of real crystal in oblique sunlight, were architecturally unconvincing, beyond baroque. The clouds by which they were coiffed were unreasonably fleecy and motionless.

The inspiration for this is drawn from our human consciousness, he thought, deliberately, making a stern effort to be calm, and as reasonable as possible in the altered state of consciousness to which he was subject, *but it's a composite. Although the initial spur comes from Shakespeare's lines, their imagery has been subjected to several layers of transfiguration and visualization, some mine and some filtered through Cerys, but by no means all. These are the Gardens of Armida, but not Tasso's, even as reflected*

*through my idea of Prospera's illusion . . . this is the work of a more
energetic reader, striving to understand something essentially alien
to its own experience, and, all things considered, perhaps doing
phenomenally well . . . phenomenally being the operative word. Oh
shit, there I go again . . . I need to find Cerys.*

He headed for the most imposing of the crystal towers,
but never reached it. Instead, after an immeasurable lapse of
time, perhaps far more and perhaps far less than an instant,
he came into a clearing between the flowery trees, where
there was a spring. There was always going to be a spring, he
knew. Springs were ubiquitous in tales of enchantment, even
ones dressed up as science fiction. There were deer grazing
in the meadow: hinds and fawns, the very image of peace,
innocence and harmlessness. There were birds singing in the
trees, and monkeys playing, leaping from branch to branch.
There were no lambs, and no lions to lie down with them—
but there was still a tension in the air, a kind of fear. It might
have been partly his own, and he was probably not innocent
of it, but it had a particular quality that wasn't his; nor was
it the ouroboros, which was still waiting, as patiently as it
could.

Simon realized that the tension belonged, primarily, to
Cerys. That made sense. If the Other was reading him, it was
also reading Cerys; if it was linked to him, and to her, it was
also linking him to Cerys.

It occurred to Simon that he really had no idea how Cerys
felt. He had talked to her several times, in his usual fashion,
more English teacher than friend, more intellectual pontifica-
tor than sympathetic ear. He had even listened to her—but
he had never really empathized with her. He had never tried
to discover how she felt. Like Felicia, he had let her down in
an hour of need, but he had done something worse than that:
he had considered her irrelevant, a mere secondary character
in a plot that was all about him. Not only had he not paid her
enough attention, but it had been the wrong kind of attention, all intellect and no heart. And she had come down here
alone, while he had been distracted.

But it doesn't matter, he thought, intent on getting a grip on himself, in the hope that he could present an echo of a sane stream of consciousness to the creature in his body and the creature wrapped around his neck. *If the alien observer is really to get a feeling for human being, it can't do it by examination of a single mind in isolation. It needs two, interacting with one another, and with a measure of tension and discord between them. It's taken what came most conveniently to hand, but there's still a logic to the selection, to the confrontation.*

Cerys was sitting beside the spring, on a grassy bank. She was dressed, seemingly, in a crimson silk robe that had nothing in common with her usual attire, and which made the revolver that she was holding in her right hand seem extremely incongruous. She caught sight of him as soon as he moved from the wooded area into the open. She frowned. There was no obvious fear in her expression, or even anxiety, but her right hand twitched slightly, as if she had had to suppress an automatic inclination to point the gun at him, as a protective talisman if not as a murderous threat.

He knew that, although everything else around him was illusion, the gun was not. The gun was real.

"You have no business here, Simon," she said.

In this instance, he assumed, "here" could not refer to a crude imaginary environment that was, after all, partly based on a hack science fiction novel he had written thirty-some years ago, but to her dream, and to her life, where he was indeed a sudden intruder, to whom she had always been scrupulously polite, and whom she had probably made a sincere attempt to like, but who remained, fundamentally, alien.

"I'm sorry you feel that way, Cerys," he said, stopping ten or twelve feet away from her. "But I was thrust into the situation. I'm just trying to make the best of it, as you are."

"You're not dead," she said. "You have no business here." Evidently, she was following a thread of dream logic . . . the dream logic of a person who had recently lost three-quarters of the people who mattered most in her life.

"Have you seen people here who are dead?" he enquired.

"Yes, of course. This is the Underworld, isn't it?"

"Which dead people have you seen?" he asked, although it wasn't hard to guess.

"James and Ceridwen."

Reflexively, Simon put his hand up to his forehead, and wiped away a few beads of sweat. He realized that it was hot here, and humid. One of the fawns wandered to within a dozen yards of him, not showing any fear of his human presence—but one of the hinds was watching, on the alert. The chatter of the monkeys seemed to increase suddenly as an invisible quarrel broke out in the dense foliage, momentarily drowning out the birdsong. Simon couldn't help wondering if the incidents were a reaction to something going on in Cerys's mind, or his own, or the tension between them.

Mortal danger, the ouroboros murmured, silently.

I know, he replied. *Don't go on about it.* Aloud, he said: "Did you see old Ceridwen, or young Ceridwen?"

Cerys seemed surprised by the question. "I only know one," she said. "Very, very old. She didn't like me, you know."

"I thought she did," Simon said. It seemed safer than simply telling her that she was wrong.

"No, she didn't. She put up with me because I was all there was. She pretended to like me, but it was just a pretense. James was the same. He was kind to me, because he thought it was his duty, but he didn't like me. No one did. They all excluded me. I wasn't one of them."

"It's true that you weren't one of them," Simon agreed. "They were all very old, and to them, you seemed very young. They weren't sure how to deal with that. It wasn't so much a generation gap as a generation abyss. But they all loved you. I didn't know the others very well, but I know that Felicia is immensely fond of you."

"You don't know anything about anything, simple Simon. You're just full of bullshit, playing with your ideas like those monkeys in the trees—all chatter, chatter, chatter. Felicia's *immensely fond* of you, because she's a daft old cow with a stupid crush, so desperate that she started simpering and salivating the moment she clapped eyes on you, even though you're just an old wreck no better preserved than she is. They all liked you, instantly, for no reason at all that I can see, fawning over you before they even met you. Go fetch him will you, Cerys. Now bugger off, Cerys, and let the adults talk among themselves. My life in a nutshell."

Simon suppressed the temptation to say that he understood how she felt, knowing that it would be counterproductive.

"I can't explain that either," he said. "It came as a complete shock to me. I certainly don't appear to have any conspicuous advantages that might lead people to like me, and I have a number of obvious disadvantages, so their reaction is, indeed inexplicable. If it's any consolation, I don't like myself very much, but I do like you, and not just because you're young and beautiful, a writer and a reader."

"Bullshit. You love yourself—*immensely*. You know you don't look like much, but you think your genius makes up for it. You're so vain that you probably think all this is yours, don't you?"

She waved her left hand at the sky, and the crystal city, the placid deer and the lush foliage: the whole illusion. Simon guessed that she felt resentful at what she construed as her own inability to construct a dream for herself without relying on imagery borrowed from a mediocre novel by a mediocre writer who had crashed into her life like a devastating cyclone. But he knew that the resentment was superficial, and that she knew, intellectually, if not as well as he did, at least well enough, that the hallucination was being manufactured by a mind far more powerful than hers, or his. She was an intelligent woman; she had to know that there was more going on here, and more at stake than her own bile and anxiety.

"Hardly any of it is mine," he admitted. "I stole every single element of my Gardens of Armida, and this garden isn't the way I imagined Prospera's illusory construction at all."

"And you're doubtless blaming me for that," she retorted, unfairly. "Well, it isn't the way I imagined it either. So whose is it?"

"You know what we're dealing with, Cerys. That's why you came down here."

"The hypermind? The collective consciousness of the universe? You don't really believe that, Mr. Cannick. It's bullshit, and you know it."

"It's not a hypermind," Simon said, unable to escape the prison of his own pedantry. "It's just a conscious mind, like yours, or the neider's, trying to communicate with other conscious minds, via an unconscious and essentially unreliable telepathic connection . . . although it is, inevitably, at least partly a reflection or a fragment of something much greater: a hypermind, if you like."

"It's just bullshit, Simon, just meaningless jargon to enable you to pretend that you know better than everyone else, that you can think better than everyone else. You can't."

The fawn stopped grazing and raised its head, looking at Simon as if interested to hear his reaction to that accusation. The monkeys had suspended their quarrel, and he could see little hands parting the foliage, and dark eyes peering through it, similarly fixed on him. The birdsong was clearly audible again, like a susurrus of background music. He had a queasy feeling in his abdomen, a sensation of imminence, or perhaps immanence. He was anxious, perhaps even frightened. But there was nothing, really, of which to be frightened . . . unless, perhaps, the manufacturers of the hallucination *wanted* him to feel frightened.

Mortal danger, insisted the neider. But it was no longer an urgent warning; the neider was resigned, and patient.

You're right, Simon admitted. *But I can't quite understand what, or even why.*

Cerys had raised her right hand from the lap of her crimson dress. She wasn't pointing the gun at him, or at anything else in particular, but the muzzle seemed to be seeking a target almost of its own accord.

276

Simon wished, suddenly, that his ever-fertile imagination hadn't come up with the idea that that the manufacturers of the illusion, however alien they might be, had to be sensitive to the same principles of narrative that he employed in his own mediocre secondary creativity. He hoped that Cerys might be right, and that it was only bullshit that he had invented in order to flatter his vanity, to give himself the illusion that he knew better than anyone else what was going on, that he had won a glimmer of understanding, a tiny victory over the implacability of ignorance and incomprehension. He hoped that because he knew that it was an unbreakable rule of drama that if there was a gun on stage, then at some point before the end of the final act, that gun had to be fired.

His throat felt tight, because the ouroboros was squeezing. It too was apprehensive—not terrified, but apprehensive. Was it also a principle of drama, he wondered, that if a character had a noose around his neck, that before the end of the final act, he had to hang himself?

He reminded himself that the neider wasn't hostile, that the last thing it wanted was to hurt him. As for the Other . . . he was no longer so sure about that one, and perhaps even beginning to lean in the opposite direction.

He thought that he needed a new argumentative tack, for more reasons than one.

"Felicia's worried about you, Cerys," he said. "She knows that you're an intelligent adult, not in need of rescue, but she can't help being anxious. She loves you, and she's afraid for you, and she feels terribly guilty about not having given you adequate support in the last few weeks, because she was too distracted by her own grief. She suggested that we could simply wait for you to come back of your own accord, but she didn't mean it; she just thought that it was something she ought to say, in order to put a brave face on her anxiety . . . on her fear. Since you came down here, the change that has overtaken this level of the Underworld has also affected the crypt, all the way up to the first trapdoor. There's nothing to be seen there any longer but impenetrable darkness. Felicia's frightened for you. So am I. I had to come down, to make sure that you were all right. I didn't know what I was going to find . . . but I certainly didn't expect this. And, benign as everything seems, it isn't making me any less anxious. How do you feel?"

"God, Simon, you're so transparent. *I've finally noticed that Cerys exists, and she's upset, so I'd better ask her how she feels to make it look as if I care.* And Felicia's no better—she didn't spare me a thought until I was gone. And as for James and his studious, scrupulous kindness, and that insane old woman who came back to life for you, with so much urgency that it killed her . . . You really are the Devil, you know, come back to collect your dues on the family pact. Honestly, I could . . ."

The hand waving the revolver swung it more wildly from side to side.

She's an intelligent adult, Simon reminded himself, *and a good person. She would never shoot anyone. The revolver is just a talisman, a symbolic shield.*

He wasn't talking to himself, but he wasn't sure that anyone else was really capable of understanding. He tried with all his might not to be afraid, because he felt sure that whatever the eavesdroppers might not be able to understand, they could surely understand that. Was anything more fundamental to the collective unconscious than fear? He had to hope so, at least, because if his own petty anxieties, and Cerys's, were reflections of the state of mind of the universe, echoes of quasi-divine paranoia, then he was in real trouble, and so was the universe. He had to hope that the greater collective unconscious was more reasonable than that, more mature, less easily intimidated.

But he knew, too, that even if the gun was just a symbolic talisman, it still had bullets in it, and that even if Cerys had no intention of shooting anyone, that might not prevent the gun going off, all the more so as she knew perfectly well that almost everything of what surrounded her was a hallucination, invulnerable to bullets.

Unfortunately, that *almost everything* did not include Simon—or, for that matter, Cerys herself.

"I'm not the Devil, Cerys," he told her, "and the family isn't cursed. There are a few unusual genes in our make-up, but that's just something we have to live with, without letting it flatter our vanity too much. It's no more diabolical than it is divine. I've been insensitive, it's true, and my arrival in St. Madoc has coincided with a whole series of events that have screwed up your life, but there's no diabolism in that. It's just life."

"If you lecture me about small victories again, I swear . . ."

"I'll try to resist the temptation. I'm sorry . . . sorry that my arrival made the impact of James's death worse; sorry that I didn't notice, when you waited for me in Raven the other night, how much you were hurting; sorry that all I've been feeding you as a palliative for your woes are lectures drawn from the cocoon of abstract thought that I've been living in for the last seven years while hiding from my own woes; and sorry that even this hallucination compounded out of a mediocre novel that nobody liked is just a garish concatenation of clichés. Do you think you can find it in your heart to forgive me?"

She lowered the gun into her lap again. "It's me who should be apologizing to you," she said. "I'm being stupid, and overreacting madly. None of this is your fault—not even this pathetic dream. The idea of a garden as the kind of illusory environment that a Prospera might construct to seduce humans was a cliché long before you, or Tasso, come to that, going all the way back to Eden. You were just doing what came naturally, and that's why I enjoyed the book. Not as much as Felicia, obviously, but I wasn't in love with the author. It's because it's a cliché that it works. I'm not at all sure that the aliens are getting a good impression of us though. The human imagination is terribly limited, don't you think?"

"Sometimes, I do," Simon agreed. "But Tasso and Shakespeare had real genius, and even I do my best, in my humble way, to broaden the sum of the human imagination."

"Spoken like a man not only content with small victories but absurdly proud of them. I prefer a little more dynamism in my life, my reading and my dreams."

"Is that why you brought a gun to this one?" Simon asked, unable to stifle the reflexive riposte.

"No. I brought the gun for protection."

"Against what?"

"Against the aliens, obviously. Just because the aliens in your cerebral fantasies never want to hurt anyone, it doesn't mean that the real aliens have to fall into line. You're just a sad old man, living on hope. If you were a passably attractive young woman, you wouldn't be able to experience the world as a benign and well-meaning place, and you wouldn't dare to project that on to the whole bloody universe. You'd know that rape is always just around the next corner, even if you have an Abbey to hide out in."

Simon couldn't help thinking about Zoe, and hence about Marianne—not to mention Angela Richardson and Megan Harwyn—and he suspected that she might be right. And yet, he reflected, it always seemed to be the men and the boys who routinely carried the guns and the knives.

While he was thinking that, Cerys said: "What's that around your neck?"

"A torque," he replied, thinking that it was best to keep it simple.

"I thought that was something that happens to airplane propellers."

"Same word, different meaning," Simon said. "A torque is also a kind of solid necklace; this one is also the neider. It didn't want me to come, but I insisted, so it insisted on coming with me."

"Okay," she said, refusing to take up that topic of conversation and taking a step back in the informational flow, "I forgive you, if there's anything to forgive. Let's stop being self-indulgent, shall we? Do you know which way to go in order to get out of here and back to the cruel world?"

Simon looked around, at all the garish flowers, the vividly green foliage, and the blue sky. The fawn was grazing again, no more than half a dozen paces away from him, but the mother hind didn't seem anxious about it any longer. Several monkeys had come down from the trees and emerged into the open, to play in the grass. Everything was serene. Needless to say, there wasn't a stairway in sight.

"Which way did you come?" he asked.

"Through a big red doorway, a kind of portico with walls like glass. Didn't you?"

"In a manner of speaking, but I was inside mine. Millions of butterflies hatched out of it and flew away."

"So which way will you head back, when the time comes? Or are you so much at home here that you're thinking of settling down? If you're entertaining fantasies of playing Adam and Eve, forget it. Even if you were the proverbial last man on earth . . ."

"I think you mean the first, unless you're mixing your metaphors," Simon couldn't resist countering. He couldn't help remembering, though, that if he ever turned out to be the last man on earth, there was one woman who wouldn't be entirely displeased . . . although, as back-handed compliments went, that one was pretty back-handed. Nor could he resist adding: "And Eve quite liked Adam; it was Lilith who didn't."

"Grandmother once said that it was a pity that I wasn't more like Lilith," Cerys observed, "but she wouldn't tell me what she meant when I asked. Rule One. Nobody tells Cerys anything."

"She meant that she thought it was a pity you weren't a clone of your mother," Simon explained obligingly. "Ceridwen was a clone, you see, several times over. She thought that made her special, sacred even. She was wrong to regret that you weren't, though. I can hardly dispute the fact that she was special given the age to which she lived, and Felicia has done well in that regard too, but they don't seem to have had much luck otherwise. Nor has Zoe."

"Who's Zoe?" Cerys asked, although Simon was fairly sure that he had mentioned the name to her before.

"My niece. The one I was hiding in Raven Cottage when she was on the run from the police. The one who hit Bernard Pallister over the head when he tried to burgle the place, looking for evidence of my being an impostor trying to usurp the Murden inheritance."

"Did he find any?"

"No," said Simon equably. "Douglas Jefferson has corrected his misapprehension. He, at least, knows that I'm genuine. He wants to be friends. He was disappointed that you turned his job offer down. He claims that it was sincere, unlike Bernard's."

"Uncle Douglas would swear blind that the sky was green if he thought that he could make a profit out of making someone believe it."

"I did get that impression," Simon admitted. "On the other hand, even habitual liars tell the truth sometimes, especially when they think that there's a profit to be made out of a well-timed revelation. Are you only sitting around here because you don't know which way to go in order to get out?"

"No, of course not. I'm waiting for the alien to show up."

"In order to shoot it?"

"Don't be ridiculous. The gun is for protection, in case of attack. If the alien doesn't attack, I won't shoot. But I'm not going to give you the gun. I couldn't trust you to use it, if the necessity arose—and in any case, I still might want to use it on you." She was obviously joking, or at least pretending to—but the fawn had raised its head again, and the monkeys had stopped gamboling and had turned to stare, curiously, at the crimson dress.

"I'm not going to attack you, Cerys," Simon said, quietly.

"That's what they all say. Usually, it's true, but it's wisest to take no chances."

"Do you call coming down into the Underworld on your own, expecting to confront an alien, taking no chances?"

"No, I call coming down into the Underworld expecting to confront an alien while carrying a gun taking no chances . . . perhaps a little optimistically."

"You think? But the gun hasn't been much use to you, has it?"

"I haven't met the alien yet."

"Actually, you have. We're inside it, and, more worryingly, it's inside us, subjecting us to scrupulous observation from every possible angle. Imagine being a bacterium on a slide under a powerful microscope. Just because you can't see the alien, or recognize it when you see it, doesn't mean that it can't see you. Except that it's a psychic microscope, and *seeing* isn't exactly what's going on. It's our minds that are being examined—but not the conscious part, which is separate and shielded, just the dark part."

"The dirty linen of our souls, being hung out to dry," she suggested, laughing. The joke proved that she wasn't surprised by what he'd just told her. She already knew, and she was complaisant, because she was interested. She had come to confront the alien, for herself, and that was what she had done. That was why she was sitting on the grass, patiently, waiting to see whether it might have any further exhibits to lay before her, as well as the convenient dead.

"Levity is good, I think," Simon opined, "provided that the alien has a sense of humor. But putting it that way makes me wish that my soul had put on clean underwear before I ventured down into the darkness. I haven't even changed my jacket and trousers. I like your crimson outfit, though."

"Of course you do. You'd like it if all pretty girls walked around in clinging crimson silk. Would you believe me if I said that it wasn't my idea? Not consciously, anyway."

"It would be impolite not to believe you," Simon observed, without actually answering the question.

"Yes, it would," she said. "So, according to you, nothing else is actually going to happen? We're just going to sit here exchanging polite chitchat while some invisible monster listens in on our unconscious, probably bored to tears?

Talking to the dead was better, even if it was only James and Grandmother. The alien couldn't manage Wild Merlin, then? Or even Saint Madoc? It was depressing for me to discover how little imagination I had, so you must be devastated. Except that the real you, unlike the pseudonym who wrote *The Bells of Ys* and *The Garden of Armida* when he still had a little energy left, is just a boring old fart who likes a quiet life, writing books nobody wants to read while listening to popular classics, and your idea of a good time nowadays is screwing a centenarian."

"That just about sums me up," Simon acquiesced, meekly. "Would you prefer it if the garden were full of rampaging dragons and blazing red stars were falling from an angry sky?"

"I don't know. I'm not quite sure what kind of mood I'm in at present, now that I've stopped being angry—which is odd, don't you think?"

"Perhaps. In fact, now that you mention it, I'm not at all sure what kind of mood I'm in either. Perhaps we're not in any mood. Perhaps our moods are being leeched away and bottled by the alien observers. Perhaps, when we go back, we'll never have moods again, because the dark part of our minds will have been smoothed out and scrubbed down by the cosmic superego, reduced to bland virtue forever."

"Which is a prospect that would appeal to you, I suppose?"

"I don't know. Perhaps that's what this health inspection is all about. Perhaps the aliens who have temporarily taken control of the cauldron are galactic health and safety officers, responsible for the cleansing of the unconscious urges of all dangerous species, spreading virtue, peace and harmony throughout the cosmos. Perhaps we've been selected as the nuclei of an angelic infection, which is going to spread throughout the entire earthly noosphere, not forgetting the dark minds at the earth's core."

"Now you're just being ridiculous. What happened to your famous author's conscience? If the cosmic mind were able to entertain a *deus ex machina* like that, it would mean that you'd been wrong all your life. Then I'd have to give you the gun so you could shoot yourself."

"I'm not that vain. I'm not the kind of person who would rather die than admit that he's made a mistake. If I were, I'd have been dead long ago. If it really were possible for the alien intelligence here present to work a benign miracle, I'd just shrug my shoulders and say *mea culpa*. But you know full well that I was being sarcastic, and that I wouldn't want the human race to be tidied up by hypothetical cleaners of the collective unconscious. That's our job, and even though we're lousy at it, and making painfully slow progress, I think it's worth persevering. Small victories, hard won, are the best denouements, from a moral viewpoint, even if they're not what most readers actually want, most of the time."

"For someone who isn't vain, Uncle Simon, you do a hell of a lot of showing off. Do you think that the alien intelligence here present, as you put it, is going to think better of the whole human race if you can pass this weird exam, give us a tick, if not a gold star, and pass on to Alpha Centauri? If so, I might be letting you down—a scarlet woman holding a gun. The Whore of Babylon and the Beast rolled into one. Still, it could be worse—suppose the gateway had opened up while you were down here with Megan Harwyn."

It did, Simon remembered, and thought: *But let's not paint her black just yet, even if what Douglas Jefferson said is true. I've forgiven Angela Richardson, after all, and if Megan really were planning to make a bid to secure the Murden inheritance for her grandson, before or after my death, she'd only be doing exactly what's been done for me, so what grounds would I have for complaint? It's not as if I even want an Abbey, or seven million pounds. The only part of it I wanted, and the only part I really treasure while it's in my grasp—apart from Felicia, who was an unexpected windfall—is the puzzle, the enigma, the chance to confront the alien and achieve some small cerebral victory of understanding. I don't even want to save humankind, which, in all honesty, isn't really a species worth saving. But I'm not going to say all that aloud to Cerys, because . . .*

He realized, after a slight pause, that he couldn't actually think of a reason, but he certainly wasn't going to admit that his imagination had run dry.

"Okay," said Cerys. "I'm bored now. If neither of us can make something happen, and the alien here present has no such intention, we might as well start looking for a way out of here. There was a way in, so there must be a way out."

Simon wasn't at all sure that the second part of that remark was necessarily true, and the first part sounded, to him, ominously like tempting fate, or even famous last words.

Perhaps the alien observers were bored too, or perhaps they had accepted Simon's careless judgment that, in all honesty, humankind wasn't a species worth saving, because that was the moment that the clichés exploded.

The monkeys suddenly scattered, yelping madly, and the hinds suddenly panicked and fled, but the poor little fawn, isolated and confused, and, in its innocence, not having a clue what to do, simply looked at Simon with its tender, innocent eyes, as if appealing for protection. And in the meantime, the lion, which was certainly in no mood for lying down with lambs, and didn't care in the least about the ecological absurdity that had commanded it to lie in wait in the trees when it ought to have been stalking gazelles on a savanna, hurtled forward with the first of two mighty bounds that were aimed to land squarely on the back of the helpless fawn.

And Simon, without an instant's thought or an atom of intelligence, bounded himself, to the fawn's defense, as if there were anything he could possibly achieve—except, absurdly, what he did achieve, which was to get between the fawn and the lion in order to intercept the predator, and absorb the shock of its impact and its attack himself.

He had no time to reflect, sourly, that he had been warned, or to hear the neider say *I told you so,* if it had been so inclined.

Nor did he have the time actually to get to grips with the lion, because he also got between lion and the muzzle of the revolver with which Cerys was reflexively taking aim at the predator, so that when she pressed the trigger, with a panic-stricken gesture as ridiculously futile as his own, the shot hit him squarely in the back, and the world ended.

And as his conscious mind formed the ridiculous, fugitive thought that the world had just ended, he imagined that he saw, or at least felt, a red star hurtling out of infinity, faster than light, and crashing into his soul.

XXI
Giving up the Ghost

The world really did end. Fortunately, Simon thought, stubbornly, it was only an imaginary world, which was capable of ending without transmitting any significant damage to the stone cocoon in which the illusion of the Gardens of Armida was contained. The illusion simply collapsed, like the insubstantial pageant it was, leaving not a rack behind . . .

Except, of course, that Cerys, save for her red dress, was not an illusion, and nor was the gun she was holding. Nor was the bullet that had struck Simon in the back. That was solid metal, capable of smashing his spine, or of passing through the ribs to either side, ripping through the lungs and blasting an exit wound the size of a fist as it emerged again. The bullet was perfect capable of killing him, if not instantaneously, very rapidly indeed — which was why he was not at all surprised to find that he was dead, lying face down on a cold stone floor, in exceedingly deep darkness.

So Eve was right after all, he thought, stubbornly, *Hell is just a place that neither earthly not celestial light can penetrate, where the only existential condition is loneliness, and the only torment tedium. She felt lonely, poor thing, because her mother was dead and her daughter had left her and wouldn't speak to her any more, and was bringing up her granddaughter to dislike and despise her. So, it was an easy exaggeration to make. But I shouldn't be here, not because I don't deserve to be in Hell — because, let's face it, which of us doesn't? except, perhaps, Felicia—but because it isn't custom-designed for me, because I don't suffer from loneliness . . . not in the sense that I don't feel lonely, because I do, being only human, like everybody else, but because I have a defense against it, a shield and a talisman. I can endure loneliness, because I can live in the world of my own thoughts, creatively, self-indulgently and pedantically, because I'm a writer, and even when my keyboard is buggered up by blood, so that I can't actually get the words from my mind on to the screen, I can still plot, and reason, and invent crazy hypotheses. And if I have to do that forever, on my own, in the dark, well, it won't be any worse than many an insomniac night I've spent, and might well be better than that, more like waking up in the morning when I edge slowly back from dream to reverie, and my creativity is at its peak. It's not so bad. For me, at least, it isn't really Hell at all—so up yours, God, you got it wrong again . . .*

Alas, it was too good to be true, even though it wasn't really good at all, in spite of his heroic pretense. When he floated up from the ground, he saw the Black Monk. Even though there was no light at all, he saw the Black Monk, black on black. There was nothing unreasonable about that *per se*, given that he was dead, and so was the Black Monk, but the fact that he could see the Black Monk meant that he wasn't in Hell—not, at least, the kind of Hell he had imagined that he might be in a few moments before.

Respectful of the principles of cliché, therefore, he said: "Where am I?"

"Lying on the floor of the cave beneath the crypt," said the Monk, unhelpfully. She was speaking in Ceridwen's voice—the voice of young Ceridwen, the goddess of the cauldron of Annwn, although, in fact, it was not noticeably different from his stored memory of the voice of the old Ceridwen, who had recognized him as her several-times-great-grand-nephew. Only the appearance would be different, and he knew that, in this instance, the beauty wouldn't even be skin deep.

He resisted the pedantic temptation to tell her that he wasn't lying on the floor of the cave but floating in mid-air, because he had a horrible suspicion that he really was still lying on the floor, stone dead, as well as floating in mid-air.

Ceridwen tipped back her hood in order to show her beautiful face to him anyway, which he decided to construe as an act of kindness.

"Where's Cerys?" he asked, looking round even though he knew that he wouldn't be able to see her, even if she were only a few feet away, or directly beneath the feet that he sensed vaguely, although he couldn't see them either, and wasn't entirely sure that there would have been anything to see, if there had been any light to reflect.

"Asleep," said Ceridwen. "She was very tired. She'll be fine. Don't worry about her."

By way of experiment, Simon put his hypothetical hand up to his hypothetical throat. The ouroboros was still tangibly wrapped around his tangible neck, but it felt inert, as if it were dead too. He hoped that it was just pretending.

"You're speaking a lot more clearly now than you were a little while ago," he observed to his interlocutor.

"Yes, I am," she agreed.

"A better quality of hallucination," he judged. "Is that down to me, or is it just easier to delude the dead?"

"A little of both."

"I am dead, then?"

"That depends how you define *dead*. Yes, you were hit by a real bullet, which smashed the uppermost lumbar vertebra and then went on to do further damage to your viscera. If the shock to your nervous system hadn't blasted the processes in your cerebrum productive of conscious thought, rendering you effectively brain-dead instantaneously, the internal bleeding would have killed you in a matter of minutes. So, in that sense, you're dead."

"But there's another?"

"Obviously, since here you are, seemingly intact and arguing."

"Seemingly being the operative word. I'm a ghost, like you and Glyndwr."

"You are, indeed, a ghost of sorts, but not like me or Glyndwr. You might be more accurately regarded as a kind of holding facility for an exact image of your consciousness and personality, constructed out of the exotic matter that invaded and possessed your body and brain when you descended into the darkness. In many ways, you're a better ghost than the version of me you met before, in Raven Cottage, but, unlike that version, you won't be able to exist outside the darkness, unless we contrive a means to re-embody you."

"Who's *we*, exactly?"

"Exactitude is a trifle difficult to provide, but in essence, we're what you described a little while ago as *the aliens here present*—the observers employing the device you call the vitreous cocoons, or the cauldron of rebirth—with a little help from the ouroboros round your neck. We're very grateful to you for bringing it, but you'll get your reward, because we have a far better chance of employing the means to re-embodying you with its help than we would have had without it."

"I see," Simon said, although he couldn't help remembering the old joke about the blind man who said "I see," when he couldn't see at all. "And does *a means to re-embody me* mean that I'm going to be reborn?"

"No. That's a little beyond our scope, even in the presence of a convenient womb, and it's not what you'd want to happen anyway. What we're aiming for is resurrection, but we can't just wave a magic wand. It's a difficult process. We're not entirely sure that we can manage it, even with the help of the creature you call the neider, which knows far more about engineering human flesh than we do, but we think there's a reasonable chance. We can't promise you that you won't sustain some permanent damage or metamorphosis, mentally if not physically, but we'll do our best to ensure that you're still recognizable as you, to yourself as well as other people. And if we do succeed, you'll be able to claim some of the credit, for making the introduction, as it were, between the collaborators in your resurrection. We were already in contact with the neider, obviously, but it had been a direly difficult conversation, if you can even call it a conversation, undermined by suspicion and fear. That hasn't entirely dissipated, by any means, but you've certainly provided what promises to be a very useful link, given time, effort and good will."

"I'm providing your part of this dialogue as well, aren't I? Just as I did when I first spoke to the Black Monk in Raven Cottage?"

"Of course. You're the one who understands your language, so you have to provide the words, and even the concepts, to a considerable extent . . . but that doesn't mean that what your hearing isn't true, in essence. Specifically, and most pertinently, it doesn't mean that you can't come back from the dead. That's a rare privilege. No one will ever believe you of course, and if you try to persuade them that it's true, all but a few of them will just think that you're crazy."

"No change there, then. How long is it going to take?"

"As long as it takes. We've never done this before, so we're working in the dark . . . as you can see."

I'm supplying the jokes, too, Simon thought, *but that doesn't mean that they're funny. That one, admittedly, wasn't.*

"This is all your doing," he said, aloud. "That illusory lion was yours. You got me killed."

"That's true—but in fairness, we had no way of knowing that Cerys was going to shoot, no way of knowing that you were going to jump in between her and the lion, and no way of knowing that the shot was going to hit you fatally if you did. We didn't set out deliberately to kill you—in fact, that's the last thing we wanted. But yes, we do feel responsible, and we're doing everything possible to repair the situation."

"So, you produced the illusory lion to pounce on the illusory fawn in response to the provocative remark Cerys made about you needing to make something happen in order to maintain her interest?"

"Not exactly. We were having too much difficulty following the thread of your conversation to react specifically to anything she actually said. We had a better grasp of her emotional responses to the fawn, and we were attempting to complicate them a little. To tell the truth, we were astonished by both your reactions, given that you both knew that the fawn and the lion were illusory."

"It wasn't our conscious minds that reacted. I'm ashamed to say it, but I didn't think. I just reacted, in a completely foolish manner, as if I could scare the lion away from the fawn or wrestle it successfully. That can't have given you a good impression of what human intelligence is worth."

"We gathered from your reactions that you seemed to think that you were somehow on trial, individually or collectively. You aren't. We were just trying to understand, to find some means of productive contact with human minds, plus a means of securing a better connection with the neider, with the aid of its human associates, and thus the commencement of communication with the intelligences that inhabit the Earth's core."

"Why?"

"Because you, the neider and the core intelligences exist."

"Simple curiosity?"

"Oh, more than that. Call it sociability. We enjoy communication. It's difficult, but rewarding. Perhaps more rewarding precisely because it's difficult. It broadens the mind, literally, and in so doing, makes the topography of various collective and collaborative unconscious knots more elaborate. There's a sense of achievement in that."

"Did you manufacture the vitreous cocoons?"

"Not the ones on your world, or the ones on ours, but we're hoping eventually to develop the capability to manufacture them, so that we can continue the slow work of their distribution. For the time being, though, we're just employers, as your species will one day be, with the assistance of your neighbors in the planetary core and elsewhere in your solar system."

"There are others?"

"Not many, but some."

"But you're from further away?"

"Much further. Not even in your galaxy, although we're in good contact with entities that are. Communication isn't easy, but we consider it a useful endeavor. So do some of them."

"And have you tried to communicate with humans before?"

Ceridwen paused before saying; "Yes, several times. It didn't go well, I'm afraid. As I say, it isn't easy. Things can go wrong . . . obviously, or you wouldn't be dead. Sometimes, things go wrong on a larger scale. We feel remorse about that . . . but we still think the endeavor worthwhile, and we persist."

"And members of some of the other species you've contacted agree that it was worthwhile persisting, in spite of the costs—but some don't?"

"That's correct. It's hardly possible to seek informed consent for our attempts, though. We take the view that the advantages to be gained, in the longer term, make it worth persevering, even in the face of initial adverse reactions."

How much of this am I making up? Simon wondered. *How much of it is just a story I'm telling myself, to while away the time of my death? But they must feel that even this petty communication is worthwhile, or they wouldn't be taking the trouble.*

"So what happens next?" he asked. "If you succeed in resurrecting me, that is . . . or, come to that, if not?"

"We'll assess the situation, in collaboration with the neider. For the time being, once we've withdrawn the dark energy into the portal, it will be easier for us to build up the link we've made with the core intelligences, via the neider. We'll attempt to provide intelligence that will help with their projects . . . including their project to build bridges to the surface ecosphere and the human species. That might be a slow and difficult process, though. As you know, it has hit snags in the past. If we can't resurrect you, we'll develop other links . . . but the neider is very insistent that we do everything possible to preserve you, as an individual. It seems to feel a certain responsibility toward you, as well as considering you to be a significant element of its long-term plan."

"Which is?"

"The neider will doubtless explain that to you, when it can."

"How long a term are we talking about?"

"For the explanation, perhaps months. For the plan itself, much longer; very long, by your standards. Far longer than a human lifetime, although it has been trying to extend that lifespan, for selected individuals, with scant success but sufficient progress to raise its hopes for the future . . . barring disasters. Unfortunately, even without hitches in interventions by distant intelligences, disasters are by no means uncommon, here and everywhere else. We live in a turbulent universe at present, alas!"

"At present? You think that your efforts might one day smooth it out?"

"We hope that it might be possible, in the fullness of time, to bring a little more peace and serenity to the universal unconscious, without reducing it to tedium. Perhaps that will prove impossible, and it certainly won't be our generation, or even our species, that succeeds, but we think we can make a contribution."

"Small victories?"

"Exactly. And this isn't just a story you're making up while playing with ideas; it's an accurate reflection of the way of the world, the nature of existence, the essence of creativity and the esthetics of story-making. We've been trying to get that across to you."

"But I would say that to myself, wouldn't I?"

"You would—but thousands wouldn't. Whether that's a cause for self-satisfaction or not, it isn't for me to say; but if it is, it's some compensation for having died, don't you think?"

"Am I going to remember this, if and when you put me back into my body—or reflect me back, if that's a more accurate way of putting it?"

"If you don't, it won't be our fault, and I see no reason to suspect that you might not. It's your consciousness that we're carefully preserving, after all. You're not dreaming, Mr. Cannick; you really are dead, and you really are a ghost, of sorts. As I said, all of this is a rare privilege for you. However stupid it was to jump in front of that bullet, you might yet have reason to be grateful for the impulse."

"But I need to be careful next time, unless I happen to be in your special darkness again."

"Indeed—but how likely is it that you'll ever see another lion pouncing on a fawn in the Gardens of Armida, in the relatively short time your resurrected self will still have to live?"

"And how long is 'relatively short,' in human years?"

"I can't tell—we've never done this before, and we're having to study human anatomy and physiology as we go along, albeit with the neider's help. Even if we don't make any mistakes, I don't think we can guarantee you more than another century. Your species isn't natural selection's finest work, by any means, and as for the way you look after yourselves . . . but I'm not here to judge. The neider might be able to improve on our work, though, if its current projects bear fruit. It's got problems of its own, but if it pulls through, you'll find it an immensely useful friend. And your species isn't helpless—it's woefully inept, but it's not incapable of making progress. There's hope. There are no guarantees, but there is hope. That's the voice of experience talking."

"Or my own, pretending to be the voice of experience in the hope of spinning a convincing yarn."

"You're certainly providing the words, and the concepts—but you're not alone. At the very least, you're tapped into the collective unconscious of our species, and perhaps to the universal unconscious. As above, so below."

"The document from which that quote is taken is a hoax, a fake."

"Of course it is—but that doesn't mean that it can't provide useful instruments for thought. Don't you pride yourself on being a fake yourself? And aren't you vain enough to think that, even as a fake, you have a small contribution to make to the sum of useful knowledge and insight?"

"Touché. On reflection—even if that's all it is—it doesn't seem to be that bad being dead . . . but I wouldn't want to stay this way forever. How's the resurrection coming along?"

"All things considered, not bad. No disasters yet . . . and if the job eventually turns out to be not quite perfect, well, you were hardly perfect before, were you?"

"Maybe not—but I was all that came to hand when the neider was in urgent need, wasn't I? And if what you're saying can be taken seriously as anything but a whim of my fugitive consciousness, then I really have helped you achieve something here, haven't I?"

"You have, indeed, been a heroic catalyst. Without you, and your particular relationship to the neider, this adventure wouldn't have worked out nearly as well as it has, from our point of view, and even more so for the neider's, in spite of its anxieties. It's only one small step in a long journey, but at the risk of sounding like a cliché-factory, every journey consists of a vast number of small steps, not one of which can be omitted if you're ultimately going to get to where you're going. But don't rest on your laurels. There's a long, long way to go. You won't see the future yourself, but you can still help to lay foundations for it, even in a little village at the arse end of nowhere, whether you inherit the custody of the cauldron or not."

"You think I might not?"

"How can I possibly tell? In that matter, I only have your perspective to go on. Your guess is as exactly as good as mine—there's nothing I can add to it, from the dark depths of a distant galaxy, and the bosom of matter that has very little in common with yours."

"Well, I'm glad I've been useful to you. I suppose you'll have been useful to me too, if you succeed in bringing me back from the dead, although, if it weren't for you, I wouldn't have needed resurrecting, would I?"

"Don't harbor too much resentment, Simon. If you have to stay dead, that will just be an unfortunate accident, of a kind that happens to everyone sooner or later. But being dead and coming back is something else entirely: a unique experience, for a human, or very nearly. If it works, even if the repair job isn't perfect, you'll have every reason to be grateful to us, and to be glad that it happened. You'll be grateful forever more to Cerys for shooting you, and to the imbecile impulse that caused you to intercept the bullet. The fact that almost nobody will ever believe you might put a slight dent in your triumph, but you'll know the truth . . . several truths, in fact."

"But none that are actually useful for any practical purpose."

"You aren't exactly a bundle of joy and gratitude, are you? I'm almost tempted to offer to make a few temperamental tweaks in your personality when we decant you back into your body, but you wouldn't want that, would you?"

"Certainly not. I wouldn't recognize myself. I wouldn't even ask you to relieve Cerys's anxieties before you pull your intrusive darkness out of her. But you can set my mind at rest a little if you can assure me that she isn't going to suffer any ill-effects from the memory of having shot me in the back."

"I can't assure you of that—but you can probably trust her to find a way of coping with it. In all likelihood, if she sees you alive and only slightly sore, she'll probably convince herself easily enough that she can't possibly have shot you, and that it must have been an illusion. I can't say that it's impossible for the adventure to have done her harm, but I'm prepared to take your word for it that she's an intelligent woman, and I'd be inclined to think that it will have done her more good than harm, even if she decides that the whole thing was a hallucination . . . as, in fact, apart from shooting you in the back, it was."

"You should have left her out of it, though. Using her as bait to bring me down here wasn't kind?"

"We didn't drag her. She came down of her own accord. All we did was collect the windfall. And if you hadn't come down after her, we'd have sent her back unharmed and no worse for the experience . . . barring disasters and mistakes. As things turned out, though . . . we're not sorry. Not as glad as the neider, perhaps, but not sorry. Are you, now you've had a chance to think it through?"

"I don't know. That rather depends on whether I stay dead. What will happen to my ghost self, if your attempted resurrection goes awry?"

"It isn't going awry. We're nearly there . . . near enough for me to say that your heart will be beating again before much longer. There'll be some residual soreness, but everything will be in working order, and a week's rest should bring you back to a physical condition slightly improved on what it was yesterday. As to what would have happened to your ghost . . . we'd have had to improvise. We'd have been very reluctant simply to pull out and leave you to vanish, but providing you with the means of some kind of continued existence would have been a technical challenge, and you might have found the result less than satisfactory. As I think I've told you before, being an earthly ghost has its tribulations. Mercifully, though, we're almost ready now to attempt the reverse transfer. You might feel a slight discomfort . . ."

XXII
The Foundations of the Future

"Slight discomfort" turned out to be something of an understatement, although it would probably have been a good deal slighter if the impatient and distraught Cerys hadn't shaken Simon so violently while trying to wake him up. The bottom half of his spine felt very painful, and his guts felt as if they'd been ripped apart and stitched back together again. But he was in one piece, his heart was beating forcefully, and he was capable of rational thought. Almost as soon as the rational thinking began, the background agony began to fade, and the gratitude he felt for simply being alive and embodied made the aching seem more tolerable. He opened his eyes and saw cerulean blue.

After a minute or two of holding still and blinking, he began to discern the vitreous cocoons, exactly as they had been the first time that he had seen them: pale and lovely, with no hint of ominous darkness. He was still lying on the floor of the cavern beneath the crypt.

"Thank God," Cerys said. "I thought for a few minutes that you were in a coma. Do you know how long we've been unconscious? I don't have my phone."

Simon lifted up his left arm, on which he was wearing a battery-powered wrist-watch. "It's two o'clock now," he said. "It must have been about eleven when I came down. I don't know how long you've been down here." He couldn't help feeling a considerable amazement; the adventure had seemed to him to last a good deal longer than three hours, even if the two periods of unconsciousness had been brief.

"I came down a little after nine," she said. "I remember coming down the steps, and feeling dizzy and faint when I got to the bottom . . . but the blue seemed darker, and then everything turned purple, and then blood red, and it was as if a door opened . . . unless I dreamed that as well . . . You wouldn't believe the crazy dream I had while I was unconscious!"

"Actually," said Simon, sitting up, very carefully indeed, "I might. But let's not dwell on it. I need to get you back to the chapel. Felicia's waiting up there. Although, the way I feel, it might be you who has to get me back up to the chapel. Do you still have the lantern you came down with?"

"Yes. It's right here. Have you hurt yourself? Did you fall?" She looked at him with exceeding anxiety as she asked the latter question, as if she were terrified of the possible answer. She was still holding the gun in her right hand, but whether she knew that it had been fired, he couldn't tell.

After a moment's hesitation, he said: "Yes, I did. I hurt my back, and I feel a little fragile, but it's okay now. I can climb the stairs. You go first, and I'll follow. Don't worry. Everything's fine. It's over now, at least for the time being."

Cerys took his word for it, and turned in the direction in which the steps were located. She picked up the lantern as she did so, but then she hesitated, unable to see where the foot of the staircase was. She waited until Simon had come to his feet before moving forward, under his gentle guidance. Once she had found the lowest step, however, she went on ahead.

When she reached the trapdoor in the floor of the crypt, she let Simon through, and then lowered it. She still had the keys to the two padlocks in the pocket of her jeans. Both of them required double-locking once the catch had been clicked shut. While she fumbled with the first, Simon leaned against the wall of the vestibule, through which air was filtering weakly.

The ouroboros round his neck spat out its tail and became a blind snake, or perhaps a blind eel. It slithered into one of the cracks in the wall, and was gone in a trice. Simon took its gratitude for granted; he had felt not the slightest twinge or whisper in his mind.

If Cerys noticed that the creature was gone, she made no more comment than she had made down in the blue, when she must have seen it. She preceded him up the second flight of steps, switching off the electric lantern as she emerged into the chapel, where bright afternoon sunlight was streaming through the stained glass windows. Everything was silent and still.

Again, Cerys waited for Simon to climb out of the gap, and she lowered the trapdoor, drew the keys from the pocket again, selected the right one, and sealed the burly padlock. Simon watched her do it.

Only then did he turn toward the benches, where there were two recumbent bodies on the second and third rows, both apparently fast asleep.

The sound of the trapdoor closing must have woken at least one of the sleepers, however, because Cerys had no sooner taken a single step toward the aisle than Felicia hurtled forward and threw her arms around her, sobbing, and punctuating her tears with incoherent exclamations of joy and relief.

Cerys looked at Simon over Felicia's shoulder. Simon said nothing, but hoped that "I told you so" was written all over his face in ironic smiles. A full three minutes must have passed before Felicia managed to control her effusion, finally turned to him, and said, wrathfully: "What the *hell* took you so long?" By that time, however, the second of the two recumbent figures had come to his feet, and was rubbing his eyes. It was Douglas Jefferson.

"What are you doing here?" Simon demanded of the intruder, as he wrapped his arms around Felicia, and her anger immediately turned to ardent affection and blissful relief, the tears and sobs flowing abundantly again.

"I saw the gardener take the two old women into Raven Cottage from the window of the Mermaid," said Jefferson, mildly. "Eventually, curiosity got the better of me, so I went over and rang the bell, and asked him what had happened. He was a trifle reluctant to talk, but he told me when I insisted, politely. I didn't like to think of Felicia being on her own, so I came over to offer my support. The gardener had left the gate unlocked, and the door to the house as well, so I came all the way through to the chapel. I'm sorry if you think that I was out of line in doing so, but it wasn't until long after nightfall that the gardener finally came back to check in, and to ask for further orders. Felicia didn't want to leave the chapel, so I sent the gardener back to your cottage and I sat with her to keep her company. She finally fell asleep, overcome by sheer exhaustion, at about eight o'clock this morning . . . by which time I was extremely tired myself, having had very little sleep the night before. Felicia flatly forbade me to try to go down after you, and she pointed out, quite accurately, that the impenetrable darkness made it impracticable for anyone who hadn't been down there before to find his way. I intended to summon help when I woke up, but I'm delighted to see that there's no need."

Simon said nothing. The realization that he had been in the Underworld for twenty-seven hours, not three, was still sinking in.

Eventually, it was Cerys who spoke: "I'm so sorry," she said. "I had no idea. It's not Simon's fault. We were both unconscious. I think there was some kind of gas down there . . . and Simon fell and hurt his back. But I don't think the gas has done any lasting damage."

Simon's gaze went back and forth between Felicia and Jefferson.

"Don't be angry with him, Simon," Felicia said. "I was, when he first turned up, but . . . well, I was really quite glad to have him with me when so many hours went by, and I began to think that the horrible darkness had swallowed you up for good. He talks far too much, but it was far better than silence, especially after dark."

"I was able to keep Felicia supplied with tea and biscuits," Jefferson supplied, helpfully, "and answer the phone . . . although I fear that Megan Harwyn wasn't exactly pleased to hear me answering it late yesterday evening. She left a message for you, but it's rather terse. It would doubtless have been more detailed if she'd reached a more welcome ear, but I explained the situation to her and told her that Felicia was very distressed, so she settled for—I'll try to remember it word for word—'Tell him that Zoe's fine, but to ring me *immediately*. It's *very* urgent. If I don't hear from him tonight, I'll come back tomorrow.'"

"Damn!" murmured Simon.

"Don't look daggers at me like that," begged Jefferson. "It isn't my fault that she wouldn't tell me any more. She really has no reason to be so hostile to me. But I'm sorry that I didn't come to fetch Felicia to the phone."

"He's right," said Felicia. "It's not his fault. I was . . . distraught. I can't blame him for not wanting to fetch me. And if what he's told me is true . . . and I have no reason to doubt it . . . well, I'm not sure that I would have wanted to talk to Miss Harwyn, even if I hadn't been as upset as I was."

Simon was still looking at Douglas Jefferson. "And what was it that you told her?" he asked, frostily.

"I told her what I explained to you . . . that I'd managed to convince Bernard Pallister that his conspiracy theory was nonsense, and that there's no point whatsoever in his trying to impede the progress of her brother's will; that I had no intention of doing so myself, and no ambition beyond trying to patch up my relationship with the family in order to co-operate with any future ventures that you might have; and that the only person who can possibly have any grounds or a reason for challenging the terms of the will is . . ."

He stopped, and turned round. The door of the chapel had just opened, and Megan Harwyn was standing in the doorway, her expression rigid.

"Don't let me stop you, Dougie," she said, after a slight pause, in a studiously mild tone. "I'd be fascinated to know who it is who might have such grounds or a reason, in your fertile imagination."

Having recovered completely from his momentary surprise, Jefferson smiled, and said: "The iron law of coincidence seems to have relieved me of the necessity, my dear Megan. Please don't hold it against Mr. Cannick that he hasn't responded to your urgent message; I've only just been able to give it to him."

Megan's gaze swept the assembly, while she appeared to be making a swift decision. Then she spoke to Felicia. "I'm truly sorry, Felicia, but I need to take Simon away. I've just driven from Southmead hospital in Bristol. His mother is dying and she's asking to see him. Even if I drive as fast as the roads permit, we might not get there in time, but we ought to try. Marianne and Zoe are with her, but she was very insistent that she'd like to see Simon, if possible, and convention demands that others try to satisfy a dying person's last wish, if they can. The car's on the bridge, ready to go."

Simon straightened up, wincing because the movement sent a sharp spasm of pain across his lower back. He looked down at Felicia, who was still in his arms, with her arms wrapped around his torso. She released him immediately.

"Go," she said. "I'll be fine. Cerys can tell me what happened, and she can keep me company until you get back, no matter how long it takes."

Diplomatically, Douglas Jefferson did not say a word. Simon limped toward the door of the chapel, but had to make a detour to the bathroom before completing the journey to the car, still in some discomfort. He sat down very gingerly in the front passenger seat and fastened the seat belt. Megan waited until she had actually pulled the vehicle away before she said, laconically: "You seem to have hurt yourself."

"Cerys shot me in the back," Simon said, with equal laconism.

Megan barely shot him a glance before returning her eyes to the Morpen road. After a pause, she said: "How serious is it?"

"Mortal, to begin with, but I had good help. I'll be all right, I think."

They must have driven at least two miles beyond Morpen in an easterly direction before Megan spoke again, presumably because she was waiting for a further explanation of what had happened in the underworld, which he did not feel competent, as yet, to offer.

"Zoe's fine," she eventually said, succinctly. "The money has been delivered and she's given a statement to the police, with a solicitor present; they haven't charged her, but they told her that the investigation's ongoing. I was still with her when she went to see her mother. It was tense, but I think my presence prevented any possibility of an explosion, and Marianne got the call from the nursing home to say that Angela had been taken to Southmead by ambulance while I was still there. I drove them both to the hospital, and waited outside the room—they actually have a Death Row there now, it seems, so that the dying don't have to do it in public, or on a trolley in a corridor—until Marianne asked me to call you. I rang the cottage, but only got Edith, who gave me a rather garbled account of what had happened. I phoned Felicia's mobile, but it was switched off, so I tried the landline and got Dougie, which threw me off my stride slightly, and I gave him a minimal message, which he evidently passed on, somewhat belatedly. I stayed at the hospital for a while, hoping you might call back, but there really wasn't anything I could do to help there, and I figured that if you did reappear, the fastest way of getting you to Bristol was the BMW, so I took a nap to make sure that I was fit to drive and then came back. That's it."

She paused, and then continued: "It doesn't take a genius to work out what Dougie must have told you, although I have no idea how he found out, but whatever edifice of lies he's built on it, it's all hot air. I never had the slightest intention of challenging the will, on any grounds whatsoever. Everything I've said to you has been the truth, and anything I didn't mention, I only left out because it has absolutely no relevance to you, or to anyone else but me. You seem to have forgiven your mother for what her mother forced her to do with you, but I'm not so sure that my daughter would forgive me. I didn't leave her in a doorway, but I arranged an informal, technically illegal, adoption as soon as she was born, because it would have been . . . inconvenient for me to keep her. The decision was all mine, not pressured by anyone else. I didn't know then that she would grow up to be so similar to me, physically, but I don't think it would have made any difference if I had known. I've never made contact with her, although I've always known where she was, and she hasn't tried to track me down. She's respectably married now, I think, with two children. I keep a discreet eye on their progress, at long intervals. Did Dougie tell you how he found out?"

"He said he's known from the beginning. Apparently he thought that he might be the father, and it was only after some years of discreet observation that he realized that she was a parthenogenetic birth."

"And he's kept quiet all these years? The bastard. Typical Dougie, though, gloating privately because he knew a secret even while he was still a regular client. It was a low blow, though, telling you that I might challenge James's will. Dai must have told him that you and I were getting along tolerably well, and he must have thought that it was worth trying to drive a wedge between us while I was out of the way. He wants to be your new bosom buddy, I take it, now that he knows that attack isn't a viable option?"

"That's right."

"And is it going to work? The wedge-driving, I mean?"

"I don't see why it would. I can hardly blame you for not wanting to tell me about that particular aspect of your past, and if you did have a hidden agenda, and wanted to put in a claim against James's estate for your grandson, you'd only be doing what Eve did for me. If you do want to do that, go ahead. I won't think any less of you."

She shot another quizzical glance at him, but then seemed to focus her attention more intently on the road. After another pause, curiosity got the upper hand, and she said: "So why did Cerys shoot you in the back?"

"I'm not sure. She thinks it only happened in a dream, and she's right—but the dream and reality overlapped in complicated ways. I know what I saw, but as to what actually happened, and why, especially behind the scenes . . . that's a different matter. As I'm clearly not dead now, the temptation is to believe that it was all illusion, in the interest of messing with my head in order to measure the response, but . . . well, as usual, I can think of too many hypotheses to be able to settle on any one of them . . . which is reassuring, in a way, because it makes it all the more convincing that I'm really myself, or at last recognizable as myself."

"You seem more than a little disorientated to me."

"I'm just tired, and a little shaken up. Why do you think I'm disorientated?"

"Well, you do have a habit of talking garbled nonsense, but it's not usually this bad. You seriously expect me to believe that you got shot in a dream, and killed, and that it might actually have happened, even though you clearly haven't died?"

"No, I don't seriously expect you to believe it, but it's all true—probably. It's possible, I suppose, that all of it only happened in the dream, but to be honest, the one thing of which I *feel* perfectly sure is that I really did get shot, that I really did die, and that the aliens really did resurrect me—and I know that's three things, not one, but you know what I mean."

"If only. Forgive me, but I'm having immense difficulty believing any of it—even that meek, mild Cerys shot you, let alone that you died and came back to life again."

"It seemed to be an accident—that I did something utterly stupid, and got in the way of a bullet she was firing at a lion."

"There was a lion in the cave under the crypt?"

"The lion was an illusion. The bullet wasn't."

"Why do you say that it only seemed to be an accident?"

"Well, for one thing, meek, mild Cerys had just spent what seemed to be a long time letting out all her suppressed anxieties and resentments, and beneath that polite exterior, she associates my arrival in St. Madoc with a series of disasters that have ripped through her life, reducing its ordinary fragility and uncertainty to utter chaos. She knows, consciously, that I'm not to blame for that, but unconsciously, she might have been looking for an excuse to shoot me, or at least somebody, for days, just as a means of lashing out at evil circumstance. If so, she might feel better now, killing me having been cathartic—all the more so as the fact that I'm still walking around, just a trifle sore, means that she doesn't even have to feel unduly remorseful about it."

"You really do have a twisted mind, you know. And the other thing?"

"The aliens were feeding me a story—a story rather neatly adapted to all the theories I'd been spouting in recent days to myself and others about the deep roots of stories in the collective unconscious. They've been observing for days; the session in the underworld was just the concluding phase of the program, the experimental phase. The impulse that put me in the path of that bullet makes no sense, consciously or unconsciously, in terms of my character and habits. Maybe it really was just an idiot reflex springing forth from my personal unconscious, but maybe it was a sudden poke in the eye with a sharp metaphorical stick, because the aliens wanted to kill me, in order to put me back together again."

"Why would they want to do that?"

"Perhaps just to see whether they could do it, or perhaps to take a crash course in learning what the neider already knew about human physiology, hands-on. Or, more worryingly, perhaps because they wanted to make a few alterations to the said physiology and to the apparatus and architecture of my personal unconscious. They even admitted having tweaked me a little, making out that they were just doing me a favor, by way of saying sorry, even though their admission that they felt some responsibility for what had happened seemed to me to be dripping with hypocrisy. They didn't even promise me that I'd be the same when I woke up—just that I'd be recognizable, to myself and others."

"The twists just keep on coming, don't they? Of all the words I could think of to describe you right now, 'recognizable' is just about the last that would come to mind. I hardly dare ask any more questions, for fear of uncovering further layers of bizarre complication. At any rate, you're back, and Cerys too. Is it over, for the time being?"

"For the moment, perhaps. It'll never be over—and I mean *never*. But the vitreous cocoons have been restored to what appears to be their resting phase, for now. The next time the neider makes contact, it ought to be equipped to be a great deal more articulate, but that might not happen for months, if what Ceridwen's ghost told me can be trusted . . . yes, I know, further layers of bizarre complication. It was the original Cerdiwen, the one associated with the cauldron by legend, but in a sense it was also the Ceridwens your genealogical research uncovered, and probably many other rebirths as well, and to cap it all, she was dressed up as the Black Monk. There are always too many images, too many symbols, too many possible interpretations. It's a psychic labyrinth. But that's just the way the world is: the world of unconscious mind, that is, on every scale from the personal to the universal. It's an uncomfortable truth, but, try as we might to avoid it, it's the truth."

There was another silence. They were barely half way to Carmarthen. Bristol was still a long way off. Figuring that it was his turn to be inquisitive, Simon said: "Do you know what happened to Angela?"

"Not exactly. Marianne couldn't get much out of the doctors except the usually defensive gobbledygook, but Angela's rheumatoid arthritis was apparently atypical, and developing oddly. Marianne gave me a line about the arthritis only being one effect of a deeper underlying condition—heritable, but she said that she'd already told you that you and she are both shielded by a gene that you inherited from your father, and she got from the long-gone Mr. Richardson. Anyhow, Angela's condition was already producing symptoms of senile dementia, and also affecting the curvature of her spine, like the dowager's hump produced by osteoporosis . . . both common symptoms of what used to be called simply 'old age.' Apparently, it was the spinal effect that went critical, causing a sudden total paralysis of the lower half of the body, with various side effects. Her brain is still working, after a fashion, but her organs are shutting down. She's on artificial dialysis, but it's only a holding measure. The prognosis is that she's unlikely to last the day. She's signed a DNR, so if her heart flips, they won't attempt what I believe the current euphemism calls 'heroic measures.' Sorry."

"Did Marianne say why she wants to see me?"

"No. Probably a dying whim. Or maybe she's taking a leaf out of her mother's book, and saving yet another great family secret for her dying breath . . . no, sorry, forget I said that. Not an occasion for joking."

"It's okay," Simon said. "Even bad jokes ease tension, I do it myself . . . even when dead."

"You might not want to tell that story to too many people. Where you're concerned, I can take anything aboard now, and just nod my head, but you might want to use the soft pedal with Marianne and Zoe. I'm sorry, by the way, for taking that out of your hands, but . . . well, I'd like to say that I was just being kind, or even that I just can't resist interfering, but . . . put it down to cynicism, if you like, but I've known a lot of junkies in my time, and I know that handing over cash to them is generally not a wise thing to do, no matter how controlled they seem on the surface. I didn't want to let her out of my sight until the money got to where it was supposed to go. If you want to take offense on her behalf, or your own, feel free. For what it's worth, having spent all day yesterday with her, I think she's okay, and that I was probably being overcautious. But once the drugs start messing with your head—and from what I gather, the new generation of synthetics isn't much different from the older products—things can go bad very quickly."

"You did the right thing," Simon told her. "You were protecting me from my own naivety . . . trying to, anyway. Thanks."

After another pause, she said: "Felicia might not be quite as forgiving as you, and Dougie's a smooth talker, quite persuasive once he gets his foot in the door. He's probably sabotaged that newly hatched friendship, given that it was precarious anyway, because she still had suspicions about my having designs on you . . . which will probably be in full bloom now."

"Probably," Simon admitted. "But if, in fact, you don't raise any objection to James's will, Jefferson's insinuations will wither away, and as you have no intention of trying to seduce me away from Felicia, time will ease that anxiety too, to the extent that it can be eased. To the extent that it can't, it's her problem, not yours."

"Or yours?"

"Perhaps I should have said 'our problem' . . . but in any case, not yours."

"If only it were that simple. She's always been contemptuous of me, because of what I used to be, and now she can add to that the knowledge that I had an illegitimate child, and abandoned her . . . she really is going to think that I'm scum . . . and might not be wrong about that. Even you . . ."

She left it at that, evidently content with the dangling implication. Simon felt a sudden twinge of pain in his spine, and said: "Even me what?"

She hesitated, although he knew that she was not usually one to put a brake on her mouth when it wanted to run away. Then she said: "Even a saint like you, who makes such a big thing about having forgiven his mother for dumping him, can't really approve of it. And a few minutes ago, in the same self-sacrificing spirit, you were saying that you wouldn't blame me if I did try to claim a share of James's inheritance for his great-grandson. Well, I won't, and although I could think of a few mealy-mouthed reasons to excuse that omission, the simple fact is that I've never wanted anything to do with my daughter or her children. I never wanted her, and I never felt any remorse about not wanting her, even when I found out that she was all me, a twin one generation removed. If she ever finds out who and where I am—which is not improbable now, knowing Douglas Jefferson—and writes me a letter, I won't go to see her, and when I'm on my deathbed, I won't summon her so that I can say I'm sorry with my dying breath. Because I'm not sorry—not because she's had a better life without me, but because I simply didn't want her then, and I don't want her now. And I don't believe that even you won't think less of me for that. And for some reason—God alone knows what—I actually care about that . . . and if I ever have a gun, and Dougie Jefferson wanders into my sights, I won't be shooting at imaginary lions."

Simon laughed.

"You think that's funny?" she snapped, incredulously.

"No. It's just a weird coincidence . . . if there's any such thing as coincidence. "When I was dead, you see, and I really ought to have had other things on my mind, I was intensely worried about the possibility that Cerys and I might have given the aliens a bad impression of humankind. I thought that they might think less of us because my reflex action, on seeing an illusory fawn threatened by an illusory lion, was to leap forward in order to wrestle the lion with my bare hands—and because Cerys shot me in the back. I thought that they would think that, as a species, we were both violent and stupid—the worst combination that my feeble imagination could conceive. And when I voiced that anxiety, and they said that they weren't there to judge me, or the human species, I thought they were just being hypocrites. I thought they couldn't possibly simply mean that they weren't judging me, that they wouldn't think any less of me. Perhaps, though, it's the simple truth. Perhaps they weren't judging me. Perhaps they weren't even the kind of entity that thinks in terms of less or more. So, for what it's worth—and where I'm concerned, you can take anything aboard now, remember—no, I don't think any less of you. I don't think in those terms at all."

"Jesus," she said. "Whether you actually mean that or not, you really are one of a kind."

"That's probably true—but not in the way you think. You're probably in a better position than me to confirm or deny the hypothesis, but I'd be willing to bet that it's not particularly unusual for a prostitute who falls pregnant by accident, presumably because of the not-quite-legendary defective condom, to find it difficult to care about the child that results, knowing only too well where the baby came from. It seems to me to be a perfectly natural reaction. Not the only one possible, obviously, but not abnormal, not monstrous, definitely not inhuman, and nothing on which I have any kind of entitlement or inclination to pass judgment. Or maybe I just find it difficult to care about anyone or anything, and thus have a natural sympathy with anyone else who feels the same."

"For someone who finds it difficult to care, you sure as hell put up a good pretence: Felicia, Zoe, your mother . . ."

"I do," Simon agreed. "Put up a good pretence, that is . . . some of the time. At other times, I don't even care about that . . . or whether you might think less of me in consequence."

She seemed uncertain as to whether or not that was a joke. Either way, she didn't laugh, but she did say: "Well, you're not boring . . . some of the time, at least. As I said before, if you were the last man on earth, I probably wouldn't regret that you weren't someone else, even though, etcetera."

"Etcetera," Simon agreed, and closed his eyes. He didn't intend to go to sleep, but when he opened them again he found that they had already passed through Pontarddulais and were on the M4, traveling at eighty-five miles an hour in the outside lane, in frank violation of the law asserting that it was for overtaking only—although, he quickly noticed, they were certainly doing a lot of overtaking.

"Sorry," he said.

"What for?" Megan countered.

"I shouldn't have dropped off. I shouldn't even be tired, having spent much of the last thirty hours unconscious."

"I thought you'd been quite busy, even when you were dead."

"Not all the time. Being a ghost isn't a full-time occupation. The Black Monk explained that to me the first time I met him."

"Even so, even illusory resurrection must be tiring. How's your back?"

"Not so bad. We seem to be making very good time."

"I'm a very aggressive driver. I have the points on my license to prove it—but it's practically impossible to lose your license these days, if you stay off the booze and manage to avoid killing anyone. Anyway, I have the excuse of a family emergency. If the police stop us, they're more likely to give us an escort than a ticket. You'll have to keep pretending that you actually care, though."

"I'll do my best."

"It's good enough. You still have me fooled."

"Good. We do need to get there in one piece, though. I've already died once today; I don't want to do it again."

"I said aggressive, not crazy. Trust me, I'll get you there in one piece. If you're hungry, there's a packet of crisps in the glove compartment, and a bottle of water."

"I'm okay, considering that I haven't had anything to eat or drink since the day before yesterday. The resurrection must have topped me up."

"I must try it if I ever get the chance. Presumably, I didn't miss it by much. The weirdness had already started when you took me down there—but neither of us had a gun. On the other hand, there are any number of ways of killing people."

Simon made no reply to that. Megan attempted a different conversational opening. "I only caught the tail end of Dougie's speech in the chapel, and I gather that you hadn't been there much longer. Do you know how he came to be there?"

"He barged in uninvited—but he did keep Felicia company during what turned out be a long vigil, and she was grateful to him for that. So am I. And for what it's worth, he told Bernard Pallister that his wild hypothesis about you being behind a plot to produce a fake candidate heir was utter nonsense."

"I don't feel any necessity to be grateful to him for that. Does that mean that Dougie and Bernard are friends now?"

"Jefferson seems to think so, but he might be just being optimistic."

"He might. Look, I know I'm prejudiced, but if I were you, I'd be very careful of him. Now he's decided to be friendly he'll play the role with conviction, but you can be absolutely certain that any deals he offers you are purely for his benefit, however he packages them."

"I had gathered that," Simon assured her. "But I know nothing at all about managing estates, agricultural schemes, development plans or any of that. I don't even know what objectives I ought to have, if and when I step into James's shoes. I'm going to need all the help I can get."

"From Dougie?"

"Among others. Including you and Cerys."

"Cerys? Even though you think she's harboring all sorts of subconscious resentments against you? And Dougie, even though you know full well that he's a snake in the grass."

"You know the old proverb about it being better to have equivocal characters inside the tent pissing out than outside pissing in. Jefferson might be useful. So might Pallister. If I have you close at hand to keep an eye on them for me . . ."

"A force in reserve to keep them in line, if necessary," Megan was quick to add.

"That probably won't be necessary. If metaphorical muscle is required, I already have the neider, with whom communication ought to be easier in future, when Melusine comes back."

"When? Not if?"

"When. The future has a very long way to extend, and I don't even have a set of plans for the rest of this year, but if what I learned when I was dead is true, it might soon be possible to start laying the foundations. It certainly won't be easy, but what is?"

"Do you really think we're equipped for making grandiose plans for the future? Apart from Cerys, every one of us is over or within spitting distance of threescore years and ten?"

"The neider is a great deal older than that," said Simon. "From that viewpoint, you and I are invigorating new blood. In any case, time will tell."

XXIII
Last Words

When they reached Southmead Hospital, they found that Angela was still alive, conscious, and seemingly quite calm. Marianne came out of the room in the corridor that Megan had described as "Death Row" and greeted Simon with a handshake. Zoe followed her, and, once again, preferred a non-nonsense hug. A young woman holding a baby emerged in Zoe's wake, who only contrived a nod when Marianne introduced her as Krysten, Zoe's daughter.

She wants to see you on your own, Marianne told Simon, speaking rapidly. "She's very insistent, and we feel that we ought to humor her. She's talking—volubly, in fact—and seems to think that her mind is perfectly clear and rational, but it's not. She refused a morphine injection today, just as she did when you came to see her in the nursing home, but she doesn't seem to be in any pain, just spaced out. She knows she's dying. The nurse offered to send for a priest, but she nearly threw a fit. She only wants to see you, she says. If she's got any confessing to do, she wants you to be the one to hear it. Bear with her, will you?"

"Of course," Simon said.

He went into the room. As soon as she saw him, Angela told the nurse to go, ordering her rather than giving her permission. "This is private," she said. The nurse acquiesced without any sort of resistance or any sign of disapproval.

Simon sat down beside the bed. He didn't ask how she was feeling and she didn't thank him for coming. She was propped up against a stack of pillows, but the distortion of her spine gave her a strange stance, and her face, although relaxed, was gray and wizened. Her hands were lying on the bedspread, but when he reached out, offering to take the nearer one and hold it, she shook her head.

"No point," she said. "No feeling. Just look, okay?"

"Okay," he said.

"Dying isn't so bad," she told him, speaking quite clearly and succinctly. "Not this way, at any rate. I don't need pain-killers any more, because I can't feel a thing beneath the waist, and precious little below the neck. I have the impression of a slight soreness in the back, but I think that's a phantom pain—you know, like the pain amputees sometimes think they can feel in a missing arm or leg. Apart from that, I haven't felt this good in . . . well, forever. Except for my head, I think I'm pretty much all phantom now. It's wonderful—except, of course, that when the missing body shuts down, I'll be dead. But it's the ideal scenario, isn't it—not being able to feel a thing when you die? Anyway, that's why I wanted to see you."

"Pardon?" said Simon, having lost the thread of the argument.

"Because of the last time. I wasn't myself then. You must have thought that I was completely mad, raving like that. I wanted to see you again so that you could see me as I really am . . . when I'm not in pain, that is, calm and thinking clearly. I wasn't then, you see . . . calm, or thinking clearly."

"I did realize that," Simon assured her.

"No, not then, *then*. When my mother took you away and left you in Birmingham city center. I wasn't calm. I wasn't thinking clearly. I was fourteen years old, and not capable of thinking clearly, even at the best of times, but it was anything but the best of times. I thought then that it was the worst, but little did I know. Anyhow, things were bad. I wasn't myself. I'm not trying to duck out of anything, mind, to say that it wasn't my fault, because it was . . . my fault, that is. All my fault. Mum was right about that, although I hated her for it at the time. If you knew how close I came to murdering her . . . but that wasn't over you. That was just things in general. You were just one of those things . . . and when she took you away, to be perfectly honest, I was more relieved than heartbroken. I was angry, of course, but I was always angry. Anyway, I didn't want you to come so that I could say sorry, or to ask you to forgive me, or because I've got another message from Hell . . . I just wanted to see you, once, while I wasn't out of my mind on pain or painkillers. I wanted to see you with calm eyes. I'm sorry if that doesn't make any sense to you, but it does to me, and I thought you might be prepared to make allowances and indulge me."

"You don't have to apologize," Simon told her. "You haven't done anything wrong."

"I've hardly ever done anything right."

"I mean that it's perfectly reasonable for you to ask to see me."

"Not everybody thinks so—but I can't complain. Everybody's being very kind, for once. It's because I'm dying. When I was in terrible pain, but not actually dying, they all hated it, and it was just one more thing for them to add to the list of things they hated about me, but now I'm dying . . . in a way, I wish I'd done it a lot sooner. Only it doesn't last, does it? This way of dying, beyond feeling, isn't natural, is it? It's just a freak of my condition, a small mercy before I actually kick the bucket. Except that there are no small mercies, are there? There's nothing small about it. It's just short. Too short. Oh, and I wanted to thank you, too, for being kind to Zoe. Not that the little pothead deserves it, but that's not the point. Marianne says that she was out of her mind, and would have been sure to do something stupid if you hadn't calmed her down and helped her out. So she's grateful, even though she always says that she washed her hands of Zoe twenty years ago, just as I washed my hands of her at much the same age. But she didn't, really, and, to tell you the truth, nor did I. You can't really wash your hands of your children. You can try, but the stain never goes away. It's not dirt, you see, not something that can be washed off. You probably think I'm rambling, that I'm still feeling the after-effects of the drugs, or whatever the side effects of my arthritis was doing to my brain, and I am rambling a little, no two ways about it, but it isn't drugs or dementia, it's just that I haven't got much time. Actually, my mind is clear, clearer than it's ever been—much good it's going to do me now. What do they call that, when everything finally comes together when it's too late. The iron of faith?"

"The irony of fate," Simon suggested.

"That's it. Are Marianne and Zoe still outside?"

"Yes, and Krysten and the baby. They're all there. Four generations. And an extra cousin from St. Madoc, Lilith's grand-niece."

"Really? They wouldn't let her in, before. They probably didn't know that she was family. Anyway, I'm glad they're there—not here, mind, but there, all together. They're having to pretend, you see, that they get on, out of respect for the dying. I don't care, obviously, about them having to be nice to me, but I would like them to get on with one another, a little better than they always have. Marianne says that you wanted that too, when you tried to patch things up between her and Zoe. I'm glad about that. It's selfish of me, I suppose, to want them to be all right, when it's probably mostly my fault that they aren't all right, because I couldn't get on with Marianne and washed my hands of her, and started the whole snowball rolling, but I wasn't thinking straight in those days. In fact, I've never really been thinking straight, although, obviously, I didn't realize it, because you always think that the way you're thinking is straight, except when you're not on drugs or in agony. Sometimes even then—young Zoe probably thinks that she's thinking straight just because she's a primary school teacher when she isn't off her head, but she isn't. I never was, although it's only now that I can see it. Perhaps you have to be dead, or almost, to be able to see life from the right angle. Except that . . ." She stopped, and waited for the prompt.

"Except what?" Simon asked, obligingly.

"Except that, if Marianne can be trusted—and although she's always been a bitch, she can usually be trusted—you have your head screwed on. Her phrase, not mine. She puts it down to your being a writer. She's always been a reader, so she thinks a lot of writers. Personally, it's always seemed to me that writers were crazier than most, to judge by what they write. But you were kind to Zoe, she says, even though she was an absolute bitch when she took you to see her—she's a fine one to talk—and had no reason whatsoever to help her out. So you must have a good heart. Didn't get it from me, I fear—must be from your real mother. We lucked out there, didn't we? If you believe what you see on TV, most foster mothers are even worse than real ones, so we were lucky. Isn't there an old Chinese proverb about an eel in a bag of snakes, but if you're lucky you might just catch it?"

"I believe the saying is that hoping to find a good woman is like trying to find a single eel in a bag full of snakes—but it adds the rider that, even if you succeed, all you have is a wet eel by the tail."

"That's it. Well, we got the eel, and that's why you're not a snake, like practically every other man I've ever met . . . or Marianne, or Zoe. Don't know about Krysten, but I've heard that baby bawling, so probably her too. You might be just pretending, of course, the way Marianne pretends, and even I used to pretend sometimes, but even if you are, it's okay. Pretending works, and I'd still be proud of you, even though I have no right. It's just that it's difficult to keep the pretense up. I am making sense, aren't I? I am thinking clearly, and not just deluding myself?"

"You're making perfect sense," Simon assured her. "Better sense than I've ever made, in fifty years of writing and hundreds of books."

"I thought so. I knew I was right to ask you to come. I knew you'd tell me the truth, because you don't have any reason to lie. They're all pretending, you know. Pretending to be nice, pretending to be sorry that I'm dying, putting on a show because they think they're being watched, and judged. But that's okay. Pretending works, while you can keep it up, and it isn't so difficult to keep it up when you know that it's only for a matter of hours. They all know that I won't last the night, and they're all out there congratulating themselves because I insisted that I had to talk to you on your own, letting them off the hook. If they're really lucky I'll pop my clogs while it's just you and me, and they won't have to pretend any longer with me. But it would be nice, wouldn't it, if they could keep on pretending to like one another for a little while longer? I'd like that. I'd like to think that coming together in order to wait for me to die helped them to repair things a little between themselves. That way, I'd feel that there was some virtue in my dying, and believe me, there wasn't a lot of virtue in my living. You don't believe in anything, Marianne says, and that's another reason why I wanted you here. Would you believe that the nurse asked me whether I wanted to see a priest? A priest! 'Why the Hell would I want to see a priest?' I said to her, Hell being the operating word. Is 'operating' the right word? It doesn't matter—the point is that I wanted someone with me who doesn't believe in Hell, someone who could put his hand on his heart and tell me that the agony wasn't ever going to start again once the bliss has finished killing me. You don't believe in Hell, do you, Jason?"

"No," said Simon, "I don't believe in Hell."

"My mother did. But not fire and brimstone; she believed that Hell was the ultimate darkness, absolute loneliness. Marianne says that you kept her company when she was dying, that you held her hand. Is that really true?"

"Sometimes," Simon confessed.

"She'd have appreciated that . . . while it lasted. I bet she never said so, though. I bet she never uttered a word of thanks."

"She had difficulty speaking toward the end," Simon told her, "but yes, she did thank me, repeatedly, in action as well as speech."

"Must have mellowed in her old age, then. Never thanked me, the bitch, whatever I did for her. Not that I'd have held her hand, even if I'd been able to get up the stairs. You know that she used to be a whore, don't you . . . yes, of course you do, you said so last time. Well, I don't hold that against her; she had to get by, and I'm in no position to cast the first stone in that coconut shy, or any other, but it soured her, you see. It made her hard. It made her hate people . . . all people, including me, and sometimes, I thought, especially me. I didn't understand that, then, but now . . . now, I'm beginning to wonder whether I haven't been a little more like my mother than I thought when I swore that I wouldn't be. Doesn't matter on my account, obviously, but I sometimes worry that I might have passed it on. Has Marianne told you, by the way, that you don't have to worry about ending up with my disease? They've even done tests on her DNA to make sure, and they checked the sample that your friend got from you. I've got two defective genes, it seems, although, to be honest, it could have been a lot worse, as the disease didn't kick in until I was sixty-odd. But Richardson had two good ones, and so, it seems, did the scumbag who fathered you, so both of you, being their children—really their children, not like Zoe, who seems to be all Marianne's and not Rob's at all—are safe. So you see, even absolute bastards can be good for something. Mother didn't have it either, because her father was sound too . . . but she sure as Hell didn't catch an eel by the tail when she fell pregnant. She got bit good and hard, and I got the poison. Can't complain, though. Most of my fuck-ups were all my own work, including you . . . not that I'm calling you a fuck-up, just that you were the result of one of mine. Obviously, you're not a fuck-up, or you wouldn't be here, pretending to be kind to a stupid old woman you haven't known for sixty-eight years, who never called you Jason until last week. You don't mind, I hope? I know you're really Simon, and that's fine, but in my mind . . . even though, to be honest, you've been mostly out of mind while you've been out of sight, but whenever you popped into it, you were always Jason. I didn't have any other name to think of you by, you see. I didn't know who you really were. Now . . . well, I still don't, really, but at least you don't believe in Hell. That's something, isn't it?"

"Yes, it is," Simon confirmed.

"I could never see the point of confessing to a priest. I know they say that he can absolve you of your sins, but that's bullshit. Nobody can absolve you. You can't even wash your own hands. You have to carry your stains with you. You certainly can't put them in a cardboard box and let your mother carry them away. You can forget them, for a while, but they're always there. But there isn't any Hell to punish you for them, and certainly not a Hell that's just darkness and loneliness. That, I could cope with. Couldn't you?"

"Yes, I could," Simon assured her.

"There you are—far more use than any stupid priest. You can't absolve me, but what does it matter? I don't even want to be absolved. I can carry my sins, but maybe not all at once. My legs are no good, you see, nor my back. I can only carry things in my heart, and I can't feel that any longer. I know it's still beating, because I'm still talking, but I can't feel it any more. I can't feel anything down there. If I pissed myself, I wouldn't know it. They say you do, you know, when you die, and worse. You can't die with dignity, it's always disgusting. But at least I can't feel anything. If only I'd stopped feeling years ago. If I had my time over again, do you know what I'd do?"

"No," said Simon.

"I'd kill myself at thirteen, so I wouldn't have to go through an entire lifetime of failure and humiliation. Other people don't say that, you know. They think they'd be able to avoid all the mistakes they made, and have a much happier life. That's bullshit. They'd just have made different mistakes and ended up just as unhappy, just as humiliated. But I shouldn't be saying that to you, should I? It's depressing, and people don't like you to be depressing. But if I had committed suicide at thirteen, you wouldn't exist, so I can tell you without hurting your feelings. I'm not hurting your feelings, am I, Jason?"

"No, you're not hurting my feelings," Simon assured her.

"Good. That's why I wanted to see you—because if I said all this to Marianne, it would hurt her feelings. Zoe wouldn't care, of course, but she'd pretend, because it's what she does. But you don't have to. You know that, don't you? You don't have to pretend with me."

"I know," said Simon.

"Good. Do you know when the last time I talked like this was?"

"At a guess," Simon said, "never."

"That's right. I thought you'd understand, even if you wouldn't even exist if I had my life over again. But you can't, can you? Have your life over, that is. You have to live the one you have, no matter how shitty it is. But yours isn't shitty, is it? Mum saw to that. It was a gamble, but she got the eel. Your life isn't shitty, is it, Simon?"

"No," said Simon, "it really isn't."

"Zoe says that you've got a girlfriend, but that she's a hundred years old. She's such a little cow. She's thirty-eight, you know, but she thinks she's still a teenager."

"She was telling the truth," Simon admitted. "I do have a girlfriend, and she is a hundred years old."

"Do you love her?"

"I don't know. Time will tell."

"Does she love you?"

"I don't know. I think she'd like to."

"Well, that's a start. More than I ever managed. I did love people, at one time, but I never wanted to; it always caught me on the hop, at inopportune moments. Is that a word?"

"Yes."

"Good I'm still making sense, then?"

"Perfect sense."

"Good—because I have the feeling that it isn't going to last much longer. What was I saying?"

"Love always caught you at inopportune moments?"

"Exactly. Always bad timing, always the wrong men. Especially Richardson—but don't tell Marianne that. She's never forgiven me for driving him away, and she's not wrong—not wrong about me driving him away, that is, not about not forgiving me. She should have forgiven me. The world would be a better place if we all forgave one another, and ourselves—but it's not easy is it?"

"No," Simon agreed. "That's why we invented God to do it for us, but nobody really believes any more that he can, let alone that he might. We have to go unforgiven—but there's no Hell, of any kind. Trust me. I've been dead; I know."

"Perfect sense," she said. "I knew I was right to ask for you. But you'd better let them back in now. Zoe and Krysten can come in first, and Lilith's grand-niece. There's no reason to stop meeting new people just because I've only got five minutes to live, is there? Marianne can hold the baby, and you can talk to her outside for a few minutes. Will you give me a message for her, in case I go beforehand?"

"As above, so below?"

"No, that one was for you, although, to be honest, I really don't think it meant anything. Tell her that I never washed my hands of her. Never. No matter what she thinks."

"I'll tell her," Simon promised.

He went to the door of the room and beckoned to Zoe. "Your turn," he said. "Be kind. Or if you can't be kind, pretend."

"I can be kind," Zoe assured him. "Even when sober."

She went in. When she was seated by the bed, Simon went out. A nurse hurried over to check that everything was under control. Simon reassured her.

"She'd like to see you too, Krysten," he said to Zoe's daughter. "She suggested that you give the baby to Marianne for a few moments."

Krysten handed the baby over to her grandmother.

"She'd like to meet you as well, Megan," he added. "She wants to thank you for driving all the way to Ceredigion and back to fetch me."

Megan nodded, and followed Krysten.

"You were in there a long time," Megan commented.

"She had a lot that she wanted to say," Simon explained.

"Things she didn't want the rest of us to hear?"

"Obviously. There are all sorts of things that people only feel comfortable confiding to a stranger. But she asked me to give you a message."

"Oh?"

"Yes. She asked me to tell you that she never washed her hands of you, no matter what you might think."

"She was just showing off, trying to make herself look good in your eyes, because you don't know her. She's pretending to be a mother now that it's too late, and she thinks she can put one over on you."

"I did get that impression," Simon agreed, "but it would be understandable, and forgivable, if it were true. She's only human. I like her."

"Why wouldn't you? It can't cost you anything now. No, forget I said that. I'm just stressed at the thought of having to arrange another funeral, and having to go through the whole empty ritual all over again. It might be some time before I can accept your invitation, if it's still open."

"It is."

"Well, I'll try, when Mum is safely buried. Will you come to the funeral?"

"Yes, of course."

"I'll invite Megan too—that way you might get a lift."

"Wise move."

"Are you and she . . . ?"

"No. Just friends. Zoe's probably told you that I have a girlfriend. It's true, even the bit about her being a hundred years old. You'll meet her, when you come to visit."

The baby whimpered, and Marianne bobbed her up and down a little. "How much money did you give Zoe, to get her out of trouble?" Marianne asked.

Simon thought about saying that he hadn't given her any, given that it was the literal truth, but it would still have been dishonest.

"It doesn't matter," he said. "She was in difficulties, so we helped her out. We're family, after all."

"We? You and Megan?"

"That's right."

"She'll have to pay you back—every penny."

"She's promised to do that. Will you do me a favor?"

"What?"

"Don't give her a hard time about it. It would make me feel bad. The weeks I've spent in St. Madoc have opened my eyes to the potential value of family relationships, and I don't want to spoil any of the few that I have. As I told you on the phone, I'm glad that Zoe thought she could come to me. I'd like her to feel glad that she did. Can you help me with that, please?"

"I suppose so. I'm not sure I'd really be doing you a favor though. You might be better off keeping us all at arm's length, Zoe especially. To be honest, I'm surprised that the conversation you've just had with Mum hasn't sent you running for cover from the family curse. She must really have been putting on a show. Dying is obviously bringing out the best in her."

It was at that moment that Krysten came hurtling out of her great grandmother's room and ran along the corridor calling for help. Megan followed her out and caught Simon's eye. She shook her head. Apparently without thinking, Marianne simply handed the baby to Simon and ran in. Simon stood there, gazing at the infant in stunned surprise. The baby stared back for a few seconds, and then started wailing.

"Don't take it personally," said Megan.

"I won't," said Simon, as Krysten arrived back, still running. The nurse and a doctor followed at a more leisurely pace, doubtless knowing full well that there was no earthly need to hurry on Death Row.

Simon handed the baby back to her mother. "I'm sorry," he said.

"It's not your fault, Mr. Cannick," she assured him. The baby stopped wailing, but there were still tears streaming down Krysten's face, provoked by the sight of death.

Zoe emerged from the mortuary chamber. She looked at Simon. "She went with a smile," she said. "She almost seemed glad to go."

"She said something," Megan put in, "but I wasn't close enough to hear what it was. Did you hear, Zoe?"

"Yes," said Zoe, "but it didn't make any sense."

"What did she say?" Simon asked, curiously.

"I can't be absolutely sure, but it sounded to me like: 'I can cope.' Does that make any sense to you?"

"Actually," said Simon, "it does. Perfect sense."

It was, he thought, an exceedingly tiny victory over evil circumstance, but it was a victory. And it did make perfect sense.

A PARTIAL LIST OF SNUGGLY BOOKS

LÉON BLOY *The Tarantulas' Parlor and Other Unkind Tales*
S. HENRY BERTHOUD *Misanthropic Tales*
FÉLICIEN CHAMPSAUR *The Latin Orgy*
FÉLICIEN CHAMPSAUR *The Emerald Princess and Other Decadent Fantasies*
BRENDAN CONNELL *Clark*
QUENTIN S. CRISP *Blue on Blue*
LADY DILKE *The Outcast Spirit and Other Stories*
BERIT ELLINGSEN *Vessel and Solsvart*
EDMOND AND JULES DE GONCOURT *Manette Salomon*
RHYS HUGHES *Cloud Farming in Wales*
J.-K. HUYSMANS *Knapsacks*
JUSTIN ISIS *Divorce Procedures for the Hairdressers of a Metallic and Inconstant Goddess*
VICTOR JOLY *The Unknown Collaborator and Other Legendary Tales*
BERNARD LAZARE *The Mirror of Legends*
BERNARD LAZARE *The Torch-Bearers*
JEAN LORRAIN *Masks in the Tapestry*
JEAN LORRAIN *Nightmares of an Ether-Drinker*
JEAN LORRAIN *The Soul-Drinker and Other Decadent Fantasies*
ARTHUR MACHEN *Ornaments in Jade*
CAMILLE MAUCLAIR *The Frail Soul and Other Stories*
CATULLE MENDÈS *Bluebirds*
LUIS DE MIRANDA *Who Killed the Poet?*
OCTAVE MIRBEAU *The Death of Balzac*
CHARLES MORICE *Babels, Balloons and Innocent Eyes*
DAMIAN MURPHY *Daughters of Apostasy*
KRISTINE ONG MUSLIM *Butterfly Dream*
YARROW PAISLEY *Mendicant City*
URSULA PFLUG *Down From*
JEAN RICHEPIN *The Bull-Man and the Grasshopper*
DAVID RIX *A Suite in Four Windows*
FREDERICK ROLFE *An Ossuary of the North Lagoon and Other Stories*
JASON ROLFE *An Archive of Human Nonsense*
BRIAN STABLEFORD *Spirits of the Vasty Deep*
BRIAN STABLEFORD (editor) *Decadence and Symbolism: A Showcase Anthology*
JANE DE LA VAUDÈRE *The Demi-Sexes and The Androgynes*
JANE DE LA VAUDÈRE *The Double Star and Other Occult Fantasies*
RENÉE VIVIEN *Lilith's Legacy*
KAREL VAN DE WOESTIJNE *The Dying Peasant*

www.ingramcontent.com/pod-product-compliance
Lightning Source LLC
Chambersburg PA
CBHW051637180726
48284CB00006B/1761